EARTH
PROTECTION
FORCE

tim eichholtz

LifeRich Publishing is a registered trademark of The Reader's Digest Association, Inc.

LifeRich Publishing books may be ordered through booksellers or by contacting:

LifeRich Publishing
1663 Liberty Drive
Bloomington, IN 47403
www.liferichpublishing.com
1 (888) 238-8637

ISBN: 978-1-4897-1748-1 (sc)
ISBN: 978-1-4897-1747-4 (hc)
ISBN: 978-1-4897-1746-7 (e)

Library of Congress Control Number: 2018945703

Print information available on the last page.

LifeRich Publishing rev. date: 07/19/2018

ONE

As far as we know Earth is the only planet in our solar system that has life on it in this remote section of the Milky Way galaxy. We hear stories of people who claim they have been abducted by aliens. Many of us think they are crazy. Most of them do not want to repeat their experience. As far as the rest of the world is concerned, the existence of aliens has not been proven and many of us do not believe that it does exist. In the twentieth century we had advanced our technology to the point that we have developed our own space programs. We monitor space for signs of intelligent signs of communication and we are sending out signals into deep space in hopes that we get a response. If there are alien races out there we are taking a 50 - 50 chance that the return message will be friendly. We are now fifteen years into the twenty-first century and the message has been received. Will we get the response we want? Are they friendly?

Here I am, sixty-seven years old. I should have retired by now, but here I am still working. Being a specialist on computer projects, I am a contractor working at home and there are many nights that I need to work late. I am working at my computer on a project plan for a customer who needs it tomorrow when I get this strange feeling that someone is watching me. I know no one has walked into the room, as I can see the door to my office in front of me. Also, there is nobody else in the house. I look away from my screen, and slowly start looking around the room. I don't see anything, so I brush it off, and go back to work. I start getting this strange feeling again, and it starts getting stronger, and the hair on the back of my neck starts to stand up, since I know there is someone in the room with me. I look away from my screen again, and start to look around slowly, only now I am ready to jump out of my skin. I slowly start looking to my left, and then I see someone, out of the corner of my eye. Now my heart is beating so fast I can feel it, since what I am looking at doesn't appear to be human. There are differences in the complexity of his skin and in the shape of his head. He is about six feet tall, with broad shoulders, and appears to be wearing a uniform. I push back in my chair, startled, but he raises his hands in a peaceful gesture, but says nothing. Still startled, I don't know what to do. If I try to get up to run, I must go right past him, and that puts him at the advantage. I don't have anything to grab as a weapon to defend myself, so I just sit there in my chair, holding on tightly to the arms, and every fiber of my being is as tight as they can be. The stranger doesn't move and neither do I. We stare at each other for a few more seconds, and he finally speaks, with what sounds like a deep male voice.

"Hello Chris."

I am startled that he knows my name. I start to reply, but he says, "Don't worry; I am not here to harm you."

I finally get my voice back and say, "Who are you, and what are you doing in my house?"

"My name is Kleg, and I am here to discuss an opportunity with you."

"Well, before we discuss anything, we need to come to an understanding on a few things. First off, you don't appear to be human. And second, why me? Thirdly, why should I trust you? So, let's start with my first two questions, where are you from, and why are you here to see me?"

He stares at me for a few seconds, as if he is gathering his thoughts trying to formalize a proper response.

He finally comes back, "You wouldn't understand if I told you, but let me try. I am from a galaxy that is some distance from your planet. First, I would like to tell you more about why I am here, and it will help explain why I am here to see you."

Based on your Earth time, my world was at peace tens of thousands of years ago, and we lived in harmony with our surrounding worlds. We were highly advanced, according to your standards. Technologically, we had advanced to the point where we no longer needed armies, or weapons, as we had nothing to defend; we were all one people. With our mental capacity and technology, we could help people of our world that had issues, and were able to establish harmony for our world. Our surrounding worlds were just like us, and we shared our knowledge with each other. We lived like this for thousands of years, and lost our perspective that bad could still happen.

One day, about five thousand years ago, our galaxy had visitors, and we welcomed them with open arms. They initially came as friends, and in our gullibility and innocence, we welcomed them. For about five hundred Earth years we lived in peace with them, but during this time they were also planning how they would destroy us. We had already shared our knowledge and technology with them. It was at this point, we became aware of their deceit. At first, we thought we could use diplomacy, and bring about a peaceful resolution. Little did we know, they did not want to coexist with us, they wanted to destroy us. Having laid our cards on the table, we also exposed the fact that we knew what they were up to. They turned completely violent, and started attacking our outer-galactic planets, destroying them one by one. We were defenseless, and they just walked all over us. The inner-galaxy planets started building ships and weapons for defense. At first, they were crude, and we really didn't know how to defend ourselves. We lost over half of the galaxies before we developed better ships and weapons. Our defenses became better, and we could slow their progress. The war lasted for five hundred Earth years before we could stop them, and we were able to develop a truce. The battle was quite costly as we lost over three fourths of our Federation. We could maintain a quasi-peace for about two hundred years before the war broke out again. In the meantime, we had developed better ships and weapons, and within a short period of time we were able to defeat them, and push them out beyond our original borders.

We were completely crushed when we saw the destruction they had done to our friends. There was nothing left but ruin. They had killed off entire populations, and our planets were wastelands. There were scattered bands of the enemy left behind to execute guerilla warfare against us, and it took us another hundred years to wipe out these bands, while maintaining our borders against further invasions.

For the next thousand years we worked on repopulating, and rebuilding the galaxies that had been destroyed, and we continued to develop our defense systems. As we did so, we developed better weaponry than what our enemy had, and they no longer sought to attack our solar systems. They didn't try to establish relationships with new galaxies. They went in violently, and just started attacking and destroying. These galaxies were caught defenseless. Many had not developed space travel, and thus had no planetary defense systems. Destruction was in days, entire planet populations gone. As many of these galaxies did not know of our existence, they could not reach out for help. They saw no hope for survival, as the Morians came to destroy everything in their path. Many of these worlds had not developed much further than your own planet.

We decided that we needed to help these other worlds, but

we needed to develop a plan as to how we were going to do that. We couldn't just take our ships and go to these worlds and fight the Morians. This would have left our galaxies defenseless, as it takes most of our fleets to fight them. We couldn't interfere with the development cycle of these worlds and provide them with the weapons to defend themselves, as many had not come to peaceful terms within their own planets. We were afraid that after fighting off the Morians, they would now use their new-found weaponry and turn on each other. Another thought we had was, if the Morians found out that we were helping these other galaxies, they would turn back to us, and we would have another war with the loss of many lives.

We had many things to consider.

Was the planet advanced enough to be able to defend itself?

Were they peaceful or were they like the Morians?

If they were advanced enough to defend themselves, would they eventually use their new-found knowledge, and weaponry and turn against themselves and then possibly against us?

If we decided to help them, what do we give them? We didn't want it to be identifiable enough where the Morians would figure out that the source of their newfound defenses came from us.

Do we have enough time to do what we need to do, without a great loss of lives?

A lot of things our galaxy council had to consider before we could do anything. It didn't take them long before they came to a decision. First, we would build up the federation defense shield. Our shield was very strong now, but it was aging. We had to develop a stronger shield, or defense parameter to keep the Morians from attacking.

In our research labs, we had some new technology we had just developed. It was a force field, but we didn't know what range of space it can protect. In the lab, nothing could penetrate it. It would hit the field and the shield would absorb the impact.

Our first thought was that this would be fantastic to help

defend these new galaxies. We could set up these defense barriers for these galaxies, and it would stop the Morians from attacking and the planets would be ignorant that we had done so. We needed to test this out quickly.

The Federation of Galaxies thought this would be a fantastic idea, but we would use it differently. Our current defenses were more than strong enough to hold back the Morians. Instead of using this new technology to better increase our own defenses, they felt we could set these new defenses up around these galaxies that were being attacked by the Morians. This way the new worlds didn't know they were being defended, and the Morians didn't know where this defense barrier came from, as nobody else had such a barrier.

This took us about fifty years to get the barriers in place. Slowly, the Morian attacks stopped, and peace was once again established. But it was a false peace. In the meantime, the Morians were trying to figure out where these barriers came from. They knew the planets, and galaxies, the barriers were protecting were not developed by them. They were not developed enough to do such a thing. The other thing that gave it away, was that these barriers were all the same, so where did they come from?

It took the Morians about two hundred years before they found a weakness in the barrier. With a great deal of effort, they had found a way to punch a hole through the barrier and allow a small ship to get through. The barrier was self-healing, but not fast enough. With one small ship at a time they came through until they had amassed a small armada. It was large enough to destroy the galaxy they had just entered. With this newfound weakness, they began attacking these defenseless galaxies.

That peace lasted about two hundred years. We had grown wiser over these past millennia and finally realized we could no longer just stand by and let the Morians destroy galaxies. If they continued to marauder and destroy worlds, eventually it would come down to a war just between the two of us, and we were not evil enough to fight on their terms. For the first time, we were afraid. We had the intelligence and weaponry to defeat them, but we did not want to be the only ones left. We decided it was time for us to take a stand. We took the defense barrier we had supplied to all the other galaxies and added it to our defense parameter. We had figured out the weakness in the barrier and had fixed it. We had continued to make ships of all kinds. In your world, they are command centers, battle stars, battle cruisers, destroyers, hospital ships, star fighters and much more. We had ships almost above our ability to man them. We made it well known to the Morians that we would no longer stand idly by while they went about destroying worlds.

For the next two thousand years, we were at war. We made alliances with other galaxies, some good, and some not so good. The bad ones turned on us, and joined the Morians. We supplied all of them with the means to be equal with us, militarily. Out of it, we came away with a stronger Federation of Galaxies. We could set up barriers around worlds that were not ready to make such decisions, like yours. You and other worlds never knew that there was this struggle for good and evil beyond your planet. You had not advanced to a level that you could understand or participate. Also, even now, you are still struggling among yourselves with internal strife and wars. But we saw something in your humanity that was worth watching. You had good in you. You have a spirit that searches for a greater presence and peace. If it had not been for what we saw in your world, we would have left you alone. But, the Morians are the reason we are here now, and *they* will not leave you alone.

Finally, I get an opportunity to speak and I say, "But how do I know you are not the Morians? This has been a great history lesson and I would like to believe it. It doesn't explain why you are here, nor what you expect from us, and, especially from me?

"These are all good questions, and concerns. As I have already told you, my name is Kleg. It is hard to translate into your language. Why I was sent here and why you, I will get to that later.

I assure you I am not a Morian. Once you meet a Morian, you will know they are Morian, because you would be dead soon, if not already. My race is known as the Hypertheans. As you can tell from our history, we are a peace-loving race that had to come to the reality they had to defend themselves. We have lived in harmony with other races for many millennia. It wasn't until we met the Morians, did we have to develop weapons and a defense system. Out of the wars we fought, we felt we had to develop a set of rules by which we would fight, and exist, to keep from being like the Morians. We had to establish a base line by which we could measure ourselves. You have what is known as the Geneva Convention. We have something like that. As you have battled against many nations who do not honor your Geneva Convention, the Morians do not honor ours. When you fight with the Morians, do not expect any type of mercy, as they have only one rule. Destroy everything in their paths, life or habitat.

"As I was saying about the two-thousand-year war, your world does not live in harmony yet. In fact, it will get worse before it gets better."

Kleg pauses for a moment to gather his thoughts and then he continues.

"Your entire world is made up of good people. You haven't come to the point where all of you are willing to work together. Several of your nations are working toward that goal, and your United States is leading in that effort.

Your country is an advanced nation technologically, but over the last ten to fifteen years you have taken your efforts towards paranoia. The internal strife you have within your own country, and with many countries not liking you, you haven't taken the time to figure out how to fix it. You are too busy trying to stabilize your own political processes, and giving away your money to countries that use it against you. You don't know where to focus.

Anyway, about five hundred years ago, when we realized we couldn't stop the Morian alliance from entering your galaxy, even with the barrier set up, we started sneaking in ships and leaving them at the outer end of your solar system, where even your current technology cannot detect them, and far enough into your galaxy where the Morian alliance cannot see them. About one hundred years ago, we completed giving your solar system an armada of ships. When it was time for you to defend yourselves, and become part of our Federation, you now have the means to do it. We thought we had about another two hundred years to go, before the Morian alliance would be attacking your galaxy system. But, based on your efforts to try and communicate with other worlds, they have discovered that life does exist within your solar system and you have advanced to the point where you are communicating out into space, and they are now turning their focus on your planet where the signals came from, Earth. Now we only have about twenty to thirty years to prepare your world for battle.

Suddenly I am the one sitting back and trying to take all this in. In my mind, I am asking myself a lot of questions. *Twenty to thirty years… I am sixty-seven, and in thirty years I will be ninety-seven. What good will I be in this effort? Will I even be alive at that time? How do you convince people, even in twenty years that this is real? Then again, is it real? How can we bring about this harmony he speaks of? Even if we survive, what will we do with all this newly found technology? Will we use it to destroy ourselves? Or, will this supposed war last so long that when it is all over, we will no longer be a people with differences? That is, should we win it?*

I finally say, "Okay." I pause and exhale. "Let's just say, for arguments sake, that everything we have just talked about is true. Let's start with a few earthly facts. One, I am sixty-seven years old and in thirty years I will be ninety-seven. On Earth, even sixty-seven is approaching an age where your mind and body is not good for any kind of military activity. On top of that, I don't have a military mind. What good would I be to you? Or, is my part in this effort over before then, and you have moved on to other people on the planet?"

"I know this is an awful lot of information to take in, but I plan on having you as part of this effort for an extremely long time."

I look at him surprised and say, "Long time? And how far out there is that? And by the way, how old are you, and how long have you been fighting in this war?"

"I am seven thousand Earth years old and I have been fighting in this war for around five thousand years."

"So, are you immortal?"

"No, I will die eventually, and I can also be killed, but not easily. To answer your question, our health system has developed far beyond yours. We have basically eliminated most diseases and ailments that exists in our world. We will be able to provide you cures that will bring you back to a physical condition of a healthy thirty-year-old person, and we can prolong your existence to several hundred years. You will not be immortal, and yes, you can be killed."

"Okay, I will absorb that as we go through this. So, if I agree to this, and we only have about twenty to thirty years, how do we convince people, even in twenty years, that this is real?"

"That will be the difficult part. The Federation of Galaxies chose you for something other than diplomacy. We will have a Federation delegation that will be responsible for convincing your world to be a part of this, and they are good at it. In about three months, your world will know of our existence, and you and I will have our hands full. I believe we can start training your fleet in about a year."

"You have hit me with quite a bit to think about. I would like to think about all this overnight. Can you come back tomorrow? At least, if you disappear now, and then reappear tomorrow, I know I haven't dreamed all this. I want to write all of this down, and review it with you, to make sure I have everything in my head correct. Don't worry, I'm not going to tell anybody about you. Even if I did, nobody would believe me, and I would be the crazy one."

"Until tomorrow," and he disappears just as he appeared.

TWO

I have recorded everything that happened yesterday, but I'm still not sure this is all real. Is the planet on the brink of extinction? I still haven't figured out why they chose me. I'm not a military strategist; I'm not an Einstein; nor am I a leader of people. I don't have great thoughts that people listen to, and most the time the only way I get people to do things, is say, "Just do it".

Oh well, we will just wait and see if Kleg shows up today. If not, then I am the crazy one.

It is about two-thirty in the afternoon, and still no Kleg. I am beginning to wonder if I was dreaming the whole thing. Instead of driving myself crazy, I bury myself in my work to get my mind off it. I am going through some e-mails that just came through, when I start having that strange feeling again. I turn to look to the same spot where I saw Kleg yesterday, and there he is, standing there again.

"Greetings Chris."

I say "hello" back to him, and decide to ask him a question.

"Kleg, is this the real you standing before me, or is it some kind of a projection?"

"It is the real me. I can move from one location to another, but only for small distances. My transportation vehicle is out in the front of your house."

I turn to look out my window to see what is out there, and all I see is a car. I turn back to him and say, "Am I able to see it?"

"Yes, it resembles one of your Earth vehicles. It is what you might call a shape-shifter."

"Are you a shape-shifter?"

"No, what you see is the real me."

"Kleg, I am going to take a leap of faith and believe everything you have told me. But I still have my doubts. I am not sure what to ask you to show me as a sign of good faith on your part, but I have a thought."

"Good, I am glad to hear that you are willing to trust me. What is it you would like me to do to show you that this is real?"

"I would like to travel with you in your car out front to see this armada."

"Before I can do that, I need to physically prepare you for travel in space." He proceeds to pull something from his waist area and sticks out his hand to give it to me. It is a device about eight inches long, one-inch-wide, and less than a thirty-second of an inch thick. He tells me to take it, and then lay it on my right wrist."

At first I pull back, hesitant to take the device and then say, "Why? What is it going to do?"

"Don't worry, it won't hurt you, nor will it take control of you. It will form as a bracelet around your wrist. It is a computer device, and will analyze your physical conditions. It will start analyzing your health condition, and will start adjusting your DNA to improve your health. It will give you a tingling sensation as it starts this process."

"I take it, and hesitantly lay it on my right wrist, and it begins to form a band around my wrist. As it completes the circle, I feel it join, and then I feel tiny prickly objects contacting my skin, and I get a sensation I can't explain. I look at Kleg and ask, "What's going on?"

"This is your life support and knowledge system. Right now, it is analyzing your physical condition and correcting your physical issues. You will no longer have high blood pressure, high cholesterol, diabetes, and all your other issues, some you may not even know about. As we move into space, it will provide you with the air you need to breathe, and provide you with a space suit, should you move into the vacuum of outer space. Your very existence from this point on is tied to this device. Neither you nor anyone else will be able to remove it."

It was a wonderful feeling. I felt like I am getting young again. My energy levels were increasing, my mental capacity to remember things is returning, and increasing. It is like I am totally healthy, and never had any ailments.

He looks at me and says, "Are you ready?"

"I feel like I'm ready."

He tells me to go out to the vehicle out front, and get in on the passenger side when the door opens. He will be in the driver's seat.

I get up, and go out the front door, locking it behind me, and then go to the passenger's side of the car. The windows are very dark, and you can't see inside the vehicle. Suddenly, the passenger door pops open and I look inside. It's not like anything I have ever seen before. Strange instruments are across a dashboard that is shaped in a semi-circle facing the passenger's seat, and the windshield is more like a visual display. I get into the passenger seat and the door closes by itself. I look at the door, and everything is smooth and soft, no door handle, no buttons for anything. When the door closes it completely seals itself. I no longer see any seams. I look over at Kleg, and he is smiling at my wonderment.

He says to me that I will soon get used to what I am looking at, and asks if I am ready.

"I think so."

I look at the console in front of us, and see that there is no steering wheel. It is like sitting in a sports car with bucket seats, and the dash has this wrap-around console, but instead of being flat, there is a surface that protrudes out like a semi-circular surface of an instrument console. Kleg puts his hands on it, punching in some instructions, and the vehicle begins to move into the street. It has this whirring sound, like an electric motor winding up to full power. The vehicle maneuvers through a couple of streets, and then onto a street that is long, and not currently used for traffic. There are no houses that line the street, so we will not be seen. The vehicle begins to change shape. It now takes on the shape of a slick aircraft, but not like any I have seen. It has a long-pointed nose that will slice through the air with little to no resistance from air flow, and the wings just form out of the body in one smooth motion, slanted at about a thirty-degree angle. There is not a tail fin, and now it looks like it is made of polished metal. It feels like we are just hovering above the ground. Kleg looks over at me, and tells me to lean back in my seat. As I do so, we start moving. It is an instant rush as the thrust is instantaneous, and I feel the g-force pushing me back in the seat. The climb becomes almost vertical as we reach space in about two minutes, and then I feel the release of the g-force from my body. I look around and see we are in space. I let out a "Yahoo," and have a big grin on my face as I have done something I never thought I would ever get to experience, space travel.

"Can I ask you another favor? When we reach a distance the Earth is from our moon, would you stop and turn the craft, so that I can see the Earth?"

"Sure."

When we are there he turns the craft so that I can see Earth. Just like the astronauts that have been here before me, seeing the Earth is an awesome sight, and I can't stop looking at the beauty of it.

Finally, Kleg breaks the silence and says, "It's a beautiful sight, isn't it? The first time we saw it, we could hardly believe that such a world would exist. Are you ready to continue on?"

"Sure, I imagine I will see the Earth from this perspective many times."

Kleg tells me to hold out my right arm, he reaches over, and touches the wrist band a couple of times and I start feeling a rush of knowledge start to flood over me, and as I look down at the console in front of me, I begin to recognize all the instruments and their readings, and I'm finding that I know what to do with them all.

I look over at Kleg in amazement and he says, "Let's see if the wrist band works for you. Take us to location ANTRIP1."

Since space is three dimensional, we need three points for an exact position. To keep from saying the three points for a position, the Hypertheans have come up with a new measurement that is equivalent but requires less time to say. I look at the console in front of me, reach out, and key in the coordinates that he has given me. Then I ask him for speed. He tells me take it to presser 54.6, and I do it. I look at the instruments, and make a couple of other adjustments, and we are on our way. Kleg looks over at me, and tells me that the wrist band is working as expected. I continue to feel the flood of knowledge filling my brain with information that I will need to accomplish whatever my mission is supposed to be.

We continue traveling for about four hours before we reach the outer parameters of the fleet. The fleet is well past Neptune. As we are approaching I just instinctively bring the speed down to presser 2. As we continue our approach, I see lots of ships on the horizon in front of us, even in the dark of space. I look down at my instruments, and determine that we are still about twenty minutes away from the ships, and realize that they are monstrous in size. I looked at Kleg to ask the question as to the size of the large ships, and the answer suddenly comes to me. I already know the answer. The largest ship, the command ship, is about five miles across. This is the only one that is oval and circular in shape, and must be about one-mile-deep at its highest point. The ship is still dark, as it has not been powered up yet. We are close enough now that I know what each ship is. I see the command station, which is the one I will be on, battle stars, battle cruisers, battle support destroyers, hospital, supply, and botanical ships, and many others.

I look over at Kleg and say, "I believe. Now what do we do?"

He takes control of the vessel we are in, and we head for the command station. As we approach the station, I see him tap a spot on the console, and it sends a signal to the station. A large door begins to open. As we approach and enter the landing bay area, he tells me we are here for a single purpose, and that is to get me a travel vessel that is the same as his. As his vessel enters the bay area, the lighting in the bay area comes on. As we are coming in, I can see many different types of vessels inside, fighters, shuttles, and a few other travel vessels. There are so many of them, I can't begin to count them, as the bay area is extremely long and large, by any standard that I have seen. We stop in front of one of the travel vessels, and the doors open on Kleg's vessel. We get out of his vessel, and start to walk over to one of the other travel vessels. It is then that I notice, I am walking on a vessel in space. This ship has artificial gravity, and I feel comfortable walking.

I say to Kleg in a surprised voice, "Artificial gravity?"

"Yes, and it is set to mimic your planets gravity, so that you will feel comfortable walking on it. You will also notice, you are walking in an atmosphere being generated like yours. That is thanks to your arm bracelet."

"Come on over here." As we approach one of the travel vessels, he says, "This one is yours. Come, and stand here, and place your bracelet close to the vessel."

Kleg tells me to say these words, "Command ownership, Chris."

I walk over to the vessel, place my bracelet close to the ship, and announce, "Command ownership, Chris." As I stand there waiting, I hear a voice come back from the vessel saying, "Ownership established."

Kleg now tells me that this vessel will only respond to my presence, and my commands. No one can touch or enter the vessel, without my permission. This will be your vessel that you will use to travel back and forth to Earth. Kleg now tells me that we need to take our vessels and go back. I get in my vessel, and he gets in his, and we fire them up, and leave the bay area. As we exit the bay area, I look back and see the bay doors start to close, and the lighting powers down. I feel like the proud owner of a new car, but this isn't a car. This is a travel vessel, and it goes into outer space, and I will be the only human on Earth that will have one, but nobody will know that.

"Kleg, we have a four-hour trip back to Earth, can you tell me what are our next steps?"

"I will need to spend the next year with you. You need to quit your job. Don't worry about your financial situation, I will take care of that. Tonight, you will receive a call offering you a position as Project Director over a new project. They will want to interview you tomorrow morning. You will accept the interview, and when they make you the offer, you will accept it. They will not have a clue as to what just happened. You will be told to report to an address in two weeks at eight o'clock to start work. You will give your current employer the appropriate two weeks' notice, and you will work through these two weeks. The place you will be reporting to will be out in the middle of nowhere, so that we can go unnoticed. Bring your travel vessel to this location, and we will store it in the garage there. I will take you back to your place of residence, and then you will drive your Earth vehicle to this location. You and I will be the only ones in the building."

We arrive back on Earth, store my vessel and he takes me home. Kleg travels off in a different direction, to take care of other things before the call that is to occur tonight, and before the interview tomorrow morning.

I go on in the house with the excitement of a young man who has just landed his dream job. I can't even seem to settle down, as I have so many things going through my mind. My wristband is still downloading information, and I am starting to wonder how much of this I will be able to absorb.

I go to my office, and start recording more of what has just happened to me. I start to think about the resignation letter I need to write. I write the letter, and store it on my PC to send out tomorrow. Now I look at the number of e-mails that I have received, and try to settle myself down. I need to answer these e-mails, or they will ask me what I have been doing all day. I start going through the e-mails one by one, and I get lost in the amount of time that has gone by. I am suddenly startled by the phone ringing. It is about seven-thirty in the evening now, and I answer the phone.

"Hello Mr. Graham, this is Robin from the Pacific Employment agency. Mr. Graham, are you open to considering another position?"

"I am always open to considering new positions. If I consider them to be worth pursuing, I will consider the position."

"I have received a strange request for a new position, and they only want me to offer the position to you."

She runs through the job description and then asks me if I would be interested.

"Sure."

"Can you come by at eight o'clock in the morning for the interview?"

"Sure, I'll be there."

This is going exactly as Kleg has described it to me. I show up at the designated place for the interview, I go in, and meet Robin, and we sit down and talk about the position as the project director for the new project. After my interview with her, she asks me if I am interested?

"Yes, I believe I am."

"Can you wait here for a couple of minutes. I need to go and make a phone call."

She comes back in about five minutes.

"You have the job Mr. Graham. When can you start?"

"I would like to give my company two weeks' notice and then start."

"Your new employer is okay with that, and you will be receiving a call from them later today with more information."

I know I won't receive the call, as I already know what I need to do. I send in my resignation to my company, and then finish out my two weeks. In the meantime, Kleg has been doing some things to set up the fake organization that I will be working for. We need to make it look legal on the books. Kleg tells me to come to this location, which is way out beyond the outskirts of town. It is not that large a facility, but Kleg must feel this will do.

I go inside the building, and Kleg is there. We greet each other. We sit at a folding table and start to discuss what we will be starting to do. He starts off by telling me that we will be going up to the command station and moving it into the asteroid belt, when she is ready. There are enough asteroids in there that we will never be detected.

For the last two weeks, he has had teams of the Federation on the ship prepping it for operations. When we have the station in the asteroid belt, we will be using it as a training facility for me and for the rest of the team, once we have selected the team. He tells me to go and bring my travel vessel around to the back of the building. We will be leaving for the base station in about thirty minutes, and we will both be taking our own travel vessels.

I am so excited about this, and nervous at the same time. This will be my first time that I will be taking my vessel out into space, but I now have the knowledge to operate her, and all its instruments. Kleg tells me we will be up there about two weeks before we will be coming back to Earth.

It is about five minutes before we are to get into our vessels and head into space. Kleg comes over and tells me where our launch area is, and how to take off without setting off any alarms in American airspace. Once we reach space, we will then need to travel toward coordinates ANTRIP1. This will take us to the command station. Speed will be at presser 146.9 and we will be there in about two hours.

I climb into my vessel, start up the engine, and move it to the strip where we will be taking off. I go over the instruments and set them for space travel, and then set the coordinates for where we will be going. I watch as my vessel changes its shape into a streamlined flying vessel. I let Kleg know that I am ready, and then move the vessel forward down our runway. In a matter of seconds, we are airborne and headed for space. It takes us about fifteen minutes to exit the Earth's atmosphere before we are in space. Kleg now tells me to increase speed to presser 146.9, and head towards the designated coordinates. I bring up a display that shows me everything behind me, and I watch the Earth get smaller and smaller until I can no longer see it. I now focus my attention forward, and go over my instruments. I set the vessel on autopilot as we move towards our destination. I watch as we travel towards the command station, and see nothing but space and stars. The brightness of the sun dims as we move further and further away from it. The only light I have is the glow from my instrument panel. I look over the instruments to become more familiar with them, even though I know what each one is for. This helps me pass the time as we travel towards the station. Before long, I feel my vessel start to slow as we approach the command station. I see it coming up before me but I am surprised, as this time I see that it is lit up, as an active ship. I see fighters flying in and out of the landing bays, along with other aircraft. I ask Kleg about this, and he tells me that we now have about twelve thousand Federation planet personnel onboard getting it ready for occupancy, and travel to its new location. The fighters and other crafts are going through their startup processes, as they are being taken out on test flights to make sure they work properly. It will take another week before she is ready to move, but they are working on it around-the-clock to get it ready.

We turn off our autopilot controls and bring our vessels into the designated landing bay, and dock our vessels. The landing bay is all aglow with lights and people moving about the deck doing their jobs. I notice that they are all wearing some type of uniforms, and I realize that Kleg's clothes matches what they are wearing, but to varying degrees. I feel out of place in my civilian clothes. I also see that there are several different looking species, so I am assuming they are from different parts of the galaxies. We step out of our vessels, and everyone stops what they are doing, and looks at me. I am the first human they have seen, and then they come to attention, and salute. I assume they are saluting Kleg, but he looks at me, smiles, and tells me they are saluting their new commanding officer, me. I give the look of surprise, then come to attention, and return the salute, and tell them to carry on. They return to their duties, and one of the Hypertheans comes over to Kleg, and a heads-up display appears from his wrist band, and Kleg motions for me to come on over. He introduces him as Taylor, and that he oversees getting the ship ready for us. All the ships technology is a little dated, since the ships have been sitting here for five hundred years. The crews are updating the hardware and software, bringing her up to standard with the rest of the Federation fleet. I shake hands with him, and he gets right down to business. On his display, he is pointing out that the ship is at 82 percent ready, and that she will be flight ready in seven days. Kleg tells him thanks, and he turns to salute me, and I return the salute, and he moves back to whatever he was doing.

I follow Kleg, and we move towards a shuttle tube that will take us to wherever we want to go. We step into the next available shuttle, take a seat, and I sense in my brain Kleg say

"Command center". The door closes on the tube, and we start moving towards our destination. The tube comes to a stop, the door opens, and we step out, and start walking down a hallway towards the command center. For some reason, I feel I know where it is located. We pass through the door, as it automatically opens, and I am looking at a very large room, about the size of a large auditorium, but it is in a semicircle. Again, this room is full of activity. In the middle of the room is a large oval shaped table, about twenty feet in diameter, and has a command console that surrounds it. It has a 3-D hologram being projected up from the surface, presenting everything that is moving around the ship for about one-light year in distance. This is completely adjustable for any distance up to about one thousand light-years. I move toward a spot that is a little bit elevated, and for some reason I know that this is my station. I sit in the chair, and look at all the instruments that surround me in this area. Again, I notice that I know what the purpose of each of the controls and what the instruments are for. I look up at the hologram before me, and start to study the chart of each of the objects that are being projected. I recognize what each of the objects are that are presented. I see the Earth, moon, sun, planets, the asteroid belt, and the ships that are part of our fleet, and other objects, which I am not familiar with. I stand up and tell Kleg that I would like to see the bridge. He nods, and we start going down the hallway again towards the shuttle tube, and get in the next shuttle. We get in, and take a seat, and I surprise myself, and in my brain I say, "Bridge," and off we go. Shortly, the shuttle comes to a stop and we step out, walk a short distance, and pass through a door into the bridge. In the bridge area, there is a large display screen that is curved, and we can see all the areas outside of the ship. There is a captain's chair, and in front of the chair, are the stations for the helmsman and the bridge officer. Other stations around the bridge are weapons control, bridge communications, science station, operations status, and other major operations. The captain's chair faces forward. He has a quick view of all areas outside the ship. I am the one in charge of the fleet, but this captain will be in command of this ship. I will maintain this as my flag ship. According to the traditions on Earth, we name each of our ships, and since we are just getting started, none of the ships have been named yet.

Kleg now takes me to my stateroom. It is a good-sized room, with a desk, a round conference table, easy chair, a couch, and is well decorated. This is the area of the ship that is designated as admiral country. There is a conference room just off the stateroom, where I will be meeting with other captains and admirals, as we move things forward over the next several weeks and years. Everything here is well decorated for a person from Earth, and suited for a person from the United States.

Kleg says he will give me time to relax and tells me he would like to meet with me in one hour, in the conference room. He said he will bring Taylor, so that I can be brought up to date on everything.

I agree, and he leaves me in my stateroom for the next hour. I am finally alone, and the enormity of the situation is finally starting to set in on me. I start asking myself questions like, "Am I up to the task?" "Has the federation chosen the right person for this job?" and "What am I doing?" Finally, sanity starts to return, and I tell myself that I didn't choose to do this. I was chosen by the Federation, and they certainly must know more about why me than I do. I am proud to be here, and I am sure that I will gain greater confidence as the day's progress. I go into my sleeping quarters area, and look around the room. The bed is against the wall with sheets and a blanket on it. There is an area to sit and relax. One of the walls appears to be a display, as it is showing a soothing image of a green field with a stream running through it. As I look at the bed again, I say to myself, I doubt that I will be doing much sleeping here. Against the wall next to the bed appears to be several drawers. I go over and try to pull one open, but it does not respond to my pulling on it. I finally realize that all I must do is think the command "open" and whichever set of drawers I want to open will open. I look in the drawer, and see that there is a change of undergarments, and they are all correctly sized for me. I think "close" and the drawer closes. Next to the drawers is a door, and as I approach it, it slides open automatically, and find that it is a closet for hanging clothes, but the closet is empty.

Now I notice another door on the other side of the room, and go over to it, and the door automatically opens when I am close to it. It is my own private bathroom. It has a shower, wash basin, and all the necessary items for personal care.

I see there is another door. I approach it, and it automatically opens, and it leads out into my stateroom.

In my stateroom, where the desk and chair are located, the desk has the proper electronics built into it for the study of situations. I have learned from my wrist band that all communications will be processed through my wristband. There aren't any broadcasts of messages over a PA system. They come through the wristband and my brain hears the message. My desk has a heads-up display that appears at my command and shows me things like a computer screen. There is not a keyboard as I communicate to the computer through my wristband. We have no need to carry tablets as our wristband handles it all.

The stateroom also has a good-sized leather couch and a coffee table, that is off to the side on the left. On the right side of the room is a credenza looking table, and I go over to see what is there. On top of the credenza is a tray, with a pitcher of water, and several glasses to drink from. I go to the door that enters the conference room and enter. There is a long table in the room that will sit forty people, and enough room for chairs along the wall. I assume this is for staff people to sit, when we have large meetings. These chairs will roll out from behind the wall, when needed. Behind a partition is a coffee bar area, where people can get coffee, water, or a non-alcoholic drink while we are in meetings. The large table appears to have the capability of having a holographic projector, that we will use during our discussions.

While I am perusing the stateroom, another person comes in, dressed like a steward. He sees me and apologizes for barging in on me, and starts to leave.

"No, please come in."

He introduces himself as Harold, and will be my personal aide. Harold is from a planet that is very peaceful. This is the reason they have chosen him to serve in a service capacity within the fleet. He is there to get me anything I need, while I am in my quarters, stateroom or conference room. He tells me that he will address me as admiral whenever we are together.

"I am glad to meet you. While you are here, would you bring me my special tea."

"Yes sir," and goes behind the partition, and comes right back out with a cold can of the tea I like to drink. I am no longer surprised at anything they do.

"Thanks," and I stand there looking around the room.

He looks at me and says, "Is there anything else I can do for you sir?"

"No thanks," and I start to head back to my stateroom through the same door that I initially came through, but it does not automatically open.

"Sir, this is a magnetically sealed door for your protection and privacy. You are the only one who can go back through that door. Since you are new here, you must use your bracelet to open it, the first time."

From this point forward, when I am close to the door it will open for me. I do that and the door opens for me, and I start to go back into the stateroom but stop, turn and ask.

"Harold, if I was to need you, how am I to get a hold of you?"

"Just think it and your wristband will call me. I will be there as quickly as I can."

"Thanks," and head back into my stateroom.

I go over and sit in the lounge chair, and set my drink on the table next to the chair. I looked around the room wondering what I was going to do next. I then think to pass a message to my wristband and say, "Computer, take notes to discuss at my upcoming meeting with Kleg. List each as an item for discussion."

1. Uniforms for officers, enlisted, and civilians.
2. Create Uniform Code of Justice manual.
3. Recording of year, date and time. How will we do this since there is not a time zone?
4. Naming of our ships and numbering of our vessels.
5. Selection of crew.
6. Training of crew.
7. Assignment of crews.
8. Status of fleet.

End of list.

THREE

I am sitting in the conference room when Kleg and Taylor come into the room. We greet each other, and they come over and sit at the large table close to me.

"Gentlemen, let's go to my stateroom and conduct this meeting in there. I would feel much more comfortable in there around my smaller table than this humongous thing, since it is just the three of us."

They smile and agree, and we get up, and head for the door. As I move toward the door, it opens, and we enter my stateroom.

Kleg says, "I see you have done a little exploring since I left you. That's good."

"Yes."

"I also met Harold, and we spoke for a couple of minutes. May I offer both of you something to drink before we get started?"

They decline and we sit at the table.

Kleg begins the meeting with a statement that they would like to update me on the readiness of the ship.

"Good, I would like that."

Taylor activates the console on the table we are sitting at, and brings up a hologram of the ship. He starts the discussion, starting with the exterior of the ship, and moves inward. It takes him about two hours to go through a brief update as to what is 100 percent ready, and what areas are not. I am asking questions along the way, and both Kleg and Taylor answer each of my questions. As he finishes this update, I ask that they highlight the areas that are not ready. The hologram changes and the areas that are not ready are now red, so that I can visualize the sections.

"How critical are these areas to us being ready to move the ship?"

Taylor answers, "Only these two areas are critical," as he points them out.

"How soon will they be ready?"

He tells me that they are pushing as fast as they can, but believes they can do it.

"What is the problem with these areas? Do we need parts, or more personnel to accomplish the task?"

"It's a personnel issue, sir."

"Can we move some personnel from the non-essential areas to assist them in getting these areas ready, or are the issues so specialized that we don't have the additional personnel to shift around?"

"We can shift some of the personnel around, and it will help quite a bit."

"Is there any reason why we can't make that happen to relieve some of the stress on this group in meeting the deadlines?"

"You say the word, and I will make the adjustments."

"You don't need my permission to shift personnel around, Taylor. You are the one in charge of getting this ship ready. Take care of it.

Is there anything else we need to discuss on getting the ship ready?"

They both respond with a "No."

"Good".

"Taylor, would you mind if I could have some time with Kleg? I need to ask him some questions that doesn't relate to the ships repairs."

He gets up and leaves the room.

I look at Kleg and ask, "What just happened here? The question of getting this ship ready and making these minor decisions should not be brought to me."

"I don't understand what you mean?"

"Kleg, both you and Taylor looked to me during the whole meeting as if I am the one in charge for all decisions. We have junior officers to make sure these types of things get done."

"You are the one in charge. This is your fleet. You are the one who was selected by the high command to run this fleet and to protect this sector. You need to realize that we are here to follow your orders. You have received enough information from your wrist band to reply informatively, with confidence and with authority. The group of Federation personnel that are aboard this ship all know that you are in charge. Even I report to you. We just need to know how you want to run things."

I sit there for several seconds, taking all of this in and think to myself, WOW.

"Kleg, we have the chain of command so that all of the decisions do not fall on one person. If this is to be my fleet, I want us to follow a chain of command. Please make sure that all follow this process and I believe we will make much better progress.

Now, I have several other questions I would like to ask. I have several of them stored on the computer, but I have had a couple more that came up during the meeting.

"From everything that I have learned, the team that is aboard this ship is only here to get her ready, and move her into the asteroid belt. After that, I assume they will remain to assist in the training of the Earth team, when we start bringing them up from the planet. Is this correct?"

"Yes, that is a correct assumption. They will be assisting in booting up the other ships systems. They will get them ready to respond correctly to human commands that will be needed after the initial boot up. They will also start the system enhancements, along with the needed hardware replacements and upgrades."

"Computer. What was my first question I have?"

A computer voice comes back with, "Uniforms for officers, enlisted, and all civilian personnel."

I look at Kleg to further clarify the question.

"My question is this, since we are starting off in a cooperative relationship with the Federation of Galaxies, are we now a part of the Federation of Galaxies?"

"Yes, but we are still in the initial phases of getting your relationship, responsibilities and membership setup."

"Kleg, so that we can properly identify ourselves while aboard our ships, I would like for all of us to wear the appropriate uniform for our ranks and responsibilities. I have noticed that the Federation personnel aboard have on a uniform, and I also assume that they represent their ranks and responsibilities."

"Yes, that would be an appropriate thing to do. I will make sure that we issue the correct uniforms to everyone, when they are trained, but we will get you yours now."

I smile and say "Thanks."

"Computer. What was my second question?"

The computer comes back with, "Create Uniform Code of Justice manual."

"Again, I want to clarify the question with this statement. As a military command, we need a set of rules we need to follow. On Earth, we call this our Uniform Code of Military Justice. I don't know if you have anything like this, or if you have developed to the point where you know how to act without these types of regulations. We, as a world, have not developed to the point where we don't need regulations, and sometimes culturally, do not find it appropriate for our beliefs. We either need to develop a set of regulations that all of us can follow, or hopefully, you already have such a manual from the federation that we will need to follow. I am hoping that it is the latter, so that we all follow one common set of rules."

"You have asked a very good question. We do have such a manual. During your military training, we will go through these regulations that we have established. As you have stated, we had to go through a similar process that has been very painful through the years. We expect, and demand, that all regulations be followed, and that punishment for disobedience is firm, final, and just. You will need to learn the entire manual for this fleet, as you are the final authority as to its execution. Should your fleet fail to follow our code, we have a tribunal which will make the final statement as to what punishment you will have on your fleet."

"Thanks."

"Computer. What was the third question?""

The computer comes back with, "Recording of year, date and time."

"How will we do this since there is not a time zone out here?"

Before I can explain the question Kleg comes back with this answer.

"All the different planets in the Federation have different ways to record their planets cycles and rotations. We have all come to an agreement for the space Federation that we would all use a common recording process. We know that all creatures have different needs for sleep cycles, so we allow for this to occur. As far as what we do to record when things happen, we have a common measurement which meets all our needs, and again, keeps things common for the entire Federation. We call it the star date. Our current star date is 1492.67. You and your team will learn more about how to measure this during your training. As far as your twenty-four-hour Earth cycle, we agree to abide with your twenty-four-hour clock. You can decide what the actual time is later."

"Computer. What is the fourth question?"

The computer comes back with, "Naming of our ships and numbering of our vessels."

Kleg again smiles at the question and answers, "We know that you Earthlings like to name your vessels. We also name our vessels. I can provide you with the rules for naming and numbering of the ships."

I smile and say, "Thanks, we as earthlings thank you."

"Computer. What is the fifth question?"

The computer comes back with, "Selection of crew."

Kleg looks at me a little confused and I give him this explanation.

"We as a set of individual cultures and countries, still are not at peace with each other. I think for us to become a working team throughout the fleet, I feel we need to have mixed crews, not allowing any one nation to have complete control of a ship or a fleet."

"I understand, and it is good thinking. You are in charge, so it is your decision."

"Computer. What is the sixth question?"

"Training of crew."

I tell him there is no need to answer this question. I have received my answer from the above questions.

"Computer. What is the seventh question?"

"Assignment of crews."

Again, I tell him there is no need to answer the question.

"Computer. What is the eighth question?"

"Status of fleet."

"Currently the Hypertheans are only working on this ship. This is the only one we are activating now."

"Computer. What is the ninth question?"

The computer tells me that it is at the end of the list.

"Ok, then, what are our next steps?"

"The most important step is to get you trained to handle this fleet, and be ready to defend your world. Right now, we will start with what you are defending. To you it is known as the solar system. This is probably mind-boggling to you right now. Since the Earth is the only planet that has a civilization on it. For now, your solar system is outside the reach of what your world is capable of defending. We, the Hypertheans, will take the battle to the Morians, further away from your solar system. This will give you more time to set up your defenses, and to identify any outliers that may be trying to come in through a back door."

Kleg activates the console on my table, and then brings up an image of millions of stars.

"This is what you have identified as the Milky Way system, of which your sun is among them. Your sun is right here."

He points to it on the hologram.

"Your Milky Way is over one hundred thousand light-years in diameter and has a depth that ranges from ten thousand to thirty thousand light-years in size. It is impossible for Earth to defend your Milky Way system. Therefore, you have this quadrant of space to defend. It is very strategic for the Federation and, of course, very important to you, as it represents your world's very existence."

Kleg reaches again for our sun, and takes it between his first finger and thumb, and expands the hologram to the point where the Milky Way disappears, and our solar system is the only thing that is now displayed in the hologram. It amazes me to see our solar system in this 3-D perspective, in full color, and representing our planets true position at this very moment.

Kleg now points to where we are currently positioned, and where we will be moving the command ship within the asteroid belt.

"Your defensive positions will extend out from your sun for three light-years, with a circumference of six light-years.

Everything from your sun will be broken down into quadrants, and will be identified in sectors. These sectors will be extended out two light-years, beyond your defensive positions around your sun. Everyone on your staff will need to know these sector numbers, and positions by heart, so that you can respond quickly, to where that is visually in your mind."

As Kleg spoke this, the process of the sectors was being represented on the hologram, and the outer defense parameter appeared as a globe around the solar system, making it very apparent the enormity of the effort that was before us.

As I am studying the hologram, I ask Kleg a question, "If the Morians were to come straight at us, which direction will they be coming from?"

Kleg points in a direction, and explains, "Morians have excellent strategies, and will more than likely come at you from many directions."

"I agree, but I just want to know where they are in space. I would like to be able to set detection buoys in each sector, to about ten light-years out from our defensive position. This will help us to be aware of any traffic that will be passing through that sector. This will also help us identify friendly from foe, since they might go through one of our sectors, and in what direction they will be traveling in. While we are at it, we might as well set buoys up within our solar system as well. We need to protect everywhere we are. I would like to get this done as soon as we can. Is this something your people can do for us, or do I need to wait for my team to be trained before I can get this done?"

"This is a very good idea. I believe we can assist you with this one. I will speak with Taylor, and see how quickly this can be accomplished."

"While I am thinking about it, I would like to change the subject for a moment. Kleg, as a matter of curiosity, where do you call home?"

Kleg brings up a hologram of the Milky Way again and then

shrinks this on down to where we see three other galaxies, and he points to one of them.

He pauses and says, "My home is here, and is about three hundred thousand light-years away from here."

He then points to another galaxy. This one is two galaxies further out from his home.

"This is where the Morian home world is located. It is about five hundred thousand light-years away from here."

"Kleg, how long does it take you to travel the three hundred thousand light-years to get here?"

Kleg answers without looking away from the hologram, "About two of your Earth years, but for me it's only about one month."

"How many different races of planets are in the Federation?"

"There are about three hundred different planetary systems that are part of the Federation. Most of them come from our galaxy and fifty or so come from these two galaxies," as he points to them."

I get up and walk around thinking about what I am looking at.

"I assume that our ships will have good sensors that can reach out a couple of light-years, and tell us what is moving around us. The buoys we will be setting up will give us better detection capabilities out another ten light years, but how do we know what is traveling out beyond the ten light-years? You have been out here in space a lot longer than we have, what do you do?"

Kleg now looks at me and says, "Don't worry about what is going on out here in this space." He waves his hands in the hologram, referring to the space between the galaxies. "We have a presence in here, and our communications are developed way beyond what you can think about. Messages will travel through space at speeds one million times the speed of light, and you will receive information that will keep you well informed. All you need to be concerned about is what will be happening within your ten-light-year area - for now."

I realize that I am exhausted at this point.

"Kleg, we have been going at this for over eight hours now. Can we call it a day?"

"Sure, I am used to going at things at my pace, and I'm not used to how you humans function yet."

"Can we take a walk about the ship. I know we won't see everything new, but you can point out different areas to me as we walk."

He motions toward the door, and we leave and just start walking. As we are walking, and just chatting about nothing, he points out the officers eating area, the captain's quarters, officer country, and many of the different functioning areas as we go along. One of the areas I see is something like an Earth naval ship area, we call CIC. Kleg tells me there are two of these areas aboard the ship, one is for the ship itself, which is what we are looking at, and the other is for me, and the control of the fleet. We come to an area that is labeled "Communications," and I ask if we can go in here. The room is wide enough apart that there is a long walk way down the middle for three to four people to walk side by side, and not bump into each other. Along both walls are communication stations where communication teams will be sitting and communicating with the fleets of ships, home worlds, the Federation, and monitoring other communications that are going across the airways. The room must go back about one hundred and fifty feet. There are only about ten people in the room monitoring and sending communications, mainly communications back and forth between the Federation stations. As we turn to leave the room, I tell Kleg I am ready to head back towards my quarters. We take a different hallway, and he continues to point out the different areas. Not every space is enclosed as we pass several open areas that just represent sitting areas where people can sit and read or just have conversations and relax. We reach my quarters and I realize that it is time for me to eat supper. I invite Kleg to join me for a meal. He respectfully declines, as it is not his meal hour yet, and he has other matters to take care of. Some of the items are what we had been discussing during our long meeting.

"Okay, and by the way, I have made the decision on how we will handle time in the fleet. We will use our twenty-four-hour clock, and our time will be measured in Zulu time. Will that work for you?"

"Yes, and I will relay that to the rest of the crew on board, and make sure that all clock measurements are set accordingly."

I go into my stateroom, and ask Harold to please come into the room.

"May I help you sir?"

"Yes, I would like my meal here in my stateroom in about thirty minutes. Is that possible?"

"Yes sir. I will have it here for you at that time. Is there anything in particular you would like to have?"

"No, just a meal."

"Very well sir. I will get it for you."

I go into my quarters and wash up and then come back out of my stateroom, sit in my chair, relax, and let the information I have received today just flow. One of the things I am noticing is that my memory retention has increased dramatically. I also believe I am getting a photographic memory. I am clearly recalling every detail of all the images I have seen today.

Shortly, Harold comes into the room with a cart of food floating in the air, along with some other items. He goes to my table, sets out the tablecloth, dishes, silverware, and a drink of ice tea. He sets the tray of food on the table, and tells me that the table is ready for me. I go over to the table to eat, and he moves to put the food on my plate. I tell him that will be okay as I can do that. He then takes the cart and moves to my sleeping quarters.

I look at the food that has been prepared for me and find

it to be a well-balanced meal. I put the portions of food on my plate, and begin to eat. Shortly, Harold comes out of my quarters.

"Your uniform has been laid out for tomorrow, and I have prepared your room for the evening."

"Uniform, what uniform?"

"From the discussion you had with Kleg this afternoon, you talked about uniforms for humans to wear. Kleg asked me to make sure that you had the proper attire for your rank, and that you will need to start wearing it."

"Okay, thanks."

I finish my meal, and Harold comes and removes the dishes, and tells me good night. I have taken a seat in my lounge chair and just sit back with my eyes closed for a few minutes just relaxing. I hear a beep and realize that I have an incoming message I command my wristband to show the pop-up display and I see that it is providing me with information about what is going on back on Earth. I listen to this for about thirty minutes, and then I send some emails back home to let folks know what is going on, without telling them too much.

I now head for my bedroom area, enter, and prepare myself for bed. After I am ready, I sit on the bed, lay back, and before long I am asleep.

At 0600 the next morning I am up, dressed in my new uniform, and go into my stateroom. I find Harold there preparing my table again for breakfast.

"What would you like for breakfast?"

I let him know and then ask, "Would you ask Kleg to join me here at 0800."

At 0800 Kleg enters my stateroom, and I motion for him to sit.

"Kleg, I know you have an agenda for me, and I hope it matches what I have in mind. But first, let's go through what you have laid out for me today."

Kleg starts going through the schedule, and it appears to be very busy but thorough.

"Did you have something else you would like to discuss?"

"Yes, but it is not the first item you have on the schedule, but my second item will be more involved. That will be around the selection of the crews for the ships. From what I have calculated, we will need about one million men and women to properly man our ships. As I think about it, I feel we will need to approach the world back home, and let them know of the situation. This is where the difficult part will come into play. We will need to include all the nations, as this threat involves them also. I know we will receive resistance and many will believe this is a hoax. It will be slow going at first. Some nations will tell us that they will take it from here, and will want to be in control, and I assume that the delegates will address that. I have many concerns, but we will just have to address them as they come."

"Thank you for bringing this up. We will start addressing this tomorrow. I will make sure that it is on our schedule."

As Kleg stands up, he motions for me to follow him, and he says, "First off on our schedule, is a meeting with Taylor so that he can give us an update on the progress they have made since we last met."

We head off down the hallway to meet with Taylor, and thus began my day. I will have basically a day of training about space maneuvers, understanding space issues, along with many of the complications of living and operating in the darkness of space, with only the distant stars as light. Over the next six months, we will be going through these routines to make sure that I am comfortable with the whole process. When it comes to battle tactics, I will automatically react to them without thinking, but training is coming.

The first week passes, and Kleg now tells me that there is a delegation from the Federation coming that will be addressing all the nations back home and getting them onboard. He tells me that he had received a message last night that they would be here soon.

I look at him a little confused and say, "How long have you had this discussion planned, if it takes two Earth years for you to travel from your home world?"

"No, it is nothing like that. Since we are in space and are working with many worlds, our delegation is coming from a visit to a world that is close to yours, relatively speaking."

I accept this answer, and we continue with our discussion.

With the week having passed, Taylor has all the critical areas ready for us to begin our movement towards the asteroid belt. I discuss with Kleg who should captain the ship to the asteroid belt. At first, I think about Taylor, but Kleg tells me that he does not know anything about flying the ship, as his responsibilities is like a chief engineer. Then I ask Kleg about himself, he smiles, and says that he would be honored to take the ship to the asteroid belt.

"Good, it is settled. You are the captain of the ship for the movement to the asteroid belt. You know what you need to do to get the ship underway. Go ahead and assemble your crew."

"Yes sir."

Kleg has taken off to assemble his crew that will be used to move the ship from our current location to the asteroid belt. In about two hours, he comes to me in my stateroom, and the doors sensors tells me that Kleg is outside of my stateroom.

"Enter."

At my command the door automatically opens, and Kleg comes in, and I motion for him to sit at the table, and I join him there. Kleg gives me an update that he has assembled his crew, and all are working on making preparations for getting underway. He then tells me we will be getting underway at 0900 the next morning, and he asks me if I would honor him by joining him on the bridge at 0800.

"I would be honored."

The next morning, I pass through the door to the bridge at

0800 and I see that it is alive with activity. People are moving about checking on instruments, talking with the different departments, and then I hear someone shout, "Attention on deck," and everybody in the room snaps to attention.

"Carry on," and they go on about their duties.

I see Kleg at one of the stations discussing something, and when he has finished he comes over to me and says, "Good morning sir. Did you sleep well?"

"I slept fine. Did you get any sleep?"

He tells me that he got some sleep, but he spent most of his time down in engineering.

"Problems with the engines?"

"Not anymore, they are working perfectly now."

"Are we going to be ready to get underway at 0900?"

"All systems are a go for a 0900 departure."

"Well, I'll let you get back to it. You have a ship to get underway. I will be walking around and observing, making everyone nervous."

Kleg smiles and returns to what he was doing.

As 0900 arrives, Kleg comes over to me, and tells me that the ship is ready to get underway.

"Let's take her out Captain. You have the con."

Kleg moves over to his captain's chair, and sits in the chair. He looks around the room and tells his first officer, "Let's take her out."

The helmsman enters a few commands at his console and enters the course for getting underway. Slowly the ship starts to move as we move away from the rest of the fleet that is waiting on crews to get them underway. There is clapping and cheers as the ship makes it first movement in quite some time, also with a large amount of enhancements that are being tested for the first time.

As the ship begins to pick up speed, Kleg says, "Helmsman, come to course ANTRIP 0.52, speed Presser 15.1."

Again, I see the helmsman enter in the new course, and

then he moves his throttles to bring the ship to a speed of presser 15.1.

As we view the movement of the ship through the monitors, I see the fleet get smaller and smaller behind us as we move away. Since we are underway, and it will take us about twenty hours to reach our destination, I tell Kleg that I am leaving, and I head for my command station.

I walk into the command center, and the place is abuzz with activity. I see Taylor at one of the stations working with a couple of other crew members, and they seem to be working through some problem. I head for my chair, and take a seat. They have the hologram display system up, and I key in a few commands at my station, and what is in front of me begins to rotate to where I am viewing our solar system. I watch from my chair to where we are heading. Everything looks normal from my perspective, so I slowly look around the room at the activity that is going on. It appears that this is also a shakedown cruise, as everything does not appear to be working properly. At some of the stations there is only a single person, and things are working normally. Others have two to three people leaning over the station, and the group is in deep discussion as they touch screens, buttons, and move about to resolve the issue. Taylor finally sees me, and comes over to greet me.

"Good morning sir. How are you today?"

"I am doing fine. It appears we are having some shakedown issues. Anything I need to be aware of?"

"No sir, these are not issues that are causing major problems. We will have everything fixed in here by the time we arrive at the asteroid belt."

"Good. What about in other parts of the ship?"

"More minor issues, but you don't need to worry. The ship is doing beautifully for our first run in quite some time."

"Very well, carry on."

"Yes sir," and goes back to helping with the problem he was working on.

I watch for about another ten minutes, and then decide to walk about the ship and observe for myself. As I walk down the halls, people pass by, going about their normal routine, while others are rushing to get somewhere. I step into the communication area, and see the normal number of people in the room, and everything is working as it should be.

I leave the communication area, and then I head for the engineering deck. The doors automatically open for me, and I enter the engineering bay. I hear the hum of the engines running, and I see people at their stations monitoring their processes and making sure that all the systems are operating at peak performance. The chief engineer is two levels down, and I can hear him yelling at someone about some process that needs to be adjusted. I just smile and turn and leave the area. I am very proud of what I have seen, and that the crew is working well together, even though it is not the crew we will wind up with.

I return to my stateroom, sit at my desk, and start working through a process on how we need to approach the countries on Earth. Over the past week, Kleg and I have had several lengthy discussions on how we need to ask the delegation to approach each nation. With 228 countries in our world now, and with a population of just over seven billion we should be able to recruit the one million people we need to man our ships. We have also decided to give some of the countries points, as they are more technically advanced than others, and will be easier to train.

We have also decided to set some guidelines around how things will work within the command structure.

1. There will not be a political agenda, therefore, no countries will be involved in the selection process, or in the direction as to what we will be doing in space. We are there to defend this solar system and Earth. And,

we will not have any influence on the political agenda of the planet or countries.

2. Since all the ships belong to the Hypertheans, or, should I say, the Federation, no nation has any say as to what or how we will be doing things. I, as the sole person appointed by the Federation to be in charge, will have single control and direction for the fleet.

3. All nations will have a seat on the Federation council, but because we are new, and the size of our world is small in comparison to the other worlds in the Federation, we will not have much influence in what is happening within the Federation.

4. Because we are still a world in conflict, we will have a staff of fleet marshals to maintain order aboard the ships, and the Earth bases. These marshals will be well trained in self-defense, and no one aboard any of the ships, or bases, will have any type of weapons. In the fleet, there is not a need for personal weapons, as the Morians do not want to capture our ships. This also cuts down on the chance of mutinies aboard any ship.

5. Selection of our high-ranking staff will come from those countries that have a naval presence on Earth, as they will be best skilled in understanding what we need to do out here.

6. Our fighter pilots will be selected from all countries that have fighter planes. These pilots will have to learn new skills for fighting in space. Where we will be, there is not any light to see the enemy by. They will be fighting, and flying, mostly by instruments.

7. Since we have a need for people with hydroponics and farming skills, medical skills, food services, and other types of non-military services, we will select these roles from all the civilian populations.

8. We will also train, and provide, medical knowledge and instruments for those countries that agree to be a part of the Federation.
9. All ships captains will have a counselor assigned to them to provide guidance, and offer alternative views. These counselors will come from the Federation.
10. All who are selected and agree to be a part of the fleet, must resign their positions they have on Earth. Their allegiance will now be to the Federation, and will only take orders from their commanders in the Federation.
11. All who agree to be a part of the Federation, will receive new uniforms that will be appropriate for their rank and title.
12. Travel to and from their assigned duty stations will be at designated departure points, and they will bring nothing with them. There will be a screening process to make sure that these rules are followed.

We will have base stations on Earth, in selected locations around the world. These base stations will be ten thousand acres of land each, and will be given to the Federation by each country. This property will be part of the Federation, and not ruled by any laws of that country, but we will respect their laws, while we are off base. We will protect these bases by the same type of technology the Federation uses as galaxy barriers. There will be a no-fly zone established at ten miles out from these barriers. Warnings will be given to aircraft approaching the no-fly zone, and they will be destroyed if they do not move away. Federation ships will approach aircraft while in the no-fly zone, and escort them out of the no-fly zones. Hostile actions on these Federation aircraft will be an immediate destruction of the aircrafts.

These bases will be for military training for those individuals who volunteer for Federation service, and will be a boot camp for enlisted and an officer candidate school for officers. The bases primary function is for transport up to respective duty stations, and for leave back home. The base will also support the delivery of supplies. These supplies will be screened and processed before shipment by designated base personnel. These bases will be in remote locations in the respective countries where there is minimal air traffic. This will allow for Federation crafts to enter, and leave, the airspace with minimal impact on that countries air traffic. These Earth bases will be the only location within the fleet that will have armed men defending these locations. Since the bases are protected by a dome shield, this protection area will be at the entrances of the bases. I have decided to have a Marine corp general in charge of all the Earth bases.

Approaching the world with this information, and convincing them that we are real, will be the most difficult of these tasks. Within the week, we will be receiving a delegation of Federation representatives that will be approaching the people of Earth with this information, and convincing them that we are serious and that our need is immediate. I am relieved that I am not the one that will be doing this job. I will have to go and appear before the United Nations, and show them that a human being is in charge of this process. But the first appearance to all the nations will be via holograms, in front of all the nation's leaders.

The twenty hours have passed, and we have arrived at the asteroid belt. Because the *Hyperthia* is so large Kleg begins to maneuver the ship through the rocks. He is using a tractor beam around the ship to grab each one, and maneuver it out of the way, and then place it back in its location. This will eliminate any appearance that a path was cut through the asteroid belt. We finally arrive at the location, and set the ship in its holding position, while we will be in the asteroid belt.

I go to the bridge and someone let's out with, "Admiral on bridge," and I tell them to carry on.

Kleg is finishing up with the stabilization process. After he finishes, I tell him "well done." He thanks me, and turns to his first officer, and tells him to take over. He sees I am looking at the display in the direction of Earth, and pauses to allow me to look at it. I turn to him, and let him know that I am ready to move on.

"Were there any problems with this shakedown cruise?

"We had some minor ones, but Taylor will be taking care of them."

"How did you like handling the ship?"

"It felt good. This was my first time to captain one this large. It was a little bit different than what I am used to."

FOUR

The week has passed, and we know from communications with the Hyperthean delegation ship, that they will be arriving at our location within the hour. I have continued my training with Kleg, and he is pleased with my progress. He tells me that I am learning faster than he anticipated. With this progress, we need to step up the training schedule, and get our crews selected as soon as we can, once the delegates work out the details of how we will work together.

"When you say 'selected,' have they been selected like I was, or are we on our own in the selection process?"

"Some of the high-ranking officers will be recommended to you, as well as doctors, nurses, and others. The rest will be selected by us, meaning you and me, or they will need to volunteer."

The delegation arrives in the shuttle bay, and Kleg and I are there to greet them. We welcome them aboard, and we show them to their quarters where they will be staying while they are onboard to allow them time to freshen up from their long journey.

"We have arranged for all of us to have a meal together, and it will be held in our delegates eating area. We will be gathering in their lounge area around 1800, and will be sitting down for our meal at 1900."

They agree to the arrangements, and we go our separate ways.

At 1755, I show up in the lounge area, and see that Harold and several stewards, have done a very nice job in setting up the tables. He knows and understands the culinary requirements of each of the individuals that will be served tonight, and has them sitting in designated spots. There are seven members of the delegation, each is a representative from different galaxies. Harold has assigned me a spot between two of the delegates, and Kleg is between two on the other side of the table. We have conversations before the meal starts, and some of the conversations continue into the evening.

The next morning, we meet with the delegation at 0900, having given them time to clear their heads, and start discussing what they will be doing to convince the nations to be proud to be part of this effort. They tell me that the first meeting will be individually, with the leadership of each of the countries, but it will be with a hologram, projected into the area where they will be.

They have done their research on each country, and some will be acceptable, while others will be hostile towards it. They know when their cabinets meet, and they will be joining them when their meetings have started. At the appearance of the delegates in the room, all doors will be sealed, where no one can enter or leave. All communications with the outside world will be cut off. This will help in preventing any interruptions. Once order has been restored, the delegation will then present their intentions before each of the country's leadership. One of the primary requirements, will be that all citizens of that country will know of the meeting, and know the purpose of the Federation. Everything will be known to all. It will take several hours of discussion, and the delegation will assemble again to present their observations. For those countries that will show good faith and intention to be part of the Federation, the delegation will start appearing before their leadership in person, but with caution. Some of the countries will be hesitant at first, but will come around, while others do not want to have any part of it. We will exclude them from being a part of the Federation, but they will get the benefit of our protection. They will be excluded from receiving the technology benefits that will be provided to those countries that will be part of the Federation, but they will receive all the medical benefits. With 228 countries to cover, it will take the delegation about three weeks to visit with each country. It is anticipated that about two hundred countries will be open to further discussions. The other twenty-eight will be removed from the list for discussions, and will be revisited in about six months, to see if they have changed their minds after they start seeing what is going on in other countries. If all goes as planned, we should be able to start talking with potential personnel in about three weeks.

At 1300, the delegation started holding their meetings, and started with the United States. As expected, it created quite a stir when they appeared in the Oval Office. It created another stir, when they found out they were locked in these chambers, and that there was no communication with the outside world. After about a minute, they finally settled down enough to take a seat, and hear what the delegation had to say. It took the delegation about twenty minutes to present their case. The delegation told them that they would give the cabinet twenty-four hours to think about what has been said, and then the delegation would return to discuss what the nation would like to do at that point. Then the delegation disappeared, just as quickly as they appeared, and the doors unsealed, and communications was returned. Then the delegation went to the next country, doing the same thing, over and over. They did twelve countries that afternoon, and then would do another twelve countries the next morning, before they started revisiting each of these twenty-four countries over the next twelve hours. So, for the next three weeks they kept this routine up.

As countries began to agree to be part of the Federation, Kleg and I began working with them. We provided them with the initial guidelines, which we had developed earlier in our process. So far, we have not had any nation object to these guidelines. A few wanted to negotiate them, but we stood firm. As part of our agreement we had one of the Hypertheans aboard ship, who was a doctor, go down to Earth, and started sharing medical knowledge. He provided cures for many of the medical issues that people had, new medical procedures for evaluations and treatments, and many, many more things. As the delegation began to move down the list, there were some countries that were very doubtful, and refused to be a part of the Federation, others rejected the thought completely. Some refused to be dictated to by the initial guidelines, and bowed out. Of the 228 countries that the delegation spoke with, forty-two refused to be part of the Federation. This would not create a problem, as down the road, over half of them will become part of the Federation, as they see the benefit. Some of the nations who refused, would have individuals who wanted to be part of the crews. We gladly accepted them into the Federation.

With all the citizens of the Earth knowing of our presence, and our intentions, it was very difficult for the countries who held out to stand apart from being part of the Federation. Several of them bowed to the pressure of their citizens to be involved with the Federation.

The first crew we train will be for the command ship. It will take about twenty-five thousand men and women to fill the roster for the command ship. The first person I want, is the one who will captain this ship. I have interviewed, and have spoken frankly with many of the potential captains, all of whom will eventually command a ship in the fleet. Of them all, two of them has stood out as potential captains for the command ship. The one I am leaning toward is a female, who shows strong leadership, and is fair. She knows how to stand her ground. She will proudly accept the position, even though it is not a forward combat ship. This command ship has more armament than the total sum of two entire fleets, but it is not intended to be in a forward combat position, but in the end, she will see lots of action. She will be my captain.

I will also be selecting my assistants, who will be working directly with me. I will need someone to handle my communications out to the fleet and back to Earth, liaisons for my admirals, my executive officer, and several others. They will also be going through the training with this group of trainees.

Training twenty-five thousand crewmembers will be a tedious task for the Hypertheans, as this will be the first crew to be trained. The first part of their training will be a boot camp for both officers and men. This will be different than the boot camps they went through to get into their militaries on Earth. This boot camp will teach them things about operating in space. After they complete this training, they will be trained in shifts, officers in one section and enlisted in another. Some of the enlisted training will last about six weeks, and the rest of their training will be on-the-job. Officer training will take about three months, with the captains training being the most intense. After all the training for the personnel of the command ship is completed, we will be at full complement, and the command ship is ready for service.

We have also selected a name for the command ship. After many names were considered, we have narrowed it down to FCS *Hyperthia* (FCS-2014). Federation Command Ship *Hyperthia* in honor of a galactic friend, who saw Earth as a potential for this honor. In a ceremony, Kleg turns over command of the ship to Captain Jennifer Faraday. She accepts command of the ship.

In the days ahead I watch the officers and crew work together. I see the pride and dedication of this new crew, taking on their responsibilities with energy and enthusiasm. The Hypertheans that were aboard will remain for some time to continue to assist the crew in the months ahead.

Next, we started selecting individuals that would meet the needs of our fleet, as far as our food supply, water creation processes, waste disposal, etc. We have sixteen large ships that are our farming-based ships. Before we can start selecting these individuals, we need to select our crews that will bring these ships to life, and keep them functioning. We first began by selecting our captains, officers and enlisted. Among the selection process, I have selected someone that will oversee the entire hydroponics fleet. That person will be Carla Lewis. She has overseen food distribution for a large food distribution company before coming to us, volunteering her service. Before they can bring the ships to life, they will need about three months of training on the entire process. Because these ships are hydroponic-based, there is no soil to plant the crops. They will require lots of water with the proper nutrients to grow these crops. Since these ships will produce the food supply for the one million men and women, with differing food requirements, we will need agriculturists to man our fleets. The men and women who will handle the production of our food supply will come from the civilian sector on Earth. They will receive minimal military training, but they will learn how to survive aboard the ships and will take their orders from the officers on board these ships, however, the officers and men will not be telling them how to do their jobs. Each ship will have a civilian farm manager in charge of the civilian workers.

There will also be men and women aboard, to package these finished goods, and store them for transport ships, that will take them to the other ships in the fleet that need the goods.

As we completed this selection process, we have brought them all aboard the command ship, and started their training. Even though the command ship is large, the training area is not large enough for all the crews at once. It will require around twenty thousand officers, enlisted, and civilian personnel to man these ships. It is quite intense, but all will go through the process with great enthusiasm, and are eager to start a new adventure. They complete their training, and upon graduation, they are ready to take their positions onboard their respective ships. These ships will be known as FFSs, Federation Food Ships. We will allow the civilians aboard these ships to come up with the names for these ships. There will be a selection process by a committee on each ship, that know the naming restrictions, and will make sure that the names comply.

As this group begins its training, we began the selection process for admirals, officers and enlisted to man the combat ships. This process will take quite some time, due to the large roster we must fill. Some will not make it, and we will have some making the roster, who we will have to release later in the process. We have developed a method by whom, and how we train this crew.

The first group will be combat crews for the battle stars, and the fourteen selected admirals. They will start coming aboard to start their training soon. It will take six months for them to complete their training, the fourteen admirals will only require three months of training. The pilots for the fighters on the battle stars, will begin their training three months later, and will complete their training when they are aboard their assigned battle stars.

The next day, I am on the introduction schedule, to greet these trainees. After I am with them for an hour, I go to meet with Captain Faraday and we have our daily update.

After our meeting, I ask my second to make sure we have a shuttle for my staff and Kleg to take us around to the food supply ships for the next week.

"I will make sure that the shuttle craft is ready at 0800 in the morning."

I now address my communication officer and say, "Will you

send a communiqué to the sixteen ships, letting them know that we will be coming? Also, will you have some photographers come with us to take pictures of our progress for the folks back home?"

"Yes sir."

The next morning my staff, Kleg and I leave, and it will take us about four hours to get to the first ship, and as we enter their shuttle bay, we see that the crew is lined up to provide the proper greeting allowed for my position as senior fleet admiral. I am pleased to see that Admiral Lewis is there. We go through the greeting process with the captain of the ship and the civilian manager, and explain to them that I would like to see the ships' operation from both of their perspectives. There will be some discussions with both, and one-on-ones. Their relationships are still new, so no disagreements to discuss and resolve. This is my first tour of one of our food ships, and it is quite impressive the way the Hypertheans have put these ships together. The military staffs report no problems with any of the ships. I then meet with the civilian staff, and we walk through each of their stations. We see the water with its nutrients being combined, and flowing out to the planting area where they will be growing their crops. The ship has only been active for about three weeks, and I already see little sprouts growing in many of the sections. The people who are taking care of this process are very pleased with the new processes they have learned, and the results they have seen.

We follow this process with the remaining fifteen ships, and the results are the same on all the ships. As we leave each ship, we are thanked by the officers, enlisted, and civilians for the opportunity to serve in this adventurous capacity.

We return to the command ship after being away for a week. I go to the command center, and watch the duty crew as they monitor all the processes. I look at the hologram being displayed, and see all the active ships on the screen, and everything looks normal.

I then meet with the delegation which is still aboard the ship, and we go over how negotiations are going with the nations. Five more nations have agreed to be a part of the Federation, and this allows more men and women to be selected for the fleet. A couple of these nations have difficulty culturally, with women in authority, but they will allow men who are not as culturally challenged, to be a part of the Federation. One nation has decided to drop from the Federation. There had been some crew members who had been selected from this nation, and they were given the choice to either stay with the Federation, or to follow their nation's lead. Ninety percent of them decide to stay. The delegation will continue to work with all the nations in getting them properly involved and introduce them to new things every day.

FIVE

Kleg informs me that it is time for them to start training me on situational warfare. Eventually, when the rest of the admirals and captains are trained, we will go through many weeks of war games that will be set up by the Hypertheans from real-world situations.

As I start this training, I am horrified by what I see, in just the first day of training. How they fooled the Hypertheans into thinking they supported life for so long is beyond me. The Morians are animals, and have no respect for life. The brutality of their torture when they capture someone alive is beyond belief, and they are experts at keeping someone alive as they extract information. When they have the information, they continue the torture for pure enjoyment. We will train all crews to kill, or be killed, and that they should consider suicide before capture, even though we are not so inclined. It will be the most merciful way out, because you are dead anyway, and you don't want to go through their torture process. As I go through more of the training, I become more callous towards the Morians. I finally notice how I am feeling, and I make a commitment to myself, and on behalf of humanity. We as humans can sometimes turn monstrous also when we see monstrosities as these, but we also have a good side, that hopefully will override our anger and disgust. My commitment is that we will treat all Morians humanly and with respect. But from what I have learned, should the opportunity occur to capture a Morian, it will probably not happen as they will kill themselves before capture. They think this is more glorious than the humiliation of capture. Regardless we will act humanly always, but we will fight to win.

I have finished this training, and I am more confident on how to deploy the fleet, have battle situations in my head, and in the ship's database of knowledge. It has been three months since I started this training, and the combat crews are halfway through their training. The admirals will complete their training next week. I will require the admirals to go through two months of this training, so that they are also aware of what they will be getting into. These two months will be their "hell week" of training. Next week I will have a special meeting with all my admirals.

I call my admirals together, and I will tell Kleg I would like to meet with them alone. As they have all gathered in the conference room, I ask all of them to take a seat, I am still standing.

I say, "Computer, secure all doors and shut off all video and voice." The computer comes back with doors secure, and all recording devices are turned off.

I started talking with them as I nervously pace back and forth, pausing at times to look at them directly.

"I have brought you together, because I wanted to have a private meeting with you. This is our first opportunity to sit, and we can talk about this whole situation as just humans. I am going to lay everything I have out before you, and then I want to hear your comments. One of the first things you may be wondering, is why you were chosen for your assignments. For me, that is easy. You were chosen because of your specialties, and you are the best. Fourteen of you will each command a fleet, and you all came from differing naval branches. For me, space is like naval warfare, not like the army, where you are fighting ground forces. On Earth, you had water that your fleets floated on, you had sea battles, or trained for battles that were with other ships, missiles, and planes. You also had subsurface vessels, which were also at your disposal. Out here there is no water for your ships to float on, or submerge in. Everything out here is a space battle. That is why you were chosen, because you know how to fight in these similar conditions. As all of you know, my military experience is very limited, having been over forty years since I was in the military. So, you may be asking yourselves, why am I in charge? The only answer I have for you, is that the Hypertheans put me in charge. Why, remains to be seen. Just like a president is the commander in chief of all branches of the military, most do not have any, or much military experience, but they have the guidance of experienced military leadership to help them make the final decisions. I am in the same boat, with one exception, I won't be replaced by someone else in four to eight years, so I guess you can say that I am a military dictator, at least out here. My plan is not to act like one, as I didn't and don't have the ambition for this type of role. But, I am the ultimate authority. Just as my assignment has no expiration date, so are yours, and all the rest of the crews'. Any can resign at any time, and others can be dismissed. These wrist bands that have been given to each of us, have different levels of knowledge. I know what this one given to me does, and I have some knowledge of what yours gives you. I have had mine on for a while, and I am still getting information downloaded into my brain. It sort of scares me. If it can download information into my brain, can it also take over my brain? I have the knowledge on how to fight in these conditions, according to the Hypertheans, but I don't have the experience to execute these battle plans, but some of you do. As it has been said, we will fight like we are one, but we will each die individually. I need to know I have your support, but I don't want that answer now. We have just come together, and we don't know each other that well. We need to learn to trust each other. We don't know the Hypertheans that well, and we don't know the Morians at all. I have been with the Hypertheans longer than any of you, and I have not found any reason not to trust them, or their reasons for wanting to save us. I haven't been to the Hyperthean world yet, but our delegation has, and from what I hear, there are no red flags.

Next week, you will be going into more training about how the Morians fight. This will be the start of your "hell week." I have already gone through this training, and it is not for the weak of heart. At first, I became calloused about how I felt, but then I made a commitment to myself and on behalf of mankind. That commitment was this, we as humans can sometimes turn monstrous, especially when we see monstrosities as these, but we also have a good side, that hopefully will override our anger, *but*, I don't want that to become a weakness so that we lose the battle, or war. My commitment is this, we will treat all Morians morally and with respect, should the opportunity be availed to us. We may regret that, but we will try.

Now as to why I called us all together. As I have said, we don't know each other that well. I want each of you to talk about your careers, your families, and what you believe. I will start with myself, and then we will go around the room. I also want to hear from you as to what you think about this whole thing, and how we can work together."

I started talking about myself, and spent about twenty minutes sharing information. Then we started around the room, and each admiral told us about themselves. This gave all of us an opportunity to know a little about each other, and to start to build some relationships.

At first, the admirals were stunned, but they slowly started talking about trust, not only for each other, but also with the Hypertheans. In the end, we all agreed to trust each other, and we would trust the Hypertheans. I was glad of that, as I think I have found a friend in Kleg, and I hate holding this meeting without him. Now they were starting to fire off questions at me about the upcoming battle. I told them that the training they will see next week is just the beginning. Later we will be going through battle scenarios, and this was where I wanted their expertise to come into play. The battle scenarios will help us fight against the Morians, and how to maneuver in space, but we have also been through battles, and we may have some scenarios we might want to try also. At least, with these scenarios we can try many different things without losing any lives. We may find we have some tricks that work better than what the Hypertheans have gone through. After all, they aren't the only brains in the room. They laughed a little and began to relax more.

We stayed in the room discussing, and debating things for over eight hours before we decided to break it up. It was good having all of us together as we started to get to know each other better, and we also gained respect for one another. I told them that we would continue to have these meetings and discussions, at least weekly, as we all progressed through our training.

The admirals started going through their training, and half of them come out of the first day of training and vomited. They had difficulty with what they saw, and what they had to commit to. I will speak with them, and give them the opportunity to back out of the program, and resign their commissions, if they so wish. Eight of them refuse to surrender to such brutality. The rest would like to think about it overnight before they give an answer.

The next morning, after I have met with Captain Faraday, I meet with the admirals in my state room to discuss their answers. Some of them have decided to stay in the program, and the rest still have some reservations. I tell the admirals who have agreed to stay to return to their training. After they leave my stateroom, I ask each of the remaining admirals what their reservations are. Most of them express disgust at what they have seen, along with fear, with the thought that they might have to take their own lives. I tell them that all of us have the same concern, but if we lose the war, or if you are captured, all our deaths are inevitable, plus the death of the rest of mankind. They think about it a little longer, and all agree to stay on. After that, I tell them to return to their training.

I ask Kleg to have his people keep an eye on these admirals who just left my stateroom, and to report back to me if they have any concerns. If their weakness continues to show, I will need to replace them before they complete their training. Kleg agrees with my decision, and has each of them monitored. I also ask that all the admirals be monitored, to see if any weaknesses show up. The admirals finish their training, and all complete the process with a strong conviction towards victory. I still have reservations for a couple of them, and I will work with the counselors who are being assigned to them. I want them to monitor how they will work under pressure. I ask the counselors to encourage them, and make sure that they keep their heads on straight.

The first group of officers and enlisted, who will man our battle stars, have graduated along with half of the transport fleet. The transport fleet will need to supply these ships when they go into service.

This is only a tenth of the battle star fleet that will be deployed now. I am hesitant to give this group of men and women the training the admirals have just gone through. I want them to assume their commands with enthusiasm, pride and excitement, not with fear of what might be coming. I will introduce them to a less violent training of what might be coming at some point in the future. Next week we will begin training for the other half of the battle star fleet, and the rest of the transport fleet.

I asked Admiral Matt Duffy to come to my stateroom. He arrives in about five minutes, and I ask him to be seated.

"Congratulations on being one of our new admirals. I also want to let you know that I have selected you for a special assignment, based on your knowledge and skillset."

He looks at me with a sign of pride and at the same time discomfort.

"Yes sir."

"Matt, I am giving you the transportation fleet. It will be made up of 420 transport ships. These ships will have minimal armament for your ships protection. These ships are transport ships, and are not built as a fighting craft. Hopefully, your crews will never have to use these weapons, but you can ward off a small attack, and wait for stronger defenses to arrive. You do have half of your crews trained, and they are ready to take their place in the fleet. You will need to be able to move crews to their new stations, and move supplies and food to each of these ships on a regular basis. In two weeks, we will have seven of our battle stars ready to be manned, and we need to move crews to these stations. You will also need to have your crews shuttled to their ships tomorrow, and have your transport ships here in two weeks, ready to transport these men and women to their new duty stations. Do you think that is possible?"

He lets out his breath and says, "I will make sure that it is done."

"I also want you to have your crew take over the shuttling of crews from Earth to the *Hyperthia.* I have other responsibilities I need the Hypertheans to be doing."

"I will take care of it immediately."

SIX

I now ask that Marine Corp General Mitch Sullivan come to my stateroom. As Mitch arrives, I offer him something to drink.

"Coffee, black please."

"Mitch, I need for you to take immediate command of the bases that are on Earth. They are being set up. Currently, we only have one base set up. And Mitch, we will need to use this as our example for getting the other bases ready. We have thousands of men and women that will be passing through our gates, and I need those bases to be very secure, and to make sure that nothing goes wrong down there.

I need to ask a couple more things of you. Since we are both brand-new at this space thing, I need for you to be prepared for anything that might happen at our bases. I am not at all comfortable with all the countries that have sworn allegiance to us. Also, there are still radicals down there that will be against this. Please set up a security process for both inside and outside the dome to prevent any attacks. I am authorizing you to use whatever means necessary to protect our bases, within reason. I will deal with the diplomatic issues afterward. As you also know, I am an American, and have a great deal of trust in our marine corps. I need for you to train a group of marines, that will be needed to be aboard our ships, to repel Morian boarders. Can you do that for me?"

"I will get right on it, and give you regular updates on a weekly basis."

"You have your own travel vessel at your disposal. You will need it to make trips back and forth to the command ship, and to the other bases. I will see that you get the training to fly it."

I gave him his orders, and one of our pilots will fly his vessel and take him to the base in Texas. They leave the next day.

Each of the Earth bases will vary in size, but they will generally occupy about ten thousand acres of land. We are currently looking at forty-two of these bases around the world to be set up. We will prefer these bases to be located somewhere where there is minimal air traffic, and in friendly territory. The first US base is in a remote location in West Texas. The base will be about five miles off I-10, where the only life is rattlesnakes and jack rabbits. We are provided this land quickly, and the Hypertheans set up the security parameter in about forty-eight hours, before anyone even knew what was going on. There is only one entrance to the base that is currently guarded by a trained team of the Federation guard. We do have a secret escape route, but only the commands of each of the bases will know where it is located. There is no way that an intruder can enter the base, from the ground or from the air. The defensive parameter also has shields that prevent even satellites from seeing what is going on at this location. From the ground parameter, people outside can only see about ten feet into the dome. So basically, all they see is barren land. The Hypertheans have a protective barrier around the whole base, almost like a dome. Within the dome area, the temperature is always at seventy-two degrees, no matter what the temperature is outside the dome. Also, within the dome the grounds are lush and green, making it a beautiful environment in which to live and work.

The gate entrances are protected by a double barrier zone that can allow entrance and departure from the base. While one barrier is down the other is up. The gate entrance has two access areas, one for men and women to pass through, and the other for deliveries to the base. No private vehicles are allowed on base, and the trucks making deliveries, can only go so far before their items are offloaded into a warehouse, within the first dome area. All the contents will be inspected before movement from this secure warehouse. The men and women who pass through the gates can pick up base transportation to where they are going. While on base they will be in uniform, and easily identifiable. The security on the base will be strong, and people who are in the wrong sections of the base, without proper clearances, will be detained and interviewed by base security.

About two thousand acres of each base will house the buildings for training of men and women. This section will be known as the Federation Academy. While men and women are at the academy, they will not be allowed to leave this section of the base, as it is like boot camp. They will be undergoing intense physical and mental training, for duty stations that will be in space. The academy buildings are quite futuristic, since much of their training will be on equipment that is unknown to Earth.

Another five thousand acres of the base will be for our transport ships, and military ships leaving the station. Even though there is a barrier around the base, our ships have the proper security codes to pass in and out of the domes. There is a contingent of fighters on the base, which is used for protection of the base, should an aircraft or unknown object enter our restricted airspace. They are also there should the Morians attack Earth.

The rest of the base is for housing of base personnel, warehouses for maintaining supplies that can only be obtained from Earth facilities, and offices for personnel who will work on the base. Civilians will be used on the base, but only after they have received the proper clearances and training. There will be a building that will have locker areas, where they will change into proper clothing to be on the base.

It will take about six months for the Federation to get each of these bases built. At that point, they will leave and the bases will be completely manned by Earth personnel.

SEVEN

Each of the fleets will have ten battle stars, sixty battle cruisers, three hundred battle destroyers and one hospital ship. A battle star will carry a crew of three thousand, with seven thousand pilots for the fighters. A battle cruiser will carry a crew of two thousand. Destroyers will have a crew of two hundred and fifty, and a hospital ship will have a crew of two hundred, with a complement of four hundred doctors, nurses and staff. We will have fourteen fleets in total. For all the fleets, we will require around one million crew members. It will take five different training sessions aboard the command ship to train each section of the fleet. It is estimated that it will take three and a half years to train all fourteen fleets. There will be an admiral for each fleet, one admiral for the hydroponic ships, one admiral for the transport fleet, and one general for our Earth bases. There will be a set of transport ships located with each of the hydroponic ships, and there will be four hundred and twenty transport ships manned by a crew of forty officers and enlisted per ship.

After graduation this Friday, I will meet with the admirals and captains of the battle stars that will be deployed. I also get to meet with the officers of these ships and will speak with each of them on what I am getting ready to do. We have fourteen large sectors that will be assigned to each fleet. For the first six months, theirs will be the only ship that will be patrolling these assigned areas. Then, they will be joined by a second battle star. Until then, they will need to train their pilots as fast as they can, and have them out on patrols. Soon, they will be joined by the rest of their fleet. I told the admirals that I would meet with them at 1800, to discuss their missions further, and give them their sealed orders.

I meet with the admirals, and we go over their missions in detail. I tell them that there has been an overabundance of captains trained with this first class. These captains will become the captains of other ships, when we have our other crews trained, and available for assignments. These captains will shadow you, and will gain the valuable experience they will need to command their green crews, when they are available. As time goes by, we will also be reassigning experienced members of your crews out to these new ships, to make sure we have a balanced, experienced crew for each ship. Even though we do not expect any trouble now, they need to be on alert for anything. Since this is our first time in space, we don't know what "out of the ordinary" is about, we need to be monitoring everything. We will learn over time, but for the time being, everything is out of the ordinary, until we can establish what is ordinary. I told the admirals not to get comfortable with being with their fleets for the next six months. They will need to depend on their captains to handle the day-to-day assignments. For all of us, we will be going through battle scenarios that have been provided to us by the Hypertheans, from their actual battles with the Morians. The Morian attack plan will remain the same as the actual battles we will see, but how we handle our attack plan will be what we will be going through. I have downloaded to each of the admirals their assignments, and told them they were not to open them until they are in their staterooms on their battle stars. I also downloaded the next set of orders to all the admirals, and told them they could open this set of orders now. This told them which battle star was their new command post, and who their battle star captain was.

I congratulated each of them on their new assignments and their new captains. I also told them that they would all be assigned a Federation counselor, who would be there to advise them on situations, and to be their advisor. All captains would also receive a Federation counselor for the same purpose. They would be there to advise only, and not to give orders. Next, I downloaded the orders they were to give to their captains, which also included the names of the officers and crew for each battle star. I asked each of them to meet with their respective captains at 2000 hours, and give them their assignments. They all needed to have their crews ready to deploy to their ships in two days. This gives them one month to get their ships ready for deployment to their assigned stations. At that point, I released them.

EIGHT

As we approach the time for the crews to deploy to their assigned battle stars, the activity around the ship is running at a frenzied pace. Crews are trying to find which launch bay they need to be at to catch their ride.

Admiral Duffy has done a great job in getting his transport ships ready for their jobs. With his base of operation on the *Hyperthia*, he has his own section of the ship. He has sent some of the transports to the food supply ships, to get the necessary food for the battle stars. He has also sent some to the Earth base stations to get different supplies. He already has transports in the bays of the command ship to pick up crews, and ready to take them to their duty stations.

As I sit at my command seat in the ready room, I watch the hologram of the solar system, and see all the ships moving around doing their jobs. I am also watching the ready room crew moving about the room, or sitting at their stations making sure that everything moves smoothly. I ask Captain Faraday to join me in the ready room. She comes in shortly, and comes over to me to see what it is that I needed.

"May I help you sir?"

"I don't need anything in particular, but I wanted you to see the activity that was going on out there, from my perspective."

This is a new perspective for her, as she watches ships that are close to the *Hyperthia*.

"What do you think of all of this?"

"Mind-boggling. If you don't mind, I think I will go back to my bridge, and watch everything from a close-up perspective. Besides, I need to work with Captain Kensington to make sure things are ready in flight-ops."

Captain Kensington is our flight operations officer for the *Hyperthia*. He commands the two hundred launch bays aboard the *Hyperthia*, and they are all large enough that they need a flight operations officer over each of them. Captain Kensington stays very busy, with the two hundred flight operation officers that report to him. I smile, and thank her for her time, and she departs the ready room to return to the bridge.

All the crews have boarded their assigned transports, and the transports are ready to take the crews to their new posts. I receive word from all the admirals that their crews are ready. I signal Captain Faraday that the admirals are ready. She confirms the signal, and the next thing I hear is Captain Kensington giving the order to launch the transports. As I watch the holograph before me, I see the transports leaving the command ship, and heading out to where all the rest of the ships are kept. They will arrive at the designated battle stars in about five hours, where the Hyperthean startup crews have started the initial boot up of each of the ships systems. Everything is now ready for the Earth crews to take over the rest of the ship startup.

The transports arrive at their designated battle stars, and enter the landing bay areas. As the crews depart the transport ships, they are greeted by the Hypertheans. From here they will take their designated personnel to their duty stations, and they will complete the rest of the ship's startup. As these human crews are trained, they will take over the responsibility of the startup of the rest of the ships in the fleet. The Hypertheans will remain aboard the battle stars for a few days, to make sure everything has started up properly, and then they will return to the *Hyperthia*. The crews that have taken over each of the ships will be responsible for the ships upgrades.

All the admirals are now in command of their fleets, one battle star, with work to be done. All the crews have been moved to their duty stations, and their ships are at full operational status. After two weeks of upgrades being accomplished, they are waiting to travel to their new assigned areas. This will occur tomorrow. I ask all the admirals to return to the *Hyperthia*, after they have reached their new areas. It will take the ships anywhere from a day to a week, to reach their assignments as some must travel further than others.

I want the admirals here at the *Hyperthia*, because it is time for us to start our battle training scenarios against the Morians. I will allow the admirals half a day to work with their ships on their duty assignments and work with the new officers that are in training for the next battle stars. During the second half of the day, we will be working with Kleg, and other Hypertheans, going over battle scenarios from their past battles. The first couple of weeks we will be watching reenactments of some of their worst battles, and learning strategies that will help us defend our solar system better.

The first day of our training, we are in a training area that looks like the ready room, except there is only the holographic table with the command consoles around the table. Kleg starts off the training telling us about how the Morians will start off with a crude strategy using a direct attack approach, knowing that they will be pushed back. This can give us a false sense of pride, and hope in that we have defeated the Morians; but it also shows the Morians any areas of weakness we may have. Then the Morians will come at us with a slightly different approach, but still a basic simple attack. Again, they will be pushed back, and we will experience losses in each case. The

Morians will be looking for more of our weaknesses. The third time, will be a totally new sophisticated approach, and if we are not ready, they can punch some significant holes in our fleet, make us appear weak, and staggering from the blow they have just dealt. With two strong push backs on the Morians and this staggering blow, we may feel we want to take the offensive, but we need to be patient, and hold our ground. They are expecting an offensive at this point, and if we go charging at them, they will destroy the ships by totally outnumbering us from the sides. Space is like an open sea, we have no place to hide and neither do they. The only advantage we have is our stealth capabilities to hide in plain sight, but so do they. We must use our advantage, along with our superior technology to know where they are. They will also use light bombs against us to see if they can illuminate us. We don't want to group up, we need to keep separated, so that the Morians cannot come charging at one spot. We can use that as a ploy to get them to come charging in, and we surround them and destroy the attackers.

After a half day of reviewing these original attack processes by the Morians against the Federation, we are all exhausted. I invite all the admirals to have dinner with me in my admiral's area. We will allow the ship officers to eat first, and then we will gather at 1900 for our meal. I invite them to join me in my stateroom for drinks and to talk at 1800.

The admirals start gathering in my stateroom, they are keeping Harold busy taking their drink orders. They are gathered about the room in groups talking and laughing about different subjects, other than the day we have just gone through. It is good to see them enjoying a lighter side and building on their relationships. They need these moments to maintain their sanity. It also helps me maintain mine.

It has been three months since I have been back to Earth.

We have completed our training on war tactics against the Morians. In the meantime, several more crews have graduated from our academy, and are being deployed out to our ships. We now have two battle stars in each fleet deployed, and we will start training men and women to meet crew requirements for two battle cruisers per fleet. After they complete their training, we will then train crews for seven destroyers per fleet. When they have completed their training, we will start the cycle over again, until the entire fleet is trained and all ships are manned.

It is now time for us to start our war games. The Hypertheans have ten war game scenarios for us to go through. It will take us two weeks to go through a scenario, and then another week to debrief. They will give us another week to take care of some business before we start our next scenario. During the first two scenarios, we fail badly. The Morians destroyed all fourteen fleets within three days, and are attacking Earth on the fourth. We did not work well as a team, and several of the admirals went off on their own, disobeying orders, thinking they had the better plan. This brought about a reality check, and taught us all a lesson. We work as a team or we die. The second scenario we did a little better this time, but it took the Morians a week to destroy most of the fleets, but they didn't get to attack Earth before the scenario was up. By the third scenario, we are getting better at our defenses, but we lost half of our ships, however we pushed the Morians back.

After the fifth scenario, we are doing much better at working as a team and at our defenses. We continued working together, and discussing our strategies and how we can improve on what we are doing.

At the eighth scenario, Kleg tells us of a weapon that each of the battle stars have, and is also on the *Hyperthia*. It is like a strong laser beam. No matter what shields, or the thickness of the ships, this beam will slice ships in half, destroying it completely. Each of the battle stars has one of these weapons, while the *Hyperthia* has ten of them, because of our size. The reason we had not been told about it, is that it is a last defense weapon, and we must learn to fight as if we didn't have it.

Once you use this weapon, it will basically leave your ship defenseless for about ten minutes, while the ship's power builds back up. It is basically for a one-on-one battle. This is a new weapon from the Hypertheans, and they are working on building a power supply that is dedicated to the weapon where it does not leave the ship defenseless. It will take time for them to put together such a power supply, and find a place to put it on board each of the ships.

It has taken us ten months to complete all the war games, but we have come together as a team, and have built strong allegiances with each other. Whatever differences they may have had on Earth, they no longer exist here in the federation.

When the admirals have finished this training, it is time for the captains of each of our ships to go through the same training.

NINE

We have been getting this fleet ready for the past nineteen and a half months, and the fleet has also accomplished quite a bit. We have trained two more sets of crews, and each fleet now has two battle stars, two cruisers, and fourteen destroyers. All the transport crews have been trained, and we have all the transports in service. The next training classes have started for two more battle stars, and they are in their third week of training. The last of the Earth base stations are being built, and we should have a full complement of bases in operation in the next two months. General Sullivan has done a great job with the security of the bases, and in getting all the other bases ready for operation. He has his operation working like a Swiss watch. There have not been any incidences at any of the bases, so we are in great shape with our cooperation with each of the nations. Some of the nations are questioning the secrecy we are maintaining, but we assure them we are not trying to hide anything, and they are welcome at any time to come by and review our operations.

The hydroponic fleet is also doing great, and all military crews and civilians are still excited about their assignments.

The civilian crews are learning new processes every day, and this will help in improving crop growth back on Earth.

We have also invited civilian delegations to come up to the *Hyperthia*, and we have stated we would be glad to give them a tour of our ship, plus other ships in the fleet. We would especially like for them to see our hydroponic ships in action. We have had most of the nation's take us up on the invitation, and we are scheduling their tours.

So far, we have not seen any Morian activity, or any other unusual activity. The fleet is getting used to being in space, and doing patrols in their respective assigned areas. The crews have gone through lots of training, and plenty of drills. We need to keep our fleets sharp, and our senses peaked.

It is now time to move the *Hyperthia* out of the asteroid belt and back out to where the rest of the fleet is waiting to be deployed. It will take longer to shuttle our forces between Earth and the *Hyperthia*, but we will adjust for that. I have instructed Captain Faraday to get the ship ready to get underway in one week. She is excited about this as this will be the first time that the *Hyperthia* has moved since we moved into the asteroid belt. This will be the first time she has taken the ship out. I have informed my staff of the movement, and they have informed their respective commands. All commands are making their proper adjustments to schedules to account for the change in location, and for the greater distance of travel when they need to come to the *Hyperthia*.

The week has passed, and it is time for the ship to move. I have instructed Captain Faraday that we will be leaving at 0800, and she has informed me that the ship is ready to get underway. I am at my command station, and she gives the order to get underway. I am watching my screens as I see the ship start to move, and Captain Faraday maneuvers the ship out of the asteroid belt. It is a graceful move for such a large ship, and well executed. She now gives commands to bring us to location ANTRIP1, and a speed of presser 54.6. It will take us about four hours to get to the rest of the fleet.

The time goes by without incidence, and Captain Faraday brings the *Hyperthia* into location and secures the ship. I was watching the bridge off and on during the flight, and it appeared that the entire crew did well and were all smiling when they brought the *Hyperthia* into station, including the captain.

Another sixteen and a half months have passed, and the last sets of crews are finishing their training aboard the *Hyperthia*. I have decided that it is time for some crew rotation. Some of the men and women have been out here on station for just over three years. They are my most experienced crews. Instead of sending this last set of graduating men and women out to man the last of the ships to be deployed, I have spoken with the admirals, and we have decided to move the crews around, to allow the more experienced men and women to be intermixed with the less experienced crews. The admirals speak with each of their captains, and transfer orders are generated, and the transfers are done. We now have well blended crews aboard each of our ships.

The ships have settled into their routine, and I have decided it is time to move the *Hyperthia,* again. We have been on station here for two years, and all our ships have been deployed. I meet with my staff to discuss where we can move the *Hyperthia*. We have located a suitable place where we can be strategically located, and accessible by all the fleet. I meet with Captain Faraday to let her know of our decision, and give her the coordinates to move the ship. I ask her how soon the ship will be ready to get underway. She tells me that the ship is always ready to move. I let her know she can take the *Hyperthia* out in the morning at 0800. Our new location will place us halfway between Mars and Earth.

The next day we are underway to our new location, and it will take us two days to arrive at our new coordinates. We arrive without incident, and this is the first time some of the crew has seen the sun, and Earth in a couple of years. After we secure our location, I let the captain know that I think we can allow one fourth of the crew to have some leave. I ask her to do this in rotations until all who want to take leave can do so. I also tell the other admirals to do the same.

I feel that I need some time off too. I take my travel vessel, and head for the base located in Texas. I tell General Sullivan that I don't want any type of ceremony for my arrival. I depart the base in civilian clothing and take one of the cars in the parking lot that has been set aside for my usage. It is my travel vessel. I leave, and head towards Houston, and arrive, having enjoyed the scenery. Many things along the way appear to be different, but it has been a while since I have traveled this route. I relax my guard some, but always remain vigilant.

I enjoy the two weeks I have taken, and then return to the base the next day, and meet with General Sullivan. I am back in uniform now, and decide that I would like a tour of the base. The general plans for this, and I ask if we can start with the academy. I want to meet with the officer in charge.

As we arrive at the academy, I look at how well the grounds have been laid out for the cadets. The academy has its grounds divided up for the training of officers and enlisted personnel. I meet with Captain Alonzo who commands the academy. I let him know how pleased I am with the layout of his academy and that I would like to visit the enlisted side of the academy first. As we go into the training area for the enlisted, there are many cadets moving about going from one class to another. As one of them spots my uniform, he lets out with, "Attention on deck," and snaps to attention. As the rest of the cadets hear the words they also snap to attention.

"At ease, and carry on."

As we continue down the hall, I hear someone behind me whisper, and catch what he is saying. "That's Admiral Graham."

Another one says, "And who is he?"

The first one says, "Idiot, you better not ask that question again. He is the admiral in charge of the entire Federation fleet."

He replies, "Holy cow," and they scamper off down the hall to their classes.

I smile, and we continue down the hallway.

We walk into one of the classrooms, and it is filled with about two hundred students. They are all gathered in pairs around about one hundred pieces of equipment at separate tables. They are being instructed in the operation of the piece of equipment, and they all seem to be quite involved in what they are doing. No one notices that we have entered the room, and Captain Alonzo is a little upset that no one has noticed us, and starts to bark out an order when I wave him off.

"It's okay. Let's continue to see more of the classes."

We go from room to room, and see cadets being taught different things about the jobs they will be performing.

We now go over to the officer side of the campus, and we go from classroom to classroom. We see potential officers being trained in different aspects of the career paths they have chosen to follow. Some will be line officers, others supply officers, personnel officers, and on and on the list goes.

After we finish at the academy, I tell the general that I would like to see the supply operations now. He takes me over to that part of the base, and I see huge warehouses with bay doors open, and with transport containers lined up outside each of the doors, and they are being loaded up with supplies that will be delivered out to the fleet.

I ask the general, "Are we having any problems with the process that is in place?"

"We have had our snags with some of the deliveries that come in, but we are working on those logistic issues."

"Good. I would like to see the other end of the warehouse where the supplies come in."

We go around to that section, through the inner dome of protection, to the warehouse. I see many trucks backed up to the unloading docks, where they are having their goods offloaded from the trucks.

"Have you ever had a problem with someone trying to smuggle something in with the supplies?"

"There have been a couple of incidences, but we caught it before it got past our check points."

"What was being smuggled?"

"Once it was some drugs, and the second time it was a firearm."

"Were you able to track what truck and company these items came from?"

"We did that, and the FBI was able to identify who was doing the smuggling, and who it was intended for in the fleet. The individuals in the fleet have been removed from duty and are spending prison time now in one of our brigs. They will be receiving a dishonorable discharge."

The general now takes me to flight operations, where I see transports taking off, and landing every thirty seconds.

"Our bases are considered the busiest airfields, anywhere in the world. We have more transports taking off and landing in a twenty-four-hour period, at the rate of twice that of the world's busiest commercial airport. Our air traffic controllers are the best trained, especially, with the instrumentation that they use from the Hypertheans. There has never been an incident at any of our bases."

Next the general takes me to the base boot camp area. There are three sections for training at this location. One section is for enlisted personnel who are joining the military, another section for Officer Candidate School, and the third section is for civilian training of personnel. All will receive a uniform to distinguish the officers, enlisted, and civilians from each other. We are requiring the civilians to wear a uniform, not just to distinguish them from the military personnel, but also it helps them when emergency situations occur in space or within the dome, as the uniform acts as a space suit when needed. They also love it that they get a uniform, because it gives them a sense of pride and belonging.

I have seen the base, and it is time for me to head back to the *Hyperthia*. I say my farewells to the general and his officers, and head to my travel vessel. In about five minutes I am off, and headed back to space and for what is waiting for me there.

TEN

The federation personnel have been with us for about ten years now. Our fleet personnel have been trained, and all the ships have been deployed to their assignments. We also have all our counselors in place, and it is time for the federation team to leave for other assignments. I am pleased with the counselor that has been assign to me. Her name is Patsy, and is someone that can sense people's feelings. She will work well with me, when I am meeting with the rest of my staff and visitors.

I have spoken with Kleg, and in about a month several ships will be arriving to take the Federation personnel to their new assignments. Kleg reports that he is very pleased with the personnel that will be taking over this fleet. There will be some sad moments in our good-byes, when the time comes.

I let the rest of the admirals know that the Federation personnel will be leaving, and we will be on our own in defending our solar system. They all let me know that they are ready for the challenge, and will prove they are up to the job.

About a week before the Federation ships are to arrive, the federation personnel are ordered to return to the *Hyperthia*. As I watch the personnel arrive, I see the excitement in their faces that they are going home. Some of them have not left us since they arrived ten years ago. For us, it is a long period of time, but for them, it has only been about five months. Some are sad to leave, because they have made some good friends with us. In the overall scheme of things, this will be a good transition for all of us.

I meet with Kleg several more times during the week, As we talk, we both have mixed emotions about his leaving. He knows that we will be okay, and will perform well when the time comes. He lets me know that we will not be alone when the battle comes, but we will have to have a strong defense, until help arrives if we need it. We discuss our friendship, and that we will stay in touch with each other through the coming years. Kleg lets me know that he will be visiting us off and on, and that I will be making a trip to the Federation planets soon. I let him know that I am pleased to know that, and will look forward to the trip.

The day has arrived for the federation personnel to depart, and I can't believe the number of ships that have arrived to take them home. It appears they have brought about a hundred extra ships that they will be leaving with us. These ships are about the size of our destroyers. Their armament is small, and they look more like exploration ships. The ships taking the crews home are in several different docking areas, and the number of people that are moving about remind me of ants, moving about in an orderly manner, going to their assigned ships. It takes about six hours to get all the federation personnel into their ships. Kleg will be one of the last ones to get into his departing ship. I am there to see Kleg and Taylor off. Harold will remain with me at my request, and he was pleased that I had asked for him. I say my good-byes to Taylor, and we give each other a man hug, and he turns to enter his ship. I look at Kleg, and I tell him that I am grateful for this experience, and the opportunity that he and the Federation has given to me.

He looks at me and says, "It is without a doubt that the

right choice has been made. You will do well. I am pleased to have met you, and our friendship will last for a long time. The Federation has asked me to express their great pleasure in you being here at this location. They welcome you to this team, and are very confident in your abilities."

Kleg and I give each other a handshake, and then a man hug, as he turns to go to his ship. As he reaches the doorway, he turns, smiles, and waves a good-bye to me, and I return the wave.

I yell to Kleg, "What are the extra ships for?"

He replies with a smile, "You figure it out, "and turns to enter his ship.

ELEVEN

It has been fifteen years since I was first contacted by Kleg, and we have not had a single incident occur with the Morians. To keep ourselves busy, we have established planetary bases on the moon, Mars, and Neptune's moon Triton. These bases have been established as research and exploration areas for NASA and other space organizations. We have negotiated with them, and have allowed them to have some of our transport ships for travel to and from these planetary bases. The most impressive base that has been set up by NASA is the one that is on Mars. They continue to search for the presence of life on the planet, but so far, they only get indications of liquid carbon dioxide in the colder regions of the planet or some form of it having been on the planet millions of years ago. What they have established on the moon is strictly a base for experiments and travel to Mars and Triton. We have provided them with the equipment they are using, which is far more advanced than what they originally started with.

All the bases that have been established have a dome over them, which allows them to establish an atmosphere and a livable environment. At first, they only had the domes with the surfaces original soil. They soon learned, that the soil is not suitable for a base surface. It is too granular and sharp and destroys equipment. It was also discovered that many of the people were coming up with new diseases, and they had to find new cures for their ailments. We had to help them establish a safe surface, from which they could work while inside the dome. Once we had this established, the strange diseases stopped being a problem.

The Triton base was the most difficult to establish. This was because of its distance from the sun. The temperatures are extremely cold, and quite challenging for our scientists. We had to establish a livable environment for the research facility. Within the dome, we needed artificial lighting, that would illuminate the entire dome area. Next, we had to build heating generators to produce the heat needed. It had to be comfortable, but also large enough to heat the entire surface of the dome to keep it from icing up on the inside. Once they had this problem worked out, then we could set up the necessary modules inside the dome for their experiments.

We had also attained some scientific ships, that were delivered to us when the Hyphertheans left. We have asked for volunteers from Earth to man these ships. It does not take long before these ships are fully manned by men and women from all over the Earth who are eager to take on this mission. We have decided to call these missions our *Star Trek* missions, after our Sy-Fi TV and movie series. They will have a five-year mission to explore some parts of the Milky Way system, and return to the fleet. We have also established a base station, that is in rotation about one hundred and fifty thousand miles above the Earth. It is quite a site to see, and we are able to observe the Earth and moon, from that perspective. God has made quite a beautiful place that we call home, and it helps all of us to keep everything in perspective. We have had cameras set up to transmit live videos of the Earth to all the ships in our fleet. This allows all crews to be able to see the Earth. They have all marveled at the sight, and what it means to them.

The nations on Earth are still having their differences, but with the establishment of the Federation, many of the differences have been resolved. However, we continue to have some major differences between some of the nations. The Hypertheans have also provided us with other delegations to help in resolving these problems, but for these major differences we have come to a standstill. The delegation is strong, and is training our people in better delegation processes.

When the first exploration ship was ready to be commissioned and launched from the station, we thought it appropriate to name it the *Star Ship Enterprise*. I was there for its commissioning and launch, and I was honored to be there. As we established this exploration program with all the nations of Earth, we all agreed that I was not in charge of this operation. The ships already came with the best technology for these types of missions and should any of the ships run into problems, our fleet will be there to assist, and potentially rescue, if necessary.

As we are approaching our sixteenth year in space, the communication area in the *Hyperthia* has received a communique from the Federation. It has been marked urgent. I am awakened from my sleep by a beeping sound. I recognize the sound, indicating that there is an urgent communication. I bring up my heads-up display and as I am reading through it, I see that the Hypertheans are reporting that there are Morian ships moving in our direction. They indicate that they should be reaching our outer parameter within the next three days. I contact my communications officer, and tell him that I want an immediate video conference with all the admirals in my conference room in ten minutes. Also, have Captain Faraday there. Everyone is there, and I explain the situation to them.

"Admiral Perry, I want your sixth fleet brought to full alert.

I recommend that you be ready to send out scout patrols once the sensors start picking up movement in your sectors."

"For the rest of us, please bring your ships to condition three, and be prepared for anything."

"Captain Faraday, I want you to move the *Hyperthia* out to a point that will be closer to Admiral Perry's sector."

I want all leaves canceled, and have all personnel return to their duty stations immediately."

Everyone says, "Aye-aye sir," and they go to do their job.

I leave my stateroom, and I am heading for my command center when I hear, "Set condition three throughout the ship, this is not a drill, set condition three throughout the ship."

People are now scrambling to get to their duty stations, ready for anything.

As I enter my command center, people are moving to their stations, and I take my place at the large area where the hologram of the solar system is set up. I command my wristband to bring up the command centers communications and I start listening to all the conversations going on throughout the fleet. I watch as Admiral Perry's ships turn red on the hologram. I notice the rest of the fleets go to condition three, as each ship turns amber, until every ship in the fleet is at condition three.

I then instruct the CIC officer to bring up the grids where we can see all the detection buoys overlaid on top of the ships. Currently, all the buoys are green, as they have not detected any disturbances. Admiral Perry deploys his ships across the grids, to be ready for anything. Now we play the waiting game.

I now call the communication center.

"Communications."

"Yes sir."

"Please send a message out to our scientific vessels and the established planetary bases of our situation, and tell them to be on the lookout for anything suspicious, and to let us know of their current situation."

"Yes sir."

The Hypertheans continue to monitor the ships, but they have not been able to find the rest of the Morian fleet. They know that it should be close by. These small ships do not have the communication band width, or fuel to travel great distances. Every hour we are receiving an update from the Federation about the location of these ships. We continue to monitor their paths, and plot their locations every time we are given an update. I receive a message from Admiral Perry that he is sending out two video drones, for each of the sectors that we anticipate the ships to pass through.

As the first day passes, all the transports are returning crews back to their ships, bringing all ships back to full complement. The *Hyperthia* is moving at flank speed to be on location near Admiral Perry's sector by noon tomorrow. Captain Faraday has given instructions to Captain Kensington to get all fighters ready for deployment.

He has instructed all fighters to be ready to go on his command.

Captain Faraday has also told Captain Kensington to get fighters out around the ship. She wants a full complement of fighters out, looking for anything that might be suspicious. The first day passes, as we continue to monitor the movement of the Morian ships.

They slowly pass through each sector, looking for signs of communications or movement within that sector. Then they slowly move to the next sector, doing the same thing.

At the end of the first day, we receive a transmission from the video drones that they are on location, and are sending out five-second videos every fifteen seconds.

By noon of day two, the *Hyperthia* has arrived on location, and sets out to move slowly through this area. We don't want her to be a stationary target. We continue to receive messages from the Hyperthean High Command that the Morian ships are still moving in our direction, as they slowly pass through each of the sectors. We are becoming anxious as they approach, and I feel sweat beads running down my face. This waiting game is just killing us. I take my watches four hours at a time, but instruct the CIC officer to call me immediately if anything comes up. Day two passes without an incident.

Day three is here, and Hyperthean communications tells us the Morian ships should be entering our first outer zone in about three hours. I have the communication center relay this information to all commands. One hour before they enter the first zone, we send commands to the video drones to send images constantly. For the twenty drones we have deployed, we now have a continuous feed on twenty displays around the command center, and all are being monitored. The video drones will also send us a signal when they detect any movement in the areas they are monitoring. If things work correctly, this should coincide with a signal that we should get from our detection buoys.

Our protection barrier is still active, but the Morian ships will have to pass through two of our monitored sectors before they arrive at the barrier. I ask the command center officer to bring up the protection barrier on our display, and indicate each of the buoys as a green "X". He does so, and I see all the buoys now coming up on the display. They are all green, except for one which is flashing yellow. It is in a sector that is over three hours away from where the Morian ships are approaching.

I get the attention of the commend center officer, and as I point to the flashing buoy I ask, "Mister Skinner, what is the story with this buoy?"

He looks surprised and is immediately talking to someone on his headset.

"That buoy went yellow yesterday, and we have a repair drone on its way there now to fix it, sir. The barrier is still working, but it is a weakness. Since the barrier was still working and this sector was not a concern, we did not feel it was necessary to report it."

"Mr. Skinner, when we are at condition one, we report everything. Nothing is insignificant."

"Yes sir."

"Let's speed up the process. I want a video drone there, to make sure we do not have any problems. I want both of those drones there within the hour, understood."

"Yes sir."

"Inform Admiral Coats of the situation, and ask him to look into it. This buoy is in his zone of protection."

As the first enemy ship enters our first outer detection zone, the detection buoy sends us a signal of movement within that zone. The zone cube turns a bold blue, and our first signal location of the Morian ship is pinpointed within the cube. The ship continues to move, as if it did not know that it had been detected. From our training, we also know that the Morians do not care if they are detected, since their ships are on suicide missions. For them it is an honor to die this way, and their only purpose is to gather information for their fleet. Now the buoy has detected movement, the video drone does the same. The video drone is now moving towards the Morian ship, and the buoy sends out a second alarm when it detected the video drone.

As the video drone moves towards the Morian ship, the second Morian ship has entered another grid. The grid is on the other side of the defective buoy, and it now lights up on our display. This cube now goes bold blue, showing where this Morian ship is. The second video drone is deployed to where this Morian ship is moving. We are now noticing a pattern in their approach and know that the defective buoy appears to be key in their approach. I bring Admiral Coats' fleet to full alert. He now orders his fleet to take appropriate action and sends fighters to the defective buoy, and orders four destroyers to move closer to the buoy.

It takes about thirty minutes before the video drone is close enough for us to see an image of the Morian ship. As the display of the image becomes clearer on our display, we identify it as an unmanned scout, but well-armed. The video drone stays far enough back, but the enemy scout is aware of its presence. It remains curious of its intentions, but does not take any hostile action against our drone. I remain cautious as we monitor this scout, and wonder why the video drone has not been destroyed. I believe their intention is to draw our attention away from something else.

As the second video drone approaches the second Morian ship, we also quickly identify it as another unmanned enemy scout. Again, the video drone approaches this second ship, but remains far enough back to be out of harm's way. We also realize that this scout is aware of the other drones' presence. Again, the hairs on the back of my neck are telling me to be cautious.

Even though the enemy scouts are still a couple of hours away from the barrier, I am still concerned about the buoy that has malfunctioned. This is too much of a coincidence for me.

Meanwhile, the enemy scouts continue to move at their steady pace, as they move from the first zone, into the second. The next buoy has come to life, indicating that they are in this zone now, as the first zone goes quiet. On our display, the cubes change their lights to reflect this movement. The video drones continue to monitor the enemy scouts without any incidences.

They are now one zone away from the barrier now. They continue to move in a straight line, giving no indications that they will be deviating from this path. This cat-and-mouse game continues for another hour.

As the enemy scouts enter the third sector, the repair and video drones have reached the failing barrier buoy. The video camera is rolling as they approach the buoy, but still no indications of any problem.

After about thirty minutes into the third sector, the enemy scouts stop. They stay in this location for about another thirty minutes, and then suddenly they make a turn towards the video drones monitoring them, and fire two shots. The video drones disappear from our displays, and the screens go dark. Our buoys are still working, and we can still track them with the buoys. When these video drones are destroyed, Admirals Perry and Coats are ready to bring their fleets into action. I tell both to hold fast, don't deploy any of their fighters yet. These are only two enemy scouts, and they still must pass through the barrier shield.

I now order the rest of the fleets to condition one and to standby.

Since these two video drones have been destroyed, we are receiving a communication from the Hyperthean command that they have detected an anomaly just outside our detection buoys. They give me the location of this anomaly. It is at this point that I realize it is in a direct path with the defective defense buoy. We now suspect that this is probably the cloaked mother ship for the enemy scouts.

The two enemy scouts have now changed their direction and are now heading towards the buoy we are concerned about. As these enemy scouts make their turn, they are picking up speed and should be at the buoy in about two hours.

As the repair drone approaches the buoy, it sends back an indication that the buoy has been tampered with. As it sends this message, both drones disappear from the screen, indicating that they have been destroyed. Admiral Coats is also aware of what has just happened, and orders his fighters and destroyers to move in closer and to be ready to fight. I also advise that they be cautious, since these drones were destroyed on this side of the barrier.

I also request that the fifth fleet send out twelve more video drones, four defensive drones, and six more repair drones to see what is going on. I tell him to send the video drones in first. I want to see where these drones are being attacked from. I also request that Admiral Perry send out five more video drones to catch up with the enemy scouts and this time, to set them to be in evasive mode and with shields.

The first three video drones and one defensive drone arrive near the damaged buoy, and they are set close together. This will allow them to provide us with a 360-degree view of the area. That way when they are fired upon, we should be able to detect from what direction the enemy is firing. Their shields are up, and the defensive drone is directly below them. All sensors on the video and defense drones are set to ultra, so they can detect anything out there. As they move in closer, there is no indication of movement or anything out of the ordinary. They continue to move in closer and are now passing through the debris field from the destroyed video and repair drones. The drones are now close enough that the video drones are showing that one of the panels on the buoy has been removed. With no indication of the enemy, we now send in two of the repair drones with another defensive drone. These drones approach slowly, as the video drones continue to monitor the area. As the repair drones approach the buoy, one of the video drones is catching an anomaly, at 11:00 to port from the video drone. Immediately, the defensive drones move into action and start firing in that direction. They are now receiving return fire from the direction of the anomaly. Three of the defensive drones are firing at the enemy drone. It is uncloaked at this point, and we see it on our screens. The firefight continues as fighters are starting to move in. One of the repair drones has been destroyed, but the video drones remain intact because they are protected by a force field that is preventing the shots from the enemy drone from penetrating and damaging them. The enemy drone also has a protective field around it, but the defensive drones continue to fire on it. With each direct hit on the enemy drone, we are seeing that the force field is weakening, but the enemy drone continues to fire at our drones. It also has become apparent that the enemy drone is not only firing at our defensive drones, but also at the buoy with the open panel. We give orders for the drones to move around the buoy, and protect the area of the open panel from being hit by enemy fire. It takes about two minutes before the fighters arrive. The enemy drone has detected the presence of the fighters, and now turns its attention to defending itself against a fighter attack. This proves to be ineffective because the fighters destroy the drone in about thirty seconds.

We have seen our first action, and it is against a drone. It still concerns me that this drone was on our side of the barrier. I want to know how many other drones might be here and how long they have been here.

The repair drone has moved up to the buoy now and is examining the area around the open panel. The repair drone has a video camera installed, and we can monitor the repairs. As the drone is inspecting the inside of the buoy, it notices something out of the ordinary. The camera zooms in for closer examination, and it has determined that it is booby trapped. Should the trigger be activated, it will destroy the buoy and will open a hole in our barrier. This explains why the mother ship is located at the distance from this location and why the enemy scouts are moving in this direction.

Admiral Coats orders the fighters to move back to what we consider is a safe distance in case the buoy does explode. I also request that Captain Faraday get a spare buoy from our repairs section and have a ship take the spare out to this location, at maximum speed. We don't want to have this area open for too long, should the drone be unable to defuse the bomb.

The fighters are now at a safe distance, and the drone is given the command to defuse the trap. We feel confident that the drone will be able to defuse it. All our repair drones have the intelligence to remove items that don't belong in what they are repairing. The drone begins to work at removing another panel. With this panel removed, it sees the booby trap more clearly. As it examines the circuitry, the drone reports back that the buoy will have to be shut down for thirty seconds in order remove the trap and another thirty seconds to bring the barrier back up. I look at my display, and we determine that we have between two to three minutes before the enemy scouts will arrive at the open hole in our barrier. This will be a very tight window, but I send the order for the drone to shut down the buoy and remove the device. I order Admiral Coats to spread his fighters between the two buoys to defend the open hole, in case the repair drone does not get the repair done in time, or at all.

One of the drones is now reporting two more anomalies appearing, about a mile to either side of the fighter protection. Admiral Coats is also reporting that he has four anomalies showing up within his fleet. I start to give the order to bring all fleets to general quarters, when Captain Faraday also reports that we now have five hundred anomalies around the *Hyperthia*. I now give the order to bring the fleet to full alert, and for all commands to general quarters. While I was giving this command, Captain Faraday was giving the order for shields and general quarters. All the ship's weapons are now trained on the anomalies, and the order is given to open fire. This feels like a battleship firing on row boats, because we have over fifty thousand cannons on the *Hyperthia*. The Morian drones have their shields up also and are now returning fire on the *Hyperthia*.

Meanwhile Admiral Coat's enemy drones have uncloaked and have opened fire on ships in his fleet. The fighter protection around the repair drones has kicked into full throttle, and the first shots from the enemy drones were near misses. The enemy drones start laying out a spread of fire at the fighters. One of the fighters has received a hit. and the pilot ejects his escape pod before his fighter explodes. Another fighter receives a minor hit, but can continue in the battle. Our pilots engage the drones and return heavy fire, and the fire fight is on. Within thirty seconds one of the enemy drones is destroyed, and about fifteen seconds later the second drone is destroyed. We only loose one fighter and another fighter has received minor damage.

The drone shuts down the buoy, and we notice immediately those two sections of the barrier go down, as red lights are flashing and an alarm is going off. I order the alarm to be turned off, as we continue to monitor the progress of the repair drone and monitor the fight that is raging around the fleet. The drone has removed the booby trap and has stowed it away for evaluation. It is now in the process of putting all the connections back in their proper places. The drone has completed this in about thirty seconds and is now in the process of starting the buoy back up.

Admiral Coat's destroyers have taken on the drones in his sector and because of the destroyer's superior firepower, they can destroy the drones quickly, with little damage to the fleet.

With all the activity that has taken place in the last couple of hours, our adrenaline is high, and we are watching for anything. In the command center, all screens are abuzz with activity, as well as the hologram I am looking at.

The two enemy scouts are aware that the barrier is down and have increased their speed to get to the hole before the barrier can be repaired. With their increased speed, we will be cutting it close to see who gets there first. As the enemy scouts are approaching the open hole in the barrier, our fighters have also arrived at the same time. Just as the enemy scouts start to make their turn to enter through the hole, they are trying to do it before the buoy comes back online. Just as they pass by the barrier, the buoy that was being worked on comes online, and the barrier is reactivated. The enemy scouts must have been given an order to start firing wildly as they pass by the barrier, and their rounds are barely missing the fighters that are there to intercept them. The fighters on both ends of the repaired buoy are engaged with the enemy scouts. The firefight is on, and within a couple of minutes the enemy scouts are destroyed. At this point, the Morian mother ship turns and heads back to wherever it came from. The Hypertheans will continue to monitor its movements until it disappears.

The repair drone finishes making the repairs to the buoy, and the buoy goes green on our display. We continue to leave the fleet at condition one for the next several hours while we continue to monitor for more enemy drones that may be out there in our sectors.

TWELVE

After we debrief on our situation, we have come to the following conclusions.

1. The Morians know we are here and probably has for quite some time since there were drones on our side of the barrier.
2. They now know we are defending this solar system.
3. We performed well in this situation, but we will need more drills. Our response time was slower than I would like for it to be. We had gotten lax in the past sixteen years, waiting for the fighting to begin. Well, it has started, and we need to be better prepared for it now.
4. The Morians have tested us for weaknesses, and they probably found some. We need to find them too, and correct them.
5. The Hypertheans have reviewed the videos we had of the drone that was inside our barrier and have determined that the drone is an extremely old one. They have determined that it was placed in our solar system long before the barrier was set up. There is no telling

how many of these drones have been placed in our solar system.

6. We will now begin searching for others. We will search for them within the asteroid belt, and we will survey all planetary moons, planets, and everything we can think of. We will also start looking for anomalies within the solar system.

As one of the first steps in finding other drones, I have asked General Sullivan to send up a couple of ships into the Earth's atmosphere to search through the Earth satellites and see if there are any of them hiding in a dormant state with other satellites. After a two-day search of the satellite field, they did turn up one there. It was still inactive, and we took it further out into space and destroyed it. I tell the rest of the fleets to save the next drone we find. We need to discover where the power supply is in the drones and remove it. Then we can analyze its program to see if we can modify it for our purposes and then we will send them back to the Morian fleet and do some damage there when they come to fight. We can make them very nervous, so that they can't trust which of their drones they control and which ones we control.

Within a month, the fleet has discovered eighty-eight of these drones. At least thirty of them were in the asteroid belt, and one was within two miles of where the *Hyperthia* was based. Most of the remaining drones were discovered on moons, or planets, disguised as large rocks on their surfaces. We have discovered how to remove their power supplies, and our computer specialists are still working on breaking down the code that controls the drones. They feel they should be able to break the code in the next couple of months. I tell them to get help from the Hypertheans because they probably know more about this code than we do. I certainly hope they can break it before the Morians move in for their next attack. I would like to have these drones as part of our arsenal. The fleet is now doing a secondary sweep of the solar system to see if they can find more drones, now that they know what they are looking for.

The secondary sweep does turn up two hundred more of these drones. We now have them all stockpiled on our moon base, Moon Base Alpha.

I ask the fleet to do a third sweep and to keep doing them until we come up with a sweep of zero finds. They continued doing the sweeps, and it was not until the tenth sweep that we came back with zero finds. I thank the fleet for being persistent in their sweeps. Even though we have not found any more drones, I am not convinced that we have located all of them. In total, we found four hundred and twenty-seven drones, and it still bothers me that we found a drone in our satellite field. That drone could not have been placed there after the barrier was set in place. We have only had satellites around Earth for about eighty years now. Of all the sweeps we did, we did not include Earth. This will be difficult, since the Earth is populated. We need to work through the Earth delegation, make them aware of what we have found, and that we need to do a sweep of Earth for any dormant drones. We know what the drones look like and how to detect them even if they are completely buried. It takes a couple of weeks to work through the details of how we will do this, without alarming the populous. I will have General Sullivan do the searches, according to what we have worked out with the delegation.

General Sullivan conducts the sweep, and it takes him about a month to complete it. With this sweep, he finds about sixty drones on Earth, some in plain sight and some were buried beneath the soil. So, this now brings our count to four hundred and eighty-seven drones. I ask him to complete two more sweeps, just to make sure that we have found all of them. We don't want the Morians using these drones for attacks on the Earth population, or having some kids finding them and getting hurt.

We don't find anymore, and Earth is now aware of the

skirmish we had. Now we have a concerned populous. They are pleased with the victory we had in this skirmish, especially since this victory was for all of Earth. With this skirmish, people are volunteering in droves, wanting to be part of the fleet, and to get in on the fight. We have no problems with that since we will probably need them soon. They have also been made aware of the sleeping drones that we have located. Now there are bands of people out looking for other drones, just in case we have missed one or two. I am hopeful that none of these bands will find anything. I am fearful they will not turn them in, or will accidently activate one, and set off a rampage by the drone that will cost Earth a lot of lives. General Sullivan did secondary sweeps that netted us another twenty drones, and he is confident these are all of them. If there are any left, it will be extremely difficult for anyone to find them.

Now we wait. Will the Morians attack, or do they know the stakes are high, knowing the Federation is involved with us now? Do they care? Probably not, at least they haven't in the past. Now we start more war games to freshen up on our skills, and to better prepare us for what is to come.

THIRTEEN

After taking a short breather from this small brush with Morian drones, we have redistributed the fleet to better protect each of our quadrants of space. We are still leery of our confidence to protect our solar system. We have never been in a space battle before, even though we have been trained well by the Hyphertheans. There is a difference from being trained and experiencing it. Our fighting will need to be reactionary from our training. Since it has been several years since we went through the training, we continue to have drills. We will start again with the training and keep doing it until it is no longer reactionary but just part of our being.

It has been a month since our encounter with the drones, and everything is too quiet. It feels like the quite before the storm, and I don't like it. I have brought the admirals and their counselors aboard the *Hyperthia* to discuss some new strategies. As our meeting starts, we lay out some options to get better information as to where the Morians are located. Even though the Hyperthean communication system has kept us well informed, we are all still a little uncomfortable with how the Morians remained so stealthy until the last moment. Then we were placed on the defensive way too quickly. One of the suggestions that came up was to send some of our destroyers out beyond the shield to scout for us. After about an hour discussion, we decide this was way too risky, since it would thin our fleets. The destroyers are not fast enough to get away if they ran into anything. We go through several different scenarios throughout the rest of the day and came away with nothing. We then adjourned for the day, and we will continue our discussion the next day at 0900.

As we continued our meeting the next day, one of the admirals comes up with the idea of building some scout ships. From our discussion the previous day, it became apparent that the thing we need are scouts out beyond the barrier. The problem is that we don't have any ships that fit that bill. At this point, everyone is jumping in with ideas on what we need to do. After discussing our options for the rest of the morning and into the afternoon, we finally agreed on developing a scout ship with the following requirements.

1. Strong hull and shield to withstand an attack for some time. The Hypertheans had provided us with the metallurgical formulas to create the metals we need to build and repair our ships right after we first became part of the alliance.
2. Shields that are better than our current ones.
3. A new communications process that would send out messages in bursts. They need to be hidden in the current communication bands and would be undetectable.
4. The ability to cloak the scouts and not create anomalies that could be detectable.
5. Speed. They need the ability to outrun anything out there.
6. Minimal weaponry. These ships are being built for scouting and speed, not to fight.
7. Crew size–fifteen.

We are estimating that we will need about ten thousand of these scout ships and that we want them in the next twelve months. We have all agreed on this and have created the order to have these ships built.

While we wait for the designs to come back, we are also having our scientists work on better shields. Our technology group needs to develop the requested communication process. For the cloaking process, we are turning to the Hypertheans to assist us in this area.

We have been waiting for six months now. Neither we, nor the Hypertheans, have heard, or seen any sign of the Morians. We have been diligently running our drills and getting more efficient at them. The fleets have been redeployed to better protect our universe, but we are not feeling comfortable yet. Currently we have about five hundred scout ships in many stages of development, and the Hypertheans have provided us with the specifications for our new cloaking process. From what we see in the specifications, the scout ships will be able to cloak for the full time they are on patrol and will not create any anomalies. The Hypertheans could deliver this for us, because we have kept the ship size small. It does not require a large power source to generate the cloaking process. We have also been able to make some improvements in the engines for the scouts. With these improvements, they will be able to outrun anything they encounter. This is good, and we are pleased with the progress. The technology team is not quite there with the requested communication band. They are telling us they are making good progress and are confident they will have it for us in the next three months. I have also requested from one of our builders that they deliver us a prototype ship for us to run some tests with. We will have this ship in the next couple of weeks, but without the communications we have requested. I have told them this is fine, since we are not interested in testing that yet.

In the meantime, I have received some very sad news. General Sullivan has sent me a communication that he is announcing his retirement at the end of the year. He tells me that his second will be a good man to replace him. I have met General Todd, and he is a good man and has served General Sullivan well. But still, I will miss Mitch. It has been awhile since I have been to Earth, and I need to speak with Mitch just to make sure everything is alright.

I make my travel plans for the next day and arrive at the Texas base. I am greeted by Mitch and General Todd, and we head towards his office. I look over at Mitch, and he seems to be tired. We go into his office, and I ask General Todd if I can have a few moments with Mitch before we start. He agrees, leaves the office, and closes the door.

"Mitch, are you feeling okay? I noticed you are looking a little tired."

"Don't worry about me, I am fine. I was ready to retire twenty years ago when you approached me about this assignment. Now I believe I have accomplished everything you have asked of me."

"Yes you have, and you have done an excellent job. Is there anything else I need to be aware of on a personal level?"

"No, I am in good health. I just want to enjoy some time with my family, and just to be with them, that's all."

"I can understand that. I know I haven't been with my family as much as I should, and I need to. I know I am not indispensable, and I have good men in the fleet who can handle things without me. The Hypertheans keep telling me that they still need me."

I pause for a few seconds, and then say, "Okay Mitch, I will accept your retirement, but I'm not giving up on our friendship."

He smiles at me and reaches out his hand to shake, and says, "Never."

"Okay, before we start crying on each other's shoulders, lets get Todd in here to discuss how we are going to transition this retirement."

We both laugh, and ask Todd to come back into the office.

FOURTEEN

We have been told that our first prototype scout ship is ready for test flights. It is currently being loaded into a cargo transport that is bringing her to the *Hyperthia*. It should be here in a couple of days.

The cargo transport has arrived, and it will take a couple of more days to get it ready for her maiden voyage. We are all excited to see what the scout ship looks like. On the day of her maiden test flight, I finally get time to go down and have a look at the ship. She looks just like the models that have been presented to me, but she is a little bigger than I had presumed. She sure looks nice, sleek and stealthy. Commander Owen will be our test pilot. He is currently going over every aspect of the ship with a fine-tooth comb to make sure she is ready for her initial flight. Commander Owen will be taking four other crew members with him on this test flight to make sure all the systems are working well. Two of the crewmen will be for engines, one for structural integrity, and the other for the new cloaking process.

The crew is now ready to take the scout out for her initial test flight. They have completed the preflight checklist, and we are ready to watch her leave the docking bay. They fire up the engine, and it is purring like a kitten. After a couple of minutes, we see the ship start moving down the launch bay and out of the *Hyperthia*. As they get it just outside the bay, they turn on stealth mode, and it vanishes right before our eyes, and we wait. A couple of minutes later she reappears about two miles away from the *Hyperthia* We are now ready to see how she handles speed. They take her up to presser 60, and she has no problems. They now increase the speed to Presser 100, and she continues to move and respond with no problems. They now increase the speed to presser 175, and they are now going faster than anything in the Federation. They are now holding her at this speed to see how long she can maintain it. They keep her at this speed for an hour, and the engines are performing well and within specs. They have now circled the galaxy twenty-five times in two hours, and are ready to bring her back into the launch bay. As the commander slows her down, he notices a slight vibration. He is not sure what it is, and he reports it to the safety team.

We are pleased with the test flight, but we still have ten more test flights to go before we approve her ready for service. The safety team has been going over the ship, but has not been able to find anything wrong with her. They still believe that Commander Owen noticed something, but they are still looking for the problem.

The next five test flights will be with the ship uncloaked, and we will be testing the endurance of the metallurgy of the hull and the engines' ability to maintain the speeds at presser 200. The commander starts the second trial, and circles the galaxy at presser 200 and maintains that speed for two days. At the same time, we are testing our sensors ability to detect and track a ship moving at that speed. Our systems are working well, and we can track the ship without any problems. With the special tracking device that was installed on the ship when it was built, we can see it on our screens even when cloaked.

We will be testing that out when we test out our cloaking runs after these tests.

When the two-day run comes to completion and Commander Owen is bringing the ship back in, he does not notice any problems with the ship like he did the first time. We will give the ship a rest for a week while the ship is given a complete inspection inside and out. We analyze the ship's logs and watch the crew for any side effects of traveling at that speed for a prolonged period.

The week has passed, and the reports are starting to come in. Everything checks out at 100 percent cleared. This is good news. We clear Commander Owen and his crew for this next test flight. They will be starting the next test flight tomorrow.

For test flight 3 through 5, we run the ship and crew through the planned tests. Everything and everyone performs beyond our expectations. On the fifth test flight Commander Owen took the ship to presser 250, which was just beyond ship specifications. We were quite impressed with the ship to handle that speed and to know that she could do that speed without any problems.

Now we are ready to test the ship over again, performing the same tests as runs 1 through 5, but this time the ship will be cloaked during the entire test. We have also asked that one of the Hyperthean cloak developers be present for these tests in case we run into any problems, and they have agreed.

Commander Owen is now ready to start run 6. He makes the run as instructed, and we also test the ability to see the ship on our systems. We cannot see her nor can we find her in the conventional ways. However, the tracking device we had built into the ship is working perfectly. We can see her as she moves about the test flight. We have also checked with the Earth's non-military systems to see if they can see the ship as she is moving about during the test process. They cannot find her.

The tracking device is not a conventional one. It has been designed to send a blip over our new communication process once we have it. We hear the team is almost ready with the new communication system, and we should have it next week. For today we had it modified to transmit over our standard encrypted systems.

As Commander Owen brings the ship back in after completing test run 6, he gets that feeling again that something is not quite right. The engineers start going over the ship as usual, but still cannot pin point what the problem is that Commander Owen is noticing. As we go through our thought processes, we conclude that what he is noticing is in the decloaking process. The first time he noticed it, the ship had just decloaked and this time it was when it decloaked. We report this to the Hyperthean engineer that is aboard the *Hyperthia*, and he begins analyzing the cloaking system. In the meantime, we have grounded the ship until we find out what the issue is with the cloaking system.

The Hyperthean has been working through the process for two days now and has not been able to find anything. He is now consulting with his counterparts, and they are also running tests back in their labs. By the time day 6 arrives, they think they have found the problem. It is within the shutdown process of the cloaking system. They are glad that Commander Owen felt whatever it was that he felt because within six months, this glitch would have caused the cloaking system to fail completely. They are now adjusting the process in their labs and should have a corrected solution for us within the week.

Since this is a programming problem, and nothing to do with the structural integrity of the ship, we are continuing to build the ships back on Earth. We have also learned that the communication team has the communication system completed, and is sending us the first prototype to be installed on our test ship. We should receive it and have it installed by the time the ship is ready for her next test flight.

The test ship is now ready to test all systems. The communication system is now installed, the revisions for the cloaking device has been corrected, and we are now ready to begin test 7. The ship is ready to begin its test run, and this time, we will do it with the full crew compliment of fifteen.

Commander Owen takes the ship out of the bay and goes to the outer parameters of our galaxy to begin his test run. He cloaks the ship, and we lose the visual on our radar systems. We still can see the ship with the detection device, but this time through the new communication system. Commander Owen takes the ship to presser 200, and begins his test runs. Everything is working as expected. The communication system is sending messages, and even we are unable to detect that messages have been sent. As Commander Owen completes his test run and shuts down the cloaking system, he does not feel any problems with the ship.

The final runs are completed with no problems. We are now at month eight of asking for the completion of the ten thousand ships that we had asked for. Now we know that they will not be completed in time. With the unexpected delays and the problems we have encountered during the test runs, we will only have about two hundred ships ready by the end of the twelve-month period. But we can now create an assembly line process and get the rest of the ships ready by the eighteenth month. We will have to live with this, and we will soon have our scout ships ready to do their jobs.

Now we have another mission to complete, and that is to get crews ready to man these ships. We will select commanders, communication officers, and engineers from the fleet for the training. Each crew will consist of fifteen personnel with each cross trained in other duties aboard the scouts, in the event personnel become ill or injured. They will all be volunteers for the positions, because these ships will be taking on the most dangerous mission of the fleet. They will be out there patrolling alone, with no help from the fleet. Even if we wanted to help, it would take too long to get there. The advantage they have is cloaking and speed. They will be on patrol for thirty days at a time. Each of the fourteen fleets will have one thousand and forty-eight scout ships, with seven hundred and four of them on patrols at one time. We will vary routines when a scout is relieved, so that we do not establish any patterns that might be traceable. We will keep forty ships in reserve in case of necessary repairs or replacement.

We will start sending two scout ships to each fleet as soon as they arrive, and the crews are ready to take their stations. By our twelfth month, we will have deployed twenty-eight scouts to each of the fleets, and by our thirteenth month, we will start receiving one thousand six hundred and thirty-three scouts for all our fleets.

Excitement continues to build as we build these ships, and we have more than enough personnel who are volunteering for the positions aboard our scouts. We will need one hundred and fifty thousand personnel to man these ships, and we will also need one hundred and fifty thousand new replacements to take the positions these people held within the fleet. We will also need another fifty thousand support personnel to maintain the scouts.

We will get forty scout ships on board the *Hyperthia* to train the crews that are volunteering to man these scout ships. With the number of crews that will need to be trained, we are also developing simulation areas aboard the *Hyperthia* for the training of these crews. We will keep forty of the ships here for training purposes until all the crews are trained.

With five thousand ships out there beyond our outer parameters, I hope we don't have anything that will go bump in the night. However, we have our patrol areas well defined. We should have ample warning in case they run into anything.

FIFTEEN

The eighteen months have passed, and we have trained and deployed all our scout ships out to their patrol areas. It has also been very quiet. We have not had any encounters with the Morians, nor has the Hyperthean High Command had anything to report to us. It is extremely quiet for them too. They have extended patrols out further into space, and have not encountered any problems. They have seen how well our scout ships are performing, and have requested that we provide them with a copy of our blueprints for the ships, so that they can develop some of the ships. We are pleased to provide them with a copy of the blueprints, and we are also sending them ten of our scout ships for them to have. We have also volunteered our manufacturing line, if they want our help in making more of these ships, since we already have the fabrication process in place. They have graciously accepted our offer, and have sent us a request for fifty thousand of our ships to be made for them, with some modifications. Mainly they want the readouts to be in their language, so that they can understand what all the instrument readouts mean. We laughed, and said we would oblige them.

With the scouts on patrol in the twentieth month, we have encountered something strange with one of the patrols. It has gone silent. We continue to get our blip signal from the ship, but the ship is not moving, nor can we raise it on our communication system. We have ordered another scout to go out and see if it can contact the scout, but it will take a week for the scout ship to get there. We continue to monitor the situation and have ordered the thirteenth fleet to go to alert level 2, because the scout ship is from its fleet. We have not noticed anything out of the ordinary, but we are keeping our alert up.

The week has passed, and the scout ship has arrived at the location where the other scout ship is located. It has been scanning the entire area for any possibilities of Morians, but it has not found anything. The scout ship is not moving, and still cloaked. Any attempts to communicate with it have gone unanswered. The commander has pulled alongside the scout ship, and one of the crew members is attempting a spacewalk over to the ship. He is tethered to the scout, and is moving over to where the other ship is presumed to be. The only way he will know he is there is when he bumps into it. Then he will have to figure out what part of the ship he has bumped into, before he can figure out where the hatch is, so that he can get inside the ship.

He has gone about four hundred meters from his ship, when he finally bumps into the other ship. It takes him about an hour to figure out how the ship is oriented, and eventually finds the hatch that will allow him into the ship. He enters the commands to open the hatch from the outside, and ties the tether to the ship and enters the hatch and closes it. He activates the command to fill the chamber he is in with air, and it functions properly. He is now able to open the inner hatch and go inside. He checks the air, and everything checks out as it should. He removes his helmet, and starts calling out names, but no one answers. As he goes throughout the ship, he does not find anything to be out of place, and even the table has food on it, as if someone had been eating. As he completes his search, he does not find any of the crew aboard. He has been in communication with his crew this whole time, but finally must tell his captain that it appears that the crew just vanished.

The captain asks if the ship is still functional. The crewman examines the controls, and all the instruments, and reports that he does not find any problems with the ship. The captain tells him to remain onboard, decloak the ship, and that he is sending over five more crewmen to take the ship back to base for examination. The commander of the scout ship reports back to the thirteenth fleet the situation, and requests that a new ship and crew, come out and replace this patrol. He will be escorting this ship back just in case there are more problems encountered.

The thirteenth fleet admiral acknowledges the request, and sends out a new patrol with instructions to be very diligent, and to report the slightest thing they see or encounter immediately.

"Don't delay in the slightest, in case this becomes an issue, and we need to respond to their assistance immediately."

I have instructed the admiral that when the scout ship comes back to the fleet to have it brought immediately to the *Hyperthia* for a full investigation. He acknowledges the request.

It has been ten days since we have found out that the crew is missing from the scout ship, and we have informed the families of the fifteen crew members that they are currently missing, and that we do not have any other information we can give to them now. The two scout ships have reentered the galaxy and are now on their way to the *Hyperthia*. They should be here in the next four hours. We anxiously wait for the ship to get here, so that we can start going over the logs to try and determine what has happened to the crew.

The two ships have arrived, and I have ordered that we have a secluded bay for the ships to enter so that we have no interruptions, or interference for the investigation. We have a contamination crew go over the two ships before we allow the crews to disembark their ships. The contamination crew does not find any type of contamination, and we let the crews come out of the ships. We have them report to a containment room so that they can be examined by a medical team. The crew is examined, and are given a clean bill of health. Now they need to be debriefed. Each of their statements is taken, and we will combine what they tell us with what we get from the logs of both ships.

The investigation team enters the scout ship, and starts pulling all the logs of the ship. They will go through each of them with a fine-toothed comb to try and find out what happened. As they are going through the video log from inside the ship, they see that the crew members are doing their jobs as normal, and the next instant they are gone, vanishing into thin air. Now the investigation team is trying to figure out if the video log has been tampered with in any way, to see if some of the video has been deleted. So far, they are not finding any evidence of it. We are sending a copy of the video log to the Hyperthean High Command to see if they have any clues as to what is going on here.

While we do our own examination internally of the ship, the Hypertheans have sent one of their own ships into the sector where the crew members from the ship disappeared. As they have told us, this is the first time they have seen anything like this, and this is their first time to do any patrolling in this sector of space.

The crew and the scout ship are released from the debriefing, and are returned to the fleet to resume their duties. We are keeping the ship that had the missing crew on board the *Hyperthia*, until all the investigation has been completed. This will probably take about six months.

As we continue our investigation, the fleet continues its duties as normal, and the scout ships remain on patrol, except for the sector where the incident occurred. Besides, with a Hyperthean ship in there now doing its own investigation, we don't need a scout ship in there. So far everything remains quiet. It has now been two years since the encounter with the Morian drones, and neither the Hypertheans nor we, have encountered any type of problems from the Morians. This concerns all of us. The Hypertheans are more familiar with them and their tactics, and they have been keeping a close watch on them, but they have not found anything that would raise an eyebrow.

The Hyperthean ship has been on patrol in this sector now for three months, and has not found anything to explain why crew members would just vanish. They are continuing their sweeps, only now they will be trying something new. They will be running their patrol in cloaked mode for a couple of weeks, to see if they can spot anything that way, since that was the way we were running our patrol when our crew disappeared.

The Hyperthean ship has been running its patrol for a week now, when I receive an urgent message from the Hyperthean High Command. The message reads as follows:

> Admiral Graham,
>
> Please send a scout ship into the restricted area immediately. We have lost communication with our ship in that sector. Proceed into the sector with your cloaking device off. You have the coordinates for our ship. Proceed with the utmost urgency and caution.
>
> Hyperthean High Command

I get in contact with Admiral Coats of the thirteenth fleet and make him aware of the message that I have just received. I tell him to send two scout ships to the designated coordinates for the Hyperthean ship, and to take the utmost caution in doing so. He acknowledges back, and tells me he will keep me informed of the progress of the ships on an hourly basis.

It takes a week for the scout ships to arrive at the coordinates that were provided to us by the Hyperthean High Command. The scout ships have attempted to communicate with the Hyperthean ship, but they are not getting any response. The Hyperthean ship is still cloaked, and we are not familiar with this style of ship. The scout ships are requesting the specifications for the ship to try to find a way to enter the ship. We contact the high command, and they send us the specifications for their ship that includes where we can make entry. We forward this information to the scout ships, and they start the process of trying to determine which way the ship is facing. It takes them about two hours to determine the orientation, and now they are sending over a couple of men in suits to enter the ship. They enter the ship with no problems and start their search for the crew. They continue reporting back that they are not finding anyone. They go to the command bridge and turn off the cloaking device. The scout ships approach the ship more closely now that they know where it is. They send over about ten more men to search the ship, because it is much larger than our scout ships. It takes them about two hours to do a total search of the ship, but again, they do not find a soul. Three thousand crewmen vanished without a trace. They report this back to the thirteenth fleet, and Admiral Coats relays this message back to me. It is now my responsibility to report back to the Hyperthean High Command. I tell the High Command what we have found, and offer them our condolences for the loss of their people. I also let them know that we will bring their ship back to our fleet and await their instructions as to what they want us to do.

In the meantime, I have instructed the thirteenth fleet to set out buoys warning ships to stay out of this sector until further notice. There is something going on in this sector that we do not understand. For the Federation, we will be doing our studies outside of this sector until we understand what is going on and what has happened to our people. The Federation has sent three more ships to do their own studies.

SIXTEEN

Time continues to go by, and we have not heard, or seen, anything from the Morians, nor have we discovered any new information about the restricted zone. We continue to monitor all space and are starting to get bored after being hyped up a couple of years ago with the possibility of a war. Now we have concerns on two fronts and don't understand what is going on or why. It is very perplexing to me. I need to have time to think. I decide to take a couple of weeks leave to think things out.

I have decided to go to a secluded spot where I won't be bothered by people. I have gotten permission from one of the ranch owners in the Davis Mountains of West Texas to camp along one of their streams. I set up camp, had a fire going, and was just sitting back relaxing and enjoying the outdoors again. I had not done anything like this since I was a kid and was wondering why I had not done it more often. It was peaceful, just the quiet sounds of the stream flowing, birds chirping, a ground squirrel now and then, and a soft breeze blowing through the trees. I enjoy this setting for a week. Then I had to get back to reality. I start to break out my computer when I hear a noise. It sounds like someone is coming down the trail towards my camp. As the sound approaches, I see it is one of the ranch hands on horseback. We exchange greetings.

"Howdy, how are you doing? The boss wanted me to check up on you. He wanted to make sure that everything was okay out here."

"Everything is fine. I have been enjoying the solitude of the moment. Almost forgot there is a world out there."

"Yeah, this peacefulness can do that to you. That is why I enjoy being just a cowhand. Is there anything you need?"

"No, I'm good."

"Okay, I will check back with you in a couple of days."

He turns his horse to leave and heads back up the trail. I continue to listen to him leaving, and then I reach for my computer and open it up. I start looking at my hologram, and pause for a moment, wishing I didn't have to get back to this reality.

Before I can get started with anything, my communicator chirps and lets me know I have an incoming call. I let out a groan and pick up my communicator to answer the call.

"Yeah, Graham here."

"Sir, this is Commander Steele, I am sorry to bother you Admiral, but one of the scout ships has found a small device in the lower left quadrant of the restricted zone. They are requesting permission to enter the restricted zone and pick it up. What are your orders?"

I am a little concerned about them finding this device just within reach of the restricted area. I feel it has been planted there but by whom, I don't know.

"Commander Steele, please tell the scout ship to approach the object with extreme caution and to make sure that their cloaking process is turned off. Tell them that when they have the device to get out of the zone immediately. Also, inform Admiral Sapp of the sixth Fleet of this, and tell him to send out a destroyer to meet with the scout ship to pick up the device. They are to place the device in the confinement box and to activate a shield around it. The destroyer is to bring it back to the sixth fleet. I will let them know what to do when it is back with them."

Commander Steele acknowledges the message and signs off.

I think about the find for about a half hour, and I am trying to decide if I should stay here and think, or to return to the fleet. I find that I am thinking more about this find. I get frustrated with myself and decide to return to the fleet. I know that my mind is no longer clear, and I won't be able to concentrate on what I intended the trip for.

I start packing up my camping equipment, and in about an hour I am ready to head back to where I parked my car. I turn one more time to make sure I have everything and that my campfire is out. Everything looks good, and I start to head up the trail. It takes me about an hour to get back to the ranch house. I let the owner know that I need to leave earlier than I expected and that I left the campsite in good condition. I thank them for allowing me to do this, and I appreciated it very much.

They let me know that I am welcome to come back anytime. I ask if I can leaved my camping gear here at their place, because I really don't have the room for it now in my car. They tell me that it is not a problem, and to come back soon.

I get in my car, and drive up the road and out of sight of anyone. I have a long straight stretch of road in front of me. I now command my vehicle to get ready for flight, and it changes into my travel vehicle. I take off and head for the *Hyperthia.*

I contact the base in Texas, and let them know that I have just taken off and am heading back to the ship. At the same time, I let the *Hyperthia* know that I am returning to the station.

The destroyer has returned to the sixth fleet and has turned over the device to Admiral Sapp to hold until further orders from me. I let Admiral Sapp know that I would like for it to be turned over to the scientific ship *Vega.* They will take it and do whatever they can to investigate the object. From the report I have received, it is a round orb that is about two feet in diameter. There does not appear to be any seams that allow us to break into it. By the weight of the orb, it does not seem to be solid. They have tried a torch on it, but it does not react to heat. They have done everything they know of to try to get it to react to something.

Finally, I tell them to just store it someplace, since it does not seem to be of any importance.

Things within the fleet have returned to normal routine patrols. We continue monitoring the restricted area but nothing changes. It has been six months since the Hyperthean crew disappeared, and still we haven't seen, felt, or heard a sound from anywhere. The Hypertheans continue their monitoring process, and still have great concern for both crews.

SEVENTEEN

It has been a long stretch of silence, but we now have a scout ship that is patrolling near the edge of the restricted area. It is reporting that it has picked up something strange on their screen just on the other side of the restricted zone. When they went to visual, it appears to be a gold piece of foil and a crank.

I don't know what to say at this point, but that this is the strangest thing I have had reported to me since I became part of the fleet. I don't know what it could possibly mean. I tell them to get both objects and to bring them back when their patrol ends.

When they return, they turn the two objects over to the scientific vessel that has the orb. When the scientists bring the two objects into the room where the orb is stored, the orb becomes active and begins to float and rotate very slowly. When the scientists see this, they go over to look at the orb. It suddenly stops spinning, and then a hole appears on the side of the orb near the top. Then they notice that the hole is about the size of the crank they brought into the room, and appears it will fit. They are eager to put the crank into the hole to see what happens, but they realize they must do things in proper order and have every step recorded.

The next day they take the orb into a concealed area, just in case it is a bomb. If it explodes, it will be confined there with minimal damage. They now have the orb and the crank in the concealed area and are taking it one step at a time.

The first step is to place the crank into the hole and see if it really is a fit. As they do so, they find that the crank does fit, and they start to twist it until it slides completely in. They stop there and give a sigh when nothing happens. Now they are ready for the next step, to twist the handle to see what happens next. They start to twist on the handle slowly, and as they complete the first turn, the top of the orb opens and shows a bunch of gears and two sets of tumblers. The gears are turning slowly inside as the first set of tumblers starts to slowly turn and change with each rotation of the gears, until it finally comes to a stop. The tumbler now shows a set of symbols which, for us, has no meaning. The scientists have decided to stop as this point, since it has brought about significant progress in getting us some answers. The scientists take a picture of the inside of the orb, and send it off to the Hypertheans for analysis, and hopefully, they can give us some answers as to what this means. We still do not have an appreciation as to what the gold foil is for, but I imagine we will find out some day. In the meantime, we wait on the Hyperthean Federation to come back with an answer.

It has been a couple of days since we sent a copy of the image off, and we are now getting a response back. They have asked us to stop any further testing on the orb. They are sending a Hyperthean ship to us that will join us in the investigation. They are pulling a ship from their fleet that is the closest to us, and it should be there within the week.

This really concerns me that they are doing this, and especially since they are not giving us any further information. I relay this message and information, to the rest of the admirals within the fleet and to let them know that this ship is coming. I soon receive the star coordinates from which direction this ship is approaching, and let Admiral Yashurio of the third fleet know that they will be approaching us through his sector within the next four days.

The Hyperthean ship arrives, and it is in a class I have never seen before. The ship docks with our scientific ship over in the sixth fleet, and I am there to greet the captain of the ship. The captain and his staff bring a shuttle over to the flag ship and docks. As the captain comes aboard, I am surprised and pleased, to see that it is Kleg. As we approach each other and give salutes, we smile at each other, and give each other a hug. I introduce Kleg to Admiral Sapp, and explain how it is that I know Kleg. After our introductions, we head towards the Admiral's stateroom and sit to start discussing things.

I start off with asking Kleg to please bring us up-to-date. We want to know what is going on, and why the Hyperthean High Command has sent his ship here.

Kleg responds by leaning forward, and says as he points to an image of the symbols, "Chris, the symbols on these tumblers are ancient symbols used in writings that we have not seen for tens of thousands of years. They were first discovered on a planet that was civilized at one time, but all the residents of the planet had longed vanished with no indication as to where, or why they disappeared. There was no explanation as to what had happened to them, and our archaeologist have not made much progress in deciphering the symbols or their language. They are excited in your find, and want to be present as we continue our research."

"Kleg, you, and your team are more than welcome to be here. If we can come together with your archaeologists and have them tell us all they know about this planet and lost civilization, I would very much appreciate it. I am very concerned how this relates to the restricted area, our lost crews, and this missing civilization. I want to understand how all this ties together, and how we get our people back. I also want to bring up some of our finest hieroglyphist and archaeologist to work with your team. Together I hope we can come to some meaning to all this."

Kleg agrees, and we set up our meeting for the next morning. Now we just sit back for some idle chatter for the next hour or so, and I ask Kleg how it is he came to be captain of this ship.

"It had been awhile since I had been here, in Earth time, and I wanted to see an old friend."

"Well I am glad that you did. We have a lot of catching up to do."

We continue our conversation, and he tells me about his adventures since he had left us, and I catch him up on what has been going on around here.

The next morning we meet on his ship, he shows us around, and explains the workings of this scientific ship. It is far more advanced than anything we have put together, and we all agree we should bring the orb with the crank in it and the gold foil over to this ship for the studies to begin. The scientists, and those who will be joining from Earth, will work together on Kleg's ship, and Kleg has set up living quarters for all of them. It will take another day or two for me to gather the hieroglyphist and archaeologists from Earth and get them up to the ship. But I am sure they will be more than willing to come and study something new.

After contacting one of the universities in Great Britain, and talking to their archaeological department head, they were more than eager to participate in the study. Within three hours they had a dozen different professors and archaeologists more than willing to participate in this endeavor.

I spoke with Kleg and the head of his research team, and they felt that twelve would be too many. They recommended that we cut it down to six of the top people from around the world. I agreed with that, and I let the university know of the decision. I told them I wanted the selection to be fair, and

I wanted the best from both fields no matter what country they were from. Within the hour, they sent me the list and where they were from, along with their resumes and character references. I showed them to Kleg's team. They reviewed them, and agreed to the selection.

I let the university know that I would like for them to be available to come up here within the next twenty-four hours. I also told them where they needed to be to board a shuttle that would bring them to our location.

In the meantime, they have brought the orb over to Kleg's ship and have noticed that the symbols in the orb have changed by one symbol. They record the change, but they do not know what has caused the symbols to change. In the meantime, it has provided them with another symbol to study.

The six professors are now here, and we introduce them to the Hyperthean team they will be working with. They immediately start talking with the team, and are now oblivious to our existence. They start walking, talking, and heading toward the lab where they will be working. Kleg and I look at each other and start laughing. We turn to head back to what we were doing before they got there.

EIGHTEEN

The team has been working for several days now, searching through Earth and Hyperthean databases for any semblance of the symbols. The Hypertheans had already been searching their databases with no luck, and now the Earth databases have not provided anything either. They are now trying some new approaches, but are not making any progress. Just by chance, one of the professors remembers some symbols he saw once in some Aztec ruins in Mexico that resembled one of the symbols here. He asks if he can have access to his personal notes back at the university. We give him access to a computer that can access the internet on Earth, and he is able to get into the universities network and his notes. He starts going through his notes, and it takes him about a day before he finds what he is looking for. He shows the symbols to the rest of the team, and they start to study these symbols. As they study them, they do find that there is some resemblance to the symbols that are in the orb.

They continue working with this professor to determine if they have found something. As they work with these new symbols from the Aztec ruins, they get more symbols, and the Hyperthean team says that some of the symbols are close enough to other symbols that they found on their abandoned planet. Since the ancient world symbols are mixed in with some of the Aztec symbols, the archaeologists think they are making good progress now. By combining the Aztec symbols with the symbols from the abandoned planet, they are now able to start deciphering the language and the meaning of what has been left behind both in Mexico and on this ancient planet. They haven't gotten close to what the symbols mean on the orb, but things look promising.

As they continue to sift through the thousands of symbols they must work with, they are starting to decipher some of the symbols. With the progress they are making, more and more symbols are starting to make some sense. They now believe that the symbols on the orb represent some number scheme. What exactly, they are not sure yet, but they are excited about their findings.

One of the professors believes that the symbols on the orb represents coordinates of some sort. He would like to try an experiment to see if what he believes is indeed true. He would like for the vessel carrying the orb to move to a new location about three minutes away. He believes that as we do, the numbers on the orb will change indicating that it is in a new location.

Kleg orders the ship to move to a new location that he has selected. The archeologists are all excited now. As the ship moved, the symbols on the orb did change as they had hoped. So now we have some new information. The orb is tracking its location in space. But what about the gold foil and the other dial that remains blank?

We are now at a perplexing stage about this orb. We know that the dial is tracking our current location, or should we say, *its* current location in space. As the scientists studied the orb, they have discovered that there is a slot for something like a piece of paper to be inserted into. It is the exact size of the gold foil. We are extremely hesitant to take the gold foil and insert it in the slot. As we think through this whole thing, we feel it is some sort of trap or setup. We find the orb at one end of the restricted zone, and the gold foil and crank at another end. Coincidence? I don't believe in coincidences and neither does anybody else.

We look at what we have so far. An orb, a crank, gold foil, a planet with no people, crews that vanish into thin air, symbols from that planet that matches the orb, and similar symbols from an ancient Aztec ruin. My inclination is to let Kleg, and his ship take it back to the planet where the race disappeared and let the whole thing play out there.

I have a meeting with the admiralty and Kleg. We discuss the whole thing as I have just laid it out. The archeologists disagree, but the rest of us agree. We come to an understanding with the archeologists. If they want to travel with Kleg's ship back to that planet to continue "the adventure," they can. Kleg agrees. They are in total agreement with that decision and are ready to go.

Kleg gets his ship ready to get underway, and we again say our good-byes. I tell Kleg I would like to be kept informed of their findings. The archeologists are onboard and ready for this new adventure. If they go and come right back, they will be gone for five Earth years. They have been told this, and they are ready to go. Those who have families are being allowed to take them too, if they wish to go. There were several families that thought of this as an expat assignment and were eager to see new worlds.

Kleg's ship leaves, and we now return to business as usual. We still have the restricted zone, and we still have not heard anything from the Morians. We send our scientific ships back out to explore new worlds within our galaxy, but it will take them about a year to get to where they were headed. We say our farewells to the captains and their crews, and wish them good sailing into their new adventure.

NINETEEN

It has been about one and a half years since Kleg's ship left, and they should be reaching this abandoned planet soon. About a week later, I get a message from Kleg that they have arrived at the planet. They have been joined by several other ships and more of their own archaeologists to see this orb and to see what happens next. They have all traveled to the planet and are setting up a lab there to continue their experiments and investigation.

I send Kleg a communique wishing him and the others well and to stay safe, and make sure that nobody there cuts any corners. He sends me a smiley face and a thumbs-up. I see that he has taken on some of our earthly ways.

They have tried cutting a piece of foil the same size as the gold foil, and insert it into the slot. It starts to take it in, but it's as if it knows that it is not the material it was designed to take, and returns it back out the slot. At least they now know that the slot is designed to accept something, not just anything. The only thing they can assume is the gold foil. Also, through the past year and a half of travel, the dial in the orb has changed with every parsec that they have traveled.

They are now at a point where the only experiment left is to try to insert the gold foil into the slot of the orb, and see what happens. They have established a safe zone just in case it tries to do something. They are standing by, and they have one of their drones' ready to insert the gold foil. The foil goes into the slot, sits there for a couple of seconds, and slowly begins to accept the gold foil into the orb. The gears are turning in the orb, and then the piece of gold foil comes back out with something written on it. As they return to get the gold foil, they see that it is a message, and it is from the captain of the Hyperthean ship that vanished. They are totally shocked to think that they are still alive after this long period of time.

The message simply says, "Take the dial out with symbols on it by pulling straight up on it, remove the blank dial in the same fashion, and insert it in the slot where you removed the first dial. When you have done that, take the first dial, and insert it where the blank was. Then turn the crank one revolution to the left."

As they examine the message they can only come to one conclusion. They will be providing the source on the other end the location of the orb. They are not sure how to handle this. This can be friendly, or this can be very dangerous. They decide that they want to have a couple of cruisers standing by, and they also want to have armed forces in the area, just in case there are armed forces that appear.

The cruisers are now standing by, and the armed forces are ready. They have the drone pull the dial from the location as instructed. Nothing happens at this point. With another arm, it pulls the blank dial from its location, and again nothing happens. It now inserts the blank dial in the location of the first dial, and then the other dial in the reverse location. Again, nothing happens. Now comes the moment of truth. The drone is instructed to turn the crank ever so slowly, until it reaches one full rotation. Now things begin to happen.

The gears continue to turn inside the orb, but now a beam

of light starts protruding straight up out of the orb, to about a height of twenty feet. It starts as a straight beam, and then starts to spin around in a circle, until the circle has flattened out to 180 degrees, and extends out the same distance. It holds this rotating beam, and then the air around the orb begins to spin itself as if it were a whirlwind, and then suddenly stops spinning. The armed men who are surrounding the orb are now at a full defensive position, waiting for anything to happen. The cruisers in space are now at full alert, and ready to fire and destroy this orb, but all are holding their fire as nothing more has happened.

Suddenly, the captain from the Hyperthean ship steps through the beam, and onto the ground. He looks around in disbelief, and then releases something that goes back into the beam. He steps forward, and tells everyone that it will be okay. Security forces rush forward, and pull him away from the beam to a secure area. They immediately start to question him. He tells them that the crews from his ship, and the Earth ship are all well. Now he lets them in on more news. There are millions of people that are trapped inside this other dimension. They came up with this orb to see if they could get back to their correct dimension. They are people from Sporta, and are known as Sporians. He said that in about another minute, people will start coming through this portal one at a time. They will be sending his crew first, and then they will send the Earth crew through. Then they will start sending through the people from Sporta.

As the captain indicated, people started coming through the portal one at a time, and it takes several weeks for millions of people to pass through the portal. As the last person comes through the portal, one of the Sporians activates a button, and there is an explosion on the other end that closes the portal.

Someone yells at him, "Why did you do that?"

"It has been a place where nobody deserves to be, and I wanted to make sure that no one can go back to the other side.

We have looked into our realm for thousands of years, and it was nothing but dark space. Everything was dark. We couldn't even see the stars. Nobody else needs to go through that."

The people from Sporta are thankful to be back home, and have a long story to tell. All the historians and archaeologists are excited to hear their story.

The captains of both ships are debriefed, and this is the story they tell. The Earth ship captain explains that the scientists from the other side of the rift could not see our side of the galaxy, at least not anything physically. Everything to them was reversed. What was visible to us was invisible to them, and when we cloaked our ships, the ships were suddenly visible to them. They had discovered a way to open the rift into our dimension, or the dimension they were looking at, but most of the time when they would send something through, it would wind up in space. They had no way of space travel, or anyway to maintain life out in space. They had no way of finding a suitable planet through which they could go back to. When the Earth ship suddenly appeared, they tried to send a message through, but instead it grabbed all the crew, and brought them through the rift into their dimension. This was not what they wanted. They kept an eye on the ship until it finally disappeared, apparently when we turned off its cloaking device. Then a few months later a larger ship appeared in the sector, and they tried to send a message again, and again it brought back all the crew from the Hyperthean ship. It was at this point they knew they had to work on their machine that created the rift. I suggested I would like to work with them, and that I had a few ideas.

For several weeks, we worked on this device, and finally came to what we thought was a working solution. This time they would send an orb through that had two dials on it. One would indicate the coordinates where the orb would be. The second dial had a frozen set of coordinates of where their location was. Then they came up with the idea of sending a crank and the gold foil through at a different location. This was to see if the people who were from these ships would find them, and eventually figure out how to use them. They had the captain from the Hyperthean ship write a message on the gold foil that would be invisible to the naked eye. The message would only appear when it was passed through the orb. It will take about two years, but our crew is finally home, and safe.

The people that came through the rift appear to be friendly, and the Hypertheans are working with them on setting up their new world and learning more about them every day. Since we now know the full story, we have lifted the ban into the restricted area, and we have again established our patrols there.

The commander who had helped the Sporians in the development of the orb is Jeff Abatacola. He believes that he knows enough about the development of the orb that he can redevelop it and make lots of improvements to it. He is requesting to be assigned to the weapon development division to see what they can do. I agree to this assignment and ask the weapons division to assign a team to work with him. It is to be a highly classified research facility with only a select few knowing of the research.

TWENTY

So far in the last five years, we have had more excitement than we did in the previous twenty years. The Hypertheans are calling us their good luck piece. One thing about comparing time between us and the Hypertheans is that our five years is like five months to them. Since we started working with them, the Morians have been silent, except for the drone incident. We are glad to have the silence, but it concerns us. The Morians are never quiet unless they are planning something. The last time the Hypertheans had this much silence, it was the prelude to the thousand-year war. If that happens again, I know I won't be around for all of it, and I'm not sure I want humans involved in a war like that for that long. There would not be any humanity left in us, if it did. We would become a military state, and we wouldn't know how to live at peace with each other in the way God intended for us to.

Now I set the fleet back to normal status to resume standard patrols. As the fleet resumes their normal patrols and duty stations, we have had five years go by, and we start taking things easy. We have no activity from our patrols, nor are the Hypertheans reporting any activity for us to be concerned about. As I am settling in, I begin to let my mind wonder, and I come up with a question that continues to stay in my mind. It is hard to believe that in this entire world of galaxies, that the Morians are the only enemy or world, that wants to destroy the rest of us.

I let this thought work on me for several days, and then I decide to send a general message to Kleg and the high command. I tell them that I had this thought, and for them not to be alarmed; there isn't anything to be concerned about. I would like to know why I have not heard about other worlds out there that might be hostile, or friendly, that are not part of the Federation.

It takes several days to get a response back from the high command. They are sending a document that will be several hundred pages long and is marked "Classified." Now they have my curiosity up, and I am impressed that it is a document that is so thick. This had better be some good bedtime reading.

That evening I start reading through the document, and I have gotten through the first hundred pages. Apparently, there are other worlds out there that are not friendly, and there are others who are very friendly but are not part of the Federation. I am curious as to why, but I haven't gotten to that point in the document. It is about 2300 hours now, and I am tired and decide to go to bed.

I am up at 0600, and have my breakfast at 0700 with my staff, and then at 0800 it is time for muster. My XO gets all the reports from all the fleets. I then have my morning briefing with my staff, and we go over anything that is of importance. I go back to my quarters and pick up the document to see how much more I can read. I continue reading, and start to get buried in the report. I discover some things that I did not know. From the report, there is a galaxy that is well advanced in space travel but chooses to be outside of the Federation for some reason. They do make some long-distance travels, and I notice a pattern in their flights. They do have a ship that passes very close to our solar system. If this report is correct, they should have a ship that will be passing nearby within the next six months.

I contact the high command and ask why they have not informed us of the possibility of a ship passing close to our solar system. I would like permission to contact the ship as it passes by.

They are surprised that I have discovered this and that they had not seen this pattern before. The report is very old, and they only look at the document as a purely historical one. They did not realize that this was a possibility. They said that they will contact this world to see if what I have discovered is true, and if they did not mind, could their new friends speak with the ships command when they were passing by.

It takes about a week before I get a response. The race that I would be contacting are hesitant to agree and would like to know more about us.

I said that I can see their point and replied that I would also like to know more about them, especially dealing with their culture, and how to properly respond to them. I did not want to offend them in any way. I tell the high command that they have quite a bit of information on us, but if needed to know anything else, please let us know. They replied that they believe they have all the information that they need on us. They are putting together a document for me, and that I should have it in a couple of hours.

As promised I receive the document within a couple of hours. It is about four pages long. I start reviewing the document and find that the people call themselves Veltans. They generally range in height from five feet nine inches to seven feet tall. There are a few pictures included in the document, so that I will know what they look like and not be startled by them. The male species has a crusted skin layer resembling that of a reptile, while the female species has the same skin layer but is more colorful than the male. They wear clothing of a sort since their atmosphere is harsh. They would not be able to live in an atmosphere like Earth's. They do not speak a language that we could understand, but we can through a translator devise that has been provided to us by the Hypertheans.

They are an easygoing race and do not participate in any warfare. Their ships do not have any weaponry, but they have a way of not being attacked, if forced into a corner. Their customs are very formal. When we greet them, we are to bow our heads and say the word "Greetings." We are not to extend our hands as a sign of friendship, and we are not to touch them in any fashion. We are not to comment on the way they look or on what they wear. When we sit, we are to allow them to sit first, and then ourselves. When we stand up, we do so very slowly, making sure that our movements do not show any sign of aggression. When we leave a room, we are to back out of the room, and once outside the entry way, we can then turn to walk away. We do not enter any space without permission. After a while they may extend a hand as a gesture of friendship. When we accept it, we are to reach past their hand and join at the wrist at the same time. We are to take our other hand, place it behind our back, and then bow our head. We are to maintain the grasp until they release it, and then take one step back at which point we can raise our head.

I agree to all the terms which are presented in the document and send it back to the high command. I am looking forward to being able to visit with another species and hopefully, in establishing a relationship with them.

I get a response back that the Veltans would meet with me and my staff only. The ship will be passing by in about three months. They will contact us, but we are not to contact them.

In my next staff briefing I make them all aware of the possibility that we will be visiting with a race of people called the Veltans. I also make them aware of when they should be arriving and that no one is to attempt to make any contact with them when they arrive. They are to inform everyone who has access to a transmitting device that they are not to attempt communicating with them.

TWENTY-ONE

The three months have passed, and one of the scout ships is reporting that there is a ship coming up on their sensors. It is outside of the barrier, and there is no danger of it getting close. We tell him just to maintain a normal patrol, and they are not to attempt to communicate with the ship or make any movement toward it.

As the ship passes through our first sector, we do not receive any message from them. We patiently wait for their message to come, but still nothing as they pass through the second sector. They enter the third sector, slow their ship, and then finally comes to a stop, and we wait. They have been sitting still for three hours now, and we continue to wait for a message from them. Finally the communication center informs me that they have sent a message.

I bring the message up on my screen in the command center for all my staff to see.

The message reads, "Earthlings, we have been testing you, and we see that you do not desire to harm us. We will be pleased to meet with you. You may send one ship with those who will meet with us. No more than four of you may come and do not bring any weapons with you. You have one hour to accept our offer before we continue our journey. Should you accept our offer, reply with a 'yes, we accept' and you may join us in six of your Earth hours."

We reply, "Yes, we accept."

I inform the flight deck to get a shuttle ready for us, because it will take us about six hours to get there in a shuttle. I tell my counselor and two others that they will be going with me to meet with the Veltans, and that we need to board the shuttle in thirty minutes to meet their timeframe request.

We arrive near the ship about ten minutes before the six-hour timeframe expires. We inform the Veltans that we are here, and request docking coordinates. They give us the coordinates, and as we dock, we are greeted by a group of Veltans. As we are instructed, we wait to be spoken to by them. One of the Veltans speaks and says, "Greetings, and welcome aboard the Voltar."

"Thank you," as we bow our heads and wait for permission to raise them.

After several seconds, the Veltan that was speaking said, "My name is Sentur and I command this ship. Please, if you will come with me, I will take you to the place where we will meet."

As we are walking down the corridor, the four of us are examining the walls and pathways as we proceed. We thought we would have difficulties getting used to the Hyperthean ships, but this is much different. I am sure this is due to the harsh environment that they live in. These surroundings fit their culture, but still we are unsure of ourselves, and of them.

We arrive at the meeting place, and are invited to sit at the table which is before us. We go to the table, and wait for them to be seated, and then we seat ourselves.

Finally, Sentur speaks, "I see you have been studying our culture, and are trying your best not to offend us. We appreciate that."

"Yes, we have received as much information as the Hypertheans have, and we have studied it to the best of our knowledge. Hopefully so far, we have not done anything to offend you."

"No, you have done very well. Since this is our first meeting, we hope that we have not offended you in any way. We will be lenient in your misunderstandings, and hopefully you will do the same for us."

I return a smile to him, and bow my head ever so slightly.

I say, "We do not have much information about your people, so I will proceed, if I may, by asking some general questions about you, and your race so that we might learn more about you. Hopefully you have some questions about us that you would like to ask. But I am uncertain about how to do that. So if you can assist us, I would appreciate it."

Sentur gives a nod, and replies, "We hope to do the same, and to make it easier on both of us. I would like for you to ask your questions first."

I stall for a few seconds, and then ask, "If I ask anything that is inappropriate, I hope you will not be offended.

Let us know, so we can correct what we are saying to where it does not offend."

Sentur nods, and says, "Please continue."

"I have deduced from the Hyperthean report that you have been passing by our galaxy for quite some time, but you have not tried to contact us. Why is that?"

"We have come close to your planet and have examined your race for hundreds of years. We did not find you to be a threat to us, and that you were not ready for contact from a race that was far superior in knowledge to yours. Also, since we look so much different than you, we felt you would be more frightened, and would not welcome us. We were surprised when we heard from the Hyperthean command that you had ships in space, that you knew of us, and wanted to speak with us."

I told Sentur the story of how we first met up with the Hypertheans, and everything that had occurred. When I mentioned the Morians, I saw a change in his expression. This concerns me, but I continue with my story. When I get to the story about the Sporians, I see another change in expression in their faces that is a little bit different. I finish with the history lesson, and then ask, "With your permission I would like to ask a couple of questions about the story I just told."

"Please," and gives me a hand gesture of permission.

"When I was telling this story, and mentioned the Morians, I saw something in your expression that changed. Do you know of the Morians, and have you had an encounter with them?"

Sentur thinks about how to respond to this, and finally replies, "We know of the Morians, and yes, we have had an encounter with them. But this was several thousand years ago, and they have not bothered us since, nor have we had any communication with them. This is the main reason we do not wish to be part of the Federation. However, we are a neutral ally with the Federation."

I see the expression that came on his face when he spoke of the Morians, and I decided to leave this subject alone for the time being.

I reply, "I am sorry if this subject brings back some bad memories. I won't ask about them again."

Sentur nods, and says, "What was your next question?"

"I hope this next question does not offend you, or bring back some painful memories, but when I told the story about the Sporians, I saw something that you may want to ask about."

"Yes, several thousand years ago, one of our ships that was exploring, like this ship. Its crew disappeared in a similar manner. I am glad to hear this story, and I will be passing this information on to our high command so that they can be making queries with the Hypertheans."

"I am sorry to hear about that, but that is all the information

I have about the Sporians. I am sorry that I have asked so many questions, and have not allowed you to ask any. Please, ask me a question."

"I like your questions and the information that you have provided to me. I see why the Hypertheans are impressed with you. I believe that they have done it at the right time for you, and that your world has handled this rapid change well. Have all of your people made the adjustment?"

"No, there are those that believe we should not be involved with the Hypertheans or this battle. We are a race of people that have a free will. Some of our countries allow their people to express their free will while others don't. We are not forcing our free will on other countries, but we do have people that are working with these countries to allow people to express their feelings. The change is slow, but we are making progress."

"I am glad to hear that. We function the same way in our world, and we have councils that handle our differences, but we still allow people to have their free will."

"May I ask another question?"

He nods with an affirmative shake.

"We live a very short life cycle as compared with the Hypertheans. One revolution our planet as it rotates is one day for us. It takes three hundred and sixty-five days for our planet to go around our sun once, and we say that is one year. With the help that the Hypertheans have provided to us, we can live to an age of around one hundred and seventy. How do you measure your life cycles? How long do you live? And how old are you?"

"We measure our life cycle in a similar way. Our planet is very large, and takes according to your measure, about seventy-two hours to make one rotation. For our planet to make one revolution around our sun, it takes nine of your Earth years to complete. Based on our time span, we live to an age of about 200 years, which is about 1,900 Earth years.

"Wow! I guess that is why we don't do long distance space

travel. Currently we are content in getting comfortable with what the Hypertheans have provided and with our own adjustments. At some point, we will probably want to reach out further."

Sentur interrupts at this point and says, "I am sorry but we need to ask you to leave at this point. We had to adjust our atmosphere for you to come aboard our ship. We are at a point where we need to change it back for us to remain comfortable."

"I understand, and I appreciate the time you have provided to us. It is my hope that we can continue our dialog in the future, and establish some friendly relationship that will be appealing to both of us. I look forward to our next meeting."

Sentur agrees that the feelings are mutual, and that he will communicate the same to his federation. He assures me that he has enjoyed our meeting, and looks forward to continuing our conversation.

We depart the ship, and as we leave, we see their ship leave and continues with their journey.

A few weeks later we get a communiqué from the Hyperthean High Command commending us on our efforts, and the communication we had with the Veltans. They have received communications from the Veltan home world that they were very pleased with our visit, and are very interested in establishing relationships with our world.

The Hypertheans are very pleased with our efforts and that this line of communication has been established with their world. I tell them we are also pleased with this, and once we establish open communications with them, I will take things slow, and see how we progress with establishing an onsite visit. I tell them I will turn this over to our diplomatic core, once we can proceed with communications.

TWENTY-TWO

Our scout ships continue their patrols, and we still have no indications of problems with the Morians. Things are starting to become routine, but we continue our drills, sharpening our skills and scenarios. All reports indicate that the ship drills are sharp, and we are as ready as we can be.

It has been about six months since we met with the Veltans, when my communication system sounds, and I am informed that I have a secret communication coming in from the Weapons Development Center. I secure my quarters, and tell them to put the call through. It is Captain Sinisha Pavlick who commands the weapons development center along with Commander Jeff Abatacola.

"Good day to the both of you. It is good to see you again Commander Abatacola. How are you, and how do you like working at the weapons center?"

Captain Pavlick responds, "We are fine on this end, and his work is what we would like to speak with you about. We believe we have some good news for you, and rather than tell you about it over this communication, I believe it would be better if we can show you. Can you come to the center and meet with us?"

"Yes, I will clear my schedule, and you can expect me to be there within the next three hours."

I arrive at the weapons center, and am greeted by both. As we walk through the corridors towards Jeff's lab, we begin to talk.

"I am curious about the excited urgency that has brought me here."

"Rather than tell you any details out here in the hallway, I can tell you that we have made great strides into the research and development that we have been doing."

"Now you have my curiosity up. This does sound like good news. But in the meantime, Jeff, how have you been doing? Have you had any problems since your time in the rift?"

"Amazingly none. Of course, after I got back I spent quite some time with the shrinks, and they psychoanalyzed me. They found that I had no side effects from my time in the rift. I was concerned about that, and I was glad to find that I am normal."

He gives a little giggle with his response.

Both Captain Pavlick and I grin, and I pat him on the back as we enter his lab.

The lab is huge, and covers an area which I think is about the size of two football fields. There are research rooms around the parameter. The center area is mainly empty, and about the size of half a football field. He tells me this is their testing area. Now we are headed towards a large secure conference room where the three of us will be joined by the heads of his research team. Captain Pavlick introduces me to each of them, and then we sit around the conference table. Jeff takes over leading the discussion they are about to present.

"Sir, we have developed a device that is like the orb, and it works."

Jeff is so excited about his announcement, he can hardly contain himself, as he and the entire room waits to see my expression.

I lean forward in my chair, and as calmly as I can say, "Okay, you have my full attention. But why would we want a device that can send people into another dimension, or in this case pull people from another dimension?"

"I don't want to give you the full details about what we have been doing, but I want to give you the results. We have been able to enhance, and develop the technology that the Sporians had in the rift. We have come up with a twofold device that can help us move things, and people, around in the universe. We can use it as a weapon without harming life. With our development, we can move things, and people into the rift, and then move them to another location in our world almost instantaneously. This will require devices at both ends of the transportation process, but we have been able to do this without any side effects or loss of life. Secondly, we can equip our ships with a device that can be like a weapon, and again without harming life. This device works this way. On a ship that is under attack, and without hope of winning, we can use this device and aim it at the enemy ship. It will move the entire enemy crew into the rift, and we could strand them there. Once we come to terms with the enemy, we let them know that their crews are completely unharmed, and that we will return them unharmed on their world. We would have a delegate arrive at an agreed upon neutral location for the return of the crew. This delegate would have a device that would bring their crews back to them. At the same time the delegate would be able to reverse the process, and then pass themselves back into the rift unharmed, and safely back to us."

I look at Jeff and the people around the table and say, "You have tested this device, and it works. You guarantee this with 100 percent accuracy all the time?"

Jeff and Captain Pavlick respond, "Yes sir, 100 percent guarantee."

"Show me."

We leave the conference room, and head over to one of

the testing areas where they have a device set up ready for a demonstration.

"For the first demonstration, we want to show you the transport movement process. We have a receiving device set up at our base in Texas in a room outside the mess hall. What would you like from the mess hall, sir?"

I let out a little laugh and say, "Let me think of something unique. Bring me back a warm bowl of peach cobbler - with ice cream."

He grins back at me and says, "One bowl of warm peach cobbler coming up, with ice cream and a spoon."

Jeff puts on a device around his wrist, and presses a button and disappears. In about five minutes, he reappears in the same spot with a bowl of warm peach cobbler, ice cream and a spoon."

"Impressive. I noticed that you did this with a device that is strapped to your wrist. Give me a general idea on how this works."

"The team has made lots of improvements to the orb technology, and we have been able to condense the operation down to a device that we can put around our wrist. As I stated earlier, we had to have a device at the other end so that we can get there. The interim step is a little tricky, since for the first part of your trip you must go into the rift. We have placed a device in the rift that receives us there, and automatically receives instructions as to where we want to go, and then sends us to our ultimate destination. This all works fine. Once on the other end, the wrist device continues to work the same way in that it knows where you came from and once you are ready, you can return to the location where you came from in the same manner. We are working on a process where we won't have to travel into the rift to get from one location to the other, but so far we have not had much luck."

"Jeff, and to all of you, this has been impressive work. Please continue impressing me."

Jeff thanks me and continues, "Sir, the piece we would like to show you is for our ships. This device works like a laser beam, with adjustments. We can focus the beam onto a single device or a person at thirty miles, or we can widen the beam to include an entire ship. As we widen the beam, the power we need to make the device work increases. We can currently surround a cruiser twenty miles away, and move the entire crew. But this process takes about two minutes to build up the power for the beam, and to maintain it for ten seconds as we move people. Let's demonstrate it. Over there in the distance is a mock destroyer. Currently for this test we have two hundred men aboard the destroyer. They have all volunteered for this test, and know that they will be returning shortly. This device will move the men into the rift, and strand them there, until we are ready to bring them out of the rift to a new destination of our choosing. One of the questions you may have is do you send them to a different location from where you send people with your transportation process. The answer is yes. All devices have a specific location programmed into them where people will be sent into the rift. Are you ready for the demonstration sir?"

"Please, proceed."

The researchers man their places, and begin to set up aiming devices and powering up the weapon. In about one minute, I hear the beam activate and envelop the mock destroyer. Within ten seconds the beam shuts down. During this time, we have been watching the crew through monitors that are aboard the mock destroyer, and as the beam envelops the ship, they all begin to disappear, with no change in the physical material on or in the ship."

I am again impressed with what I have seen, and tell Jeff and his team the same.

"Sir, just to show you that these men are safe, please, if you will watch over there to your left. One of the team will act as a liaison, and will bring the crew back to that location, and then will return to us here at this location."

"Proceed."

The person that will act as the liaison goes over to the designated spot, and activates his device. The crew begins to appear as I was told. When all the crew has passed through the portal, the liaison immediately shuts down the portal, presses another button, and disappears. In about fifteen seconds he now appears before me as indicated.

I tell everyone that I am very impressed with what they have shown me. I inform Captain Pavlick and Commander Abatacola that I would like to continue our conversation privately.

Captain Pavlick takes us to his conference room and closes the door.

As we sit down I begin to speak, "I have been very impressed with what you have shown me today. I am also very interested in deploying your weapon device out to the fleet. But before we make that decision, I would like to ask you some serious questions."

I pause briefly, and then ask, "How much testing have you done on this, and are we ready to deploy such a device?"

Captain Pavlick responds, "We have been testing the device for the last two years, and we know we are ready."

"How safe is it?"

"With the extensive testing we have done, we have not lost or injured any personnel. We have been very careful with our testing, and we are extremely confident with the devices and their performance. We are ready and confident to have the device deployed to the fleet sir."

"How soon can you have these devices manufactured and installed on all of the ships in the fleet."

"All the ships sir?"

"All the ships. If this device works as you say, and you have demonstrated that it will, we can protect our entire fleet with it. We can show that we are humanitarians at the same time by not taking life unnecessarily."

"Thank you sir. We will have the report to you within the week."

"Captain, if I may have a word with you."

Commander Abatacola takes his cue, and dismisses himself. I again express my thanks to him for the great effort on the work.

"Captain, I want to share what you all have done here with the Hypertheans. I will make sure you and your team, gets full credit for this work. You may question why I would share this new technology. The Hypertheans over the years, have shown their great friendship with us and has shared, not only their technology, but also their weapon advances with us. I believe we should do the same with them. I will be contacting the high command and informing them of the work you have done. I am sure they will want to come and see this amazing work for themselves. Because of the distance, it will probably take them awhile to get here, but I am sure they will be in contact with you. Once they hear and see this new technology, I am sure they will want us to send the details to them. They will want to start working on it immediately, especially our transporting process. This will allow them to send someone here sooner than they will be able to physically travel.

Oh, and one more thing. I want each of the ships, and our bases, to have one of these transport devices. I want people to be able to move about more quickly."

Captain Pavlick agrees to the exchange of information and technology as I have requested.

I return to headquarters, and a couple of days later I get a communication from Captain Pavlick. He informs me that he has arranged with one of their weapon manufacturers to get the devices on board all our ships. They have agreed that all ships will be ready with the new weaponry within the next twelve months. I am pleased with the update.

TWENTY-THREE

A year has passed, and almost all the ships have been updated with the new weaponry and transport devices. A few days later, while I am in my quarters, my communicator goes off. They tell me that I have a message from the Hyperthean High Command. I tell the communication officer to put the call through to my quarters. The call comes in, and I see that it is Kleg. I am surprised to see him on my screen, but also pleased.

"Kleg, what a pleasant surprise to hear from you. To what do I owe the pleasure of this call?"

"It is good to see you too. I am calling because we need to make a request of you."

"Name it, and it is yours."

"Let me tell you what it is first, before you commit so readily."

I get serious and reply, "Go ahead."

"We have a situation in our quantum sector of space, and we would like your assistance."

"What kind of situation do you have?"

"We are not completely sure. We had three ships in that sector, and one of them sent out a distress call. Then everything

157

suddenly went silent. Our nearest ships will take about three Earth years to get there, whereas if you were to send some ships, it would only take about one Earth year. Do you think you would be willing to send some ships to investigate the situation?"

"You don't even have to ask, consider it done. Can you give me any more information on the situation?"

"Not now. You have all the information we have. I will send you the last coordinates we have on the ships. We will provide you with star maps for your ships to navigate with."

"As far as ships to send, what do you suggest I send for the situation."

"I would recommend that you send a battle star, one cruiser, four destroyers, and four scout ships. Make sure all are heavily armed. I also recommend that the battle star take at least two squadrons of fighters with them."

"If you can send me those star maps, we can start evaluating our course of action. I will gather my strategic action team, and we will start getting the ships ready to leave immediately. As you get new information I would appreciate it if you would keep me updated."

Kleg agrees, and I tell him that he can depend on us.

I call my first officer, and tell him I want the Strategic Action Team to assemble in my conference room in one hour. I then send a confidential message to all admirals of the fleet telling them of the situation, and that I will be meeting with the strategic action team at 1800. I inform them I want all of them to join by video if they are not aboard the *Hyperthia*, they are to meet me there.

As soon as I send out this message, I get an incoming call from the communication center that I have received a data packet from the Hyperthean High Command, and they would like to know what to do with it. I tell them to hold it in my classified files, and I will let them know what to do within the hour.

I now call my CIC officer, and tell him I want him in my quarters now. He responds with a "Yes sir," and within two minutes I have a knock at my door. I say, "Enter", and it is my CIC officer.

"Hi Tom. Thanks for coming so quickly. I will get right to the point."

I explain to him about the call I just received from Kleg and about the data burst I just received from high command.

"Tom, I told them to secure the data file. These are the release commands to get that data file. It will contain the star maps we need to get to the ships we select to go to the location. I want you to get that file, download it into our mapping system and have it ready for us to use in my assembly room by 1800. I also want you to study the situation, and then be ready to walk us through what we are looking at. Don't share what you are doing with anyone. Can you do that for me?"

"Yes sir, no problem."

As Tom turns to leave I say, "Tom, once I meet with the admirals and the strategic action team, I am going to give you a list of ships. When you get this list, they will know to expect this same data burst from you so that they can upload it into their mapping system. When you receive the message from them that they are ready to receive, I want you to send it to them."

"Yes sir, is there anything else?"

I tell him no.

At 1800 I enter the conference room, and I hear the command "Attention on deck."

I tell them to carry on and to be seated.

"We have an opportunity before us that will be a first. We are getting the opportunity to leave our solar system, and to go assist the Hyperthean fleet with a situation they have. This mission will last anywhere from two and a half to three years, and there is the possibility of danger involved. I have received a communication from the Hyperthean High Command that they have received a distress call. It was from three of their ships in the quantum sector. They have not been able to reestablish communication with these ships. We are their best hope for help, since we are the closest to them. We are going to help them. The situation is serious for them, and by the time we get there it will probably be too late. It will take our ships about a year to get there at flank speed. We don't know what we are going into, so we will prepare our ships to meet the worst scenario. Based on what has been recommended to me by the Hyperthean command, we will be sending one battle star, a cruiser, four destroyers, four scout ships, and two squadrons of fighters. We need to pick what ships and crews to send and prepare them to go immediately. Since this is our first mission of this type, I am asking this to be an all-volunteer crew. We may have to break up some of the ships crews for this mission. But my anticipation is that we won't be doing that. Vice-admiral Stark, I am volunteering you to lead this mission."

"Yes sir, no need to volunteer me."

I reply with thanks and continue, "Now, I have asked my CIC officer to join us. I have given him the star map to download that we just received from Hyperthean High Command. He has downloaded it for us and will display it on our hologram display now. I have also asked Tom to do the impossible in a short period of time."

I asked, "So, Tom, explain to us what you know."

"Thanks Admiral. What you see on the hologram is a display of the star map that the Hyperthean command has supplied to us. We are located here."

He points to a location on the star map.

"These are the coordinates in the quantum sector where the distressed ships are located."

Now he points to another location on the star map.

"If we went in a straight line, we could get there in three hundred days."

He draws a straight line on the hologram and continues,

"As you can see, there are some obstacles in the way. I have spoken to some Hyperthean mapping experts in the past hour, and they have told me we need to avoid these three areas."

He is now pointing out the three areas and continues, "To bypass these areas will add forty days to the travel time. So right now, it will take three hundred forty days to get to the quantum sector."

"Thanks Tom. Of course this information is very preliminary, and we will have adjustments to make as we go. From what we see, it appears that the ships will need to come from the third fleet as our beginning point. Admiral Fuentes, this is your fleet. Do you have any recommendations as to which ships we can use?"

"I would like to review this a little closer if I may. I will also need to see if I have an all-volunteer crew for these ships so that I am not pulling a command apart for the mission."

"Admiral Stark, I want you to work with Admiral Fuentes to get this done, and I want an answer in twenty-four hours. Understood admirals?"

They both reply with a, "Yes sir."

"Captain Raymond, you are in charge of the Strategic Action team. I want your team to work with the admirals of the fleet to come up with scenarios for this mission. I want our crews to be able to respond to any situation they encounter and to any situation when they arrive. Work it to the last detail. Start working it now, and you work it until they return, whenever that might be."

"Yes sir, we will start working it right away."

"Commander Hilliard, I want you to put together a communique that I can send out to the fleet on this situation. I want to make them aware of our mission. Tell them I am looking for volunteers. Explain that this can, and will probably, be a dangerous mission and that they can be gone for three years, possibly longer. Also, explain that we won't be able to accept all volunteers, since only so many ships and crews will be going, but I will be proud of all who volunteer. You know what to put in it. I would like to have that within the hour.

"Yes sir, within the hour."

"Admiral Hopper, as the fleet supply officer, I want you to immediately prepare these ships for departure. As soon as they have been selected and provided to you. I also want you to have resupply ships to follow these ships at six month intervals, until our mission is over. The first ones will probably need to leave immediately."

"Any questions."

There is silence in the room, I know there are questions, but none come. I know I will be getting a ton of them later.

"Okay, thank you for your time. You know what you need to do. Let's get the job done. Dismissed."

TWENTY-FOUR

I am in my quarters studying the star map; forty-five minutes have passed, and there is a knock on my door. I tell them to enter, and it is Commander Hilliard with the communique he has prepared. I review the message, approve what he has written, and tell him that this is exactly what I want to convey. I ask him to make this a fleet-wide communication, and to get it out immediately to all the commands.

"Yes sir, immediately. Thank you for allowing me to be part of this process."

About thirty minutes after Commander Hilliard has left my quarters, I get another knock on my door, and I tell them to enter. This time it is Vice Admiral Stark.

I have known Stan Stark for about fifteen years now. He has shown himself to be an outstanding leader with a "get it done" attitude. He puts up with no horsing around, but is well liked by the men that work for him. They will do anything for him. I chose Stan because of his leadership abilities, and he has no problem with accepting a challenge and getting the job done.

"Hi Stan, please come in. I was wondering when you would be coming by."

"I want to thank you for choosing me to lead this mission."

"Don't thank me yet. You may want to shoot me before this is over."

He laughs, and we give each other a big smile and continue our conversation.

"What can I do for you?"

"I know you have put me in charge of this mission, but how far can I go in choosing my ships and crew?

"Stan, I have put you and George in charge of putting these ships and crews together, since they are coming from his fleet. George is a good man, and I believe the two of you will work well together. But, with that said, if you are not completely happy with the selections you two have put together, I want the two of you to try and come to an agreeable consensus. If the two of you cannot do that, then come to me with your concerns.

We will work them out, and I don't believe either of you will like my decision. I'm not worried about it. I know that the two of you can work through this. As far as your command is concerned, you choose who your senior officers will be."

"Okay, I guess I am a little anxious about this mission, and I want to make sure we have the right people to get it accomplished."

"It is still too early in the process to be worried about what will happen. In twenty-four hours, you and George will settle into this. You will feel better about it as you go down the road. On top of that you have a year of travel in front of you. It will give you time to get to know your crews and to get them into the shape that you want them in. I know that, or I would haven't have chosen you for this mission.

"You're right. I am sorry to have bothered you with this."

"Stan, this is the first mission of this sort. We are going into an unknown for all of us and especially for mankind. You have a right to be apprehensive about it. He says thanks, turns, and leaves my quarters.

I know I need to watch him closely now, and need to make

sure that he is the right man for this mission. I probably have about a week to watch to make sure I am right before the ships leave for their mission. I still feel he will come around. He always has.

At 0900 the next morning, during my staff briefing time, I start getting updates on where we stand with the mission. Everyone has worked through the night, gathering information, and getting supplies ready for the ships. The volunteer list has been coming in by the thousands. From the looks of things, I believe nearly everyone in the fleet has volunteered for this mission. I am so proud and thankful for everyone who is part of this fleet.

Tom is present, and gives us an update on his study of the star maps. He has been up all night working with his team. They have studied the star maps and have mapped out a path for the ships that will reduce the travel time by ten days. Instead of three hundred and forty days to get there. It will now take three hundred and thirty days.

Tom now tells me that all the ships in the fleet are requesting a copy of the star maps. I ask Tom if their systems can handle that much information, and he informs me that they can. I then inform the admirals, and Tom, that I don't have a problem with them having a copy of the star maps but I want the route that Tom has mapped out to remain confidential. They all agree, and I tell Tom he can send the ships the star maps.

Stan and George are present, and they tell me they have been working through the night and that they have selected the ships that will be going on the mission.

"Excellent and both of you agree on this?"

They both reply with, "Yes sir."

"And about your crews? I understand from an earlier report that you basically have the entire fleet to choose from. What is your progress here?"

"Good, I am glad to hear that this is going so well. I am sure we will be pleased. When you are ready to speak with me about your selection, please provide me the list of the ships you have chosen at that time. I don't want any of this information leaking out and have crew members disappointed before we announce."

They both reply, "Yes sir, understood."

"What time do you want to meet with me to go over this list?"

Stan looks at George, and they speak softly for a brief second.

Stan replies, "How about 1600 sir?"

"1600 is good. I want to see both of you in my state room at that time."

From this point on, it is the usual routine with the usual reports, and the fleet is in great shape. With this possible mission, the morale is high, and everyone is looking forward to being chosen and hope to be part of this mission.

The briefing time is over, and I have spent a couple of hours going about the ship meeting with the officers and crew. I am back in my stateroom and start going over what I need to do with the shift of personnel and ships that is about to happen. I need to speak with George about this, but I want to wait until after the ships for the mission have deployed.

This will leave his fleet short on a few ships and men. We need to discuss how it will impact his ability to patrol. I might need to make some adjustments in the other fleets to help build his fleet back up. I will need to think through this more and discuss it with him late next week after the other ships are gone.

I also need to speak with Admiral Hopper. Since the supply ships are slower moving than the cruiser and destroyers, we need to get our supply ships moving now, before the other ships get underway. The mission ships will pass the supply ship at some point down the road, but we need to work out a schedule as to when these ships need to leave and what type of protection we need to provide for them, if need be. I don't want anything happening to these supply ships. The mission will depend on them for these supplies. I decide to set up a time to meet with Admiral Hopper at 1400 today to see where our progress is in this process.

It has been a busy day already, and it is going to get busier for the next several weeks as we move through this process. At 1400, I meet with Admiral Hopper, and we go over what he has done so far. I am pleased with his progress report, and we also go over the ships he will be using and the schedule they will be departing under. We also decide we will be sending out two destroyers with the first ships and two destroyers with the ships that are to follow several months later. This way these ships will travel together going, and coming back, and the destroyers will be supplied from the ships they will be escorting. The first ships will be leaving in twenty-four hours with the necessary supplies.

It is 1600, and time to meet with Stan and George in the situation room. I go to the situation room, and Stan and George are there waiting on me. We greet each other and are ready to get down to business.

"Okay gentlemen, I want to start off by asking if you two are still friends?"

They both laugh and have grins on their faces, and I am pleased.

"Good. The first order of business I would like to know is what ships you have chosen for this mission."

Stan looks at George and says, "I will let you answer this one."

"Thanks. It wasn't all that hard in choosing the ships, but at the same time, we wanted to look at the crews for these ships. We reviewed the battle stars I have under my command, with the list of names that volunteered and found that all the crews from all the battle stars had volunteered for this mission. Also, based on the performance of the ships with their crews, we have narrowed down our selection to the *Argentina*. All the members of this crew have volunteered. From the ship's marks and reports, they have performed well together, and we would like to keep them all together."

"The cruiser wasn't much harder, but we have narrowed it down to the *Saint Louis*. As far as working well with the *Argentina*, we found that the *Saint Louis* captain has worked well with the captain of the *Argentina*."

"The four destroyers weren't much harder. The crews from the four destroyers we chose all volunteered, however we also wanted to be fair to all the men who had volunteered in the fleet. Two of the destroyer crews we decided to keep intact and two of the crews we decided to swap out with other destroyers. What we would like to do is pull a destroyer from the second fleet and a destroyer from the fourth fleet. I will send two of my destroyers to replace the ones I am pulling."

"George, this sounds excellent, and I concur with the decision the two of you have made in this selection, but I am going to override a part of that decision. Your fleet will be drawn down to make this mission possible. One of my concerns was after these ships leave your fleet you will be unable to handle your patrol areas with the reduction in ships. I believe that the other admirals will be pleased that you have chosen destroyers from their fleets for this mission and will not have a problem with their fleet being reduced by a single destroyer to make this mission possible. We won't have a need for any swaps here. Now please continue with your selection process."

Both Stan and George say thanks, and George continues, "For the scout ships, all of the crews from every scout ship in the fleet has volunteered. Again, we have decided to split the opportunity for four scout ships between four fleets. We have decided to pull a scout ship from the first, fifth, seventh and the seventeenth fleets. With the addition of scout ships being built and the ones that we have in reserve, I believe we can replenish the missing scout ships."

"Excellent, you guys are making me proud. Continue."

George now tells me about the squadrons.

"Again, all of the crews from the squadrons volunteered for this mission. This has been a little harder in deciding. The *Argentina*, being a battle star, only has the capacity for one squadron. Stan and I have thought through this and know that you are requesting that we have two squadrons of fighters, but we don't see how this will be possible. I left this decision up to Stan, as to what he wants to do. He is in charge of the mission. Stan, I will let you answer this one."

"This will put us a little short on support for this mission, especially since, as of today, we have a lot of unknowns. My thought is that we will keep the squadron that is currently assigned to the *Argentina* with us on the mission. We know there are supply ships that will be leaving in a few days. We would like to request that you include, with that first supply shipment, a transport ship that will carry the second squadron of fighters that will follow along. They could arrive a few months behind us and assist us when they arrive."

I look at Stan and George at this point, and am silent for about thirty seconds, and finally respond, "Gentlemen, I like your plan. It has been well thought out. Let's make it so. Put together your announcements, and let's get this show on the road."

They both smile and say thanks and leave the room to execute the orders.

TWENTY-FIVE

Stan is in charge now, and he and George have informed the fleet which ships will be going on the mission. Along with that message, Stan has informed the captains of the ships that they have been selected for this mission and what ships they will command. He has given orders to each of the fleet admirals, countersigned by me, informing them of the volunteers who have been selected for the ships, stating that the admirals are to execute orders for these men to report to these ships immediately for duty.

Stan has decided on a rendezvous point where these ships are to gather and has issued orders for the ships to be there at 0800 in forty-eight hours. A supply ship has been requested to be there at the same time to replenish the ships and for making them ready for their mission. Currently the plan is that they will be underway ninety-six hours from when they gather together at the rendezvous point.

The first set of supply ships are already underway at flank speed toward their destination. At this speed, and the speed at which Stan's ships will be traveling, they should join up for resupply in about six months, which is exactly what we planned for. We are already making plans for the next set of supply ships to leave in about three months. They should meet up with Stan's ships twelve months from now in the quantum sector. This set of supply ships will have the transports with them that will be carrying the second squadron of fighters for Stan.

One of the things we need to do is get more information about the quantum sector. I also have another thought I am going to see if I can follow through on. First, I need to contact Captain Raymond and have him talk with the Federation, hopefully to get more information about the quantum sector. We need to know as much as we can.

I now put a call into our diplomatic core because I want them to work another angle for me. In about an hour, I get a message that I have a call waiting from me from the diplomatic core.

I bring up my screen and am greeted by Ambassador Vestaj of the Diplomatic core. I pass my greetings back to her and then start to ask my question.

"Ambassador Vestaj, as you know we recently met with a ship from Veltan. I know that we are starting a dialog with them, and I wanted to check to see how we are progressing."

"We are making good progress. We are moving slowly, and not infringing on their territory, and not asking anything of them they are not willing to continue to communicate with us. Why are you asking?"

"I would like to ask something of you to see if we can get some information for us."

"I see, I hope it is not too strong of a request. We are still in the very early stages of diplomacy with them and establishing our friendships."

"I don't think so, but I will let you be the judge of that."

"We have just been asked by the Federation to go out on a mission into an area where they have lost three ships. They currently do not have much information on the area. So, this was a new venture for them. From my research on the Veltans and my conversation with Sentur when they passed near our sector, they like to travel and visit new worlds. I would like to see if they have passed through, or if they have any information on the quantum sector they would be willing to share with us. Assure them we will not be using this information to stir up any problems. We strictly request it for a rescue mission. I will also provide you with the star vectors in case they are not familiar with our description of the quantum sector."

As she thinks about it she finally replies, "This sounds like it is something doable. It may take some time to get the information from them. I will discuss it with my counterparts and get back with you on how we may possibly approach this matter."

"Thank you, and I appreciate it very much. I look forward to your response. You have a good day."

"You too."

As I leave this in their capable hands, I now turn my thoughts back to the matters at hand.

The forty-eight hours have passed, and the ships have gathered at the rendezvous point. There are at least a dozen ships gathered there to make sure that Stan's ships are ready for their mission. The ships are being checked out, and they are doing any last-minute repairs that are needed, communication systems are being updated with the new technology, so that they can properly communicate with the scout ships and with us. We want to keep this mission as secret as possible because we still do not know what we are heading into. Supplies are being loaded aboard the ships that should last them for six months until they rendezvous with the supply ships that have already left. Also, the armament is being loaded to its fullest compliment, because this will be all they have until they meet up with the supply ships. The ships have also had the new trans-portal weapon installed. The crews are being trained on its proper operation and maintenance. All things are almost at the ready, and crews are excited and ready to go.

I have asked Stan to meet with me so that we can go over everything. We have a meeting set for the next day just before my staff meeting.

It is 0600, Stan has arrived with his executive officer and several others to assist me with my briefing. I also have my exec and Captain Raymond with me. We gather around the command table and start going over where we stand. Stan's exec tells us that the repairs, upgrades, and supply loading are going as scheduled, and they should be ready to get underway at the appointed time. All the star maps have been loaded into each of the ships, and they have been working with Captain Raymond studying the details of the path they need to take to get to their destination. They have discovered some new flight adjustments they needed to make and have done so. The new weaponry has been installed, and all crews have been trained on its proper usage. All the crews have reported aboard the ships, and are making their personal adjustments to their new assignments.

"Good, anything else?"

"Not now."

"Stan, one more thing, your new weaponry. It has not been battle tested, so use it only as your last resort. I don't want to sacrifice crews by not using it, but I don't want you using it if it puts ships in danger. I believe you will know when to use it, and I only want it used at your command. Understood."

"Understood."

I now turn to Captain Raymond, "Captain Raymond, do you have any new information for us from the Federation command?"

"Not a whole lot. They still only have sketchy information about what has happened. They are telling us that the ships were on a routine scientific mission, nothing militarily related. They were not receiving any communications that would indicate they were having any problems, nor were they seeing any other ships in the area. The mayday was sent only from one of the ships, and it was extremely short with no details, and then everything went silent. I am trying to get more details about the quantum sector, but they don't seem to have much to share. This is a new area of space for them, and they were there to gather more information to update their star maps."

I look at Stan now and say, "Stan, I know I don't have to tell you this, but I want you to proceed with extreme caution. The entire trip, I say again, the entire trip, and especially when you start getting closer to the quantum sector. You and your crew are taking on a mission that no human has done before. You could be establishing new friendships or creating new battle strategies and scenarios for all of us. We have also provided you with more drones to send out and more recording devices to capture every detail of your trip, both inside and outside of the ships. When you send your bursts back to us, I want you to include every second of your recordings for the strategic action team to go over and analyze to see if they catch things you might miss. I want those recordings from all ships. I want to give you as much assistance as we can. We are all in this together. This is your mission, but it is our mission, too."

"I also want to share with you that I have been in contact with the diplomatic core. I have requested that they contact the Veltans to see if they will provide us with any information they might have on the quantum sector. Since diplomatic relations are just beginning, this may take several weeks before we get any type of answer from them. I am hoping they might be able to provide us with some insight for what we are heading into."

"Everyone, from this point forward, I want all of you to be part of my morning briefing. I want complete updates on everything that you have related to this mission. Nothing is unimportant. Does anyone have anything else they would like to share?"

There is silence, and then I stand to leave the room and say, "Thanks. Good luck and may God go with us. Dismissed."

They all stand to attention as I leave the room, and as I leave, I start to hear conversations begin discussing other details on what needs to be done.

TWENTY-SIX

The day has come for the ships to leave on their mission, and there is great excitement to be had by everyone. I am in my command center, and I get a message from Stan that he is ready to get underway. I tell Stan that he has his orders, and give him a Godspeed. I am watching the hologram before me as Stan's ships get underway. They move to flank speed heading into the unknown for us. We all are envious of him, and the crews as they take on this mission. We all wish we were the ones going. The room is abuzz with the sounds from communications with the fleet, watching, and monitoring their progress as they move through space. In about an hour they will move out of our protection zone, and they will be on their own. As they approach the protection barrier, we turn off the pods to allow them to pass through. They don't even slow down as they pass into unprotected space. They are on their own now and will have to depend on each other for protection. But this is who we are.

It has been a week since I was in touch with the diplomatic core, and I haven't heard a thing from them. I am anxious to hear something, but I have always been that way. I want my solutions now, not three weeks from now, and having the patience to wait has been a struggle for me. I am getting better at it, and I know people are doing their jobs; but I need to be a good leader along with being a good commander. I decide that I want to give them a courtesy call, and I put in a call to Ambassador Vestaj.

She picks up the call and says, "Admiral, I have been expecting a call from you. How are you doing?"

I smile into the monitor, and say, "You have heard about me. I am doing fine, and we have our ships underway."

"I am glad to hear that, and I hope things are going as planned."

"Yes, as planned, no problems now. Ma'am, if I may, I know we still have plenty of time before our ships reach the quantum sector, but I was hoping to find out how things are progressing with the Veltans. Are you getting information about this sector?"

"We have been planting the seeds to see if we can approach them with the question, and we believe we are making good progress in this area. As you know, diplomacy takes time, and we don't want to hurt our chances to ask the question and to expect a reasonable response from them. With that said, I can report that we are progressing well, and that as we currently stand we might be able to approach them with the question in a couple of months. But, you also realize that they may not know anything."

"Thanks for the update, and I appreciate the effort that you have put on this. As soon as you can get any information, I would appreciate an update."

"Absolutely we will. Thank you for your call Admiral."

"Thank you again," and disconnect the call.

I am thinking, "A couple of months. I want that information now, but…"

Stan has been gone a couple of weeks now, and we are getting our daily updates from him during the morning briefing hour. He has not encountered any problems, and the supply convoy is progressing on schedule with no problems. He has been sending the scout ships out on routine patrols, but they are not finding anything out of the ordinary to report either. They have passed some new worlds that might be worth exploring, but they know this is not their mission. They just record their location for future reference for our scientific ships.

The mission is now approaching its third month, and we are not getting any new information from Hyperthia on the quantum sector. We have been in contact with them, and they with us. They want to know how our ships are progressing even though we give them weekly updates. We have also told them that if anything of importance comes up, we would let them know immediately. They tell us that they appreciate the updates but they are anxious to know what happened to their ships.

Since it is the third month and I still have not heard anything from the diplomatic core, I decide it is time for me to make a call. Just as I am about to make the call, my communicator rings, and it is the diplomatic core on the other end.

"Admiral Graham here."

"Admiral, I have some good news for you."

"Good, I am ready for some good news."

She says, "We have been working hard with the Veltans, and we have been making good progress. A couple of weeks ago we could ask them about the quantum sector. They came back yesterday with some information I believe you will be interested in having. They want you to meet with Sentur the day after tomorrow at a sector they provided to us. Will you be able to do that?"

"Pass me the sector information, and I will make sure that I am there."

She cautions, "Admiral, take your counselor with you and make sure you continue to use diplomacy in your handling of this matter."

"I understand, and I will do the best job I can, with patience. Thank you and your team for all of your hard work in getting this information for us."

We sign off, and within the hour, I have received the sector information.

I give the information to Tom, and he plots the location into the star map. He tells me it will take at least sixteen hours to get there, and it will be well outside of the protection zone. If it is the type of information I think it will be, I am willing to take the risk.

I tell Admiral Fuentes to prepare a ship for me and to have it ready to leave in ten hours. I want to be there in time. He tells me he wants to send two destroyers with me, just in case. I tell him fine, but I want them to hold back two hours from the rendezvous point. I don't want to give Sentur any sign of a hostile action.

He reluctantly agrees.

It is time to meet with Sentur, and we have traveled for sixteen hours to meet him at the rendezvous point. The ships that were sent with me are two hours behind me now, and I am there with my counselor. Sentur's ship comes onto our radar screen. He arrives to meet with me about two hours later.

Sentur and I do our customary greetings, and then we get down to business. The Veltans have passed through what we call the quantum sector several times and have quite a bit of information they are willing to share with us.

They provide me with lots of star map updates and some additional information. The sector is currently unpopulated, but they have monitored the Morians there several times. It could have been that the scientific ships had an encountered with the Morians in that sector. They have also noticed that the Morians have taken an interest in this area of space, because they have been spotted in this region with increasing frequency lately. The Veltans do not have a liking for this species but to remain neutral, he does not feel he can share much more than he already has. I thank him for the information he has shared with me, as it is more than we knew just a few hours ago.

He invites me to stay for a meal and for more general conversation for us to get to know each other better. I am anxious to get back to my ship and pass this information along, but I sense from my counselor that leaving now would not be a great diplomatic move. I agree to stay for the meal, and he tells his first officer to have their chef prepare a meal that would be suitable for our consumption. We settle in on some general conversation. I must keep my attention tuned at its peak, in order that I not say or do anything that would offend. I don't want to hurt the diplomatic relations that have already been established. In a few minutes, his first officer comes back and tells us that they believe they have selected something that would be suitable for us. I thank Sentur for his efforts and await the excellent meal that they are preparing.

About thirty minutes later, they tell Sentur that the meal is ready and invite me to an area of the ship where we will dine. We walk into the dining area, and they have the table set with the meal covered. Sentur invites me to sit in a spot and for the counselor to sit at another. They sit and then invite us to join them at the table. They uncover the trays, and we see insects of varying kinds and vegetation I have never seen before. Finally, they uncover the trays they have prepared for us, and they present us with vegetation and a tray presentation that looks like one of our salads. I am relieved. I am not certain that I want to try any of the other presentations prepared before us. We enjoy our meal and continue our conversation. When I feel it is the appropriate time to leave, I look at my counselor and she nods.

"I have enjoyed the meal, and our time together. I also want to thank you for the other information that you have shared with me, but I believe it is time for us to return to our ship."

"I also have enjoyed our time together, and I believe we are moving forward toward a long and prosperous friendship between our worlds. We are glad to share what information we have given to you, and we hope it will be helpful in your rescue mission."

"Yes, I hope it will be."

We now bow, back out of the room, and head back to our ship. We now have more information to assist us in our mission and information that I need to share with the Hyperthean high command.

I am now on board my escort ship and have rejoined my protection ships. Then we head back to base. I am now in the ship's conference room with the captain of the ship, and we are going over the information that I have received from Sentur. I have also received from Sentur the star map update that he promised and have had it uploaded into our star map system. I tell the captain that I would like to establish a link with Hyperthean High Command. I ask that he have his communication area get me that link, and when they have it, to route it into this room. About two minutes later we get a call from the communication area that they have the call ready for me. I tell them thanks and to put it through.

The screen comes alive, and I see Kleg on the other end. I greet Kleg and tell him "I have met with Sentur from Veltan. I tell him that our delegation core has been working with them for several months in establishing a relationship with them. We were able to work with them to see if they would share as much information on the quantum sector as they felt allowable. They agreed, and I just met with Sentur. He has provided me with some good information. They travel through this sector often and have provided me with more star map information pertaining to this sector. I will be passing that information on to you shortly. They have also provided me with some intelligence information. The Morians seem to have a great deal of interest in this sector also. They have been spotted in this sector by the Veltans with increasing frequency. It may be that your scientific vessels ran into some Morians while they were in this sector."

"Morians! This is news. If you can get me the map information as quickly as possible I would appreciate it. I need to get this information to others and inform fleet command. And, by the way Chris, great job on your work with the Veltans. We had completely forgotten about them, but we won't ignore them anymore."

"Thanks, and I'll talk with you later."

I now tell the captain I would like to speak with Tom in my CIC center.

He quickly brings up the line, and I have Tom on the line. I update Tom with my information and tell him that I am sending him the new star map information that we have received. Once he gets it, I want him to encrypt it and send it on to Hyperthean command. They are expecting it.

"Tom, one more thing. Get my XO, Stan, George, Captain Raymond, Admiral Hopper, Commander Hilliard, and the rest of the fleet admirals together for a conference call with me in the next fifteen minutes. Establish the comm link with them, and then pipe me into the conference call."

"Yes sir."

The staff has been gathered together, and now my comm link is ringing. I am informed they are ready.

"I have met with Sentur, from Veltan, and now we have more information on the quantum sector, and it is not all good. I update them with the information I have received, and am ready to give them new orders."

I start addressing each of them individually starting with Stan.

"Stan, you and your mission appears that you might encounter some danger. Bring your ships to full alert. Now I want hourly updates from you, so that we know you are safe. If you run into anything, I want you to report it immediately. I am also going to put together another fleet to follow you for support. If you should come upon any Morians, I want you to avoid them at all cost, until your support arrives."

I now turn to George and say, "George, I want you to work with the rest of the admirals. I want you to put together a fleet to go out in full support of Stan's fleet. I will be back at base in about sixteen hours. We can discuss at that time what you all have come up with."

"Captain Raymond, I want you and your group to start working up new scenarios with the information you have just received. I want an update when I get back to the base."

I now address the rest of those present and say, "The rest of you know what you need to do. I will get with you when I get back. That is all that I have for now."

TWENTY-SEVEN

I have arrived back at base, and immediately call for a staff briefing. Captain Raymond states that his group has come up with a recommendation.

"We have reviewed our strategies, and we believe the best approach is for Admiral Stark and his ships to stop and hold their position. We recommend that these supply ships that are out in front of him turn around and return to where Admiral Stark will be holding his position. When we decide on the new ships that will be sent out to join Admiral Stark, then they will come under Admiral Stark's command leadership. Along with the scout ships that Admiral Stark has, they will continue doing long range patrols and to watch for anything that may come their way. This is what we are recommending now, sir."

"Thanks Captain Raymond. Gentlemen, do you see any problems with this recommendation?"

There is a little conversation and a few feel that Admiral Stark should continue, but the rest believe this is a good recommendation.

"It has been several hours since my conversation with Sentur. It has also been quite some time since the incidence in the quantum sector has occurred. Since our initial contact from Hyperthia, they have not received any further communique' from that sector. I don't believe we would be going in for a rescue mission. Now, I don't see the need to send Admiral Stark on a suicide mission. I also concur with Captain Raymond's recommendation."

"Stan, I want you to find a planetoid to hide behind. Bring your ships to a halt, but keep them on full alert. Keep your scouts out on long range patrols. Recall your forward supply ships. When you have found a suitable location to hide, let us know your star position so that we can direct your support ships to you."

"Aye aye Admiral."

I now turn to George and say, "George, do you have an update for me?"

"We believe we do. We are pulling a battle star, a cruiser, six destroyers, sixteen more scout ships, and the battle stars fighter squadron. We are taking them from different fleets, and they will be assembled in our rendezvous point tomorrow. The ships will be fully manned. The captain of the battle star will be in command of this group of ships until they join up with Admiral Stark's fleet. Admiral Hopper already has supply ships waiting for them, and we should be ready to get underway in twenty-four hours. Admiral Hopper is also putting together his fleet of supply ships that will be needed to support our ships for this mission. We are ready to go."

"Good, we have been waiting for quite a long time to bring things to a head with the Morians, and I believe we are ready. Let's make this happen."

Everything is falling into place. Stan has found a suitable location to hold his fleet. The support fleet is underway making flank speed to join up with Stan in about three months.

The support ships have joined up with Stan's ships. There have not been any reportable incidents. The second set of support ships will be arriving at Stan's location in about a month. His scouts have been on long range patrols and have not encounter any other types of alien ships during their patrols. Stan has also kept fighters out on long range patrols but again, no activity.

We continue to get communications from the Hyperthean High Command. They have also dispatched their own fleet to join us in the quantum sector. However, it will take them about one and half earth years to get there. They have also tried to communicate with the Morian race, but as always, The Morians are claiming they do not have any ships in this section of space. The Hypertheans are monitoring the situation with them, and they have noticed an increased amount of communication activity from the Morian side. They are also noticing some ship movement towards the quantum sector. So, now the Hyperthean high council believes they are now playing games with all of us and that we need to be on high alert, and be ready for anything.

Time seems to be moving by slowly as we wait for the two fleets to join up. Scout ships from the approaching fleet have contacted Stan's fleet. There is excitement in the air by the crews of the ships, and us, as the two fleets come together. At their current speed, they should be joined up with Stan's fleet in the next eighteen hours. We are continuing to monitor the situation, and still everything is silent.

I have been in touch with Stan during this waiting period, and working with the strategic action team, and the other admirals of the fleet. We believe we have come up with an action plan to move forward with, when the other fleet joins up with him.

We are approaching it with the thought that they will be moving into a hostile situation. Stan is to deploy his fleet by approaching the quantum sector from three different sectoral directions. Scout ships will have been in the sector for about a week before Stan's fleet should arrive. If there are any Morians there, they should be able to spot them and get out of there before the Morians can do anything about it. If they do not spot anything, they can also report back on anything they might see of the Hyperthean ships that were lost in the sector. We believe we have worked up some good scenarios on possibilities. Stan has had his crews working and practicing different action plans and believes they are ready to proceed.

The two fleets have joined up. He has met with all the staffs of all the ships, and they have gone over the situation plan and are ready to deploy. Stan now calls me to give me an update.

"Admiral, I believe we are ready to deploy. We have gone over our strategy to move forward. We have plans for battle situations, should we run into any problems."

"Good. I'm sure you have covered all situations well. Do you have anything new we need to know about?"

"No sir, nothing new."

"Then I recommend that you get your fleet underway, and good hunting."

"Thanks," and we say our good-byes.

Stan gets his fleet underway with scouts well out in front of the fleet. They should reach the quantum sector in about two and a half months.

We continue to remain in communication with the Hyperthean High Command, and they are still reporting increasing activity from the Morian side. They also have some ships that are closer than the fleet they are sending to join us. With the increased Morian potential, they are redeploying these ships to join us in the quantum sector. They should arrive about two weeks after we get there.

Our diplomatic core is having increased communications with the Veltans, and they are aware of both our and the Hyperthean's situation in the quantum sector. They continue to want to remain neutral in this situation, but it is becoming apparent that they do not have a like, or trust, for the Morians either. We are getting more information from the Veltans, but only enough where they remain non-committal. We express to them our appreciation for the information we do receive, and we will honor their commitment of neutrality.

From a standpoint of protecting our own solar system, we are not letting our guard down. We also know that this can be a ploy to draw our attention away from protecting our solar system, and having us focus on the quantum sector.

I have met with the fleet admirals, and we have redeployed our remaining ships where we have a good balance to protect us here, should the Morians try a side approach on this front. So far, we have not detected anything, and our scouts do not report any unusual activity.

TWENTY-EIGHT

Stan is now about three days from the quantum sector, and things are starting to gain some excitement. The Hyperthean High Command is now reporting that the Morians are close to the quantum sector. Our scout ships are not reporting any activity in there yet, but their patrols out beyond the sector do show signs of ships that are approaching the quantum sector of unknown origin At their current speed and direction. They should be in the quantum sector about five days after Stan gets there. The scouts have also reported areas of space in the quantum sector where there are several debris fields, but they have not taken the time to investigate. Stan orders them to maintain their patrols, but to search for any signs of life. In a couple of hours, they report that they have not found any life signs.

Stan now has his fleet at full alert again. He brings the fleet to half speed as they approach the three designated sectors. There are still no signs of activity in the area, and the approaching unknown ships are still about five days away. Stan has his scout ships doing full searches of the entire area setting up a protection barrier around the fleet as a precaution

189

and as an early warning system should something slip by the scout ships. He is now deploying his scouts out beyond the quantum sector to search for anything and has four scouts headed toward the approaching unknown vessels to try and get more information on them and to monitor their approach.

With his defensive parameter set, Stan now sends two destroyers towards the debris field to investigate the situation. In about three hours the destroyers have arrived in the debris field and start their investigation. In about an hour he gets a report from the lead destroyer, that from all indications, these were the Hyperthean ships. He believes there were three ships, and apparently, they were all destroyed in some type of surprise attack. The skipper also reports that whatever took them out was almost instantaneous. He also wonders how they even got the short communique out that they did. Stan also reports that they did find the three ships black boxes, as they were still sending out a weak signal. He says they would be bringing them back to the battle star for Stan's communication group to study and break down the information to see if we can get any useful information from the black boxes.

The destroyers return to the fleet without incident, and things continue to be a waiting game. We know that the Morians are coming but whatever their intentions, they can't be good.

Back in our solar system things are starting to pick up now. Two of our scout ships have detected some movement, way out beyond our border protection, coming in the direction of the ninth fleet. There appears to be some ships heading towards our solar system, and they are moving at a good pace. Should they continue heading in the direction we are plotting them, they should be arriving in our solar system within the next fourteen days.

We are now anticipating a two-pronged attack. We have sent communiques stating such to Stan and the Hyperthean High Command. The Hyperthean High Command agrees with our analysis and are also preparing their worlds for some type of retaliatory strike, should such an attack occur. Activity throughout all worlds are now picking up as we prepare for an attack by the Morians.

We are continuing to monitor the movement of unknown ships from both situations, but we still are not 100 percent certain that these are Morians moving towards us; however, we have all indications that they are.

The Morian ships that are heading towards the quantum sector have slowed down, and we now anticipate that their arrival time has now been delayed by an additional eight days. Based on our current calculations, they will be arriving in the quantum sector one day before the other unknown ships arrive in our solar system. We do not find this to be a coincidence, but a coordinated attack.

TWENTY-NINE

Anticipating an attack, and playing the waiting game is quite a stressful situation. It is not one that is played well by all. A person has time to think about their mortality and ask themselves why they are here in this situation. Some of us are thinking about our families back home; all of us are scared and wishing we were someplace else. But regardless, here we are, and we will stand true to this calling, scared or not. The time has come to find out what we are made of.

Things are coming to a head on all fronts. We have approaching enemy ships here on the home front, and Stan is getting ready to face off with an unknown enemy on his front. It may be the same enemy, but we each have different battle situations. I need to make decisions which will affect the outcome on both fronts. This is not going to be easy for me, having only been in what seems now to be small earthly battles, compared to what we are starting to get into. I was only an enlisted man at the time and was not a leader of men. Now I bear the fate of a solar system on my shoulder and of mankind. I know I have the support of our human race, our leadership, and the assistance of leaders who have gone through greater battles than me, but none of us with the experience to face this situation.

The approaching ships are now close enough that our scouts have identified them as Morians. This is true on both fronts. It now appears they will be making a coordinated attack, as both approaching fleets have come to speeds where they should be arriving at both of our locations at approximately the same time.

We have instructed our scouts to play the annoying gnats game with the approaching ships. They are not to fire upon them, but get close enough to where the ships know they are there, but also not close enough to put themselves in danger. This seems to be working. When the scouts approach the ships, they send out fighters to engage our scouts, but we turn and disappear, fast enough that they can't catch the scouts. Then we appear someplace else and do the same tactic. They have finally caught onto our game and have stopped sending out ships. We are now trying a new tactic. This one I call the nipping-dog approach with the enemy scouts. We are coming in from behind, cloaked, and get close enough that they could fire upon the scouts uncloak for a few seconds, take two shots, and then turn tail and run. This approach seems to be working because the ships are now taking a more guarded approach than before. They had been charging at us full steam ahead, but now has slowed down some, and are now sending out patrols looking for the scouts. Maybe if we can keep up this hit-and-run tactic, we can slow these Morian ships enough to allow the Hyperthean ships to get here, but they are still several days away.

The ships that are approaching Stan's fleet are now close enough that Stan will attempt to communicate with them. Stan sends out four attempts before he gets a response.

His initial signal is as follows, "This is the Earth Ship *Argentina*. Will the approaching ships to the quantum sector identify yourselves, and tell us what your intentions are?"

As the communication channel opens, Stan and the rest of the bridge crew sees an earthling-looking person that is fair, but his eyes are deep and dark. Everyone on the bridge gets a chilling sensation as they look at him before he responds. He looks around the bridge before he responds, and finally greets Stan.

"This is Captain Luthian of the Morian Empire on board the *Grand Eviliatian*. What are you doing in this sector, and why do you have ships trying to provoke us?"

"We are here on a rescue mission for the Hyperthean Empire, and the scouts were there helping us to understand your intentions."

"This sector of space is restricted, and there is nothing here to rescue."

"There are no restrictions on this section of space, since it has been marked as unexplored. Where do the restrictions come from?"

"I have restricted it, and that is all that matters. You are ordered to leave."

Stan now is getting firmer in his responses and says, "We have noticed that there are no lives to save since their ships have been totally destroyed. Would you happen to know what destroyed them?"

Captain Luthian smiles, as he responds, "We destroyed them. They were violating our territory. I suggest you leave now, before we do the same to you."

"So, you admit you destroyed these ships, and killed the crew without warning?"

Luthian stands now, and looks directly at Stan, "Without warning... Yes, more than I will say for you. I think we will play a game now." And the screen goes blank.

Stan quickly turns to his captain, and calls for general quarters throughout his fleet.

Stan watches on his hologram as the Morian ships sends out dozens of attack drones. They are quickly repelled by the protection barrier that Stan has established around his fleet. The remaining drones that were not destroyed by the barrier are now attacking the barrier points. Stan now has his attack drones at these barrier points attacking the enemy drones. There is an ongoing battle between these drones.

In the meantime, Stan has ordered the scouts to attack the outer most ships of the approaching ships, do what damage they can, and then get out of there. The scout ships start making their runs at the ships, but the Morians are not holding back either. The ships are exchanging fire and after a thirty-minute battle, we have lost four of our scout ships and three are lightly damaged. But we have also had our impact on the approaching enemy fleet. The scouts destroyed one of their destroyers, severely damaged two other destroyers, and slightly damaged one of their cruisers. This encounter has slowed them down some, and we have given them a taste of dealing with humans. This has caused them to withdraw for the time being.

Our scouts that were not damaged in the battle are following the retreating fleet at a safe distance and are monitoring their moves. The scouts that were damaged are looking for survivors from the scouts that were destroyed. They are picking up any life pods they find and then returning to the fleet for repair.

About the same time that Stan was establishing a communication link with this Morian captain, we are also establishing one with the Morian fleet that was approaching our solar system. This captain looked just as grimacing as the one that Stan is talking with and just as nasty. He basically told me that we had no business to be in the quantum sector, and we were to withdraw immediately. If we did not do so, our fleet would be immediately destroyed. This will force him to destroy our solar system also.

I told him we have not done anything to provoke such a threat. I then let him know that I'd like to discuss our misunderstandings and disagreements to see if we could come to a peaceful solution in this situation.

He immediately told me that the only peaceful solution with them was for us to back down immediately, or suffer the consequences.

The impression I got was that he is only interested in the consequences.

As soon as our communication was over, I hear from Stan that he is under attack. Immediately, the enemy fleet here started their run at us, where our seventh fleet is located. Their attack drones began hitting our protection barrier hard, and we had our protection drones there to meet them. There was a battle that went on for about three hours, but we fortunately did not have a break in the protection barrier.

When the battle with Stan's ships broke down, the battle here just stops but these ships just maintained their position. That lasts only about fifteen minutes before the ships come charging in toward our barrier full steam ahead.

Captain Stillwell puts his ships on the defensive close to the barrier ready to take on the full attack of the approaching enemy ships. The enemy ships have sent out their fighters and drones. They are attacking the barrier pods trying to destroy them so that they can enter through the wall we have built up. After about thirty minutes they have destroyed one of our barrier pods, and the enemy ships are starting to come through. Captain Stillwell has his ships in position and takes the enemy ships full on. The battle is in full force. Fighters streaking around space taking on enemy fighters, destroyers, cruisers, and battle stars are maneuvering around trying to avoid other ships as they fire upon enemy vessels. It is pure mayhem. The battle has been going on for an hour now, and we have only lost two destroyers, an estimated one hundred fighters, and have some damage to other ships. As best as we can tell, the enemy has lost about seven destroyers, almost five hundred fighters, and one cruiser. We have inflicted moderate damage upon the rest of the attacking enemy ships.

As this fight continues, Admiral Stark's fleet has come

under attack at the same time. Stan has received word that the home fleet has come under attack too. When he gets word that this enemy fleet is moving in, Stan orders all his ships to come about, and to take on the incoming enemy vessels.

The Morians are very aggressive, vicious, and brutal in their approach and fighting tactics. They are charging in, with no thought on what they are doing or for their own safety. They do not have any tactics, except to destroy and kill. It seems the only thing they respect is death itself. This too can be a weakness.

Stan does not bunch his ships, but keeps them well spread apart. Currently the number of ships that Stan has outnumbers the Morian ships. But Stan is taking on a full-frontal attack by the Morians that is taking its toll on his fleet. He has now lost a third of his ships in this battle, but the Morians have lost half of their attacking fleet. It does not seem to be slowing them down. At this point I order Stan to use his trans-portal weapon on five of the closest attacking ships.

Stan orders five of his ships to ready their trans-portal weapons and to let him know when they are ready. It only takes about a minute to get all the weapons ready, and Stan receives notification that they are ready to fire. Stan orders the ships to fire at the five designated ships. The fire control systems lock onto the ships, and the weapon screen shows that it has enveloped each of the ships. When the weapon fires, there is no sound, no visible beam, just the ships going silent. Stan also orders all physical firing at these ships to stop. This should send a clear signal to the Morians that we are the ones responsible for their ships going dead in the water, so to speak. It takes them several minutes before they realize these ships are no longer functioning. Stan's communication group catches communications going out to the lifeless ships, but they do not receive a response back. The Morian fleet now pulls back to a non-firing position trying to determine what has just happened. The five ships are just sitting there in space completely dead with no response. The Morians try to make a move to go to the five ships, but Stan sends in ships to block their path. The Morian ships turn and back away. They still do not know what has happened to their ships, nor are they for sure that we are the ones who did it.

Stan now attempts to contact the Morian captain, and gets a request from the Morian captain to discuss his ships. Stan takes a firm stand, and tells the captain that the ships now belong to the Earth fleet, and the crews are no longer with their ships. If the Morians wish to continue this battle, the rest of their ships will come to the same fate along with their crews.

While I had ordered Stan to take out five of their ships, I have also ordered Captain Stillwell to do the same. The results are the same. As the trans-portal weapons fires, five of the Morian ships then go silent, and again it takes several minutes before they realize that the ships are no longer functioning. Again, the Morian ships back off to a safe distance from our fleet, and I order a cease fire.

The Hyperthean fleet is coming to the quantum sector at full throttle, and plan on being on scene within forty-eight hours. The battle has come to a standstill at both locations, and things have been silent now for about four hours. We have sent out ships to recover life pods from our destroyed ships, but we are not finding as many as we had hoped for. Crews stayed at their stations fighting until there was no hope of their ships surviving, and then it was too late for most of the crews to get to their life pod stations. Ships that were heavily damaged are now in tow and are being brought back to a base for repair. Crew members that were injured during the battles are being offloaded onto our hospital ship or on transports going to the hospital ship. Our five captured Morian ships are now in tow and are being brought back to the fleet, while the five that Stan now has are well within his protection area. When we were making our hookups to tow the Morian ships, the Morian fleets made one last attempt to stop us. They soon backed down when we threatened to take another one of their ships.

It will be another twelve hours before the Hyperthean fleet arrives in the quantum sector. The Morians must be aware of this fact, but they are still holding their ground. They still do not know what has happened to their ships or their crews. Just for our own peace of mind, and for the safety of the enemy crews, we sent in a recon drone into the rift. It has recorded that the twenty thousand or so enemy crew members that were sent into the rift had committed suicide. We were totally shocked by what we saw. As we told the Hyperthean High Command of our findings, they told us they were not surprised, this is the Morian way of life and standard for their soldiers.

THIRTY

As we wait in anticipation of the next attack, we are pulling ourselves back together. Captain Stillwell has pulled his fleet back together and is accessing his damage. The loss of two destroyers and about one hundred fighters is a small loss compared to what it could have been. The admiral is sending in his battle report to me, and I see that besides the two destroyers and fighters that has damage, he also has damage to two of his battle stars, six of his cruisers, and ten additional destroyers. The battle stars' damage is minimal, and they are currently making repairs without having to leave their stations. Four of the six cruisers are only moderately damaged, and the other two cruisers have minor damage. It will take longer to get four cruisers repaired, but the other two cruisers will remain on station while being repaired. The four cruisers should be back in action within six hours. The ten destroyers have fought bravely, but two of them are damaged badly enough that they will have to pull back. They will only be used if needed for a final death thrust. Out of the entire battle, we have lost three hundred and twenty-seven brave souls and have sustained about two thousand seven hundred and eighty-three injuries.

Stan is now sending in his battle report, and his looks worse than Captain Stillwell's. Stan's battle was the more aggressive battle, and he had less of a force to fight with, but in the overall scheme of the battle, he has done extremely well. Stan has suffered heavy losses. He has lost one of his cruisers, three destroyers, eight scouts, and five thousand fighters. Casualties have been high as the death toll now stands at approximately eight thousand, with injuries now being reported at around twelve thousand.

Overall, I feel we have done well as we have pushed back the Morians for the time being. Now we regroup and wait for the next wave of attacks to occur.

The Morian fleet facing our solar system has been increasing in size, and we are now looking at an attack from three fronts. From all indications, a large concentration of ships is forming in the sector where we have our seventh fleet and Captain Stillwell. It appears the Morians feel this is our weak point, as we have already lost several ships at this location, and they know where to hit us. There are also two other forces gathering outside of the solar system, at locations that would seem to be forming for side attacks. They appear they will be attacking the fourth and eleventh fleets. I have ordered the admirals from the sixth and eighth fleets to send in additional ships in from the side, to support our seventh fleet, should this large armada of ships attack the seventh fleet. I have also ordered the *Hyperthia* to a location to be in the center of the seventh fleet to assist in their support, and with the large amount of armament that we have, we should be able to make a difference in a battle.

The tension back on Earth is building. They are becoming aware of the battle that has already occurred at both locations and are also aware of the building forces that are gathering to attack us again. It seems so amazing to me that as this death throng builds and people are already mourning the loss of their loved ones, we as a human race are putting aside our differences, praying, and gathering to support those out here preparing for a battle that can determine the fate of mankind. We seem to do that, and now it is the world that is gathering together to watch this struggle unfurl before their eyes.

Stan has regrouped now and is preparing for the next attack from the Morians. They appear to be also regrouping their forces, but they do not seem to be getting any additional support coming their direction. This is a good thing for Stan, as he certainly does not have any additional support coming his direction from us, since we are too far away to assist him. His only hope, should he need it, is the Hypertheans coming his direction, but they are still several hours away. If the Morians are aware that they are coming, they either don't care or don't know. Our feeling is that they don't care. Right now, we wait for the next move.

We don't have to wait long before they are ready to make their next move. It has been about four hours since the last attack, and we are now getting indications that all four forces are making a coordinated attack on the solar system forces and on Stan's group. The large concentration of ships outside of the seventh fleet has started to move in on us. The two side forces seem to be holding back waiting for the large force to attack before they make their run at the fourth and eleventh fleets. As this large armada begins; it attacks on our outer parameter. They are hitting the parameter with such strength and numbers that we have two of our barrier pods fail within fifteen minutes of being attacked, and we now have a large hole in our defenses. The seventh fleet is now moving into our defensive positions and are taking on the attacking Morians with everything that they have. The Morians do not seem to be ready to take on the *Hyperthia* yet and are attacking all our other ships. But the *Hyperthia* is not to be left out of this battle, and our weapon systems open fire on the attacking ships. With the ability to deploy seven fighter squadrons at once, the Morians are now facing a formable enemy of their own. With this enemy armada fully engaged, the Morians now have brought their additional squadrons against our fourth and eleventh fleets. With the loss of two of our barrier pods in front of the seventh fleet, I have ordered that the pods in front of the fourth and eleventh fleets be turned off, so that these fleets could immediately engage the enemy at these locations. Also, should we be able to push back the enemy at these locations, we can turn the pods back on.

As the battle for our Solar System ensues, Stan is now facing a charging enemy force of his own. Both he and the Morians are charging at each other like two bulls with no holds barred. They move in on each other, and then suddenly, Stan orders his forces to divide and the Morians go through the middle with nothing to attack. Now Stan has his ships circling back on the Morians. They are attacking from the sides and back, catching the Morians completely by surprise. Now there are ships flying around in a complete waylay, attacking and fighting off each other. Stan appears to be in complete control of his fleet while the Morians are still trying to figure out what has happened and how to gain control of their own ships again. Stan is taking full advantage of this, and enemy fighters and smaller ships are falling prey to Stan's strategy and are taking heavy losses. The larger Morian ships are also being damaged in the process, but not to the extent the smaller ones are. Of course, Stan is also suffering damage. This type of fighting continues to go on for about four hours, and Stan has lost two more of his destroyers. They have caused great damage to the Morian ships. It has damaged their pride too, and you can tell it by the way they are fighting.

The Morians are not giving up easily in this process, but it is becoming apparent they are sore losers. The fatigue on our ships and crews is starting to show as the battle continues to wage. Stan needs to pull his ships back, and regain control of the battle. The Morians are learning from us and are starting to play in this battle scenario as well as we have developed it. They are now starting to gain the upper hand in this situation, and if Stan doesn't defeat them soon, we will not be the victors in this battle. We do not want that.

As Stan tries to pull his ships back to regroup and to get ready for another strike, the Morians are continuing to press the battle. With Stan trying to regroup, the Morians feel they now have the upper hand, and press the battle to Stan. It is now the sixth hour of the battle, and Stan has lost another destroyer. One of his cruisers is so badly damaged that the Morians are picking it to death, trying to destroy what life is left in it. Stan has sent in three of his destroyers and a fighter squadron to help defend the cruiser, but all that seems to be doing is delaying the inevitable. The Morians feel that they have the victory in hand, and Stan is ready to use his trans-portal weapon again, when out of nowhere, Hyperthean ships are on top of the Morian ships. A new battle front is being engaged. As the Hyperthean ships engage the Morians, you can almost hear the cheers come from Stan's ships. With the Hypertheans now in the battle, along with Stan's ships, the battle only lasts about an hour. We give the Morians the opportunity to surrender or retreat, but they refuse, and the battle continues. In the end, the Morians do fight to their last ship and never retreat, nor did they surrender.

With this battle now over, Stan has pulled his ships back together and is now in communication with the Hyperthean captain that brought in his ships. Stan is very grateful to this captain for coming to the rescue and saving his bacon. The captain was glad that he could get here when he did. He expressed his appreciation to us for coming to this sector for them. It is now time for both crews to start helping with the injured and getting them the medical attention that they need. Stan starts pulling his fleet back together and begins the needed repairs on the ships that are still capable of working.

Stan starts to open a line with me, when he realizes that we are also in a full-scale attack back here in our solar system. He becomes greatly concerned and wants to know how our battle is going. He contacts his communication group, who is now monitoring the battle that is going on back here, and he requests an update.

The battle back in our solar system continues to wage on. We now have three fleets of ships in full engagement against the enemy forces. The two side forces are trying to push the fourth and eleventh fleets toward the seventh fleet, but we are holding our own against these attacking forces. We are a much more formable foe than the Morians had anticipated. Both the fourth and eleventh fleets have suffered losses, but they have also pushed back the attacking force back behind the barrier parameter. I have given them the order not to pursue, but to defend their current positions. I don't want this to be a ploy on their part to pull us out beyond the barrier where they can now circle these fleets and destroy them.

The armada that is attacking the seventh fleet is coming at us with everything that they have. With the *Hyperthia* in the mix, they were not anticipating such a formable weapon as her. With the over fifty thousand batteries of heavy cannons pounding heavy fire on them, and the fighters being deployed, they are no match for the *Hyperthia*. They are still pounding the fleet badly, but after a seven-hour battle, they are now in full retreat and now have pulled back behind our defensive barriers.

It has been a couple of hours now since they have retreated, and we have been able to repair our barrier pods. The battle with Stan's ships is now over, and the Morians must now be aware they have lost all their ships in that battle. We are noticing that the Morians are leaving our system now. I have ordered scout ships to follow them to make sure that they are not returning anytime soon.

I am now in contact with Stan to get a status update from his battle.

"Stan, glad to hear from you and that you were the victors in this battle."

Stan replies with an exhausted sound in his voice, and on his face "Thanks Admiral. I couldn't have done it without the help of the Hypertheans."

"I am glad they were able to get there in time to help you. Give my best to your officers and men and tell them 'job well done' for me. I will get an update from you later. You get your ships back together, and then get some rest."

"Will do. Thanks Admiral."

I now establish my link with the rest of the fleet, and let them know that they have done a great job, and I give them an update on Stan's situation. I also pass along another "job well done." I am now ready to report to the Earth population what a great job our people has done, and that they should be proud of them.

The scouts have followed the Morian armada for a week now, and they do not appear to be returning to our solar system. As we settle into cleaning up from our battles and doing the necessary repairs, I am starting to receive communications from the Hyperthean High Command. They are very pleased with our performance in this battle and how well we have fought.

I have also received a communique from Kleg, letting me know that he would like to speak with me. I call him up and say, "Kleg, you know you can call me up anytime. You don't have to ask that I call you."

"It is good to hear your voice and to see that face. I am glad that you did so well with the defense of your solar system. Congratulations, and I am sorry for your losses.

You know it would be good to see you, and I am looking forward to seeing you soon."

"Thanks. Are you coming to see me?"

"You are not listening to what I am telling you."

"What do you mean?"

"We are inviting you to come to my home world to visit with

us. We want to meet with you. We want to help you celebrate your victory and to discuss a new opportunity with you."

"Now wait a minute. I don't mind coming for a visit, but what do you mean, 'A new opportunity?'"

THIRTY-ONE

The year is 2045, and we have been in space for thirty years. We have contacted three other species, other than the Hypertheans and have developed scout ships and new weapon technology. We have shared it with the Hypertheans. Our original agreement with the Hypertheans was for us to defend our solar system, however, we have gone beyond our solar system with a rescue mission, space exploration, and setting up relationships with species that the Hypertheans didn't. With the small amount of time that we have been in space, we have accomplished quite a bit during this time, not only in space, but with our own relations back on earth. The conflicts we had with each other on earth have diminished to almost nothing. I believe this was due to the realization that we have greater enemies than each other. With each passing year, more and more people want to be part of the space programs that have been established. With the medical technology we have received, and with the incorporation of our human DNA and medical issues into the wrist bands, we have been able to make it available to every human on earth. From birth, the band has been made available to all children. It grows with everyone, evaluating, and keeping the person healthy. The most amazing advancement is that it has helped in the elimination of human abuses, such as drug abuse.

I have been asked by the Hypertheans to come to their system for a visit. They said they would like to discuss a new opportunity. It will take me two years to get there and back, and I will be one hundred years old when I return. With the health improvements that I have received, I still feel like I am about forty years old, and fortunately for me, I look like I am forty. I have decided to accept the offer, and will be leaving for Hyperthia in about a month. They will have one of their diplomatic ships take me, so I will be traveling in style. I must decide who I will be turning over my command to. I have an idea who that will be, and some of my senior officers may feel they should be the one taking over, but that is the way it is.

It has been a couple of weeks, and I have made my decision as to who I will leave in command of the fleet. The problem is that he is returning from a mission and won't be back in the solar system for another six months. He is one of my junior admirals, but has shown great command skills under combat conditions, tenacity, and level headiness under pressure. He is a good administrator and knows how to delegate. Most of my more senior admirals have the same qualities, but they don't have the singularity of combat skills under dire conditions that he has exemplified. My plan is to promote Vice-Admiral Stan Stark to full Admiral, and place him in command of the fleet. I also plan on making Admiral Fuentes his second. He will oversee the fleet until Stan gets back.

I have asked Admiral Fuentes to come to the *Hyperthia* and meet with me tomorrow at 0900. I have also sent a message to Stan that I want him to call me tomorrow morning at 0830.

At 0830, I hear my comm signaling me that I have an incoming message, and I see that it is Stan and answer it.

"Hello Stan. How are you?"

"Just fine sir."

"How is your return trip going? Anxious to get home?"

"Yes sir. I haven't been away from home for this long a period before."

He pauses for a second, and continues with a questioning thought, "Why do you ask sir?"

I laugh at him, and say, "Oh, you don't have to be so suspicious. There's not a new threat. But I do have something I would like to discuss with you.

As you know I have been asked to go to Hyperthia for a visit, and this will take about two years, round trip. With my being gone, I need to leave someone in charge. I know you are still about six months away, but I wanted you to know who that will be. In the meantime, I wanted to share something else with you."

I pause for a brief second, and continue, "Effective immediately, I am promoting you to senior admiral."

I wait a couple of seconds, and am not getting a response.

"Stan, you still there?"

"Yes sir. Thank you sir."

"Don't thank me yet. It comes with more responsibility, and you may not want it."

"Yes sir, but why senior admiral? That is quite a jump."

"Stan, I didn't make this decision lightly, and I will be questioned strongly on my decision to promoting you over more senior admirals, but you will understand in a moment. This promotion may cause some disharmony among the leadership. I will do my best to address it, but I will need your help. Along with your promotion and my departure for at least two years, I am placing you in charge of the fleet. It is not a temporary change. I have overseen the fleet for over thirty years now, and I am being asked to take on new challenges. I will also be promoting Admiral Fuentes to be your second-in-command. He will oversee the fleet until you get back to the solar system."

Again, there is a pause, and finally Stan speaks, "You have

left me speechless, sir. I don't know what to say. Thank you sir, and are you out of your mind?"

"Stan, again, I haven't done you any favors. I believe in your leadership ability, and you will keep this fleet strong. With Admiral Fuentes at your side, I believe the two of you will form strong alliances within the fleet, and will keep the morale high. Please do not say anything to anyone yet, until I tell you who you can speak with. I want to speak to each of the admirals individually, and defuse any situation that may arise from my decision. I will speak with Admiral Fuentes next, and I will let you know when you may speak with him. I want the two of you to start working out how you plan on taking over command. Do you have any questions now?"

"No sir, I understand."

"There is one more thing I want to emphasize to you, and I must insist that there is no leeway in this. It is our Magna Charta statement. No matter how you or anyone in the fleet may feel, from admiral down to a civilian working for us, this fleet's purpose is to defend Earth and our solar system, from attack of races of all kinds. We are never to become involved, in any way, with the politics, wars, or defend any country, or people on Earth, regardless of our feelings, or our own personal alignments. Do I make myself clear?"

"Yes sir, perfectly."

"Stan, I will let you start speaking with your fleet in the next couple of days. I just need the time to start setting the stage for you. In a couple of weeks, I will be on a diplomatic ship headed for Hyperthia, but I will be available at any time for advice. Always remember, you are now in charge, lead without hesitation but with confidence. Make sure that your crews see that. I will be back in contact with you later today, after I speak with Admiral Fuentes."

"Thank you again for having this confidence in me. I will do my best not to disappoint you. I will be awaiting your call."

It is now time for me to make my call to Admiral Fuentes.

I am just a little anxious about this call, but I think it will go well. I bring up my comm system, and place my call to Admiral Fuentes' office. I get his second in command, and ask him if the admiral is available. I see that I have startled him when he sees me on his screen. He snaps to attention, and says that he will get him immediately. I thank him and tell him that I will be waiting here for him to transfer my call over to him. Within seconds I see Admiral Fuentes on the screen.

Admiral Fuentes says, "Admiral, this is a surprise. How can I help you?"

"Admiral Fuentes, it is good to see you. Can you make sure that we have a secure line and the privacy of the room?"

George takes a couple of seconds, and then comes back, "We are good sir."

George Fuentes is a good man and has been with me for the past twenty years. He has led his fleet with confidence and courage. His people like him, and I don't see that there will be any problems with what I am about to tell him.

"George, I am about to tell you something that I need for you to hold in confidence until I tell you otherwise."

"Yes sir."

"You may not know it, but I have been asked to go to Hyperthia and will be gone for a couple of years. I will be leaving on a diplomatic ship in a couple of weeks, and I am making a couple of changes in my command structure. Some of you may not like the changes I am making, but I am asking you to support me, and the person I will be telling you about in a couple of seconds.

I will be leaving the fleet, and I am promoting someone to be in charge. The person I am placing in charge of the fleet is Stan Stark. I have promoted him to senior admiral, and he will be over the fleet, effective immediately. I know he is still about six months away from getting back into the solar system, and he is going to need some help. With his promotion, I am promoting you to be the second most senior admiral of the fleet. You will be his second in command. I want you to work with him, and oversee the fleet until he gets back. I know I just laid a lot on you, but I want you to keep this to yourself. Now, you may go ahead and hit me with everything on your mind."

As with Stan, there is silence on the other end of the screen, as I look at a man with disbelief on his face. He finally regains his composure, and says, "You sure do know how to drop your bombs, sir."

First off, let me congratulate you on your new opportunity. I hope it is what you want. Second, I want to thank you for trusting me with this promotion and opportunity. And thirdly, may I also offer my congratulations to Admiral Stark on his promotion. I believe he will do an excellent job for you, and for us. I believe the rest of the fleet will support you in your decision."

"Thanks George. I was hoping you would say something like that. As you may have already figured out, I have informed Stan of his new job, but I must also emphasize to you, that you cannot speak of this to anyone for the next couple of days. I need an opportunity to speak with the other admirals of this change of command."

"Understood?"

"Completely."

"As I shared with Stan, I may be gone, but I am available for consultation. I still expect you to follow the chain-of-command. I will not forget the fine job all you have done for me, and for the protection of our solar system. I want you to take some time to let this soak in, and then you may contact Stan on a secured channel to start discussing how you will start making changes. This is now Stan's fleet, and I expect you to support him in all of his decisions."

"Don't worry sir, we will make you proud of us."

"Thanks George, and congratulations."

Now I must speak to the rest of the admirals, and let them know of the changes that are coming down. I just hope that these calls will go down as well as these two did. But I think I will wait until tomorrow to see if I get any calls back from Stan or George. I need to see if there's anything to settle before I move on with my calls.

I have made my morning rounds of staff meetings, and things are as calm as they should be. No one has spoken of any rumors. So, things must still be good. It is now 1000, and I need to start making my calls to the admirals of the fleet and letting them know of my decision. These calls take me the rest of the day. I finish up about 1800, sit back, and let out a sigh of relief. Things have gone better than I had hoped. There were a couple of admirals who were disappointed with my decision, especially since they were not the ones promoted to this position. They have large egos, and it has hit them hard. I told them that they are good leaders, and that I expect them to honor and support these men I have promoted. I wanted men in leadership roles that cared more about the mission, and their men, than they did about their own careers. After the dust had settled, I believe everyone is on the same page and will support Stan and George. I may have a couple of resignations coming down, but I know that I have good officers ready to step up and take their places.

I let Stan and George know that I have spoken to all the admirals and that they will have the full support of all of them in the change of command. I told them I will formulate my communique tonight and will send it out to the entire fleet tomorrow morning. I told Stan and George to think about other promotions of those who will be taking over their current assignments within the fleet.

THIRTY-TWO

The announcement to the fleet has gone over well, but some are shocked at my leaving. All three of us have received many congratulatory communiques on our new assignments along with full support from the fleet.

My two weeks have gone by, and it is time for me to catch my ride aboard the diplomatic ship. Harold, my steward, has decided to go with me as my steward. I am pleased and honored with his decision. I would have missed him. George is there to see me off and has a message from Stan for me. He has thanked me for my service and for being available to serve mankind in their hour of need. It is a very heartfelt message which I will cherish for some time to come.

I am on my way to Hyperthia. The first six months have gone by, and it is starting to be a boring passage. I get communiques from the fleet, and things are going well. Stan is due to be back in the solar system in about a week. He and George are starting to communicate more. They appear to be adjusting well to their new assignments, and Stan is eager to be there.

After his battle with the Morians, he feels we need to make some adjustments in our deployments and has patrols that are reaching out further into space. He has been speaking with George about the adjustments, and they have met with Captain Stillwell. He was the captain who defended us against the attack by the Morians in our solar system. Adam also has some recommendations he would like to add, and after several lengthy conversations, they believe they have some new strategies to put into place.

After the battles, we have several ships that need repair. The repair crews that have been working on the assessment of the damages have made a discovery. They are unable to repair the ships completely. We don't have enough material to make all the repairs. The Hypertheans are sending us more material as fast as they can, but it will take another six months to repair the ships before they are back in commission. We will move them back to the repair station near Mars, where they will have a skeletal crew on board keeping minimal systems up and doing what repairs they can. We will also cannibalize these ships to repair the ships that have less damage to bring them back to full service. The rest of the crews from these damaged ships will be transferred.

With this realization, Stan is now working with Admiral Duffy of our transportation fleet. He explains the situation to Matt, and that Matt needs to work with the Hypertheans on getting the needed supplies for the repairs on our ships. Stan has requested that Matt now put together a fleet of cargo ships that will move the essential parts and supplies that we can't get here from other galaxies. Matt will need to establish trade agreements with the other galaxies and facilities for these supplies. He will need to put together a team that knows specifically how to work these trade agreements. They will need the help from the Hypertheans, and this is where my new position comes into play. Since I have worked well with the Hypertheans for the last thirty years, I know several contacts there that I believe can help us along this line.

Stan has made me aware of another situation which can

become serious in the next ten years or so. The power for our ships appear to be burning down faster than anticipated. The power source for our ships is supposed to last us for another two hundred years.

Since the ships we received from Hyperthia are about five hundred years old, they are among the oldest ships in the Hyperthean fleet. We aren't complaining. They are more advanced than anything we could develop in the next three hundred years. With the ships being this old, the power source is also about that old. A Hyperthean engineering group is looking into the problem and has discovered that the diaplatforcite crystals used for powering our engines and providing power for ship systems are deteriorating at a faster rate than anticipated. Now here comes our next problem. These crystals are not readily available and only come from a few mining planets on the far side of the Hyperthean federation. The Hyphertheans do keep a supply of crystals on hand, but they are now building new ships to better defend their own systems. They only have enough on hand for these new ships being built. Again, Stan turns to me for a solution.

The diaplatforcite crystals were a very rare find for the Hyphertheans many hundreds of years ago. They are similar in form to our quartz. In their raw form they have no value, except maybe to a geologist. The diaplatforcite crystal has another quality that makes them very valuable. They are like our diamonds, in that we need crystals that are without flaws and to last for extremely long periods of time. Just like our diamonds, they can take the flawed crystals and cut them down to remove the flawed pieces. These smaller crystals are used to power our generators that create the same power for all the rest of our ships' requirements. With our ships, we have eight redundant systems. Should a system fail, any of the others will take over and keep the ship running. This also allows us to take a specific power source offline for repairs and maintenance. When these crystals are used as a power source, they are placed into a containment area where a stream of ionized glucocite is injected into the containment area. The chemical reaction with the diaplatforcite ignites the crystal. The crystal now glows in the shape of a small sun about five feet in diameter and puts off tremendous heat. Somehow the Hypertheans have found a way to control this ignition process and the power output. Just like our sun that gives off different types of radiation and rays, like gamma rays, the diaplatforcite crystal also gives off a special ray called alfogagam rays. These rays are harnessed and transformed into a plasma stream used as the power source for our engines. The containment area is surrounded by a barrier that has a special coolant that protects the rest of the ship from the tremendous heat and the radiation. We have four of these containment areas in engineering as redundant sources of power for the smaller crystals.

Smaller crystals are used for the four smaller containment areas and they create a smaller sun ball about six inches in diameter. They still generate a tremendous amount of heat and radiation and are maintained in the same way as the larger containment areas used for the engines. But from these smaller sources of energy, we only capture the heat from the containment areas to generate our source of power to supply the needs of the ship. Since these sources also produce a small amount of alfogagam radiation, it is also redirected to the plasma stream for use by our engines. As they say, waste not, want not.

But enough on an engineering lesson. Since these crystals are going to be a source problem for the fleet, Stan has a new problem for Matt. He needs to find a source of these crystals for us and start bringing it back to our solar system for our ships. Of course, our demand for these crystals won't be as large as the rest of the Hyperthean fleet. I'm sure it won't create a large problem.

Matt is working with the Hypertheans now to find out if they have any type of transport ships that we could have, or negotiate a trade that can be used for the movement of the crystals.

Stan and George has put together a team of officers to formulate a new division, within our command structure, for the exploration of space. About fifteen years ago, Admiral Graham worked with the Earth agencies to allow them to have ships for exploration of space. This agency is separate from the purpose of what we are out there for. We do support them with their needs and with any problems they run into. They don't have the speed or the defensive capabilities of our ships, but this is not their purpose. As was stated when they were formed, they were to use their ships to explore space to a much finer detail and to more accurately map what was there. They were to discover new worlds, but not to interact with these worlds. That is the job of the diplomatic core. They were to monitor them from a distance, no closer than their nearest moon. If they were to discover life forms, they are to only listen, to discover how far they have progressed in civilization and not to interfere with that progress. With the limited capabilities of their scanners they are to determine and log the type of minerals the life forms have, atmospherics, other chemical makeup of the planet, set up a listening post on their moon, monitor the planet from that distance, and move on to their next location.

The team that Stan and George has commissioned is to put together a plan for new exploration ships that are much faster than the earth ships. They are to have better armament. Since our section of space, and beyond, has not been greatly explored by the Hypertheans and our earth ships, we need these crystals for our ships. These ships and crews are to explore these new sectors of space, map it with a broader stroke, and allow the earth ships to fill in the details. These ships will have a much higher sophistication of scanners and are only being commissioned to search for what we need. We are not there for the conquest of space. Should they discover a planetoid, moon, asteroid, or anything that has what we need, they are to determine if the area is inhabited. If it is inhabited, they need to determine how far this society has progressed. Should they determine it is worth the risk of establishing communication without creating a shift in their societal progress, or a panic. We will send a diplomatic ship to establish first contact to show that we intend no threat to their society. If we can establish a relationship with them we would like to have and what we would be willing to trade for it. Should we determine that our first contact will create a problem, we are only to establish a listening post on their moon, mark the planet as a potential source of the mineral for future contact, and move on.

If we discover the crystals we are looking for on an uninhabited planet, moon, or object, we need to determine if another species has prior claims on the source. If we cannot find that any claims have been established on our find, we then place our claim within the federation courts. Should no disputes arise, we will have the rights to start mining the crystals we need. If we determine that there are others who have prior claims on the property, we need to establish a relationship with them and start a negotiating process for us to bargain in trade for the supplies that we need.

With the establishment of trade relationships with others, we will be able to establish our own space trade routes for our transports to travel safely.

This is a great plan. Stan and George give permission for the establishment of this division within our fleet. The only problem with this plan is that it will take about ten years to build these ships before we can start the exploration of our new space. So now Stan is going to present me with a new opportunity to explore with the Hyperthean High Command. This is the purchase of some ships that we can use for this purpose until we can develop our own.

THIRTY-THREE

I am now in my seventh month of travel to Hyperthia, and things are no longer boring for me. When I left our solar system, I was on my way to Hyperthia for my first visit to meet their people who I had only spoken with or heard of. It was also my opportunity to see new worlds first hand, to meet new races, and learn new things. I was, and still am, very excited about this opportunity. But it now appears I am also a mediator for our fleet for some much-needed items, and I still do not know what this 'new opportunity' is that Kleg wants to speak with me about. First, Stan has contacted me and explained the problem on the ships, and that we need more plating to get our ships fully repaired.

A couple of days later I am again contacted by Stan with a new issue. This time it is the crystals for our ships. This one is going to be a little harder to work out, but I have had a couple of days to think through the issue. I believe that I have come up with a solution. Now I need to explore it with the Hypertheans.

A week has passed since I last heard from Stan. I am working through some proposals for the crystals, and I want to make sure that they are sound before I present it to the high command. I have just been informed that I have a new communication request, and they want to know if I want to take it. Since I am working in my quarters, I ask if they will put it through to me in here.

In a couple of seconds, I have Stan on my screen, and say, "Good afternoon Stan. How are you?"

"Good afternoon admiral."

"I'm not your admiral anymore. You may address me as Chris."

"Yes sir, but you will always be my admiral. Chris, I have something new to ask of you."

"Stan, I'm here to enjoy myself. You are going to have me so busy I'm going to wonder why I even left the solar system."

I have a grin on my face, and Stan sees that I am only joking with him.

"What can I do for you now?"

"Admiral, I mean Chris, we are forming a new division within the fleet. With the need for the crystals we don't want to place all this demand on the Hypertheans to supply it. We may not be able to find what we need, and it may take us years before we do. We feel we need to get started in exploring our own space out beyond what the Hypertheans have explored.

It will take us about ten years to build our own space crafts for this exploration. So, we are hoping you will speak with them, and see if they will loan or sell us some exploration crafts so that we can start sooner than later. Do you think you can work with us on this also?"

"This sounds like a great plan, an ambitious one, but a good one. Of course, you don't need my permission to do this. I will add this to my list of things to do.

If you keep sending me these requests, I am going to need a team of people to work with me, and I don't know where I will get them out here."

I grin at Stan, and he does the same.

"I'll try not to come up with anything else. If you can pull these three off, you are some miracle worker."

"I am already working on a couple of thoughts and am trying to formulate them to make sure that they are sound before I present them to the high command.

Stan, how much of your needs have you communicated up to the Hyperthean High Command?"

"They are aware of our need for the plating to make repairs to the ships, so they were expecting us to make this request. They are working on sending us sheets of plating for us to use for our repairs, but that is as far as we have gotten with that.

As far as the crystals are concerned, their high command was surprised with the problems we have encountered with them. They have assigned a team of their own scientists to work on the problem, but they have not come up with a solution. They know that our ships are old. They know that our containment centers for the crystals are a little outdated, but the process is still as current as possible. It's the same process they use on their newer ships. They feel it might be with the older containment process and the software used to make it all work.

This last request I have made only to you; they are not aware of it."

"Good, let them continue to send you the plating you need, and hopefully it should arrive much sooner than you anticipated.

I am glad they are working with you on a solution for the crystals. Maybe they can come up with something that won't be too costly for either of us.

On this last opportunity, let's just keep it between us for the time being. I want to think on it, but I like it. I still have a few months before I get to Hyperthia, but I will get back with you before then with my thoughts on how we need to proceed. In the meantime, you keep working with them on the other problems, but don't you lose focus on what your primary mission is."

"No sir, I won't. Thanks for your help on all of this. I will talk with you later."

"Okay."

After I sign off with Stan, I start thinking about the situations again. With the new opportunity that Stan has provided me, I see several things I need to investigate further.

With the Hyperthean High Command providing us with the plating we need to repair our ships, I will work with them to see if we can continue to receive plating from them for future repairs. I need to see if we can place orders with them to receive plating to build new ships and stockpile for future repairs.

Over the past ten years or so, I have had the opportunity to see some of the new ships that the Hyperthean High Command has produced and some of the new technology they have. As it is with all new advances, they no longer have any need for battle stars or a ship like the *Hyperthia*. She is considered an old relic. For us, she is still quite an impressive battle station. Their new ships are extremely impressive, compared to what we have, even though what we received were quite impressive when we got them. I want to start replacing our older ships with new ones. Hopefully, I can work a deal with them to get the schematics for one of their new destroyers. If I can get it to our ship builders at the Alpha station near our moon and maybe, we can have one of these new destroyers in the next five years. We'll have to see how that goes.

In the meantime, new plating is on its' way to Earth and should arrive there within the next nine months. I will see if we can keep the plating coming. We can stockpile it at our Mars base for future repairs. Hopefully, it is the same type of metallurgy used in the building of their new ships. As it is with everything new, probably not.

On the discussion of the crystals, I believe I have come up with a plan where we can get enough crystals from the

Hypertheans, without hurting the supply for either of us. Since we believe the crystals we have are not going to fail us for at least another ten years, we are not in any current danger of making our solar system defenseless. And since the Hypertheans have an ample supply of crystals to support their fleet and to start reserving new crystals for their new ships, I believe I can work a deal with them to trade a certain number of crystals with us every year over the next five years. This will help us in the replacement of the defective crystals. Over this period, they can increase their number of crystals they need from their supplier without damaging their demand or need for crystals. I believe this can be a win-win for both of us. It will also allow us the opportunity to set up our own trade agreements with the crystal supplier for our future needs. We can ask the Hypertheans to be our intermediary handlers, if we need to. Since these crystals last for several hundred years as a power source, we should not need very many.

Should this work, which I believe it will, I can get Stan to stand down on the second part of his plan to send out ships to look for a new source of crystals. Shooting down two of his plans this early in his command can damage his ego. It can also bring into question his ability to make decisions with the rest of his staff, especially with me countermanding the suggestions and decisions he has made. I need to think of a way to make it a win for him and build his respect with his command.

Now on to the third thing Stan has asked me to do. This will take some time but my wheels are already turning. I believe I can see a way to make this work, where Stan will come out the hero and I had nothing to do with it. Umm, let's see how I can pull this off.

THIRTY-FOUR

I am about a week away from the Hyperthean home world. Things are starting to get exciting around here. I was contacted by Kleg about two weeks ago. He is going to meet me at the landing site where I will be met and introduced to some of the dignitaries. I know I will not remember all their names. I have seen the itinerary, and they have me completely busy for two weeks with dinners, meetings, and just meeting people. Everybody wants to see the earthling who defeated the Morians in two separate battles, with older ships.

I have had the chance to talk with Kleg on several occasions. We have discussed the two things that I urgently need to get some answers for, or at least, see that I am making some headway. I don't want to put Stan off much longer, or he might think I am stalling or don't want to tell him bad news.

Since we shared the makeup of our scout ships, and have built so many of the ships for them along with the trans-portal device. Kleg is confident they will not have any problems with providing us with the amount of plating that we need for many decades to come.

We have also discussed my proposal that I would like to

present for the crystals. He feels it is a good proposal and believes that the council will go for it, but he is not the one that I must sell this to. I am confident that I can do this. Kleg has shared some information with me, that even though the crystals do come from a remote location, the traders of the crystals have an abundant supply. It is almost like the sale of diamonds here on earth. It is a tightly controlled market, but they will not run out of crystals anytime soon.

The day before we arrive, I get another chance to speak with Kleg. I tell him of one of the two last things that has been requested of me. The request is for the design of their new destroyers so that we can start replacing ours.

He looks at me through the screen with a long pause and then I say, "Let me give you a better plan and purpose for what we are trying to do."

"Please do, since you are really stretching what you think we can do."

"You came to me thirty-one years ago and asked me, and all of Earth, to trust you and the Hyperthean race. You explained that we were in danger. Against all reason, we did just that. As a race, we overcame many odds and worked closely with you and your people. I believe that we have established a very close relationship and friendship. We learned a lot through these years, and when it finally came down to whether we would stand or fall, we pulled ourselves together and stood against the Morians on two fronts and won. I believe that we have shown ourselves to be friends, allies, trustworthy, and that we would never betray that trust or relationship.

You have asked me to come here, not only meet with your people, and I more than eagerly and happily do that. I also believe you are going to ask me to go deeper in our relationship and trust of each other. I am now asking the same of you.

One of the things you have shared with us is that our solar system is on the outer reaches of your exploration boundaries, and you have not explored those regions of space with any detail. With the hostilities with the Morians increasing, you don't know when you can do that.

Our proposal is this, we believe we are ready to join you in the exploration of these new expanses of space. We will continue to protect our solar system with the ships you have provided to us. But as you have shown us, our ships are very old. Even the Morians have a more modern fleet with which they have attacked us. There may come a time soon when they will be able to overpower us, just with new technology. Then the defense of our solar system will fall to you, or we will be wiped out.

I am asking that you provide us with the blueprints for your new destroyers for us to build them at our foundries back in our solar system. We will also need your new technology and to be trained on how to use this new technology for these destroyers. A few years down the road, we would like the blueprints for your new cruisers and many of your other crafts.

We also know that you have new types of exploration vessels with the right amount of equipment to travel into these new regions of space for extended periods of time. What we are also asking is that you provide us with a dozen or so of these ships so that we can begin to explore the unexplored. We will share all our findings as you have done with us. I am asking you to allow us to share with you the exciting adventure of exploring these new expanses of space."

Kleg looks at me almost with his jaw hanging on the floor, and says, "I hope you just canned that speech, because if you say just that to them, I believe they will not only do this for you, but give you everything else you just asked for without hesitation. Of course, we will need to work out certain treaties between our other communities, but I don't see that being a problem."

I am looking back at Kleg with a big grin on my face, and almost in disbelief. I thank Kleg for his time and tell him that I will see him tomorrow when I get there.

I have decided it is time for me to make a call to Stan. This will probably be the last opportunity I get to speak with him for the next couple of weeks. I punch up my comm device and call Stan. I get the communication center on board the *Hyperthia* and ask to be put through to Stan. I must have gotten a brand-new communication person in the center because he asks who is calling even though he can see me on the screen.

"This is Chris Graham on board the delegation ship nearing Hyperthia."

There must have been a higher-ranking communication officer that overheard the conversation, and who must have picked up the younger person out of their chair, threw him across the room and took over the call.

"I am sorry about this Admiral Graham. How can I help you?"

There must have been sweat running down his face by now, as he probably feels his career floating out into space now over the oversight that this younger communication person has made. They should know by now that I am not that type of person.

"It is only Chris now, since I am no longer your admiral. Will you please put me through to Admiral Stark?"

"Yes sir, right away."

My screen goes blank for about ten seconds, and then I see Stan on the screen. He is grinning from ear-to-ear and laughing.

"What is so funny?"

"That communication officer you were just speaking with is probably off changing his underwear now. You scared the belittles out of him when you called, and they made the mistake of not knowing who you were."

"I'm glad I left such a remarkable impression on all of you. Gone for a year, and nobody remembers who I am."

We stop laughing and calm back down when I say, "Don't

be too hard on them. I have some news for you, but it is still incomplete.

Stan, as you know I will be arriving at the Hyperthean capital tomorrow and will not be able to speak with you for at least the next couple of weeks. But I do want to give you a progress report on the things I have found out, and how I anticipate presenting them.

Kleg and I have put together a presentation that we believe will get you what we need in plating and crystals. I hope to have a big surprise for you regarding earth's potential for the exploration of space. I don't want to get your hopes up just yet, but I am ninety percent sure I can sell your proposal to the high command. So what do you think of all of this?"

"Sir, I really do appreciate all that you have done on this, and I look forward to our next conversation. I will put a halt to some of the things that we have put into play. I'll explain that we have received some new information that requires us to take a different path on a couple of decisions. AND, I will make sure that the communication center knows who you are when you call in next time."

I laugh and say, "Thanks Stan." and we say our good-byes.

THIRTY-FIVE

We have arrived at the space port where arriving dignitaries are greeted. It is almost at the top of one of the buildings and just off to the side is a large room which I believe is a waiting area for arriving and departing vessels. I have been given the proper attire for a dignitary that arrives, but I am not sure what to think of it. Even though I have been in a military uniform for the past thirty years, this is going to take me some time to get used to.

The ship has landed, and I am standing at the door waiting for it to open. Then I am told that I will be presented in five-four-three-two-one. The door opens and as I step out, I am greeted by Kleg and several other high-ranking officials. There is not a large crowd to greet me, just a handful of people. I wasn't sure what I was expecting after traveling for a year, but I thought it would be a little more fanfare than this. I suppose the real crowd will be at the reception later this evening.

Anyway, I hide my disappointment. Then I shake hands with Kleg and the other dignitaries who are there to meet me. Kleg presents each of them to me with their titles, which means nothing to me now. I greet them, and we start walking towards a vessel that will take us to where I will be staying. This is where we will be having our conference meetings for the next couple of weeks. As we are walking towards the vessel, I am looking around at the buildings, the vessels they use, and the sky. I can't believe how similar the sky is to ours. They have two moons, but only one is visible now. The other one is on the opposite side of their world. Their atmosphere and gravity is like ours. I do notice a slight difference in the air that I am breathing, but I don't believe that it will be a problem for me. Because of the two moons, the gravity does appear to make me feel lighter. I feel like I can move more freely and with less effort here.

As I look at their structures, I see that they are very tall skyscrapers. They are almost oval in shape, and have walkways in the sky that join the many superstructures at many different levels. They are covered with a glass-like material that provides light as you move from one building to another. As I look down, I can see vessels that travel through the air from one location to another. There also appears to be air garages for these vessels to fly into and park. Just like on Earth, a lot of people still have a personal vehicle. Also, as I look further towards the ground, I do see vessels that are traveling on the ground. They appear to be vessels for transporting cargo like our eighteen wheelers. They travel below the gardens as if they are below ground but aren't. The Hypertheans are quite advanced, compared to us. I keep taking in the sights when Kleg breaks into my thoughts and says, "What do you think?"

"I have never seen anything like this. Very impressive and futuristic for me. Do you not have individual homes to live in like we do?"

"Not anymore, but the people who handle our farming needs still do. With the increased population of our world, not only from our own growth but also with other worlds living here, we no longer have the land available for us to be able to own individual pieces of property. This is the reason you see so many tall structures. We have tried to create an environment where we can still go and get some of what we used to have, like open spaces, but now live in these superstructures. Those that have jobs live in the same superstructure where they work. This cuts down on the need for vehicles. Instead of spreading out across the land, we do our expansion up. We have created them where families can have large spaces to move around in, but also large open porches for us to be able to enjoy the outdoors also."

"Very nice. How has this worked out for you?"

"At first we had quite an adjustment to make, but we realized we had to do something. We had to maintain enough open areas for us to grow our vegetation to support our populations. Just like you, we struggled with keeping enough farming population out in the country to grow our sustenance, since many of the younger people wanted to move to the cities. We were able to find a way to do this over many years of trial and error."

We arrive at the building where we will be staying and having our meetings for the next couple of weeks. This structure appears to be for special envoys and is quite elaborate. We depart the vessel and head towards what I believe are elevators. The delegates say their good-byes at this point and tell me that we will see each other at dinner this evening.

Kleg and I enter the space that appears to be an elevator. It is a transport device that transports us to the floor where we will be staying. It is instant, and we are on the 433rd floor. Both of our rooms are on the same floor. The transport door opens, and we walk out into a large space that has several rooms for other guests. But because I am a visiting dignitary, the whole floor has been reserved so that we won't be disturbed. There appears to be only about five rooms on this floor, and Kleg's room is across the hall from where I will be. Since the buildings are oval, the area here in the middle is also oval shaped, and it could be set up as another living space but isn't. Kleg takes me to the door of the living space where I will be staying and points to the room on the other side where he will be. He provides me with the magnetic key to my quarters. Even though it is still about 1000 hours, he tells me he will come get with me about 1800 to take me to where we will be gathering for our meal this evening.

I enter my room, or should I say rooms, and see that it is quite spacious. It has a large living room area that has large windows letting in lots of light. From here, I can go out onto a large patio area that has plenty of greenery and light. There is a large patio table with chairs for six people to sit. There are also three good sized couches to sit on, with a small waterfall off in one corner with a small flowing stream moving across the edge of the patio structure. This gives a soothing sound as the water flows down the waterfall and across the stream.

I go back into the living room area. It has two large couches with what appears to be coffee tables. Off to one side is a desk structure where I can do some work. I see twin open doors that lead into the bedroom area that is also quite large. It has a sitting area, large bed, and twin doors that lead out onto the patio area.

The bathroom area is quite comfortable and good sized. The whole space would be quite comfortable for a family of six back on earth. The whole thing is very impressive, but I guess this is what they expect to provide a dignitary.

In a few minutes, I have a knock at the door. It is what I would consider to be the bellboy delivering my luggage for my stay here on Hyperthia. He comes in, and doesn't quite know what to do with my belongings. Harold comes into the room, takes my things from him, and thanks him for bringing them up. Then Harold puts all my things in their proper place, and then leaves the room. I now have several hours before we must go to dinner.

Since it is around my lunch time, I decide to go down to the main floor and see if they have anything like restaurants. I get down there, and start looking around for anything that looks like a restaurant. I must have looked like I was lost. One of the hotel employees comes up to me and asks, "Is there anything I can help you with?"

"Yes, I am new here, and I am looking for someplace to eat. Can you recommend something?"

"Yes sir. We have several places to eat here. May I recommend two of them to you that would be good?"

"Which one would you recommend?"

"I like this one a little more than that one" as he points one direction and then the other.

"What type of cuisine do they have?"

He looks at me a little puzzled and says, "What's cuisine?"

I smile back at him and say, "What do they serve?"

"Oh, they have a mixed menu, and you can pretty well get anything you would like to try."

"Can I put the charge on my room?"

"No problem sir."

"Thank you for helping me," and I head over to the eatery.

The restaurant has a few patrons in it, and the waiter takes me over to a table and seats me. I look at the menu and don't recognize three-fourths of the items that are on the menu. The waiter comes over, and asks if I have any questions about the menu.

"I hate to say this, but I don't recognize most of the items on the menu. As you may have guessed I am from Earth. Can you tell me what some of the items are, and something that might suit my palate?"

He smiles back at me and says, "Yes sir, I believe I can." As he starts off, he tells me what some of the items are, and then he names one that sounds like a club sandwich. I stop him there, and tell him that is what I would like to have. He brings me the meal, and it does look like a club sandwich. I taste it, and it does have a similar taste to one, so I go ahead and eat it. I don't ask how it is made.

I finish my lunch and go back up to my room. Since I have had a year to prepare for this visit, I decide to see if Kleg is available to come over just to talk. We haven't had an opportunity to just chat and catch up. I bring up my comm link and call up his room to see if he is there, and if he is available for a visit.

Kleg answers and says he will come over for a little while.

When Kleg comes over, we go out onto the patio area to sit. I offer him something to drink. Then we just sit and take in the view for a couple of minutes.

Finally, Kleg breaks the silence and says, "What do you think of the view?"

I pause for a second, and then say, "You know I have always wondered what it would be like to see other worlds, even as a kid. Would they be like ours? How different would the people be, not only physically but also culturally? I was very surprised to see how similar physically your world is, and people are to ours. I know from when I first met you, that your planet was much larger than ours and that it takes longer to revolve around your sun. It has been a pleasant surprise to see how similar our societies are, at least at first appearance. I hope that as time goes by, I will get to know your culture and habits better. I hope I won't offend you, or your people, as we grow to know each other. Also, having been cooped up on that vessel for the last year, it is good to see a sky and breathe the fresh air."

Kleg smiles at me, takes a drink from his glass, looks out past the patio view, and then says, "I am sure you will do fine. We know you are new to our culture. As many other races, from many other planets over the centuries, we have learned from each other. We have been able to work through many of these differences without being offended and without offending others in the process."

We are finally breaking the ice, and are starting to relax with each other. The conversation continues for the next several hours as we discuss our families, our lives as we grew up, and how much difference there is between us. But this doesn't seem to matter as we are growing closer to each other in our friendship, and we are becoming more open.

As it is approaching 1700 hours, we decide to call it an afternoon. Kleg heads for his room to prepare for the evening's festivities. I do the same and think about the afternoon and how enjoyable it was just to relax and chat. I didn't have anyone to do that with, especially as I traveled here. I need to make a note of that and make them aware that we do need some type of entertainment as we travel.

The evening was enjoyable. The next two weeks turn into a time of getting to know different levels of leadership within the council and understanding how I need to play the game to get things done. I am not a politician, but a military man, but even at that, I have had to play some politics through the years. I am still not sure why I am here. I'm not a diplomat; working with these folks is for the diplomatic core.

The two weeks are over, and I'm not sure what I am going to be doing next. There's no agenda. I have been resting up for the last couple of days, and just sightseeing their city and country side. The next morning, I am sitting in my patio area when I hear a knock at the door. It is Kleg.

"Would you mind joining me out here in this foyer area. There are some people I would like for you to meet."

As I go into the foyer area, I see about ten military types standing around talking. There has been a table set up in the foyer, and it appears we are getting ready to have a meeting. I look at Kleg and ask, "What's going on?"

"The admiral and these officers want to meet with you and discuss something with you. I hope you will keep an open mind and will be open to what they will be presenting to you."

With a slow, "Okay", I am invited to sit at the table, as the rest of them join me. This time Kleg sits next to me.

The admiral starts off the process by introducing himself,

and then goes around the table and introduces the rest of the officers to me. I greet them all, and then he proceeds.

"You have met with the diplomatic council for the past couple of weeks, and from what we have been told, you were very uncomfortable with the group."

"Yes I was. I hope I didn't offend anyone. I have been a military person for the past thirty years, and then was suddenly expected to be a diplomat. Ugh, not exactly who I am. Sitting around and discussing things, more like arguing about things, and getting nowhere. At least from my perspective, we weren't getting anywhere. If this is what you expect from me, I'm afraid I will need to turn this opportunity down."

"Well, from our perspective, we didn't think you would accept it. To be honest, when we had Kleg tell you that we had a new opportunity to discuss with you just over a year ago, being a diplomat was not what we had in mind."

I look at Kleg and he is just sitting there, stone faced, and then I look back at the admiral.

He continues, "You have proven your leadership abilities with your command and on the battlefield, and we have been very impressed. You took the old ships we gave you and defended your solar system. You also assisted us when we needed help in the quantum sector. Your people developed a new weapon which has proven to be very impressive. You came up with the scout ships that you have also provided to us and have helped us in our battle against the Morians.

Unfortunately for us, the battle with the Morians is not going as well as we would like. We have formed a special deep space division and are using the new scout ships along with some new stations we have developed. We also know of some of the tactics you used against the Morians. It has helped us some in slowing their aggressiveness towards us."

"I am quite shocked about the information that your battle with the Morians is not going as well as you would have expected. I know that from everything we have heard over the past thirty years, everything was at a standstill.

This bothers me from the aspect of the protection of our solar system. You have much newer ships and technology, and so do the Morians. You have provided us with much older ships and technology even though they have been updated as best they can, and we are not complaining about that. If the Morians can get the upper hand over this federation, I don't see that we have much hope in surviving since they know of our existence."

"We understand how you feel, but the picture isn't all that gloomy. We know of your desire to update your fleet, get better trade agreements for the crystals, replace your ships with a more modern fleet, and to have some ships for the exploration of the space beyond your galaxy. Our software engineers have discovered a small problem in the software that controls the burn of the crystals and have sent out a fix to all commands, including yours. The problem is that the damage has already been done."

I look at Kleg and he grins at me.

The admiral continues, "Don't worry Mr. Graham, Kleg came to us with your proposals, and we found them to be sound ones. Because we are the military, we can provide you with all that you have requested, and more, without having to go through the council or diplomatic core. What you have proposed is for the defense of all our galaxies and does not need council approval.

What you ask from us is in the best interest of all."

"I want to thank all of you for what you are doing. I was not expecting this, but neither was I expecting what you told me about our current situation."

The admiral says, "I do have a proposal for you. When we first approached you to come here just over a year ago, we started the development of some new stations. We are in the process of completing twelve new stations scattered throughout several locations. We want them to be stations for our cargo ships to stop at, but the main purpose of the stations is to deploy scout ships and monitor these sections of space. We would like you to take charge of these stations. If you accept, we will make you a one-star admiral in our federation. We also want it to be a multi-galaxy effort. We will fill three fourths of the stations from our galaxies. We would like for you to fill the other fourth from your experienced scout fleet. One of the stations is about three months from your solar system, so you can get home as often as you like, if you want to establish it as your base of operation."

I am very surprised by this offer. I let all that has been said sink in.

"I accept your offer, as long as I don't have to be a diplomat, and I am humbled that you consider me the best person for this job. I know I have a lot of things to consider and to think about, but I hope I can get started on this as soon as possible."

"We were pretty sure that you would step up to the challenge, and Kleg said you would accept the position."

I look over at Kleg. Then I elbow him in the arm, and say, "You were pretty sure of yourself, weren't you?"

He grins back at me, elbows me back, and says, "No, I just think you are that arrogant."

We both laugh, and everyone congratulates me on accepting this new position. Then the admiral continues, "You will have a new uniform to wear. We have instructed Harold to get you your new uniform, and we expect you to start wearing it tomorrow. We will make the announcement to our fleet this evening.

You can send an announcement to your fleet when you are ready. Tomorrow morning at 0800, we will start with having a meeting here and start going over details. Do you have any questions now?"

"I would like to make one request, if I may?"

"What would that be?"

"If you don't mind, I would like to discuss that with you privately before everyone leaves."

He agrees, and we step to the side out of hearing range of the others.

"If your command structure does not have a problem with it, I would like to name my own second in command."

"We don't have a problem with that if it is reasonable, and we agree with your choice. Do you have someone in mind?"

I look at Kleg and say, "I would like to appoint Kleg as my second in command, if you agree, and he accepts."

"Give me a second."

He pulls the other officers in the room together, minus Kleg, and discusses it with them, and then comes back to me and says, "We agree with your decision, if he accepts."

I now pull Kleg off to the side and say, "I have spoken with the admiral, and he has spoken with the other officers. They have all agreed with my request to ask you to be my second in command, if you accept."

Kleg looks at the officers in the room. They give him a nod, and then he turns to me and says, "Yes sir, I accept."

"Good, then it is settled. We will start meeting in the morning. I will see you here in this room at 0800 hours."

We go back over to the table and sit.

The admiral says, "With the need that we have, and with what Kleg has told us of your requests, we started that ball rolling a couple of weeks back. You can tell your Admiral Stark that these things are on their way to them. You can have Kleg provide them with the details of when things will be arriving and what the expectations are for transferring over the new ships."

"Thank you sir I appreciate it, and earth appreciates it."

"I think we have discussed all we need for the day. Gentlemen, until 0800 tomorrow morning, earth time."

Everyone in the room now snaps to attention, and then relaxes. Everyone is now coming over to Kleg and myself to congratulate us on our new positions and wishing us well. Everyone starts leaving, and I now can go over to Kleg. We look at each other, give each other a man hug, and we both break out in laughter.

"You old dog you. You knew about this all the time, and kept it from me. I bet you enjoyed watching me squirm through all of those diplomatic meetings."

He is still smiling, and says, "I did enjoy it, but I was under orders to keep everything to myself until we had this meeting."

"That's okay, I got even with you, I made you my second. I get to order you around now."

"I want to thank you again for making me your second. I am looking forward to this new challenge. I hope we will remain friends through all of this?"

"Kleg, we have been friends for quite some time now. I don't expect anything to get in the way of that. While I am thinking about it, I need to speak with the admiral, if you will excuse me for a little bit."

I go over to the admiral that I had been speaking with, and ask if I might have a couple more minutes of his time.

"Sure, what can I do for you?"

"Sir, I don't know the procedure here but in making Kleg my second in command, I would also like to promote him to vice-admiral. Do you know if that will be a problem?"

"Generally, we have a more drawn out process but under these circumstances I don't see that the command will have a problem with this."

"Thank you sir. If I may, I would like to tell him tomorrow morning at the start of the meeting."

"That shouldn't be a problem. I will get the paperwork done and approved."

"I would also like to ask Harold to get me a set of vice-admiral insignias that I can present to him at that time."

"Go ahead, I will authorize that."

"Thanks admiral. See you in the morning?"

"Of course, see you then."

We wrap up our time of discussing and congratulating, and then Kleg and I head for our quarters. I enter my quarters and am greeted by Harold. He congratulates me on my new position, and tells me that he will have all my new uniforms ready for me later that afternoon.

"Harold, I haven't said this often enough, but I want to thank you for all the years of service that you have provided me. You have done it selflessly, and I haven't taken the time to express my appreciation.

Harold, thank you for your service to me."

"No sir, thank you. I wouldn't have it any other way. You have treated me better that any other person I have served. The greatest honor a steward can have is to serve an admiral, and I have had the greatest honor of all, and that has been to be your steward.

Now, if you don't mind sir, I need to get you your uniforms."

"Harold, as a surprise for Kleg, I am promoting him to vice-admiral tomorrow. He will also need the appropriate uniform to wear. When you pick up my uniforms, will you also pick up a uniform for Kleg. But don't tell him about it nor present it to him.

Oh, also, get me a set of vice-admiral insignias that I can present to him in the morning. It's a surprise."

Harold smiles and then leaves the room, and now I feel I need to make a call to Stan. I go over to sit at my desk. I bring up my pop-up display and get Stan on the line.

I now see Stan on my display and say, "Stan, it is good to see you."

"And you too, sir."

"Stan, as you know, I have been in some diplomatic meetings for the past couple of weeks, and I'm glad to say, they are over. Now, don't you tell anyone I said that. Diplomatic work is for the birds.

Today I had the best meeting of all. I met with one of their admirals and several other high-ranking officers, and things are changing around here."

I went through all the discussions we had, except for how the battle with the Morians was going. I thought I would save that for another time.

I say, "Now I have some good news for you. Are you ready for this?"

"Okay, the suspense is killing me. Tell me."

"Metal plating for the ships is on the way, and you will receive enough for the next several years to meet all of your requirements. You will also receive additional plating for the new ships you will be receiving."

Stan surprisingly says, "New ships, we're getting new ships!"

"Yes, new ships. I will give you more details later, but Kleg will be working with you on the details of what you need to do to have them transferred over to you.

Now second, as to the crystals, you will have the necessary crystals to replace the ones that are going out, and you will receive enough to keep you in supply for your future needs.

Third, you are also receiving several exploration ships for the continued exploration of space out beyond our solar system.

And lastly, you can start addressing me as Admiral Graham again. Only this time I am a one star admiral in the Hyperthean command."

Stan let's out a yell, "Yahoo!!! Excuse me sir, yes sir, and congratulations, and thanks for all of the good news."

"Along with me taking on this new position, Kleg will be my second in this new assignment. You are still in charge of the fleet there, but I will be coming to you soon for some help.

Tomorrow morning at 0800, I will be meeting with other Hyperthean officers to formulate my new command. You can make your announcement to the rest of your fleet, and to Earth, about the new position that I have taken here. Please have your publicity officer contact Kleg for the details to put in your announcement. He can also give you details on the ships, and supplies you will be receiving. You can announce this to the fleet.

I know you are as excited about this as I am, and hopefully, this can help in boosting the morale for the fleet. This should make them excited.

Stan, take credit here. You worked hard on all of this. This one is all yours."

"Thank you, sir, and congratulations on your new position. And anything you need, you just name it."

"You too. Now go, and celebrate your victory."

THIRTY-SIX

It is almost time to get ready for the meeting that will be starting at 0800. Harold has my new uniform laid out. The fit is excellent, like it was tailor made. I look at myself in the mirror, and I don't see anything out of place. I then go into the living quarters where Harold has my breakfast set for me. I eat my breakfast and notice a box lying on the table. I open the box and see that it is the vice-admiral insignias for Kleg. I close the box, and then place it in my pocket so that I won't forget it.

It is now 0800, and I go out into the foyer area. Everyone is there, and snaps to attention.

"At ease," and everyone then takes a seat.

"Admiral, if you please, I would like to say something first. I need to make a proper adjustment to my staff. As you know, Kleg is now my second in command. Kleg, if you would please, come over here."

Kleg leaves his seat, and comes over to me with a surprised look on his face. He is confused about what is about to happen.

"Gentlemen, I spoke with Admiral Tern yesterday after the meeting to make sure I wasn't doing anything out of order or illegal. I found out I wasn't, and he agreed with what I am about to do. Kleg, not only are you my second in command, you are promoted to vice-admiral."

I pull the box from my pocket, open it, and present it to him.

He thanks me, and starts to head back towards his seat.

"Just a minute, I'm not through with you yet. That uniform you are wearing is inappropriate for a vice admiral. I'm giving you ten minutes to go to your quarters to change into the proper uniform, put your new hardware on, and get back out here. Harold has the appropriate uniform for you in your quarters. Now go."

Everybody laughs as he heads across the hall to his room to change.

Admiral Tern says, "Gentlemen, to give Vice Admiral Kleg the time to change and for you to congratulate him, We'll take a fifteen-minute break to refresh our drinks, and wait on him before we get down to business."

Kleg comes out of his room grinning from ear-to-ear, and I yell out, "Attention on deck, new admiral in the room."

Everyone snaps to attention, and salutes.

Kleg says, "At ease, and thank you."

Everyone grins at him, and then we all go over to him and congratulate him on his promotion. After all the congratulations are done, Admiral Tern has everyone take their seats so that we can get down to business.

"Let me introduce everyone to you Admiral Graham, since they are all new faces. It will probably take you some time before you get their names down. I would like to introduce you to your staff. I will let you know their purpose and why they are part of this meeting.

Let's start to your right. This is Counselor Centas, she is from the planet Ammolos. Her race has the ability of discernment and can advise you on anything you would like to discuss with her. Next to her is Commander Areg publicity, Captain Dreg security, Captain Sprot strategy, and Captain Vog Command

Center. These are the people who will be making up your staff from our galaxies. As for me, I am your commanding officer."

I look at my team around the table, and say," I will get to know you as time goes on. I received from Admiral Tern your personnel files last night, and I have reviewed each of them. Later this week, I will meet with each of you individually. We will get to know each other better, and you can tell me what is not in your personnel files."

Admiral Tern starts this part of the meeting by telling us where the twelve stations are located. They are all in various stages of completion, and six of them are ready to be manned. The other six are about ninety percent complete and should be ready in about three months. Each station will need someone to be in command of them, along with the proper personnel to man them. You will need about three-thousand personnel for each station. We expect to have two hundred scout ships on each station and three squadrons of fighters to protect them. All stations will have weaponry. Since these stations will also have a separate bay for transport ships, they will also have separate docking bays for the fighters and scout ships.

We have been making some improvements on your trans-portal weapon and have reduced the size of the power supply for the beam. We have added it to our scout ships, but the weapon is only strong enough to do a section of a ship. We will be providing this new technology to the earth fleet, so they can make modifications to their scout ships too.

We are now turning to you, and this team, to better improve our search areas and help keep us one step ahead of the Morians.

I pause for a second, and then ask, "How many scout ships do we have for the stations now?"

There is a moment of silence, as I wait for someone to answer my question, and finally Admiral Tern answers, "Currently we have about two hundred and fifty scout ships and crews."

"When will the rest of the scouts be ready to deploy to the stations?"

"We have been waiting for you to take command, you and your staff will need to decide how you want to deploy them. We have twenty-three hundred scouts on order. They should be ready over the next six months. We expect the earth fleet to supply twelve-hundred of the crews for these ships. They will man the stations that are closest to your solar system. The other stations are too far out for your crews to be away from Earth and families.

The fighter squadrons will have the same setup. Each squadron will have a thousand fighters. Again, the stations closest to your solar system need to have fighter crews provided by earth, and the same with the personnel for the stations. But because of our galaxies people life spans, they can be intermixed with your crews, without any problems."

I sit back in my chair for a couple of minutes with one arm crossed across my body, and the other with my hand on my chin thinking.

I then say, "Admiral, where will I be, or can I set up my own command center?"

"That is your choice. Where would you like to set it up?"

I pause for a second, and then reply, "The selfish side of me would like to set it up on the station that will be closest to my solar system, but that will probably not be feasible. I would like to study where all the stations are located, and see if we can come to a consensus on one that is strategically located and still allows me reasonable access to my solar system."

"Let me know what you all agree on. Now, I need to take my leave as I have other things to do. Keep in touch admiral."

We all stand up and snap to attention as the admiral leaves our meeting.

It is now my time to take charge. I motion for everyone to be seated again and start by asking some questions.

"Lady and gentlemen, we don't know each other that well,

and I plan on getting to know all of you better. We have a large task before us, and we have a million things to accomplish to get things up and running. I don't know how many of you knew of this assignment before we gathered in this room, or how many of you might have a problem with reporting to an earthling. So first off, I am going around the room, and ask each of you to answer me honestly. There will be no hard feelings if you would like to take another assignment. I don't want just a yes or no answer. I want you to speak honestly about how you feel about your assignment.

Counselor Centas, I would like to start with you, please."

Counselor Centas pauses for a second and then says, "I didn't know about this assignment when I was asked to come here, but I do feel it will be quite a challenge for me. I have never worked with, or seen, an earthling before I met you, so understanding your reactions and emotions will be something new for me. I do look forward to working with you and this team, and no, I do not have a problem working for you."

"Thank you Counselor Centas.

Commander Areg, how about you?"

"I agree with Counselor Centas. I did not know why I was called to this meeting, other than the admiral had a new assignment for me. Working on a new area within the military command is exciting for me. I will be the first publicity officer to learn about deep space stations, as we set up this new area of responsibility. I will learn as we go, what I can share and what I can't, and will clear everything that I release through you and vice-admiral Kleg. And I do not have a problem reporting to you."

"Thank you Commander Areg.

Captain Dreg?"

"I have heard of rumors that these stations were being built throughout many locations, but I had no idea that I would be asked here to be part of this team. My current responsibility is security. I assume that will be my responsibility here. Sir, I am honored to serve in whatever capacity you would like, and I do not have a problem reporting to you."

"Thank you Captain Dreg.

Captain Sprot, how about you?"

Captain Sprot looks at me, hesitates for a second, and then says, "I am a little surprised that I have been asked here by the admiral and have been asked to serve as part of your command. As you will soon find out, if you haven't already, I can at times get a little argumentative and will stretch my authority some. If I don't agree with your decisions, I will let you know but I will follow your command to the letter. I have heard of your reputation, but I really don't know you all that well. For now, I will accept being part of your command."

"Captain Sprot, I appreciate you being candid with me. Let me make this perfectly clear to all of you, I do not want yes men and women reporting to me. If you do not agree with what I say, or with what anyone else says in our meetings, I expect, no demand, that you speak up. But I also expect you to respect those opinions. These opinions will only be spoken of in our closed meetings, and that all of you will agree with the final decision, and will follow it to the letter. AND, you will not speak of these disagreements outside of our meetings. Any disagreement with that?"

I get a "no sir" from everyone in the room.

"Thank you Captain Sprot.

Captain Vog."

"Sir, I along with everyone else in the room did not know why I was called to this meeting. I am honored, and humbled, to be here and to take on this great responsibility that is being presented to us. And no, I have no problem reporting to you."

"Thank you Captain Vog."

And now I turn to Kleg, and say, "Vice-Admiral Kleg how about you?"

Kleg looks at me surprised, and then says, "Sir, the admiral did speak to me about why we were having this meeting and why all the rest of your team were asked to be here today. Each of you, except for me, was hand selected by the admiral to be part of this team. He felt all of you were the best to make this command a success and were the right ones to bring this to fruition. Yes, I did know that Admiral Tern would be asking Admiral Graham to take command of these stations. I was not expecting Admiral Graham to ask me to be his second, but I am honored. And I would, and will, follow him wherever he leads us without hesitation."

I look at Kleg and say, "Thank you, my friend.

Now that we have this settled, we need to get down to business. I want to say something to each of you, and then give you an assignment.

Counselor Centas, you are the counselor for this group. But if you see, or feel, anything that you think needs to be reported, please come to me right away.

Commander Areg, you are our publicity officer. Currently we do not have anything to report to the military, or to the public, since we do not know what we want to classify.

Captain Dreg, you will be the head of security for all our stations. Your assignment for tomorrow is to give us twelve names to head your security teams on each of the stations. You may want to leave three names open, because we will probably fill them from earth personnel. Also, I would like you to provide us with how you would like to set up security for all the stations. We also need to know how you would like to set up command center security to protect the information that will be provided to us by the scouts.

Captain Sprot, you will be the head of the strategy team. Your assignment for tomorrow is to provide us with a report on how you would like to set up your strategy teams. We will build upon the process from that base.

Captain Vog, you will oversee the command centers. I want you to lay out a main command center that all stations will report to, but I also want you to lay out how you would like each of the command centers to look.

Admiral Kleg, I have a special assignment for you. I want you to get us out of these diplomatic quarters and surroundings. They make me uncomfortable. Get us set up in our own meeting areas on base where we can work with some security around us. Get quarters for all of us, if you don't already have one. Then make sure you get us two extra quarters."

Kleg has this strange look on his face, and then says, "Two extra sir?"

"Yes, two extra. Harold, and your own steward."

"My own steward sir?"

"Yes, you are an admiral now, and admirals have their own stewards. So, I expect you to fill your position properly. If you need to, work with Harold on it."

Kleg smiles and says, "Yes sir, my own steward. Anything else sir."

"I would like for all of us to be in our new surroundings by 1500. You think we can get this accomplished?"

"Yes sir. I will have your vessel pick you up about 1400. Anything else sir?"

"No, and thanks Kleg. Congratulations on your promotion.

I think this is enough for the day. Each of you have your assignments. Admiral Kleg will let you know where your new quarters are located, and where we will be meeting tomorrow morning at 0800. Thank you, and you are dismissed."

They all stand to attention, and start talking among themselves as they leave the assembly area.

I see Kleg grinning, and mumbling something to himself about having his own steward.

THIRTY-SEVEN

Kleg has done everything he said he would do. We are now on the military base, and we are in our own quarters.

It is now 0800, my next morning, and I meet up with Kleg. We head over to the meeting room reserved for us, and meet up with the rest of the staff. As I walk into the room, they all snap to attention, and I tell them to relax and be seated.

"Lady and gentlemen, I know you had a busy day yesterday, at least my yesterday, moving into new quarters and completing the assignment. I appreciate that you could accomplish this task so quickly and get your assignments done. First off, let me say good morning to all of you. Do you have any questions before we get started?"

They probably feel strange having me say good morning, but it is my twenty-four-hour cycle. However, it is still all part of their same day. While I slept, they were probably going about a daily routine.

I look around the room, but there does not seem to be any questions.

I say, "Counselor Centas and Commander Areg, I know I didn't give either of you an assignment. But I would like for the two of you to be taking notes, even though we are recording these sessions. I would appreciate you doing this for me, jotting down anything you feel the recordings might miss."

"Yes sir."

"Ok, Captain Dreg, let's start with you. Your assignment was to give us twelve names that you want to head your security teams on each of the stations. You were to leave three names open, because we will probably fill them from earth personnel. You were also to provide us with how you would like to set up security for all the stations. You were also going to provide us with information on how you would set up security for the command center. Are you ready to present your assessment?"

"Yes sir, I am. I have reviewed in more detail, where the twelve stations are located, and I have come up with nine names I would like to present to the team for approval. I am sending them now to each of your tablets. As you have requested, I have left three of the slots open to be provided by your earth command. On security for all the stations, I don't have anything for us yet. I have requested a layout of a station so that I can study it in detail. I will give the team the information when I have the layout and have studied it. Also, I assume you would like to use one of the stations as our command center. That is all I have for now sir."

"Thank you, Captain Dreg. This has been a good report. Before we vote on these nine names, I would like for all of us to review the personnel files of all these recommendations and for each of you to give me your opinions. Admiral Kleg, if you will get the personnel files for each of these individuals and get them to all of us. We can review them later today. I would appreciate it."

"Yes sir."

"I like your thoroughness in your plan to study the details of a station before you present to us how you will provide the security for each of the stations. And I would like to use one of the stations as our command station. Hopefully, we might be able to decide which one that will be today. Anybody have any questions for Captain Dreg?"

Again, there is silence.

"OK then, let's continue.

Captain Sprot your assignment was to provide us with a report on how you would like to set up your strategy team."

"Our strategy team will only be based in our main command center. I would like to set up our patrol areas for the scouts in sectors like your earth patrols. I don't plan on having any overlapping patrols into a sector. Each station would have a set of sectors to cover. They will border up to a sector from another station, that way all areas of space are covered. All scouts will provide their information back to us, and we will disseminate it. Then we will provide the relevant information to each station, and high command. I already know where each of the stations are, and I have started laying out a breakdown of the sectors. I should have it ready for review by the team in the next couple of earth days."

"I like your thoughts on this. Does anyone have any questions on this plan?"

Captain Vog speaks up and says, "Yes sir, if I may?"

"Go ahead."

"How do you plan to know what will be relevant information to each of the stations?"

"At first that will be a trial and error process. As we gather more information, we can build our scenarios based on the information that we get. We don't want to flood them with irrelevant information and have them start ignoring it because most of the information is useless."

Captain Vog accepts this statement, and no one else has any questions.

"Thank you both for your comments. Captain Vog, your assignment was to define our main command center, that all the stations will report to. I also wanted you to define what you would like each of the command centers to look like for each of the stations."

"The main command center will be a strategic part of our total operation. For the main command center, I would like for it to be separate from the station command center. I would like for the strategy area to be part of the main command center. I believe this to be very important so that we can work closely together, but also separately, so that each of us can do our jobs. All command centers should be highly secure. I believe the information we gather is highly sensitive. Each of the scout ships should have a new communication band that is ultra-sensitive and that only the main command center can receive. As Captain Sprot has said, we should only share with the other command centers the vetted information that we send to them, over a different secure communication band. The station command centers will have the responsibility of monitoring their own sectors and sending out scout ships to their assigned patrol sectors. Only the main command center will have a strategy team, which may change as Captain Sprot deems necessary."

"Very good job Captain Vog. Captain Sprot, do you agree with Captain Vog?"

"I like Captain Vogs plan to have the strategy team in with the command center, and initially to have only one strategy team. As we get more into our process we may see the need to have a backup station trained to take over in the probability that we are destroyed or badly damaged."

Everyone else in the room speaks up, and agrees with Captain Vogs' plan and agrees with Captain Sprots' comments.

"Good, we have heard how everyone would like to set up their own areas. Does anyone have a problem with how each section will be ran?"

No one in the room has anything to add, and then I add, "Good, gentlemen start your processes, but I would like to add a couple of things to the process based on what each of you has said. Our area of responsibility is very important to our entire federation. The information that we receive must be handled with the utmost secrecy. With that said, Captain Dreg, I want you to set a new level of security and for it to be higher than top secret. I want complete security checks to be ran more deeply on all of us, starting with me, then on this team. Then do your team that will be protecting our command centers, everyone that will be assigned to command centers, station commanders that will have access to each command center, and all outside personnel that we allow into our command centers, including admirals. By the time we get to whichever station we choose as the main command center, I would like for most of this to be done. If you need extra security personnel to get this done, get them.

I will contact Admiral Stark and let him know of our plan. I will have him give us three names to be in command of a station, command centers, and to oversee security. Oh, I also mean for you to vet all the necessary earth personnel that will be on the stations. That includes admirals from earth.

I want everyone to consider which station we would use as our main base of operation, considering my needs. We will discuss that later for my consideration.

Let's take a break, it is near my lunch time and I am hungry. If I remember correctly, it is near your mealtime also. We will get together at 1400 to discuss our next topics."

At 1400, we are sitting around the table chatting, getting to know each other better, and getting whatever drinks we like, and then I call the meeting to order.

"We need to think about some other things now. Not only are we in charge of collecting data from the scouts that are on patrol, but we are also in charge of getting these twelve deep space stations ready to be manned and functional. From what I understand, it will take about three thousand personnel to man each station and to keep them functioning. We will have three squadrons of fighters for each station, which means we will have three thousand fighters per station. Then we have the scouts, which we will have two hundred per station. So, on top of the station personnel, we have the fighter crews and the scout crews. This means each station will house twelve thousand personnel. So, that means we must come up with one hundred and forty-four thousand personnel. A monumental task is in front of us. As I look at it, it is not our responsibility to pick these personnel, but I do want us to pick the twelve commanders who will command each of these stations.

You have nine names in front of you. I would like for each of you to start going through them one at a time, and vote with a yes or no as to whether you think they are the right person for the job. I am going to step out for a moment and contact Admiral Stark. I'll let him in on our plans, and tell him I would like three names that he thinks are qualified to take charge of one of our stations."

I leave the room and find an empty meeting room, go in, and shut the door. I bring up my pop-up display and ask for a secure line. I now have Stan on the line, explain to him the situation, and that I need three names from him that he thinks would be good to command three of our stations. I tell Stan I would like the names in the next three hours because we need to get moving on this.

I return to the meeting, and they are still talking about the first name. I think this is going to take some time. I sit beside Kleg, lean over, and speak into his ear, "How is it going? Are we making any progress?"

Kleg leans over, and says, "I think things are going well. They are having a good discussion about the first name on the list, and I believe we will have a decision soon. No big disagreements, from what I am hearing."

It takes another thirty minutes, and they are ready to cast their votes.

"Before we vote, I would like to hear your consensus on this first name."

Captain Sprot speaks up and says, "I believe that I can speak for all of us when I say that Captain Heslig will be an excellent choice. Three of us know him personally, and his record speaks for itself. We had one concern but after discussing it, we agreed that this will not be an issue with him taking this command."

All the rest of them nod their heads in agreement.

"Then all of you agree that Captain Heslig is our first choice to assume one of these stations. On your tablets is Captain Heslig's name with a 'Yes' and a 'No'. Please cast your vote now."

I see all the votes, and I show it to Kleg, and tell them that the vote was unanimous.

"Now let's go on to the next name."

We go through the same process for the eight other names, and it takes us just over four and a half hours to vet all the names. The vote is unanimous. About three hours into the process I get a message from Stan, and he has presented three names for us to consider. I lean over to Kleg and show him the message, and say, "Will you get someone to pull their personnel files so that we can vet these three at the end of these names."

Kleg takes the names and sends them off to someone to pull their files and asks that they get them back to him within the hour.

The names that Stan has presented to us are Captain James Graham, Captain Curtis Johnson, and Captain Nathan Taylor. I know two of them well, and the other by reputation only. I don't see that we will have a problem with passing all of them.

About an hour and a half later we finish the process, and Kleg has just received the files on the three new names.

"Gentlemen, we have been at this for just about five hours now, and I think we need a break. I know I do. We have received the three names from Admiral Stark, and Admiral Kleg has just received their personnel files. I would like to finish up this process today, and then we will take a break until tomorrow. Let's take a twenty-minute break, and then get back together."

I start off the discussion on these three names by saying,

"You have before you the personnel records for these three officers. I know two of them personally and professionally. Captain Graham has the same last name as mine but we are not related, so there is no favoritism shown here. As for his record, it will show he has a good command of leadership and organization. With the startup of a new station, I believe his organizational, administrative, and leadership skills will be a great asset to us.

Captain Johnson I also know personally and professionally. He has the same qualities as Captain Graham. Captain Johnson also has the quality to jump in and work on problems. He has no problem with getting his hands dirty by helping his people when the need arises.

As for Captain Taylor, I only know him professionally. I have never met him, but I have heard of him. His record will show that he commanded the battle cruiser *Berlin,* during the battle with the Morians when we fought them on the border of our solar system. He served gallantly there, and his record will speak for itself.

I will let you review their service records, discuss them, and then you can vote on each of them individually. As before, neither Admiral Kleg nor myself will vote in this process."

They begin their process of review, one at a time, and discussing each one individually. It takes them about two and a half hours to come to their conclusions. I ask them to give me a vote on each of them. They pick up their tablets and start voting. I wait a few anxious seconds, and see the votes start to come in. I breathe a sigh of relief; the vote is unanimous on all three.

"Thank you all for your time today. You have worked hard, and I appreciate the time you have put in today. I need to report in to Admiral Tern now and let him know of our selections of whom we would like to command our stations. We will give him time to consider the choices and to make sure that he agrees with them. When he does, I will ask him to contact each of their commands and tell the captains that they are being transferred to our command. That is all we want them to know for now.

Until tomorrow at 0800. You all have a great evening, and enjoy it."

They all leave the room except for Kleg, and I ask Counselor Centas to stay for a few minutes. I sit back in my chair for a few seconds and then ask Counselor Centas, "Well, how do you feel about the meeting today? Did you see, or feel, anything that we need to be aware of?"

The counselor waits a few seconds before answering, gathering her thoughts, and then says, "Overall I believe everything went well. During the discussions, Captain Dreg went deeper in his questions, but I believe it was good for the team. It made them think more deeply about the candidates. In the end, I believe it made them feel better about the decisions they made. I felt they were bonding more and becoming a closer team. I believe the two of you did well in building their confidence and your faith in them by letting them have the final decisions not countermanding the decision they had made. Tomorrow I would suggest that the two of you become a little more involved in the discussions and process, but continue to make your decisions as a team. I know the two of you have the final say in all of this, but I also see that you are trusting your team."

"Thank you counselor for those insights. We will take them to heart. If you will excuse us, I would like a few minutes with Admiral Kleg."

The counselor gets up and leaves the room, closing the door behind her. I look at Kleg and say, "Now to your thoughts. How did you feel things went? You know your people better than I do. Do you feel things are going in the direction they should be going?"

"I agree with everything that Counselor Centas said to us. As a culture, we are a little different than you and your race.

You are more demanding of us in that you expect us to be part of the decision-making process. We have societal norms where certain types of people are taught to be the ones to take charge of the situation. I believe you call them type "A" personalities. These are the ones who command our fleets. I think the way your race is put together is why you were so successful in defeating the Morians and decisively when you fought them. You can take all your qualities and have them blended together as a team so that everyone can do the right thing when the situation dictates. We are learning from your race how to blend ourselves together, but it is difficult for us. We appreciate your people, and I appreciate you especially."

"Thanks Kleg, you humble me by your comments. I hope I don't let you or your people down. Would you like to join me for dinner and some drinks?"

"I will join you for some drinks, but it is not my meal time yet."

"That sounds good. Where can we go?"

"I know just the place. I believe you will enjoy the meal, the atmosphere, and we can talk into the evening."

"That sounds good, but let me make a call to Admiral Tern and report into him what we discussed today, what we need from him, and then we can go. I don't want to worry about making this call later. You can stay as I make the call."

I place the call to Admiral Tern, and report our minutes for the day, and let him know of the twelve choices we have made for command leadership over the stations. He said he will review each one of them, but does not see any problem with the choices now. He will let me know by tomorrow morning if we can proceed.

With that done, Kleg and I head off for the evening to enjoy my meal and drinks together. We go late into the evening at the restaurant that he has chosen, just sitting around and talking.

By 0730 the next morning I receive a message from Admiral Tern that he has signed off on all our choices. He will have each of the nine commands contacted, and let these choices know they have new orders and that they are to report to me in two weeks. For the three from earth, he said he would let me contact Admiral Stark and let him tell each of their commands that these three men have new orders.

I send a reply to Admiral Tern telling him that I appreciate his quick response in getting this done, and I will contact Admiral Stark and let him know.

I contact Admiral Stark on a secure line, and say, "Hello Stan, how are you today?"

"This is a surprise, two calls from you in two days. Do you have something for me?"

"Yes I do. We have vetted the three names that you provided us, and the team has approved them. I then presented them to Admiral Tern, and I just got a message that he has also approved them. Now I need you to contact each of their commands that they have new orders and that they are to report to you on the *Hyperthia* in two weeks."

"That sounds good. I will do that right away."

"Stan, I want you to set up a secure area for five people to meet. If you want to use your meeting area, that is fine with me. It will be the three of them, you, and Admiral Fuentes. We will be having a lot of meetings to get things rolling, and we don't have time for all of you to come to us. These meetings are highly classified, so when you meet with them, they are not to discuss anything other than with the five of you.

On another note, what do you have going on today?"

"I understand, and I will make sure they understand it too. As for today, I have my morning briefing in thirty minutes, but you are lucky in that I am pretty well open the rest of the day."

"Good, what about Admiral Fuentes?"

"He will be in the staff meeting with me, and he has a couple of other things to do, but I can have him reschedule them if you would like."

"Yes, I would appreciate that. I will send you a coded

message about 0900 on how to join us. Make sure you have a secure location where the two of you can meet with us. As soon as your staff meeting is over and you get my message, please join us."

"Yes sir, I look forward to being there."

It is time for me to go to our meeting. I get there and everyone is in the room, and everyone snaps to attention. I motion for them to sit, and then say, "I hope all of you had a pleasant evening. I know I did. I also want to let you know how much I appreciate all the hard work you put in yesterday. We have another day of hard work ahead of us.

At 0730 this morning I received a message from Admiral Tern that he has approved all the names that was presented to him."

Everyone cheers, claps their hands, and have big grins on their faces.

"He has contacted their commands to let them know they have new assignments and will be reporting to us in two weeks. I have also contacted Admiral Stark that the names he submitted were approved, and they will be reporting to him on board the *Hyperthia* in two weeks. They will be joining us via video when they start their assignment on the *Hyperthia*. I have also asked Admiral Stark and Admiral Fuentes to join us this morning when they finish their morning briefings. As part of the earth command structure, they need to be aware of what is going on, but as I told Admiral Stark everything that they hear is confidential. Whatever we need the earth command to do, they will make sure that it gets done. Any questions on this?"

There are no questions.

I have transmitted the coded message to Stan early, and I am surprised to see both Admiral Stark and Admiral Fuentes on the screen, and say, "Welcome. You are here earlier than I expected, but we are glad you have joined us. Let me introduce you to the team. Everyone, on your left is Admiral Stan Stark, senior admiral in charge of the earth fleet, and the other is

Admiral George Fuentes, his second in command. Stan and George, let me introduce you to the team here. Starting on my right and going around the table is Admiral Kleg, my second in command, Counselor Centas, in charge of our wellbeing and sound minds, Commander Areg, publicity, Captain Dreg, security, Captain Sprot, Strategy, and then Captain Vog who oversees the command centers. For the two of you, I have told the room about the approved selection of the station commanders and when they are to report to us. I have also explained to them that you need to be a part of this team moving forward.

Everyone, we have our command leadership chosen for each of the stations, and we will turn to them to start getting the crews they need for the stations they will command. We now have four things we need to discuss today, no five, fighters, fighter crews, scouts, scout crews and the command center personnel for each of the stations. I just thought of a sixth, our own main command center.

For the fighters, we will need thirty-six squadrons of fighters which means we need three squadrons of fighters per station. That means we will have three thousand fighters on each station, and we will need crews for each of those squadrons. That means three thousand pilots, but also crews to maintain the fighters. Next, we need two hundred scouts per station, and there are fifteen crew members per scout. We must have bunking on the stations for up to three thousand scout personnel. That means each station must be large enough to handle sixteen thousand personnel, not including visitors, and crews for temporary housing of cargo ships that will come to each station.

Now, I don't see it is the responsibility of the station commanders to fill all these positions. For each of the stations, we will need at least twelve air bosses for the three squadrons of fighters. That will be four air bosses per squadron. With a thousand fighters per squadron that is a lot of air traffic for two air bosses to handle. I believe they need to report to the station commanders, but I also believe these air bosses should select the crews to man these fighters, and the crews to maintain them.

That is a lot to absorb, so I will give you a minute to think on it and give me your comments."

I sit back in my chair now. All are talking back and forth and then the room goes silent.

"Okay, it's your turn to talk. Give me your thoughts."

Admiral Stark is the first one to speak up and says, "That's a lot of fighters and personnel. I don't mean to sound like we can't do it, but how many fighters and crews are we going to have to supply?"

"Stan, that is a good question. You know that you have supplied me with three commanders for three of the stations. Not all these stations are going to be filled with personnel from earth, for now. Earth is only a small population compared to the rest of the federation. But with that said, Earth needs to do their part. Our plan is that the three stations that Earth will be manning will be those closest to your solar system. We plan on choosing one of these stations for our main command center. As Admiral Tern agreed, when I accepted this position, it was so that I could at least get back home occasionally. There are some of the earth crews that might not mind being away from home for five years, and we can station them on some of the stations that are further away from our solar system, and there are some personnel from the federation that might not mind serving on one of your three stations. My staff might enjoy having the company of their species. Now, to answer your question. Three stations will need nine thousand fighters and pilots plus crews to maintain them. How we are going to come up with one hundred and eight thousand fighters remains to be discussed."

Stan sits back in his chair and is silent.

I now say, "Any other questions or comments?"

Everyone is silent, almost afraid to speak basically seeing I just put down my own admiral.

"Okay, let's put on our list that we need to select one hundred and forty-four air bosses today, or at least get started on it.

Next let's talk about the scouts for a second. As I stated we need two hundred scouts per station and six thousand crew members to man these scouts. Since we don't know how many sectors each of the stations will need to patrol, we don't know how many scouts will need to be out at one time. Once we know how many ships and crews will be out at one time, we can reduce the number of berthing requirements. I also see that we will need one air boss for the scouts as they deploy and come back. These air bosses will also report to the commanders of each station, but I believe these air bosses should be the ones to select the crews for each station. Again Stan, that means you will need to come up with three air bosses for the scouts.

Any questions or comments?"

This time no one has anything to say, so I continue saying, "Let's add twelve more air bosses to the list for scouts.

The last thing we need to consider is how we need to man our command centers. I am going to leave that for Captain Vog to define for us.

Now that I have bogged us down with enough work to last for a year, we only have one week to accomplish the task. How do we want to get started?

Since all the stations are not ready, we don't have to address all of them at one time. Don't let the way I spoke with Stan scare you off. I have known Stan and George for a long time, and they know how I feel about them. They are not scared to voice their opinions and concerns to me, and I don't want you to either. We are here to work a solution, and as the saying goes, 'I am not the only brain in the room. So, let me hear what you have to say."

Captain Sprot is the first to speak up, and says, "I think we need to approach it one step at a time. We have the commanders for each of the stations. First, I think we need to look at each station and determine how complete they really are. They tell us that six are ready now, and six are ninety-percent complete. Let's start with the six they say are ready and really determine if they are fully functional now."

Kleg says, "I agree with Captain Sprot. We all know that builders tell us things are done, but we will find many things that don't work or there is work that was not finished."

I say, "I think this is a good start. Are we all in agreement?"

Everybody nods in agreement.

"To make things easier for all of us I think we need to name all of the stations. To keep things simple, rather than coming up with names for each one, I think we should number each one. Like Deep Space Station One (DSS-1) through Deep Space Station twelve (DSS-12). Anybody have a problem with this?"

They all seem to like this idea.

Admiral Fuentes says, "Instead of us naming all twelve stations now, why don't we review each of the stations. Once we determine which ones are close to being occupied, why don't we start with Deep Space Station One on down to the least ready being Deep Space Station Twelve?"

Everyone agrees with this suggestion, and we agree this will be the naming process.

I say, "Is there any way we can bring up a hologram of where the twelve stations are located out there in space?"

Commander Areg says, "Give me fifteen minutes, and I will get a holographic system set up in here."

"Good, let's take a fifteen-minute break while Commander Areg gets this set up."

While everyone is taking time for a break, I notice that Stan and George are still sitting there, and I walk over to the screen.

I say, "Stan, George, I hope I did not offend you in any way by what I said to you."

Stan looks at George, and then says, "I know you didn't offend me, and I feel you didn't offend George either.

George shakes his head no in confirmation.

"I appreciate what you said because it helped me better understand what the situation is."

"Thanks to both of you. If we have time later today I have more information I would like to share with both of you."

Commander Areg comes in shortly with a technician, and he begins to set up the equipment so that we can get a holographic projection in the middle of the conference table. Shortly he has it set up and functional, and we are ready to continue our meeting. The technician leaves the room, and we secure it again so that we can continue our discussion.

Captain Vog takes control of the holographic equipment and brings up the area of space where the twelve stations are located. We start looking at twelve globes, and Captain Vog points to the six stations that are said to be complete. Two of them are within Admiral Starks area of responsibility.

I think about what I see for a couple of seconds, and then say, "Do we know who the inspectors are on these six stations? I would like to hear them tell us what the state of readiness is of these stations."

Captain Dreg says, "I will find out, and I will have them appear before us tomorrow."

"Good. Let's move on to another subject. Fighters. We need one hundred and eight thousand fighters for all twelve stations. With only six stations supposedly ready now we need about fifty-four thousand fighters to start with. Stan, with two of these stations in your realm of responsibility, that means six thousand of the fifty-four thousand needs to come from the earth fleet. My question to all of you is where are we going to get this number of fighters? I don't see that we have this number of fighters just lying around waiting on someone to say they are needed."

Stan says, "I certainly don't have them. I am still trying to get twenty-six ships repaired from the two battles we were in, and we are waiting on twenty-seven new ships to arrive. I have crews we need to retrain for the new ships and new recruits coming in to replace the people that we lost. We lost about eight thousand fighters during the battles, and I still don't know how I am going to replace them.

I know that the Hyperthean Federation probably has their own problems replacing ships, fighters, and personnel, but from my perspective, they are better equipped to do that. Right now, we are heavily dependent on the Federation to supply us our needs."

"I see your point and feel your pain. Let me share something with all of you that I know you don't know. When I spoke with Admiral Tern about taking this position, he shared this with me. The Morians are becoming more hostile and aggressive with each passing day. Now the Federation is holding their own with them, but their fronts are starting to weaken. The Federation is trying to change some of their strategy to better improve their odds and hold the Morians off longer. One of their strategies was the establishment of these twelve stations. We are being placed here to defend this area of space to better monitor what is going on out there, and to report our information back to Federation headquarters. If the Morians can punch holes in the Federation defenses, it can provide the opening the Morians need to attack Earth. We could be left to defend it as best we can. So, with that said, it falls to us to pick up the ball and come up with plans on how we are going to get this done. I hate to say it this way, but we need to pull every string we can, scrounge where we can, politic beyond our capability, set up alliances to get what help we need, call in all the favors you have, and more. I don't know how to express the urgency of this any clearer."

I look around the room, and at Stan and George on the screen, and everyone has a stunned and shocked look on their faces. I give them a few more seconds to let what I said to sink in more deeply.

Captain Vog breaks the silence and says, "I will have for you tomorrow what we need for the main command center and what we need for the command centers on each of the stations."

Captain Sprot says, "I have lots of connections within the fleet, and I will work on getting as many fighters and scouts as I can."

Captain Dreg says, "I will get as many security personnel as we need to start getting the clearances that you asked for, and I will make sure they are deeply vetted, no shortcuts."

Commander Areg says, "As a publicity person I have many connections, not only in the fleet but in the council also. I will start pulling in favors and see what I can get for us."

Admiral Stark says, "You can count on us too. George and I will start reviewing the fleet and see what we can supply in the way of fighters, scouts and crews. We will also set up new classes for recruits so we can start pulling them in for the fleet and for the stations."

Admiral Kleg says, "I have some contacts I can make, and I assure you that I will have some results for you tomorrow."

I smile at them all, and thank them all for their commitment. Then I add, "We all have a lot of work to do before tomorrow morning. So, I will let you go for the day."

Everyone has left the room to go do their thing. Stan and George have signed off, and I am all by myself in the room. I go and close the door, and sit and stare at the holographic image that is before me. I see where the Hyperthean home worlds are, and I also see our solar system. A small dot off to the right. The stations are very small dots strategically located throughout the deep space sectors. Each station will be alone out there. Only fighters, missiles, and cannons to defend them, should the Morians attack one. No destroyers, cruisers, just the station and fighters. Not much of a defense for a Morian attack of any size. Help would be a long time coming, unless there happens to be some destroyer or cruiser in the area.

I take control of the holographic display, and zoom in where I can see the twelve stations more clearly. Still not much of a difference in size. They are now the size of a pea. I look at each one and see how they are strategically placed. Each one is about five thousand light years away from each other. Even with the speed of our ships, it will take us about three months to travel from one to another. It would take me three years to travel to each one once, and I don't see how I can be away from the main command center that long. I must share the travel responsibility with Kleg and Stan. I know the main command center will be on one of the three stations that will fall under Stan's jurisdiction. I will let Kleg travel to the stations that are closer to his home world so that he gets the opportunity to visit as often as he feels he needs. I will do the same for the rest of the staff, but I can't let them all be away at the same time.

I now zoom in further where I can only see a single station that is supposedly complete. It is a cylindrical object with oval domes coming out of the top and bottom of the sphere. The station is slowly spinning, which must be the way it provides the artificial gravity for the station. The sphere and domes are well lit, and I can see many windows on the station to allow crews to see out. I see many areas that look like landing and launch bays for fighters, scouts, and supply ships. The domes appear to be additional housing areas, recreational areas, or the station's office areas.

I stare at it a little while longer and then decide to shut it down. I secure it for the day and head towards my quarters.

Around 1800 it is time for me to give my report to Admiral Tern. I give him the update for the day, and he is pleased with the progress we are making. He sees that I am exhausted and tells me to sit back, relax, and try not to think about the day.

I contact Harold and tell him I would like to have my meal in my quarters this evening. He asks what I would like, and I tell him to surprise me. I shut my eyes, and just lean back on my couch trying to clear my thoughts from what we need to do. It is difficult, but I have almost dozed off when there is a knock at my door. I sit up and look at my monitor. It tells me that it is Harold. An hour must have passed since I told him I wanted my meal in my quarters, and I unsecure the door and tell him to come in.

Harold comes in the room with a tray of food in his hands. He sets it down on the table in the room, and lets me know he will be back in about an hour to get the tray. I thank him, and he leaves the room. I go over to the table and pull the covers off the plates of food. He has brought me my favorite meal of meat loaf, loaded scalloped potatoes, green beans, and then there is a dish of cherry pie. I doubt I could be more pleased. I start to eat, and it is taking my mind off the day as I enjoy my meal.

About an hour later there is a knock at my door, and it is Harold. He has come to pick up the empty tray. I smile at Harold and say, "You couldn't have picked a better meal for me this evening. I enjoyed it thoroughly. It took my mind off the day, and I appreciate it very much."

He smiles back at me, and says, "It was my pleasure sir. Is there anything else you need from me this evening?"

"No. You go and enjoy the rest of your evening, and I will see you in the morning."

"Thank you sir, and I will see you in the morning."

I sit back on the couch, bring up my display, and look through the messages I have received for the day. Most of them are not that important, and I give short responses to most of them. One of the messages I have received is from Stan. I open it up and start to read it.

It says, "Admiral, I want to thank you for including George and myself in the meeting today. It was an eye opener. George and I discussed it for about an hour after we signed off. Today we had a lot of the air taken out of our egos as we realized how dire the situation is for the Hypertheans, and how it can be for us. At first, we felt ashamed of ourselves, but realized we needed to get over it. We have a lot of work in front of us all.

With your permission, I would like to share some of the information with the other admirals in the fleet. George and I feel we don't want to share the weight of this burden by ourselves and get a lot of resistance from them when they don't understand the situation. As always, we will swear them to secrecy. With their support and understanding of the situation, we believe we will not receive any resistance. I believe they will want to help us in the task that is before us. Regards, Stan."

I think about it for a few minutes before I respond. I know that all the Hyperthean admirals know of the situation they are in and understand what the purpose of the twelve stations are for. I don't think we should hide this from the admirals and the marine general of the earth fleet. I have decided what my response will be, and I will inform the rest of the team of my decision in the morning.

I reply to Stan's message with the following, "Stan, I appreciate what you have shared. I agree with what you have requested. Please share what you feel is necessary with the admirals and the planet general. Let me know what their response is. I will tell the team in the morning that I agreed that you should share this with your staff.

Regards, Chris."

I close my display for the evening and decide to head off to bed.

At 0800 the next morning I walk into the conference room, and everyone is present except for Stan and George. I know they will be joining us about 0900 after their staff briefing. They are all discussing different things they have done to get things rolling. Some are joking at what they did to get the cooperation they needed to meet some of our needs. They realize I have entered the room, and they all come to attention. I tell them to be seated and to continue with their conversations. I say good morning to Kleg and the counselor, as they are the only ones that are not engaged in conversation. I look at both and ask, "How is it going?"

Counselor Centas says, "I think it is going well. Everyone is starting to get relaxed around each other, and the bond seems to be growing closer. We are becoming more of a tight knit group."

I smile and say, "That sounds great. I am glad to hear that."

I now turn to Kleg and ask, "How was your evening?"

"Just fine sir. Nothing spectacular. I spent most of the evening making contacts and seeing what I could accomplish. Since it was still part of my day cycle, it worked out good."

"That's good."

"Gentlemen, if we can, I would like to get started. We have a lot of work ahead of us today. I would like to start us off with my report from Admiral Tern.

I made him aware that we have now included Admirals Stark and Fuentes in our meetings and that I have shared with you the state of the situation our federation is in. I also let him know each of your reactions, and he was very pleased that all of you are stepping up. He also told me he will help us in every regard. If we run into any stumbling blocks, I am to let him know, and he will remove them. We have his full support."

About this time, Stan and George appear on our screen, and we greet both, and welcome them to our meeting.

"Now there is something else I would like to share with you. Last night I received a message from Stan asking that he and George not bear the entire weight of what they learned yesterday by themselves. He asked if he could share some of the information with his senior staff. He felt that, if they knew of the situation he would receive less resistance from them when he started pulling fighters, scouts, and personnel to man these stations. I agreed with him and told him he could tell them, with the understanding, that the information was highly sensitive.

Stan, were you able to share this information with your staff?"

"Yes sir. I did it this morning during my briefing with them. They were as shocked as we were when we first heard. After a few minutes of some discussion they are all on board and will work with George and myself to get you as much as we can pull together."

"Thank you both and thank your staff for all of us here.

Now, let's get to it."

The team starts giving their reports, and we continue doing this for the next week and a half. By the end of the second week, things are starting to come together. We know the status of all twelve of the stations and have named them appropriately. Stan has Deep Space Stations three (DSS-3), four (DSS-4), and seven (DSS-7). He has decided that Captain James Graham will have three, Captain Curtis Johnson four, and Captain Nathan Taylor seven.

We are also getting commitments from all commands for fighters, scouts, and personnel. The team has come up with a list of air bosses for each of the stations and are contacting their commands with instructions for them to report to us in one month. Stan and George have selected their air bosses and have them reporting to them in a month.

Captain Vog has laid out how he believes the main command center should be done and how the command centers for each of the stations should be laid out. He says, "The main command center will be large enough to handle a staff of at least three hundred, but he will start with a staff of fifty. The main command center will have its own data center, that is not connected to the rest of the station, for security reasons. I anticipate we will have around three hundred people working in there within six months. Also, this center will have a communication center that will be receiving all the information from the scout ships. We will be mapping their locations within our center. I want the center and our scout ships to have a new communication band that only we will be receiving and sending on."

We are all encouraged by the progress. Next week we start meeting with the commanders of each of the stations and sharing with them their assignments.

THIRTY-EIGHT

It is Monday morning, and it is still confusing to the Hypertheans that I am running things by earth time. Nine of the twelve captains have joined us. I expect the other three to show up on the screen with Stan and George. I introduce them to each of the team members in the room and ask that they join us around the table. As I have done for the past two weeks, I am allowing everyone to talk while we wait for Stan and George to join us. In about forty minutes the screen comes up, and there is Stan and George with the other three captains for the stations. I ask George to introduce the new team members, and then I introduce them to everyone around the table.

I ask for everyone to go around the table and give us an update on what they have accomplished since we last met. They give their updates, and I am entering the new totals into my tablet. The new captains look a little confused as to what is going on, and then I apologize to them. I explain to them the purpose of my command team of seven.

"In case you haven't figured it out, you now report to me. I report to Admiral Tern."

I bring up the holographic image of the twelve stations.

"One of the things this team is responsible for, which includes you, is to monitor and protect all this space. As you can see there are twelve stations and twelve of you. Each of you will command one of these stations. The three stations that are closest to earth will be commanded by the three of you with Admiral Stark, and one of these three stations will be home to the main command center.

When we thought about naming these stations we decided to make it easy on ourselves. Instead of trying to come up with names for each station we chose just to number them Deep Space Station One (DSS-1) through Twelve (DSS-12). I will point out each station and tell you which one is yours."

"Now here are your assignments, and they are listed on your notepads.

Deep Space Station One (DSS-1)– Captain Heslig.
Deep Space Station Two (DSS-2)– Captain Capos.
Deep Space Station Three (DSS-3)– Captain James Graham.
Deep Space Station Four (DSS-4)– Captain Curtis Johnson.
Deep Space Station Five (DSS-5)– Captain Galops.
Deep Space Station Six (DSS-6)– Captain Hilig.
Deep Space Station Seven (DSS-7)– Captain Nathan Taylor.
Deep Space Station Eight (DSS-8)– Captain Zurg.
Deep Space Station Nine (DSS-9)– Captain Dureg.
Deep Space Station Ten (DSS-10)– Captain Eltos.
Deep Space Station Eleven (DSS-11)– Captain Nurm.
Deep Space Station Twelve (DSS-12)– Captain Turog.

Two weeks ago when we were made aware of the stations only six were complete. The other six were about ninety percent complete. One of the things we did, was to get in touch with the inspectors of each station and found out that all of them weren't quite as ready as we were told. As you heard from the reports today the first six are now ready with a few minor glitches. The other six should be ready in about two and a half months. This should not be a problem and I will explain why.

We don't have the crews ready to man the stations.

The stations that are ready are three, four, six, seven, ten and eleven.

You will be with us the rest of the day to get a better understanding of what is going on.

But first let me give you an idea where each station is located, and then we will examine a station."

I take control of the holographic display and shrink it down where we can see the twelve stations more clearly.

"I want you to look at each of the stations and see how they are strategically placed. They are about five thousand light years away from each other. Even with the speed of our ships, it will take you about three months to travel from one to another. The main command center will be on Deep Space Station Three (DSS-3)."

I now shrink the image down even further where we can only see a single station.

"Notice it is a cylindrical object with domes on the top and bottom of the sphere. The station is slowly spinning which is the way it provides the artificial gravity for the station. The sphere and domes are well lit, and you can see many "windows" on it. It is to allow crews to see out. You can see many areas that look like landing and launch bays for fighters, scouts, and supply ships. The domes provide additional housing areas and station office areas.

One of the strategies the Federation command has is the establishment of these twelve stations. We are being placed here to defend this area of space and to better monitor what is going on out there and to report our information back to Federation headquarters. If the Morians can punch holes in the Federation defense, it could provide the opening they need to attack Earth and other points of interest in Hyperthean space. We could be left to defend it as best we can. So, with that said, it falls to us to pick up the ball and come up with plans on how we are going to do that.

Now that is a soft look at a station. You are a long way from any help. You have your ingenuity, experience, and imagination to protect your stations. You only have several hundred cannons and three thousand fighters to defend that station. You will have no cruisers or destroyers near you. If the Morians come your way, your defense against even a couple of Morian cruisers is going to be a great challenge for you. If any of you want to change your mind about your assignment, please speak up now."

Everyone is silent. As I look at each one of them I know they have no problems with their assignment.

"Good, then gentlemen, this is the situation. There are twelve stations. Each station must be manned by three thousand officers and personnel to keep them running. Each station will have three squadrons of fighters which is three thousand fighters and crews to take care of these fighters. We have determined you will need twelve air bosses to handle the launching and landing of your fighters. You will also have two hundred scouts with fifteen personnel per scout. This means you will need to set up three thousand berthing areas for the officers and personnel. You will also have security personnel for your stations that will report to you. We will have security personnel and a command center that reports to this team. The security and command center teams will be selected by us for each of your stations. You will also need berthing areas for visiting personnel and accommodations for cargo ships that will be temporarily at your station. That means your station will house up to sixteen thousand personnel.

After today and for the next several weeks you will be in the adjoining conference room doing your first job. We don't expect you to fill the sixteen thousand positions on each of the stations yourself. You will need help. We have selected the thirteen air bosses that will be reporting to you, and we expect twelve of these air bosses to fill your fighter personnel and fighter maintenance needs. The thirteenth air boss will be for your scouts, and has experience handling scouts. They will get your scout crews and the maintenance crews for the scouts. They will be here in about a week except for yours Stan, they will be reporting to you on the *Hyperthia*. When you go into your meeting rooms next door to you, you will find several large manuals that you can also access on your tablets. These manuals are complete layouts of your stations, and they have your names on them. For the next several days we expect you to get familiar with your station through these manuals. We expect you to know, and understand, every nook and cranny of your station as we believe this will help you to understand what personnel you need. All the stations are the same except for one which will have the main command center. We want you to work together in reviewing the stations and come up with a list of the officers you will need. When you agree, and are ready, we want you to select the officers you will need for each of your sections. Then present them to us. We will pass them to Captain Dreg and he will clear them through the security process. Once they have passed the security process and we have reviewed their personnel files, we will let you know the status of each one. Those that pass will have orders made for them to report to each of you at this location. Then with their help you can start the selection of the rest of your crews.

When you have your station crews selected, you will have them report to you here on Hyperthia. Stan for your crews on the *Hyperthia*, you will need transport ships available for each of your station crews to take them to their stations. Those of you whose stations are not ready when you have selected all your personnel will have them wait at their current duty stations until the timing is right and then have them report to your location to be ready to board transports. Once you arrive at your stations, there will be personnel there that constructed your stations. They will take your crews to their assigned work areas and will work with them for a month to work out any final glitches that you find. Then they will depart the station and return to Hyperthia.

Do you have any questions?"

They all reply, "Not now, but we are sure we will later."

"I think we have caught you up with what you need to know. Let's get back to where we are.

When we first started this meeting, all of you gave us an update on what you had accomplished over the weekend. I have compiled a list of where we are at.

For the three Earth stations, you had a need of nine thousand fighters and six hundred scouts. Of the three stations two of them are ready to be occupied, and they are three and seven. Four should be ready in about a month. Since we estimate we won't be ready to man these stations for another two months, you should have crews ready for all three stations. Based on the numbers I have just calculated you will have seven thousand fighters and five hundred scouts ready to deploy when you are ready to man these stations. Stan, do you have any idea when you might have the other two thousand fighters and one hundred scouts for your stations?"

"I am sorry sir, we have done our best to come up with this number. We will keep working on it but this will spread us pretty thin."

"Thanks Stan, I understand. If you can't come up with them we will see if we can get them from the Hyperthean fleet."

I now look at the team in the room and say, "This leaves the nine remaining stations. When we started this process, we only had four of the nine stations ready to be manned. Since then we have added two more stations that are ready. That leaves three that still need work on them. The inspectors tell us that one will be ready in a month, and the other two should be ready in forty-five to sixty days. This isn't bad for us. We can go ahead and select all our crews and have them here ready to load into transports for the long journey to these stations. The trip is calculated to take about three months to get there. By the time you arrive, the stations should be ready for you to take command.

So, for these nine stations we need thirty-six thousand fighters and eighteen hundred scouts. Based on my calculations, the fleet has committed to us thirty-three thousand fighters and the eighteen hundred scouts. Good job gentlemen."

They all have a grin of appreciation, and then I continue, "Do you see any problems in getting the remaining three thousand fighters?"

Captain Sprot says, "By the time the last set of crews leave for the last stations, we should have them."

"I like that answer. Now I have a question for each of you. Do you think we can help Stan get the additional fighters and scouts for them?"

Captain Sprot says, "I am sure we can get the scouts for him with no problem. An additional two thousand fighters might take some time. But I believe we can get them for him in the next four months."

"That sounds good. I believe we can live with that. What do you say Stan?"

"We can live with that too, and thank you. On behalf of the earth fleet, we appreciate this. We can take the seven thousand fighters and spread them between the three stations until the other fighters arrive. We will go ahead and assign a full complement of fighter crews to the stations until the other fighters arrive. They can help handle the patrols with the crews that will have fighters."

I now say, "Captain Dreg has reported that his security team has vetted all the names you have supplied to him so far. He also tells us that he has selected the security staff for all the stations, and his team is in the process of vetting them now. It should take them about a month to clear all of them, and they should be ready to go with each of their transport ships. Good job Captain."

"Thank you, sir."

Now I turn to Captain Vog and tell the group, "Captain Vog tells me that he has his team selected that will man the main command center and your command centers. He has submitted their names to Captain Dreg so that his team can vet them. Captain Dreg has told me that his team has cleared half of them and that the rest should be vetted in two weeks. Good job to you too."

He also says thanks.

I turn to Captain Sprot and say, "I think you had the easiest job of the group. Only kidding. This is the first time in history that any of us has had to set up a situation like we are now in. The strategy for this scenario is brand new, and Captain Sprot has had to come up with many different scenarios that we might have to handle. Based on this, he has had a difficult task of selecting members of his team that need to think outside the box, since everything is brand new. The strategy team will be located on station seven with the rest of us at the main command center. He presented his team to Captain Dreg, and they were cleared. Nice job Captain."

"Thank you sir."

"I think it is time for us to take a break. I have been talking for a while, and I need something to drink. After the break, all the station captains can go to the meeting room next door and start getting familiar with your manuals. For the three captains on the *Hyperthia*, you can go to your meeting room and join the other nine captains via video. We will get back together in twenty minutes."

The station commanders go into their meeting rooms, and see these three giant manuals. Each manual is about six inches thick, and they just stand there and stare at them in disbelief. Then they go over to their stack of books, open one, and start fanning through the pages. They sit down one by one, and

Captain Taylor says, "Why don't we divide and conquer. We can all get to know the total contents of these books later. We only have two weeks to figure out what we need for crews. Why don't we divide the books into twelve sections? We can review our sections of the books and in a couple of days we can discuss each section that we have reviewed and make recommendations on the number of officers we need for all the departments in the sections we reviewed. Does this sound good to everyone?"

There is agreement from everyone, and they start to divide the books into twelve sections. They spend the next couple of days going over their sections in detail, taking notes, and writing in their books on things they deem important. On the third day Captain Taylor asks, "Is everyone ready?"

They all nod that they are, and they start discussing their sections one by one, starting with the first section in the first book. They each give a synopsis of what their sections are about. They have the holographic image of a station up, and they can zoom in on the area they are discussing. They all are focused on what is being discussed and as the topic giver goes along, they ask questions. At the end of each synopsis they discuss and give recommendations on what the crew makeup should be, and they vote on the recommendations that are made. It takes them two weeks to go through all the sections and are ready to make their recommendations before us.

THIRTY-NINE

It takes three months for all of us to get everything set up for the stations. The crews have been selected, orders issued, fighters and scouts are in route to their designated stations. The seven of us will be leaving in two days for DSS-7. We say our farewells to the twelve station captains and tell them we will be in contact with them on a weekly basis. It will probably be more often the first couple of months, as we settle into our routines.

Admiral Tern has asked Admiral Kleg and myself to join him and a couple of others for dinner tonight.

We arrive at the admiral's quarters, and we are taken to a private dining area where there are six admirals waiting on us to join them. We greet each one and are seated. We eat our meal while we all are having conversations with each other. At the end of the meal Admiral Tern stands and asks if he can speak. The admiral gives a speech thanking Kleg and myself for the job we have done so far. He says that the chain of command has been very impressed how things have come together. He lifts his glass and says, "A toast to these two gentlemen."

As everyone stands they lift their glasses, and the admiral

continues, "We salute you and wish you well on this new endeavor. We look forward to your success as we all move forward."

They all say, "Here here," and clink their glasses together and take a drink.

We both say thanks, and appreciate the kind words that have been given. We sit around the table a little longer talking, drinking, and Kleg and I decide it is time for us to leave. We say our thanks again for the meal, kind words, and for the great evening.

The next day I meet with Admiral Tern for our final orders and good-byes before we depart. At 1700, the seven of us are at the departure port where we will catch a small ship out to a cruiser. The cruiser and two escort destroyers will take us to our station. The trip will take us about six months to get there. On board the cruiser are the personnel for our command center and the security team that will be there to protect the command center. Also on board the cruiser and the two destroyers are the special equipment we will need for our command center.

We depart Hyperthean space at 0200 and are on our way. That morning I meet with the captain of the cruiser, and we are in his cabin as we discuss some of the details of the trip. He appreciated the update, and I go to a small meeting room that has been set up for the seven of us.

At 1000, I ask the team to gather in the meeting room for a short meeting. We have a monitor set up for us. They have all joined me in the meeting room, and I say, "We have a long six-month trip in front of us, and it will more than likely get monotonous. We have this room dedicated to us, and you can use it anytime you need to. We know the schedule for the departure of the transport ships that will be taking crews to each of their stations. The captains of each station will be sending us messages letting us know how each departure is going and if all personnel have reported to their transports. The first transports will arrive at their station in thirty-six days.

I want each of you to be able to use this room to check in with your perspective personnel on each station and get updates from them as often as you need. Admiral Kleg, I would like for you to oversee each of the station captains and make sure things are going well with them. At 1000 each morning we will gather in this room for our morning briefing. While we are on this cruiser this area has been set as off limits to all ships personnel, except for those that need to be here.

I know that this cruiser is a Hyperthean cruiser, and it is running per Hyperthean standards. Based on that, you are welcome by the captain to join the other officers during your meal times. As for me, I still haven't adjusted to eating meals that far apart. I will join you when our meal times overlap, but at the times when they do not overlap, I will have Harold serving me in my quarters to keep from disturbing the routine of the ship. We do have an observation deck where you can sit and relax. The captain of the ship and his senior officers are welcome to join us there to enjoy themselves, have conversations, and relax. So, take the opportunity to use it. It will help you to keep from going stir crazy during this trip. That's all I have for now. I will see you all later."

The trip is passing quickly for us, as we are getting more and more involved with the stations as crews arrive at them. We are now about five days away from station seven, and Captain Taylor and his crew arrived there about two months ago. My team has already been in contact with them, making sure that the station is fully functional. Captain Taylor is now in contact with us daily, discussing what work his team needs to do to get our command center ready for us. Since we will be arriving with the special equipment that we need to set up, Captains Vog and Sprot are giving him the necessary instructions to set up the framework for our gear to go into.

We have arrived at Station Seven, and the cruiser has docked first to allow us to depart and to offload the gear they have brought for us. This takes about a day to get all the gear, our personal effects, and necessary supplies off. As the cruiser is ready to pull away from the station, the captain and several of his senior officers leave the ship and remain on the station. They pull off a short distance, and one of the destroyers pulls up to the docking station and starts offloading personnel, equipment, and supplies. The captain and his exec depart the destroyer as they arrive. The other destroyers captain and exec come over in a shuttle. The routine is the same for the first destroyer, and then they pull off, and the second destroyer does the same.

We are all greeted by Captain Taylor and his exec. We all shake hands, and they lead us to his conference room. We sit and talk for a while, and we tell him how impressed we are with the station, at least, from the outside. I then say, "We would like a tour of the station. We are eager to see it, and I know we will be impressed."

"I will be glad to show you the station, but it will take a couple of days to go through it."

"That's okay. We're not going anywhere, and I think our captains and their crews would enjoy the break. You might say we've been on the road for six months, and we all need a little R&R."

We enjoy our tour of the station, and Captains Sprot and Vog are eager to get to the main command center and see how the installation of the new equipment is going. They are ready to get the operation going and to start collecting information from the other stations that have crews onboard, and have scouts out on patrol.

FORTY

As the stations become functional, Stan is making good improvements with the fleet back in Earth's solar system. But without the material to repair the Hyperthean ships, he still has nine cruisers, twelve destroyers, and two battle stars that are out of commission. The eight lost scouts have easily been replaced. He has placed orders with Earth manufacturing for two hundred more scouts with enhancements. Stan has redistributed some of the ships to balance the fleet for the best protection possible.

He has started receiving the plating from Hyperthia and has started the repairs on the damaged ships. Along with the plating, he has received lots of supplies that will assist him for the repairs. He has prioritized how the repairs should be, so that he can get his ships back into the fleet. Last week he got a pleasant surprise when fifteen new destroyers, three new battle cruisers, and nine ships for space exploration arrived along with enough crystals to replace all the faulty ones that were discovered.

Before these new ships can be used, the crews must go through at least three months of training for all the new equipment on these new replacement ships and space trials. With the arrival of the new ships, there is quite a bit of excitement in the fleet. The fleet command center, on board the *Hyperthia*, is receiving more requests than they can process for transfers to serve on these new ships. Stan is pleased with what he has heard and plans on meeting with his fleet admirals in the next day or so to discuss how to disperse these new ships, select new commanders for them, and the crews to serve on them. They need to do this soon since they need to get the three months of training and trials finished before we can commission them for their shake down cruises.

Since Stan was surprised to see the new exploration ships, he needs to get together with his staff and decide how they will use these new ships. Once they decide, they will need to select crews for their special missions.

As far as Hyperthean history tells us, they were the first race to go into space. In the measurement of time as it relates to Earth, this was tens of thousands of years. They have explored and mapped all the space around their galaxy and several of the surrounding galaxies. They established many new relationships with many species. There were some species they were not able to establish friendly relationships with, like the Morians, but these are the exception rather than the rule. Our solar system is on the outskirts of the territory that they have explored. They have sparsely mapped our Milky Way but nothing beyond. This is one of the reasons they have allowed us to have the nine exploration vessels. Now that we have established our defenses for our solar system, helped in the establishment of the deep space stations, and set defenses in the surrounding areas, we can now do what many on Earth have always wanted to do. That is, to go into the unknown of space, explore what we could only observe, and to be the first to travel into these unknown regions of space.

Because these missions are not military missions, Stan has conferred with me, and we have agreed on what we think should be the approach for their missions. They will establish a space station that will be in orbit around the Earth. The station will only have docking ports for four exploration vessels at a time. This shouldn't be a problem since the rest of them, if not all, should be out exploring new sectors of space. All nine of the space exploration vessels will function from this home base. Since we have the experience for operating vessels in space, Stan will select nine commanders to command these ships, along with enough crews for the functioning of the ship, operations of the bridge, communications, engineering, life support systems, and weapons. We want this to be a non-military mission, so we will have Earth select nine different civilian managers as mission commanders. They will make decisions on the mission for these vessels. If a military matter comes about, the military commander will take over full command of the vessel and protect the ship from whatever the situation they encounter. The civilian mission commander will have under their responsibility, civilians for the study of the stars, mapping of new objects they encounter, crew members for the study of medical complications that they discover, botanical staff for the study of new life forms, etc. The mission commanders and military commanders will also have an additional three months of training on how to handle space exploration from a Hyperthean space exploration team. The Hypertheans know the guidelines on how we need to do this properly without damaging the eco-system that is out there.

We also don't want to limit the selection of the mission commanders or their civilian staff to a single country. Stan will be working with Earth leadership by forming an exploration council that these mission commanders and civilian crews will report to. This council will interview and select these crew members over the next twelve months. They will be notified that they have been selected to serve on these ships, and this will be the amount of time that Stan needs to build the Earth station that the ships will be stationed from.

In the meantime, Stan will select the military side of the crews for these ships and assign them, get them trained, and take these exploration ships out on space trials so that they can become familiar with the operation of the ships and their performance.

The ships will first be deployed for missions that will last five years before they return to base. Stan plans to start deploying four ships at a time, and then the next deployment three months later, and so forth until the first group of ships returns for some shore leave, replacements, if needed, and new sets of orders for their next section of space to explore.

The station for the exploration ships has been started, and from the artistic rendition that Stan sent me, it will be very impressive. It will be located half way between the earth and the moon. The middle structure will be oval. From this structure, there will be two arms that will extend out from the top side of the structure and then two arms that will extend out from the bottom side. At the end of these arms will be cages that the ships will be able to fly into for servicing and necessary repairs. When they are ready to leave, they will continue in a path out the other end of the cage. Ships that will be traveling to the base station from Earth and other ports of call can board the base station at locations on the oval structure of the station. It will take about six months for the builders to complete the station before Stan can take control of it.

With the threat from the Morians stabilized at least in our sector and the fleet now well settled, Stan has made the decision to bring the *Hyperthia* into an orbit about three fourths of the way between the moon and earth. This will become a base of operation for the fleet.

FORTY-ONE

With nine new vessels for space exploration, there needs to be a decision made on what to explore. Since this will be a combination of military and civilian personnel manning these exploration vessels, Stan has decided that the council from Earth will be the ones making the decision on where to go. Stan initially met with astronomical and scientific members from Earth seeking help on who should make up the council. After lengthy debates for the last three months, they have come to a decision. They have also decided that to help give them some guidance, they want to ask a member from the Hyperthean Space Council to be on the council. Rather than have them on Earth, they will join the meetings via video conferencing. They have also decided that there will be thirteen members on the council with the thirteenth member with no voting rights. The only time this person will be allowed to vote is when there is a six to six tie, and they will be the tie breaker. They have decided to ask Stan to be the thirteenth member. Stan won't be participating in the meetings, but should there be a tied vote on a situation, he will receive a full set of the minutes of the meetings for his review. He will then cast his vote in the direction in which he feels it should go. Should he choose not to vote on the topic, it will go back to committee for them to adjust the subject and revote, or drop it all together.

The council has started their work in the selection of the civilian crews for the nine ships. Stan has turned over the responsibility of selecting the officers and enlisted personnel to his personnel staff. The selection of both military and civilian crews will take another three months because there are thousands of people to select.

The council not only has the responsibility in the selection of the civilian crew members, but they have lots of decisions to make about where to go and how to go about it. The Hyperthean member has provided them with invaluable guidance in setting the guidelines they will need to follow and how to go about the selection of space they will go into. They have done a wondrous job in the selection of the crews and in setting the direction the first ships will take, as we step out into a new region of space.

As it is with everything in life, getting the space station ready for the exploration ships has taken a little longer than the original estimates. Another three months has passed, and it is now ready. Crews are manning the station and getting her ready to accept the first four ships for their deployment assignments. Stan tells me she is something to see and is an accomplishment that each should be proud of.

It is time for the first four ships to be brought into the docking stations. The Hyperthean crews that brought the ships to our solar system are still with the ships and are working with the military crews that have been assigned to take over. The Hyperthean crew will be bringing the ship into the docking port. Our crews will be standing next to each of the Hyperthean crews, and they will be observing them as they bring the ship into the docking station. Everyone is standing by to watch the ships as they come into the station. There are some tense moments as this is the first time we have ever docked a ship at our new station, a Hyperthean ship with an earth space station.

These new ships will have a crew complement of one hundred seventy-five. The military crew will be made up of sixty members, and the remaining one hundred fifteen members will be the civilian scientific members of the crew. As Stan thinks on the selection of the crews, especially the captain of one of these ships, he finds it a little humorous. The name of our first captain of one of the exploration ships is James H. Kirk. As he remembers stories from his father, in the late twentieth century, there was a sci-fi movie called Star Trek, and the captain was James T. Kirk. Then around 2015 there was a new type of destroyer commissioned for the US Navy, and the captain of that new Zumwalt class destroyer was James Kirk. And now, these several decades later, with the commissioning of this new exploration ship this captain will be James H. Kirk.

The first four ships will be at the space port for the next two weeks allowing the crew, both military and civilian, to get used to their new ships. They will both be going over their areas of responsibility making sure everything is in its place, and everything is in working order. The ships will also be loaded with the necessary supplies for a three-month shakedown cruise before they depart for their assigned mission. Of course, Captain Kirk is getting his usual amount of ribbing about his name once everyone learned about the sci-fi movie, and this being the first exploration ship.

Since the ships are medium sized, they do not have the cargo space for an away mission of any magnitude. With that in mind, Admiral Duffy has been working out a schedule for his transport ships to resupply these ships on a rotating basis of about every six months. This should work out fine since the ships will not be that far out on their first mission. This way it will not stress his fleet with his other supply missions. Since he now must support the fleet, three deep space stations and now these exploration ships Admiral Duffy has asked for more transport ships. The distances they must travel does not give him the time to meet the demand that is being placed on him.

Stan agrees with his argument and requests to receive fifty more transports to meet the demand, and he has come to me for help.

I go over the request with Stan, and tell him that I will see what I can do. I get in contact with the Hyperthean High Command and explain the situation to them. They tell me that they can get the Earth fleet thirty transports, but it will take a year before they will arrive in our solar system. They say we will need to build the other twenty transports. I thank them for their time and relay the message on to Stan.

Stan understands and appreciates them being able to supply them with thirty transports. He says he will get the plans for the transports to several Earth manufacturing facilities, have them built the ships in pieces, and then have the pieces sent to our assembly location near Mars.

He lets Admiral Duffy know this and tells him that he needs to inform the academies that they need so many new officers, enlisted personnel for fifty new transports, and they need to be ready to report to the fleet in twelve months.

We are going to have so many ships, beacons, and other moving objects out here, Stan is starting to feel like he is going to need traffic cops to direct traffic to keep ships from running into each other. But space is still very large, and we don't have it that cluttered, yet. Besides, the beacons are marked on all ships star charts, and they have the sensors to know the movement of all the ships that are out there.

The council has been working hard at breaking down the unexplored space into sectors for the ships to work in. Of course, with initially only nine ships to start the mapping with, it will take quite some time, decades even, before we feel we have even made a micro dent in the mapping process. It could possibly even take several decades before we get to a sector of space where there are even any stars and planetoids of any sort to start looking at. I don't know why we are in such a hurry, it took the Hypertheans tens of thousands of years to map and explore the space they have mapped. The first nine sectors have been laid out for the nine ships that we have. Each has been mapped for a five-year mission. Since what we need to start mapping is close by, it will only take about a month for each of the ships to reach their assigned areas, and then about two months to return to space port at the end of their mission. The council has decided to just lay out the first twenty-seven sectors of space now and see where we stand five years from now.

The crews are settling in for the two weeks of familiarity, and the supply load is approaching an end. The first four Hyperthean crews are departing the ships to leave port and have turned over full responsibility to the human crews. Stan is checking in with Vice-Admiral Ward, who oversees the space exploration fleet, to see how the turnover has gone. As Stan is making his call, he also receives information that the next ships will be moving into space dock in the next couple of days.

Stan makes his call to Admiral Ward and says, "Mike, I thought I would check in with you on your new ships. I hear you are getting ready to deploy four of them?"

"Yes sir. As you know, we have just finished getting all the necessary supplies on board for our three-month trials. The crews have been going over their stations with the Hyperthean crew, and we feel we are ready to test our skills."

"That's good news Mike. How is Captain Kirk doing? Is he still getting a lot of ribbing?"

Mike gives a little giggle and says, "Yes, but he is handling it fine. Since he first found out he would be the captain of one of these space exploration vessels, they have been giving him a hard time about it, but it has been in honest fun. He says he is going to keep looking to see if he can find a science officer named Spock, and everybody laughs. It keeps the mood light but he is a good officer."

"That's good. If you want I can see if I can find a ship's doctor named McCoy?"

Mike laughs and says, "Please don't. We might have to name the ship Enterprise."

We both laugh and then Stan says, "On that note, what have you named the ship?"

"She will have a hull number of 1295, and her name will be the SES Graham. Since this is our first space exploration ship, the SES stands for "Space Exploration Ship." We chose Graham after Admiral Graham. We know we usually don't name ships after living people, but we felt it would be okay since he is no longer with Earth command, and he was the one who got us here."

"That's sounds good to me. I'm sure he will be honored by it when he finds out. How did you come up with those designations?"

"We didn't. They came from the council. Since we wanted to give them some of the naming pride here, we decided not to interfere."

"We will just have to live with that. Now on to something else. Where will you be deploying the Graham and the other three for their trial runs?"

"We have looked at our options and have decided to send the Graham to just outside of the barrier protection of the ninth fleet. The other three will do their trials outside the third, fourth, and sixth fleets. They can make their trials there without interfering with any of the fleet operations. Should they run into trouble, they are close enough to the fleets that they can go in to assist the ships in fairly short order."

"Sounds good. When will they be leaving?"

"On the 21st at 0300."

"If you don't mind, I would like to be there for the sendoff, since these ships will be our first of their kind we will be sending out."

"That would be nice sir. The crew would be honored."

"Good, I will see you at the station on the twentieth."

FORTY-TWO

It is now the twenty-first, and almost 0300 hours. The crews of all four ships are at their stations ready to take their ships out of space port for their trial runs. Everyone on the Graham and the space station are a little nervous because this will be the first ship to leave the port. Everybody believes everything is going to work well in the dedocking process and hope we don't have any bumps as the ship leaves station.

It is now time for Captain Kirk to take the ship out of the port, and he is asking for readiness from all stations. As he waits, he starts getting reports back on their readiness and eventually receives word from his first officer that all stations are ready and manned for departure.

Captain Kirk now asks Mr. Shane, his first officer, "Is space port ready for dedocking procedures?"

"Yes sir, they report all stations are ready for dedocking process."

"Okay, Mr. Shane, let's take her out."

"Aye, aye sir."

He says to port command, "Port, you are clear for dedocking. All hands prepare for dedocking and leave port."

The ship begins to move slowly at first as you hear cables and docking clamps break away from the ship. Mr. Shane receives word that all cables and docking clamps have been released, and we are clear to move forward out of the port.

"Helm, departure speed."

"Departure speed set sir."

The Graham has made a clear departure from port and is ready to set course for their trial run destination.

"Helm, set course for ANTRIP 836; speed of parser 3."

"Course set in for ANTRIP 836 and bringing her to parser 3, sir."

The Graham is now well on its way to its first destination.

The other three ships take their turns at leaving port and each are on their way to their trial destinations.

It will take the Graham about a day to reach the area of space where they will be doing their trial runs. In the meantime, all the crew is starting to set up their ship's routine and checking on the functioning of the ship. Even though it is a new ship for the crew, the Graham is about two years old. She was built back in Hyperthean space, and the Hyperthean crew took about a year to get the nine ships to us in our solar system. All systems should be well broke in, but this new crew needs to familiarize themselves with the ship and how she is functioning. As with everything you take care of, you get a certain feel for the things you are responsible for. Even though the electronics say things are fine, you get used to certain vibrations and noises. If they are not there you feel something is not right. That is what this crew now needs to learn; to get the feel for the ship. Trusting their instincts around the equipment they are responsible for is vital.

The ship is now at the outer parameter of the ninth fleet and are communicating with their command center on getting the outer security measures turned off. They need to pass through and head into the area they will be doing their trial runs for the next year. They receive their clearances to pass through the security areas and are well out into an area of space where they are basically on their own. They are excited about this aspect, but also know that the ninth fleet is not that far away if they need them is a comfort.

The Graham has been on patrol for three months now, and things have been going smoothly. All the equipment has been functioning as expected. They have not run into any problems. All sensors and scientific equipment have not picked up anything out of the ordinary. It is also time for them to rendezvous with a supply ship, and sensors have the ship coming up about two hours out. They make their call to the ship and tell them they are ready to rendezvous. This resupply goes well and the first resupply of one of these ships has occurred with no problem.

Four more ships arrived at space port when the Graham and the other three ships were leaving. While the four ships were being resupplied, these four ships were leaving space port while the last ship was getting ready to enter space port for their changeover of crews. The four new ships are being deployed out to different areas of space. They will receive assignments just beyond the eighth, tenth, second and first fleets. This will give four more of our exploration ships experience with ships just outside of the protection areas. By the time all nine ships are deployed, it will give nine of our exploration ships the experience they need outside the protection zone. By the time the ninth ship is being deployed for its trial runs it will be time for the first four ships to return to space port for a month. During this month, the four ships will be evaluated by Admiral Ward's command to make sure they, and their crew, are ready for their first mission.

The four ships pass all evaluations and have been supplied with supplies for their first five years of deep space travel. They will start mapping the new space areas that have been assigned to them by the council. During this month, the crews receive two weeks leaves in rotating cycles. Then all members return to the ship to get the ship ready for departure.

They depart space port and head back to the same patrol areas where they were doing their trials just outside of their assigned fleets. This time they will travel out further. It will take them three months to reach the area of space they will need to start mapping and measuring new space with their new sophisticated instruments. They will be well beyond the protection of their fleets.

FORTY-THREE

At the same time the other space exploration ships are being made ready at the space port, Stan begins working on crews to take over the fifteen new destroyers and three new battle cruisers. His admirals have their work cut out for them, since they need to replace the crew members they lost during the battles. The ships that were damaged are being repaired with the new plating they have received and should be back in full service within the next six months. With these twenty-six ships being placed back into service and with these eighteen new ships to man, they will need several thousand new recruits for these ships. Currently this should not be a problem, as new officers and recruits from Earth are eager to serve. At the same time, we are needing volunteers for the new Mark II Scout Ships that we are putting into service. Stan is also starting to do deep space patrols with the scouts.

Since the deep space stations have been doing patrols for three months, Stan decides to ask me if I have any suggestions for his patrols. He brings up his pop-up display and places his call.

"Good day Stan. Good to hear from you other than our briefing time. What can I do for you?"

"Oh, I see how it is. You think the only time I call you is when I need something."

We both laugh, and Stan continues, "Well, I hate to say it, but I do need to ask you a question. Your stations are operational and have had scouts on patrol for three months now. Has your strategy team put into place any techniques for the patrols that might be helpful? We are starting deep space patrols, and anything you can share will be helpful."

"I know some of the details, but let me have Captain Sprot contact you and give you more details on what we have in place."

"Thank you. Now on to a more personal note. How are you enjoying your new assignment?"

"I like it. It is a big change from being Admiral of the Earth fleet. Instead of having the final say on decisions, I must let my higher ups know what I am doing, and they can countermand my decisions. I understand that, since I don't have all the information for the bigger picture. Also, their daily cycle is totally different than ours, and I must be respectful of that. I am getting used to it. I am glad our command center is on a station that is made up mostly of humans. I feel sorry for my team sometimes, but they don't seem to mind it. I have decided to visit one of the stations that is about three months away. I will be visiting DSS-9 commanded by Captain Dureg. They were one of the last ones to get to their station, and it has been up and running for only a month now. I will have a cruiser and two destroyers take me there, and I should be back on station in about six months. Keep that under your hat, since that information is confidential."

"What trip? I am glad to hear you are handling things. Best of luck to you on your travels, and I will be waiting on Captain Sprot's call."

"Thanks Stan, and I will talk with you later."

About thirty minutes later Stan receives his call from Captain Sprot. His wristband lets him know that he has a call, and he answers it. He sees Captain Sprot on the other end, and says, "Good day Captain, how are you doing?"

"I am doing fine admiral, how are you?"

"I am doing well. I'm sure Admiral Graham has filled you in on why he has asked you to call me."

"Yes. Right now, all our patrols have been routine, as you know. We have developed some strategies when a ship might run into something they need to investigate. Should we detect activity in a patrol sector, we have trained our scout commanders on routines they need to follow to get us the best information for analysis. I tell you what, let me send you the manual we have put together for the scouts, instead of me telling you the details. Is that okay?"

"That will be perfect."

"I will have it to you within the hour."

They both say their good-byes and as Captain Sprot promised, Stan has received the manual within the hour. He goes through the manual and likes what he sees. He contacts Admiral Fuentes and lets him know of the manual. He says he will forward a copy to him for his review. He says that after his review, please send a copy to the strategy officer in the command center.

With these patrols and these new guidelines, it will provide our solar system better security than we have had before.

By the time the ninth space exploration ship is released from the space port, Stan has all his military ships back in commission. The new ones have completed their trials and are now being deployed to their assigned stations within the fleet. As the new command center for the deep space scouts has been set up, it will be a highly-classified area on the *Hyperthia*. All information gathered by the scout ships will be funneled through the command center, relayed out to the fleet, and to Admiral Graham's command center. This will also give Stan the information that he needs to respond to any situation they report. Stan has also requested to receive one thousand new

Mark II scout ships for doing the deep space missions. This will help the deep space stations that were given scouts by the Hypertheans.

The new Mark II scout ships have some nice enhancements. Even though the cloaking on the ships was top notch, the Hypertheans had made an improvement to the cloak that virtually guarantees the ships invisibility, not only to sight, but to any type of sensor detection. The engines for the ship had been improved to run more silently and leaves no ion trail for detection of their movement through space. Weapons are virtually the same when the ships were first designed, but since these new ships are not being designed for battle, the armament they currently have is adequate for the challenges they might face. The ships also have the new trans-portal weapon that the Hypertheans improved for their scout ships. Communication has been improved to monitor, capture any type of sounds that they receive and to send that information on to the new command center. This new highly secure band wave is so compressed that detection of the signal is virtually impossible. It comes across basically as space noise in micro bursts. Sensors on board the scout ships have also been improved to reach deeper into space. Should they ever detect enemy activity, they will know about it at least a week before the enemy can reach their location. This will allow the passing of that information on to the command center and the fleet, with plenty of time to prepare for any situation. It also allows the command center time to send more scout ships into the area to better monitor the situation before it becomes critical.

With the orders for new scout ships going to the Hyperthean High Command and earth manufactures, Stan's order for a thousand ships is almost impossible for the earth manufacturing facilities to keep up with. With the dual manufacturing facilities and the demand they have on them, it will still take a year for the earth facilities to be able to meet the request that Stan has placed on them.

Having been in space close to forty years now, we have become more comfortable being out here. Stan is now the second person to be in command of Earth's space protection force. He is also more comfortable with his responsibilities. His command has settled in and has accepted him as their new leader. He has decided, along with his staff and the other admirals, that they can spread their fleets thinner and can provide a deeper reach into space. They have improved on the technology of the detection probes and can now spread them out to three times the distance of the original probes they had received. The sensors of the ships have been improved, and they can detect objects at greater distances now. With the scout ships out doing patrols, they are ready to cast a wider net of protection on our solar system. With the improved sensors and with ships now traveling out beyond the barrier he has decided to turn off the barrier, but also to leave it in place, should they ever need it in the future. This will allow ships to move more freely. They don't have to worry about whether the barrier is up, and that they might accidently run into it and be damaged.

Stan and his staff have laid out a plan on how they will provide this new deployment strategy. Even though he does not need the approval of the Hyperthean High Command, he is keeping them in the loop on what they are doing, since we are now part of the federation. When the Hyperthean High Command hears of the plan, they are pleased to see that Earth is willing to take this initiative and sends them their full support on the plan.

FORTY-FOUR

Ten years have passed since the deep space stations were set up. I have been able to visit all the stations. The Hyperthean High Command has seen the vulnerability of the stations, and we now have cruisers and destroyers patrolling the space where the stations are located. Admiral Stark has joined in the protection process and has sent out three cruisers and nine destroyers to patrol the areas around the three stations that are closest to our solar system.

We have only had three minor incidents with two of our stations further out, when Morian cruisers and destroyers tried to infiltrate close to stations five and six. With the help of fighters and the ships that were in the area, they could fend off the infiltrators with only minor damage to one of the destroyers and the loss of six fighters.

With the earth fleets expanding patrols deeper into space, and the deep space scout patrols both from the deep space stations, and the deep patrols from Earth, everyone feels we have a strong defense network set up. Also with the exploration ships reaching deeper into space, we are getting information from them on discoveries that continues to excite our science community. The military presence on the ships also keeps us informed of information that helps all our command centers in the analysis of data.

Scout patrols are solemn and lonely ones. They last six months and the only communication you have with anyone is with your fifteen crew members. Generally, the watches are four on and four off, and the four off you are doing maintenance on something you are responsible for. The skipper is a lieutenant, one other officer, and the rest are enlisted. The other officer oversees communications, and there is a chief over engineering. It takes them about three months to get to a patrol area and then three-months to return home. The total time you are gone is a year, home for six months, and then back out for your next patrol.

On this patrol, scout LRPC-71 has been assigned to patrol a quadrant of space designated Fox quadrant. This sector of space has been known to have Morian activity, but it has supposedly been silent for the last five years. Lieutenant Michael is the skipper of this patrol. They left our solar system about two and a half months ago, and should be reaching their patrol area in about two weeks. The trip has been uneventful. They have had drills to keep skills at their best, and the skipper has been pleased with their progress. The drills have slowed to once a week now, and their timing is still improving as they man their stations. They continue to monitor their sensors and gather information as they travel towards their patrol area. They continue to send out their reports and data collection on an hourly basis, but do not have any activity to report back to the *Hyperthia*, just general communications. Basically, just to let them know that they are still here, and things are fine.

They have reached Fox quadrant, and Lieutenant Michael has set a course for their patrols. The ship is cloaked and has been since they left our solar system. They are running at patrol speed to keep any trailing gases down to a minimum. The focus of the patrols is not on our course, but on sensors and monitoring the communication systems to see if we detect any object or pick up pieces of information that we need to pass back to the command center.

They are now in their second month of their patrol, and as usual, all systems are quiet. The skipper is starting to shift some of their watches around to break up the boredom. It is a good thing, because they are starting to get on each other's nerves. For this long a period together, I'm not surprised.

It is now the ships mid watch, things are quiet as usual, when Natalia, who is on comms, suddenly sits up in her chair and puts on her head gear to listen to something more intently. Mat is on duty at the same time, but his station is to monitor any movement or objects that we may encounter. He sees nothing.

"Mat, are you picking up anything on the sensors?"

He starts looking at the sensors more intently and replies, "No, nothing on the short or long-range sensors. What do you have?"

She calls Mr. Shaw, who is in charge of the mid watch, over and tells him that she has picked up something, but doesn't quite know what to make of it. She asks if she could wake Mr. Ezekiel, our communication officer, and see if he can help her.

Mr. Shaw turns to Mat and says, "Wake Mr. Ezekiel and tell him we have something he needs to listen to."

Mat rushes over to the sleeping area where Mr. Ezekiel is sleeping, and wakes him. "Sir, Natalia has picked up something that she needs you to listen to."

Mr. Ezekiel is blinking his eyes, trying to wake up and clear the cobwebs from his head. Then it sinks in what Mat has told him, and he quickly gets out of bed and goes to the communication area. As Mat heads back to his sensors, half paying attention to them, and half trying to hear what is going on at the communication station.

"What do you have Natalia?"

"Sir, it was just a short blurb, and I almost missed it. I

have gone back over it a couple of times, but I believe it was a communication of some sort."

Mr. Ezekiel has now taken a seat at the station next to Natalia and has put on his own set of headgear. He has started listening to what Natalia has picked up. He listens very intently for about five seconds and says, "It definitely appears to be a message of some sort. Have you run it through the decoding algorithms yet?"

"I am doing that now sir. In about a minute we should have an answer."

The minute passes, but the system comes back that it could not decode the message.

Now Mr. Ezekiel says, "Let's run it through a decompression algorithm and see if that helps."

Natalia starts the decompression algorithm subroutine, and the system comes back with something.

"It does appear to be a message sent in the clear."

"What do you have?" with some excitement in his voice.

"I only have a single word now, but I don't know what it means. I need to run it through a translator to see if it can tell us."

"I have it. You keep trying to get the whole message."

As Mr. Ezekiel takes the word and runs it through the translator, it quickly comes back as a Morian word meaning "course."

Mr. Shaw, who is the mid watch officer, and our engineering chief, is now over at the communication center intently listening to what is going on. He has decided it is time to wake the skipper and make him aware of the situation.

He now points to Phil who has to bridge watch with him and says, "Phil, go and wake Mr. Michael and inform him he is needed in the communication area."

"Yes chief, right away," and rushes off the wake him. He returns shortly, and tells him that Mr. Michael will be here shortly.

Mr. Michael arrives in the communication area and says, "Report Mr. Shaw."

"Sir, a message has been picked up, and Mr. Ezekiel is trying to make sense out of it now. Both long and short-range sensors are being monitored, but nothing has been detected. It is believed that the message was transmitted well beyond the range of the sensors. What Mr. Ezekiel has gotten so far is one word of the message, and it is "course". Sir, the translator says it is Morian."

"Thank you chief. Let's everybody get back to your stations and keep a close watch for anything that you hear or see out there. I don't want to be caught by surprise. Chief, get Stephanie up here to help with the communications area. I want Mr. Ezekiel and Natalia to focus on this message for now."

"Yes sir," and sends someone to get Stephanie out of her rack to come up and help.

Stephanie arrives at the communication area, and Mr. Ezekiel explains to her what is going on, and that he needs her to monitor the communication array while he and Natalia continue to work on the message that has been picked up.

It takes another thirty minutes before Natalia has finally found the correct decompression ratio and can now hear the full message. She runs it through the translation matrix, and passes it over to Mr. Ezekiel.

Mr. Ezekiel is intently listening to the message, and Natalia looks up at the skipper and whispers, "Definitely Morian."

Mr. Michael now turns his head towards Mr. Ezekiel and says, "Well, what does it say?"

Mr. Ezekiel looks up at the skipper and says, "On course to destination. Should arrive in two weeks. Will start patrols when we arrive."

"Sir, if I may provide a synopsis, I don't believe they realized they were sending in the clear, even though it was compressed."

Mr. Michael is now standing there thinking for about fifteen seconds, and then says, "Mr. Ezekiel, I want you to get this message off to the command center and attach this comment to it. 'After review of message, believe Morian activity in our sector to be imminent. Please advise.' Encrypt the message and get it out immediately."

"Aye sir," and begins working on getting the message out to the command center.

"Everybody, resume your normal watch. Mr. Ezekiel, I would like for you and Natalia to continue to work on the message, and see if you can triangulate where the message came from. If you can figure that out, I want you to work with Mat on sensors to see if we can figure out where that ship is going. Mat, I want you to keep a very close watch on those sensors. If you so much as detect a speck of dust that you don't believe should be there, I want you to inform me. Make sure every watch knows that."

"Yes sir."

By now all the crew is awake and talking about the message that has been received. Even though it was just a message, this has broken the monotony of the patrol, and we feel excited about this break from the routine. After about two hours of talking about it and nothing new happening, people are starting to get back into their racks or getting ready for the 0400 watch.

The *Hyperthean* command center has received the message from the 71 and has noted it in their system. They have also made the main command center on DSS-7 aware of the message. Since this is just beyond the patrol area of DSS-3, Admiral Graham has ordered the main command center to make Captain Graham aware of the information. He also requested that they send out a scout to go two sectors deeper into space around sector Fox. He also starts to have the cruiser and destroyers in that area to start patrolling a little further out.

The 71 has finally settled back down to a normal patrol, since no other communications are intercepted The sensors haven't picked up any type of activity, not even a speck of dust out of place. They complete their first six-month patrol, and it is now time for them to head back to the solar system. The three-month trip home is uneventful, and they arrive back at the *Hyperthia* for debriefing. They spend three days being debriefed, but normally a debriefing only takes one day. The two extra days this time is going over the message that they received.

Hyperthean High Command also got a copy of the message that we intercepted, and they are also showing a high level of interest in the content of the message. They are now sending extra patrol ships out to DSS-3 to assist in the patrolling of this section of space and see if they can find any Morian activity.

Our scout ship, the 71, is now in one of the landing bays of the *Hyperthia*. She will spend the next two months being gone over with a fine-tooth comb to make sure all systems and hull integrity are sound. During this time, the crew will be getting their much-needed shore leave back on earth. All the crew is excited about going home and getting to see their families for a couple of months.

Their shore leave is over, and the crew is starting to arrive back on the *Hyperthia*. Since they are crew members of one of the scout ships, they have special berthing facilities for all scout ship crews. This allows them a few more privileges than the rest of the crew on *Hyperthia*. After the crew has returned, they are called into a briefing room where we will be going over the plans for their next patrol. They are still four months away from leaving for their patrol assignment, but they still need to make their plans for being out there for quite some time.

Mr. Michael, Mr. Ezekiel and the chief have been back for about a week and have been working with the other senior officers on what they will be doing. The next patrol area will be in the Gulf sector of space.

FORTY-FIVE

They are two days away from departing for their patrol area. For the past four months, the 71 has been gone over thoroughly by the maintenance crew on board the *Hyperthia*, but also by the 71 crew. They have received a couple of new enhancements to their sensor arrays, which will give them better long-range capabilities, and the engines have also received some new enhancements. She will run much more quietly now, but she also has received some improvements in conservation on her fuel. We will need it for this patrol. We have also added some personal weapons for the crew, in case we are boarded, or if we need to board another vessel. We certainly hope not, with boarding parties in space, we do not have the element of surprise.

We are going through our inventory of supplies in our cargo hold area making sure we have everything we are supposed to have. Once we leave, there is no meeting up with a replenishment ship or getting something we forgot, like the skipper's coffee, which reminds Mat that he needs to check on that, to make sure we have that and that there is enough for him and the rest of us. As Mat finishes working the inventory check list with the chief and a couple of others, we notice two security types come on board and walk over to the skipper's safe. They enter the code to open it, then place a sealed tablet inside, and then relock the safe with a new code. They turn to leave while we are all looking at them. They nod, and leave the ship. We are all curious, but know better than to ask.

It is 0700 on the morning we are to depart. We have arrived early. We are all standing outside the ship waiting on the skipper. We have placed all our personal gear on board in our personal area. The ship is lit up, all the electronics turned on, and everything shows to be one hundred percent functional. At 0715, we see the skipper enter the bay area and comes over to us. We all come to attention, salute him, and he returns the salute.

"Good morning everyone."

"Good morning sir."

"Mr. Ezekiel, is the ship ready for getting under way?"

He reports that the ship is ready, and all systems are a go.

As he usually does, Mr. Michael takes the next thirty minutes to do his own inspection of the ship, both externally and internally. He finishes his inspection and comes back over to his crew. We are just standing around chatting and wondering why we don't just get aboard and start getting under way. Finally, we see Captain Grey, our senior commanding officer of the scouting divisions, enter the bay area, and is heading over to us. As we snap to attention, salute, he returns the salute, and tells us to stand at ease.

He walks up to Lieutenant Michael and says, "Mr. Michael, here are your orders. I wanted to deliver them to you personally. On board your ship there are more sealed orders for you. You are not to open those orders until 1000 hours three days from now. Good luck with this patrol, and God's speed."

He takes one step back, salutes Mr. Michael, and then the rest of us. Then he turns and leaves the bay area. We are all standing there a little surprised, wondering what is going on, because he never sees any of his crews off. It is as if he is saying his good-byes, or something. Mr. Michael says, "Okay, let's get aboard and get this ship under way."

We all scramble to get onboard and the chief secures the hatch. Everyone is at their stations going over their instruments one final time and reporting that the ship is ready to leave the bay.

Mr. Michael says to Mr. Ezekiel, "Report to bay command that the 71 is ready to leave the bay area."

"Aye sir," makes the request to the air boss, and then replies, "the air boss has given permission to depart the bay area down bay launch 47"

"Helm, take us out of the bay down bay launch 47."

He gets an 'aye sir, bay launch 47,' we depart the *Hyperthia*, and now set course for the Gulf quadrant. We watch the *Hyperthia* get smaller in our viewer knowing this will be the last time we will see her for the next year. We settle in now. Mr. Michael sets the normal watch process, and we begin our routine.

Mr. Michael sits at his station, takes the sealed orders that were given to him by Captain Grey, taps the pad in his other hand for a few seconds, breaks the seal, and opens the flap that is covering the screen. He pushes the "On" button, waits for the screen to come up, and enters his password to open the command app on his tablet. In front of him are the orders for this patrol, and he starts to go over them, first quickly to see what everything says, and then he starts over and reads it more slowly to absorb every word to make sure he understands his orders correctly. He looks at Mr. Ezekiel and says, "Normal patrol assignment. Nothing out of the ordinary to report." He closes the pad and settles in for his watch.

It is now day three, and time for Mr. Michael to open his new set of orders. He goes over to the safe, takes his tablet, and opens an app for security passwords. He enters his password, and as the app comes up, finds the new safe combination, and then turns to Mr. Ezekiel and requests, "Mr. Ezekiel, please record in the log that I am opening the safe at 1000 hours on the third day of our journey toward the Gulf quadrant as instructed."

"Yes sir."

Mr. Michael enters the new code into the safe, opens it, and takes out the tablet that was placed inside. Mr. Michael takes the tablet with his new set of orders, taps the pad in his other hand, as he normally does for a few seconds, breaks the seal, and opens the flap that is covering the screen. He pushes the "On" button, waits for the screen to come up, and enters his password to open the command app on the tablet. In front of him is a new set of orders for this patrol. He then starts to go over them, first quickly to see what everything says, and then he starts over, and reads it more slowly to absorb every word to make sure he understands his orders correctly, as he normally does. He lays the tablet down in his lap, and then starts rubbing his lips as he is thinking. He does this for a couple of minutes, and then picks up the tablet, rereads his orders, to see if he has missed anything.

"Mr. Ezekiel, if you please," and nods for him to come over and take a seat next to him. He hands Mr. Ezekiel the tablet with the new orders and tells him to read the orders.

As Mr. Ezekiel reads the tablet, Mat notices him raising his eyebrows, and then hands the tablet back to Mr. Michael. Mr. Ezekiel looks at the skipper and asks, "What are your orders sir?"

"For this one I believe we need to let everyone in on what our instructions are."

"Do you want me to call everyone together now?"

"I don't see any reason to delay."

He now calls everyone together around him. He says there is something that he needs to share with us. As we gather, he says, "I want to let each of you know that I believe you are the best scout ship crew in our fleet. Because I believe this, I also believe command believes that too. I tell you this because we have been given a mission that will be extremely dangerous, top secret, and we must be on our toes every minute of every day while we are on this patrol, starting now. As you know we are heading for the Gulf quadrant to patrol. Our orders have changed, and we are heading to patrol an area known as the Hotel-India quadrants. What you don't know is that these two quadrants are more dangerous than other quadrants, and there is a greater than high probability that the Morians will be in these two quadrants. It is suspected they are there, for an unknown purpose. We are to gather as much information as possible to help determine why they are there. One of the things that will help us is that an asteroid will be passing through the quadrants during the time we will be patrolling the area. Our orders are to land on this asteroid before it enters the India quadrant, and we will ride it through to the other end of the Hotel quadrant. As we patrol these two quadrants we will exit the H-1 quadrant, continue in stealth mode, and gather as much information as we can about Morian activity. I wanted to make you aware of this. This patrol will be one of the most dangerous patrols ever undertaken by a long-range crew, but I have full confidence that we will come through this and will do the best job we know how to do. So, stay on your toes and remember, nothing you see or hear is unimportant during this patrol.

Now, per these orders, we are to turn off the signal we transmit that allows the command center to know where we are. We are also to deploy the special buoy we received just before we left the *Hyperthia*. From this point on we are to run silent, our only communications will be to the main command center. That means if we receive a request to respond to a communication we are to ignore it. Any questions?"

After a pause, Stephanie asks, "Sir, do you know where the asteroid is or when we will encounter it?

"No. That is our next job. Since this mission is top secret, no one other than the high command knows of our orders so we are on our own to locate it. With that question, I would like for you, and Mr. Ezekiel, to get started in locating the asteroid and give us a plot to intercept it. Make the intercept course to occur three days before the asteroid enters the India quadrant."

Stephanie and Mr. Ezekiel reply, "Yes sir," and they start going to their screens and looking at the star charts to see where the asteroid is located. The rest of us go back to our stations and start to absorb what Mr. Michael has just told us. Stephanie and Mr. Ezekiel come back with the plot to take us to the asteroid.

Mr. Ezekiel says, "We have the new course to intercept the asteroid three days before it enters the India quadrant skipper."

"Mr. Ezekiel, please give the course correction to the helmsman."

Mr. Michael now turns to the helmsman and instructs, "Helmsman, change course to the course Mr. Ezekiel is giving you now."

Mr. Michael now turns to Mat, and says, "Mat, please turn off our tracking signal."

Mat turns off the tracking signal, and the indicator light turns red, telling him that the tracking signal is off.

"Mat, deploy the special beacon and once deployed, please turn it on."

"Aye sir," and pushes the button to deploy the beacon and activates it at the same time.

In a couple of seconds Stephanie turns to Mr. Ezekiel and says, "Sir, the beacon we just deployed is transmitting a weak distress signal. The signal it is sending says we are the ones in trouble. I don't understand sir."

Mr. Michael now interrupts the conversation and says, "Calm down people, it is all part of the assignment. Let me explain a little more.

For this mission to be a success we are hoping that the Morians will also pick up this distress signal along with our fleet. With our fleet scrambling to send out ships to search for us, we are hoping that the Morians will see this as an opportunity for them to make a mistake, and give us an opportunity to slip in, and gather as much information as we can. Unfortunately, for all of us, this will cause some distress on our families. When the fleet is unable to find the 71, or any debris, we will be reported as missing in action. It will remain that way while we are on patrol. I'm sorry, but that is just the way it must be."

We all sit there in silence as the reality of this sets in. We knew the patrol would be dangerous but with this news the reality of this has just become worse.

Mr. Michael now turns to Mr. Ezekiel and says, "Mr. Ezekiel, how long will it take for us to get to the asteroid at our current speed?"

"Five days sir."

"Calculate a new speed and course to get us there in three days, if you would please."

Mr. Ezekiel turns to calculate a new speed and course to intercept the asteroid in three days and comes back, "Sir, we need to increase our speed to presser 104, and change our course and head towards ANTRIP 972."

Mr. Michael turns to the helmsman and says, "Helm, change course to ANTRIP 972, and increase speed to presser 104."

The helmsman responds with the course correction, and the increase in speed, and we are on our way.

Mr. Michael now turns to us all and says, "We are now running super quiet and super stealth mode from this point forward. Record everything, that we say, do, what we hear, see and track. That includes everything we say and do, and be ready to transmit it instantly. I would also recommend you record any final messages you may want to send home, should the need arise." He walks to his station, sits in silence, and we all do the same.

FORTY-SIX

We have been on patrol for a couple of weeks now. A day before we reached the asteroid, our sensors and communications systems started recording Morian activity. We are all surprised that we started capturing messages this early, but remembered that our comms and sensor equipment have been upgraded. At first, it is just bits and pieces, but with each passing day the activity increases. We haven't been able to make any sense out of it, but it is recorded.

When we reached the asteroid, the skipper circled it a couple of times to determine the best place for us to set down and to make sure nobody else was there. After finding a spot the skipper liked, he set the ship down on the asteroid, and we start to settle in for the long run. We shut down the engines, but we leave all other systems functioning. We still must breathe, do our jobs, and be ready to go in an instance notice.

We have been sitting on the asteroid for two months now, recording conversations, logging, and plotting objects and ships the sensors have picked up. The communications have been deciphered, but we don't understand what they are saying. We just can't put together the puzzle they are presenting to us. The sensors are picking up ships passing by us, and they mainly appear to be cargo vessels. We have plotted the direction they are heading, and it all seems to be in the same general direction, but their destination is well outside the range of our sensors. It is all we can do to just stay put and do our assigned jobs. We all want to break loose from this rock, follow one of the ships from a distance, and see if we can find out what their destination is. As ordered, each day we are sending bursts of data back to the command center.

The command center is receiving this information, deciphering the data, and tracking all the information. They are also sending the information to the main command center on DSS-7. Admiral Graham is now in the command center daily, along with Admiral Kleg. As the information is received and categorized, it is sent on to Hyperthean command. Admiral Graham's command is deeply concerned about the reports, and they decide to increase the scout activity a little deeper into the region of space where the extended patrol range has been set. Hyperthean command is also concerned about the activity and decides to send a fleet toward the India sector. Admiral Graham speaks with them, and asks that they only send the fleet to be around DSS-3. He explains his request that he would like for the 71 patrol to continue to monitor the situation and to gather better information so we can get an idea on what the Morians are doing. As of now, we don't believe they know we are onto them. They agree with Admiral Grahams suggestion and he orders the fleet to go to DSS-3.

A couple of days ago, sensors on the 71 picked up a larger vessel. We were finally able to determine that it was a warship, probably a cruiser. It to, was traveling in the same direction as the rest of the ships that have passed by. For the past two months, we have been sitting on this asteroid, and we have tracked at least forty-two ships passing through the India sector of space. Only two of the ships appear to be warships.

We are now a week into our third month on the asteroid,

when our sensors pick up a ship that appears to be approaching us. The skipper quickly has us man all our stations in case we have been detected. It is a smaller ship, more like a Morian scout. It continues to approach our location, and its speed is slowing, indicating it is approaching us with caution. We still don't know if it has detected us. We can feel the tension building within each of us, as we sit at our stations. The skipper and Mr. Ezekiel are hanging over the sensor screens, watching the ship as it approaches the other side of the asteroid. It slows more, and then the sensors pick up a scan start up on the other side of the asteroid.

Mr. Ezekiel says, "It has begun a scan of the asteroid. They are slowly moving towards the front of the asteroid."

It will take it about an hour to finish a thorough scan of that side. The hour passes, and the ship begins its scans of the next area. When it finishes their scans of this section, another hour has passed. It will now begin to scan the next half where we are located.

Mr. Michael says, "Okay, this is what I want us to do. Shut down all systems, everything. We have enough oxygen to breathe for the next three hours without the oxygen generators on. I don't want anything running that will give off any sounds or heat. When that ship passes over us we should be cool and quite enough for them to think we are just a piece of the rock. The only thing we should have on is cloaking. Get to it."

Everybody turns in their seats and begins to shut down everything. It generally takes us forty-five minutes to do a shutdown process, but we got it done in thirty. We just sit there in total darkness, we don't even have sensors functioning, so we don't even know where, or what the ship is doing. That hour has passed, and the scout should now be scanning the part of the asteroid where we are located. Everyone is sweating, considering the darkness, looking at the hull, wondering if the ship is out there, just hoovering over us, waiting for us to make a sound. We just sit.

The second hour has passed, and the Morian ship should be completing the final scan of the asteroid by now, and we are still here. All our nerves are as tight as fully wound rubber bands, the slightest movement or sound will probably cause us to snap. The temperature inside the ship has cooled drastically. It is probably now about forty degrees in here, and we all are starting to shiver, but still, nothing has happened. We don't hear any type of sound coming from outside.

We are now at two hours and forty-five minutes, and our oxygen levels are starting to get extremely low. Some of us are starting to experience oxygen deprivation. The skipper decides it is time to take a chance, and see where this ship is.

He turns to Mr. Ezekiel, and says in a whisper, "Mr. Ezekiel, bring up short range sensors, and see if you can see this ship. Also turn on the viewer, and let's see what is outside the ship."

Mr. Ezekiel turns on the sensor array and viewer, and in about one minute it lights up the ship with a dim glow, and he looks at the screen as we all wait for his response. Finally, he responds, "It appears we are in the clear on both."

"Chief, start up the oxygen generation system."

The chief turns on the oxygen generation system at his command station and tells the skipper that it is done.

The skipper now tells him to give us some heat also.

Now the skipper turns to Mr. Ezekiel and says, "Turn on your long-range sensors and give me a full sweep of the area. I want to know where everything is, and especially that scout ship that came to investigate my asteroid."

"Yes sir," and immediately turns on all sensors and begins his scans. About five seconds later he reports that all ships are moving as normal through our area with a three-hour time delay considered. As far as that scout is concerned, he appears to have moved back to a normal travel path with the rest of the ships that are passing through. I can only assume that we were not detected when he scanned the asteroid."

"Good, but I want you to keep a special watch for any

activity out of the ordinary coming from my asteroid. We still can't rule out the possibility that they are now playing the same game we are. Since we were silent for so long we don't know what was going on. Go ahead and bring the ship back to normal status before we went silent.

Mr. Ezekiel, I want your section to start analyzing all the data we have up to the point we had to shut down, and from the point we picked everything back up. I want to know everything we can about that missing three hours. Piece it together for me."

"Yes sir," and he and his staff begin working on piecing together the information as best they can. The rest of us bring all our instrumentation back up. The ship starts to warm up, and the oxygen levels are starting to return to normal. We are beginning to relax again, but with every sound that is out of the ordinary, we all jump expecting a Morian to be there.

It takes Mr. Ezekiel and his gang about six hours to take all the information they have and replot every ship they were tracking. He calls Mr. Michael over to his plot table and shows him every ship they were tracking.

"Sir, every ship we were tracking is plotting as normal." He moves his hands in a gesture showing each of the ships movements as they were plotting just before we had to shut down to the point where we are now. "Except for one sir."

He now points to the scout ship as it started its movement toward the rock up to the point when we shut down the systems.

"I can't find any additional data to indicate that they left the asteroid. I can only assume that they are also now on this asteroid doing their own thing, whatever that might be."

"Oh great, now we are going to play a cat and mouse game with this Morian scout."

He pauses for a couple of minutes thinking and then says, "Since there have been no aggressive moves towards us, I am going to assume he doesn't know we are here. With that said,

I want you and the rest of the crew to continue what we have been doing as if they are not on this asteroid with us.

Mr. Ezekiel, I want you and your team to develop a new app for me. I want you to take some of your short-range sensors, set them to ultra-high and monitor all activity for a range of one mile out from this asteroid. If anything, anything, so much as moves an inch from where it is currently, I want to know about it. I want to be able to pinpoint their location."

"Yes sir, we should be able to have that for you by tomorrow morning."

"No sir, I want it in six hours."

"Yes sir, six hours. We will get right on it."

"I also want to know if they so much as say boo, you pinpoint where they are."

"Yes sir."

Mr. Ezekiel, Stephanie and Phil begin working on the concept for the new app they need to develop. Mr. Ezekiel has asked Mat to also monitor the communication station and sensors at the same time. It will be a little difficult, but he can do it. He puts on a set of wireless headsets and listens to the activity that the Morians are sending out. At the same time, he is watching the sensors for any activity that changes. With the computers doing the same thing, they will probably tell him about it before he can catch it with his ears or eyes.

Mr. Ezekiel and his gang have completed the app in six hours, and it is working. It still needs some fine tuning, but it works. Mr. Michael is pleased with what they have done, and tells them so. Mr. Ezekiel says they will continue to work on the app and get all the bugs out, but it will do what it was designed to do.

We are now monitoring our normal processes, along with this new app, and things appear to be normal. We still do not know where this Morian scout is. It has been two weeks since our first encounter with him.

The asteroid has now moved out of the India quadrant

and into the Hotel quadrant. We have about two months left of our patrol, sitting on this asteroid. If the Morian scout is on this asteroid with us, he has been as patient as we have been. We have not heard a peep out of him, no movement and no communications. We are getting very concerned about this. If he is here, and just sitting here monitoring the situation, and does not suspect we are here why isn't he creating as much chatter as the rest of the ships passing by? There is no reason why he, or the Morians, should suspect we are here, and have been monitoring this area of space. They have not made any type of moves or sent any communications to indicate they suspect we are here. If he does suspect we are here, this could be a long wait and see game, as we still have a couple of months left before we move from here.

We are continuing to remain on the asteroid, as it moves through the Hotel quadrant. As we approach the end of the Hotel quadrant, we have not had any movement from the Morian scout. He has been with us for four months now. We have continued to monitor all the Morian activity as they move through the quadrant, with no significant change in their movement. We have about two weeks left in our patrol, and we are one day from moving out of the Hotel quadrant when an alarm goes off on the app that Mr. Ezekiel created. Everyone almost jumps out of their skin as it goes off. Mr. Ezekiel quickly turns it off, and everyone is quickly trying to figure out what set it off. Stephanie quickly jumps in with, "We have something moving from the asteroid."

Now all sensors are monitoring a ship taking off as they depart the asteroid. We are all shocked as we determine that they had parked in a valley that was about a quarter of a mile from us. We continue to monitor the Morian scout as it moves towards the other ships, and then continues on its' route towards wherever they are going.

We all breathe a sigh of relief to know that this cat and mouse game is over, but Mr. Michael is not quite sure it is over yet. They may have left some type of detection device behind to catch us as we leave the rock. We have no way of knowing.

We are now two weeks on the other end of our patrol in the Hotel quadrant. All activity is showing that the Morian ships are entering our area at the upper end of the Hotel quadrant. All the chatter we are picking up is decreasing, as we get further away. Only our long-range sensors are picking up the movement of the ships as they enter the India quadrant.

Mr. Michael believes we are through with our patrol and instructs us to get ready to leave the rock. He instructs the helmsman to lift off very softly, and slowly, to make sure we don't disturb any of the asteroid material around us. The skipper is doing this in case the Morians did leave some type of detection device behind to pick up any movement out of the ordinary. If we do disturb something and it sets off an alarm, we probably won't know about it until we see Morian ships coming in the direction of the asteroid.

We lift off and start our turn to head towards home. We pick up speed as we leave the H-1 quadrant. We continue to monitor all our sensors, but don't detect any Morian ships heading our way. We will continue to monitor.

We have been traveling towards home for a month now, and everything appears to be good. At this point, Mr. Michael says, "Mr. Ezekiel, turn on our detection beacon. I want to let command know where we are."

Mr. Ezekiel smiles and says, "Yes sir," as he reaches and presses the button to turn the beacon back on.

As we watch, we see the red light go off, and the display goes to full green status. This is a great relief for all of us, as we feel we will reach home safely, even though it is still two months away.

FORTY-SEVEN

The Command Center has been receiving daily information from the 71, but they don't understand why we have turned off our tracking signal where we are at, or why we won't answer any calls that they make to us. Captain Grey has told them to stop trying to contact us, but they don't understand why. The crew members' families were notified that they we're missing, but nothing was given that we are dead.

The distress signal was extremely weak, and lasted about a week before it was completely gone. No one ever found the beacon that was sending the signal. We just vanished into thin air. A search of the Delta sector of space where we disappeared lasted about three months before the search and rescue efforts were called off.

It is now a year and a half later, and the command center is at their normal routine of getting coded messages from all the scouts that have been deployed. All the blips on the plots are active indicating where the scouts are currently. The person that is monitoring the blips for the deployed scouts is sitting back in his seat, when he notices there is a new blip on his screen in the Echo Sector. He moves forward towards the screen to get a closer look, and he can't believe his eyes. He suddenly jumps up, and says to the command center officer, "Sir, sir, a new blip just came on my screen. Sir, it says it's the 71!"

Many of the personnel in the command center are now racing over to look at his screen. They see the new blip, and the identification number for the blip.

Mr. Webb, the officer in charge of the duty watch says, "Ron, verify that the blip is authentic please. The rest of you get back to your stations."

Ron runs through the processes at his station and comes back, "Yes sir, authentication verifies the signal is the 71."

Mr. Webb now turns to another person and says, "Jason, contact Captain Grey and tell him that we have an authenticated blip for the 71 on our screens in the Echo Sector."

Jason makes a call to Captain Greys office, tells them of the information, and within five minutes Captain Grey is in the command center.

Captain Grey says, "Have you sent a verification communication to the 71 yet?"

"Yes sir, we have sent it out, and we are waiting to see if they will respond."

Tense seconds go by, and then a quick signal from 71 comes in verifying they are there. A cheer goes out in the room, and everyone is jumping up and down with joy knowing that the crew of 71 is okay.

Captain Grey has a grin on his face, as his face softens in relief hearing the great news.

Admiral Stark is now aware that the 71 has turned on its tracking signal, and has now entered the Command Center.

It has been a week now that everyone knows that the 71 and crew are alive and well and that they should be arriving back at the *Hyperthia* in about a month and a half. The information they sent in has been continually combined with the other information that has been received from other scout patrols. It has the high command meeting for hours on end, and new orders are being sent out to all ships in the fleets. Hyperthean High Command is now involved to a high level. It is sending six fleets of ships in our direction, and they should be arriving near the Juliet quadrant within the next ten months. It appears we are preparing for an invasion.

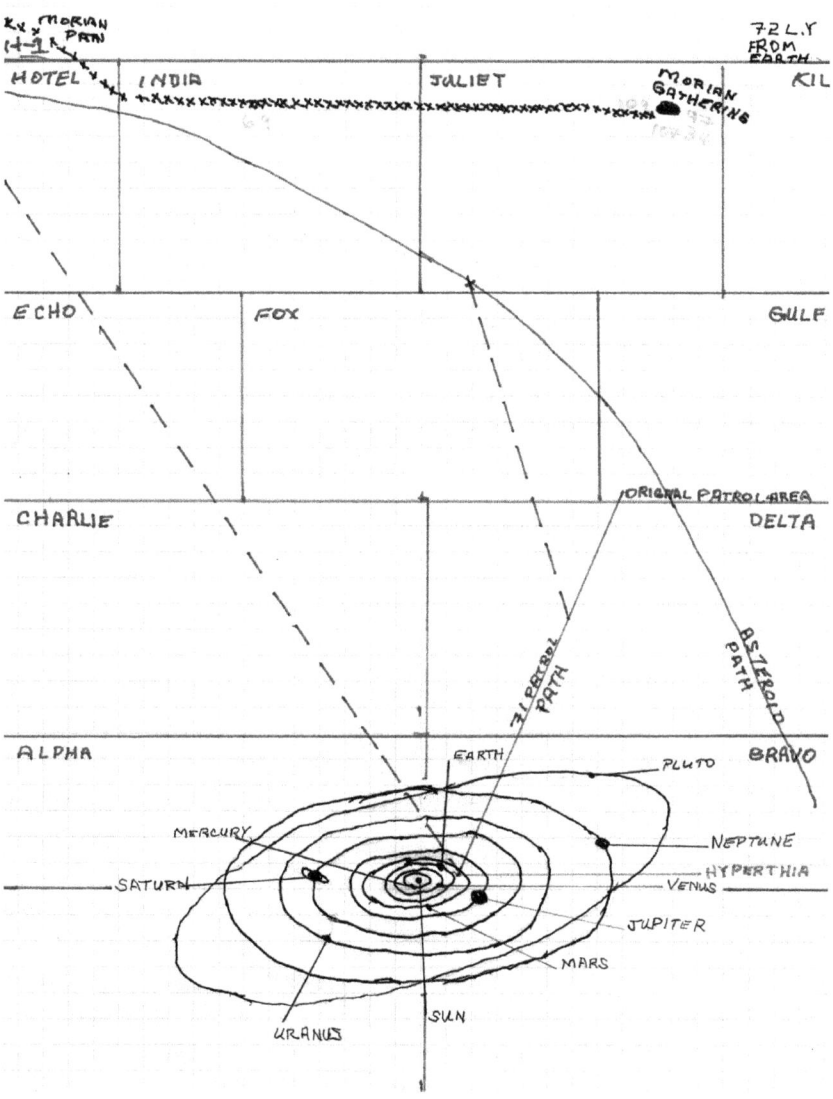

Scout travel path

FORTY-EIGHT

When the 71 turned on their tracking signal, it took about thirty seconds before they got a request to verify their signal. Mr. Michael tells Mr. Ezekiel to send out the verify burst. For the first time in over a year we feel safe again.

We are now getting regular communications from the command center telling us how good it is to hear from us. We are also happy to receive these messages, but the thing we want most is to be able to communicate with our families back home. Finally, we receive permission to talk with our families. We are to keep our conversations short, and we are not to talk about our mission. We are to do our communications one at a time and we are limited to ten minutes. Mr. Michael has decided, to be fair, to put all our names in a hat, mix them up, and to draw a name. The name he draws will be the one who will be selecting the names from the hat, one at a time.

All of us have written our names down onto a piece of paper and placed them all in the hat. He has Mr. Ezekiel mix up the names, and then he draws a name from the hat. He hands the name to Stephanie and has her open the piece of paper and read whose name it is.

Stephanie unfolds the piece of paper, and says, "Mat."

Mr. Ezekiel takes the piece of paper from Stephanie, places it back into the hat, and mixes them up all over again.

"Mat, you get the honor of pulling the names from the hat for all of us to make our calls home. So, if you would please, draw the first name."

Mat reaches into the hat, and draws a piece of paper and hands it to Mr. Michael.

He says, "Sam, looks like you get to be our first caller."

Sam is one of our enlisted members that works with the chief on the engines. He grins, and Mr. Ezekiel takes him over to the communication station, and gives him instructions on what he needs to do. Then Mr. Ezekiel tells us, "Your call will be going to the command center, and then your call will be monitored by security there. So be careful what you say. Also, in fairness to you, we will be making a call to the command center first, informing them each time who is making the call. They will first contact your home to make sure that your family is there to receive your call. Once that has been done they will put you through.

So, Sam, if you will give me five minutes, I will get all of this set up for you, okay?"

Sam is a little nervous but says, "Yes sir."

Mr. Ezekiel has Stephanie go through the process with the command center. In about five minutes she comes back that the command center is ready for Sam to talk with his family.

Mr. Ezekiel takes Sam to the communication station, and Sam tells the command center he is ready to talk with his family. At this point we all back away to give him some privacy.

The ten minutes pass, Sam ends his call, and as he is walking away from the station we all see that tears are welling up in his eyes, but he has a big grin on his face. He turns to Mr. Michael and Mr. Ezekiel and says, "Thank you, I know that meant a lot to my family, and it meant a lot to me. I will never forget it."

Sam starts to head back to his duty station and we all give

him a pat on the back as he passes by. We are all eager to have our turns to talk with our families.

Mr. Ezekiel now says, "Okay, Mat, draw the next name."

We go through this process until all fifteen of us gets a turn at calling our families, and are all grateful for the opportunity.

FORTY-NINE

Admiral Stark is now calling all his admirals and requesting that they be at the *Hyperthia* by tomorrow morning at 0800. They will be gathering to meet in the admirals' conference room.

In the meantime, he has instructed Captain Grey to download all the information into his conference room database. He also requests that Captain Grey and his top analysts, join him in his conference room in the next thirty minutes.

As Captain Grey's staff and the Admirals staff meet in his conference room, they are gathered around the holographic display of the universe. It is zoomed in on the Juliet quadrant of space, showing all the Morian activity that has been going on there. Admiral Stark comes into the room, and they come to attention, and he tells them to carry on.

Admiral Stark says, "A little over a year ago, we sent out one of our scout ships, the 71, on a top-secret mission. They did an excellent job in getting us the information that we needed. We knew they were alive, but we had to keep it a secret. Captain Grey has been downloading their information into the main command center database every day, and will share with us what all of it means. Captain Grey, if you please."

"The 71 sacrificed a lot to get us this information. From our analysis, the Morians have been gathering a large force in this sector of space."

He now points to a large mass of dots in a remote sector of the Juliet quadrant.

"We don't know how long they have been amassing this large armada of ships here, nor do we know what their intent is. The information we have gathered shows massive movement of supply ships going and coming from this sector. The Hyperthean High Command and Admiral Graham were given this information as we received it.

I have ordered a dozen scout ships to the area, but it will take them another two months to get there at max speed. We will start with four of the ships infiltrating their gathering point, four scouts are being sent to go beyond the Juliet sector to see how deep their penetration is. Then I have four ships that are setting up patrols just outside of the Juliet sector, in Fox, to continue monitoring their activity, and for relief purposes. Until these scouts get there and start sending us more detailed information, we have no idea what kind of ships they have in there, how many, or what they are doing."

Stan says, "Thanks captain for the update. Fleet admirals will be here in the morning, we will be meeting with them, and we will be giving them an update."

All the admirals have arrived at the *Hyperthia,* and are starting to gather in the admiral's conference room. Admiral Stark has been there for the past four hours, discussing different aspects of the information that has been displayed on his conference room hologram. As the admirals arrive, they are starting to be updated with the information and being brought up-to-speed. It takes another four hours to share the information and to answer all their questions.

Admiral Stark calls the room to order and addresses the room, "If I may have your attention."

The room gets quiet.

"As all of you have been updated, you know the Morians are gathering ships at a point in the Juliet sector of space that is causing great concern for us. The Hyperthean High Command has also shown great concern about this gathering and has sent six fleets of ships. They are under the command of Admiral Graham. They are near DSS-3 waiting on orders. The plan is that Admiral Graham will be sending two of these fleets to the Hotel sector, and they will be setting up a blockade preventing other Morian ships from going into the Juliet quadrant. As soon as this blockade is established, the Morians will be aware that we are aware of their presence in the Juliet quadrant. That blockade will be in place within the next three months.

So gentlemen, we must put together our own plans. We need to have it in place within three months. We need to move quickly.

I would like to have Mr. Grey go over what we have at this point."

Captain Grey explains the situation by pointing out where the Morians have gathered, and where the Hypertheans will be coming from, setting up their blockade, and stationing their other four fleets around the Hotel quadrant. He also explains what he plans on doing with his scouts, and what their purpose will be.

Admiral Fuentes interrupts and says, "Gentlemen, we plan on taking the offensive this time. We need to come up with a plan on what ships we will be deploying into the Juliet quadrant, and how we will be spreading our defenses through our solar system. It will take some time to get our ships into the Juliet quadrant, so we need to set our plans now and get our ships moving. I want to spend the rest of the day going over how we will get this accomplished.

Oh, by the way, I have also been discussing the situation

with Admiral Stark, and we do have some other concerns. As we all know, the Morians are devious, and this setup by them in the Juliet quadrant causes us some other concerns. When we set up our defenses for the solar system, we want scouts going out on deep space patrols. We want them past our solar system searching for any type of Morian activity, just in case they are planning any side attacks.

Even with all our current information we still are not certain as to their intent for being in the Juliet sector. Until we get better intel from our scouts, we are uncertain how to deploy our fleets. With that understanding, we still need to be on the aggressive side of this."

FIFTY

Admiral Stark returns to his quarters and sits at his desk. As he does so, he starts a thought to contact someone, but has second thoughts. He leans forward, puts his elbows on the desk, interlocks his fingers, and is in deep thought.

As Admiral Stark contemplates the situation, he has a lot of questions and concerns on his mind. We still do not know enough to set up a decent strategy. All we know is that they are there in the Juliet quadrant. What are they doing out there? What will we find? Don't know. We know their technology has changed as much as the Hypertheans. So, it must be far superior to what we have on many of our ships. We are just now getting some of the newer technology and ships from the Hypertheans, but we still will be no match for whatever they have, technologically. We've got to get those scouts in there to find out what they have, so we can build our strategies. Think Stan, think. We know they are in the Juliet quadrant. Scouts are on their way to find us as much information as they can. I know what I need to do. I need to reach out, make a couple of contacts, and see if we can get more information.

He places a call to the communication center, and tells them to get someone from the diplomatic core on earth.

He says to the communication center to tell them that he would like to speak with them right away.

About fifteen minutes later he receives a call from the communication center informing him that they have someone from the diplomatic core on the line ready to speak with him.

"This is Admiral Stark. May I ask who I am speaking with?"

"This is Mr. Allen from the diplomatic core."

"It is a pleasure to speak with you Mr. Allen. I don't believe I have had the pleasure of speaking with you before. What are your duties in the diplomatic office?"

"I am part of the diplomatic council dealing with relations between other planets."

"Perfect, Mr. Allen. You are just the person I need to speak with. We have a situation here, and I need someone of your qualifications to help me out."

"I will do my best. What is it you need?"

"When Admiral Graham oversaw the fleet, one of the things he did was to establish a relationship with a race of people known as the Veltans. His main contact was a person by the name of Sentur. I would like to know what our current relations is with the Veltans."

"We still have good relations with them. From our talks with them, they know that we have become close enough with the Hyperthean Federation to become part of it. They were also pleased to hear that Admiral Graham has taken a position with the Hypertheans, and that he oversees the deep space stations. They believe this will help in improving relations with other races."

"Mr. Allen, I am going to share something with you that can have grave consequences for us, and Earth, should our suspicions prove to be correct."

Stan shares with him the situation that we have in the

Juliet sector and how the Hypertheans are also reacting to the situation.

"Mr. Allen, I need you to speak with the Veltans to see how much information they can share with us on what the Morians are doing in the Juliet sector. I would appreciate it very much."

"I will do the best I can. I will contact you in a few days, once I know anything."

Stan thanks him, and they sign off.

It has been several weeks since Stan last spoke with Mr. Allen from the diplomatic core. The fleet has been getting ready for battle. All the younger cadets are excited about this possible battle, but the more experienced personnel are apprehensive. The Hyperthean fleet is moving closer to setting up their blockade, and the scouts are still about a month out before they arrive on location. Reports from the scouts still come in, but they are not encountering any activity, nor are they picking up any major Morian communications.

As Stan continues to contemplate his next move, he receives a call from the communication center that he has a call from the diplomatic center. He sits up immediately, and tells them to put the call through.

"This is Admiral Stark."

"Good morning Admiral. This is Mr. Allen."

"Mr. Allen, it is good to hear your voice. I hope you have some good news for me."

"I have news, but I'm not sure it is what you are looking for. We have spoken with the Veltans, and they have some great concerns about what the Morians are doing in the Juliet sector. About six months ago, they had one of their ships passing very close to the Juliet sector when they were approached by a Morian patrol. They were harshly asked what they were doing in the sector. They replied they were just passing through on their way home and they were instructed to take another route. They were then escorted out of the area, without any harm. They did add, that they picked up some chatter that the Morians were planning something big, but could not specifically say what that might be. I'm sorry but that is the most I could get from them."

"Thanks, Mr. Allen. Even this bit of information does help some. At least we know they are planning on doing something out there, just what is still the big question. I appreciate the effort you put into this. If you hear of anything from any other sources, I would appreciate you passing it along to me."

"You're welcome. I'm sorry I couldn't get more information for you. If I do hear anything, I will make sure the information is passed along to you immediately. Best of luck. Bye."

Stan sits back in his chair and wonders what powers or weapons the Veltans might have that keeps the Morians at bay. What are the Morians afraid of? They are not the type to be afraid of anyone, to give anyone respect, or to avoid them.

FIFTY-ONE

Two months have passed since Stan has heard anything of significance. The Hypertheans are getting closer to where they want to set up their blockade. The Morians are now aware the Hypertheans are moving in a direction that could interfere with their movement into the Juliet sector. There is a lot of communications going on back and forth between the Hypertheans and the Morians. The Hypertheans are using their best diplomacy to throw off the Morians about what their intent is. So far, it is working but the Hypertheans are seeing that the Morians are starting to have a lot of ship movement toward the Hyperthean ships. They are making counter movements to throw off the Morians. It is a game of strategy, something like chess, you need to be thinking three moves ahead of your opposition, since they are doing the same. As you make each move, you change your strategy to improve your odds of countering their next move.

Meanwhile, Stan is starting to get reports from the scouts. They are starting to pick up communications that the Morians are sending out, and the scouts are relaying them into the command center where the messages are being broken down and interpreted. As the messages are interpreted, they are coming to Stan and to Admiral Graham's command. It appears the Morians are starting to get nervous about what the Hypertheans are doing. They appear to be gathering some ships to send back along their route to intercept the Hypertheans. It does not appear that they have detected the scout ships yet.

Admiral Graham continues to get this information, and he is keeping the Hyperthean High Command informed.

The month has passed, and the Hypertheans are at the location where they plan on setting up their blockade. As they arrive, the Morians are there to greet them, but the Morians are surprised by the number of Hyperthean ships that are there. Now they show no signs of aggression, but their communications are strong, angry, and aggressive. The Hypertheans have been successful in setting up the blockade, but they are surrounded by Morian ships on three sides that are increasing in number. We are sure this standoff will soon come to a head, but the Hypertheans still have the superiority advantage of numbers and more of their ships are on their way to help, should they need it.

Our scouts have arrived on location in the Juliet sector, and they are starting to send in their reports which is helping us in understanding the situation. Reports from the scouts, that are to follow the route where the Morians are traveling, are reporting that the number of ships going into the Juliet sector is decreasing, but the number of ships heading out of the Juliet sector is increasing by the day. With the Hyperthean blockade, it appears they are sending ships back to assist in breaking the blockade.

The scouts that were sent to see if they are going deeper out of the Juliet sector, are reporting that they are finding no indication that their intent is to go deeper into space. It appears the Juliet sector is where they are planning on setting up shop.

The scouts that are in the Juliet sector are sending us some important information. The Morians have amassed about ten thousand ships in the sector. They are building a huge station that appears to be a base for these ships to operate from, like the deep space stations we have set up. The scouts report that it appears the base is only about half finished, and that they still have several months of work left before they will complete it. The Morians have established outposts around the entire area. The ships appear to be around a thousand cruisers, at least eight thousand destroyers, and a mass of other ships for a total attack operation. Since we know of no other interests in the area, we can only assume that they are establishing this base to attack Earth.

We tell the scouts, in the middle of the Morians, to pull back to a safe distance. We don't want them to be detected, but we do want to continue to receive information.

Admiral Stark pulls his staff and admirals into a meeting. With this information, he knows what he needs to do, but he wants to make sure that everyone agrees with his plan. It will be a risky one. He updates everyone on what has been going on and that the scouts on the outer patrol are reporting in on a regular basis.

"The Morians are sending at least two cruisers and ten destroyers back to the blockade area every couple of days. If they continue to do this on a regular basis we may stand a chance for an offensive."

Everyone in the room begins to look at each other, and you can hear soft chatter as Stan gives this time to soak in.

"Gentlemen please, if I may continue. As you all know, it will take us at least three months to reach the Juliet quadrant at flank speed. We don't know that the Morians have any patrols in our area, but with the blockade in effect, I'm sure it won't take them long to figure out that we also know they are there. It will take them at least four months before they can get patrols down here to watch us, and if we plan things right, we might be able to catch them by surprise. Our scouts in the Juliet sector can inform us when, and if, they send any patrols our way."

Stan looks at General Todd and says, "General, I need you to do something for us, and I need it done as quickly and as quietly as you can."

"Yes sir, name it."

"We have domes that protect all of our bases on earth. We are at a point where the likelihood the Morians could break through our defenses and attack Earth. We currently have these domes turned off, but I want you to bring them back up. BUT, here is the assignment I have for you: I want you to set up transmitters for domes around every major city in the world. I don't want them activated, and I don't want the cities to know that you did it. I don't want countries to use these domes to protect their cities should they want to go to war against each other. Also, build the power source for these dome transmitters within the protection of the domes. Also I want you, from your base in Texas, to be the only one that can activate the domes around these cities. This must be done within the next four months. Do you think you can get that done?"

General Todd looks at Stan, gives him a sideways nod of his head, and says, "It will be very hard. We don't have enough transmitters to accomplish such a task. If I can get some help from our manufacturing facilities around the world to build them, we might be able to do it. We will do the best we can sir."

"Thanks, General Todd. I know this is putting a big job on you, and we will do all we can to get the manufacturing facilities to help you get this accomplished. I want it to be their top priority.

Now gentlemen, we don't have the whole Earth protected with these domes, so now it falls to us to figure out how we will protect the rest of Earth."

Stan continues as he paces back and forth in front of them, "We know, from the information that the scouts have provided us, they are sending ships back towards the barricade that the Hypertheans have set up. This is reducing the number of ships that they will have in the Juliet sector. We can also surmise that the blockade will come under attack long before we can get ships to the Juliet sector. With that assumption, depending on how the battle goes there, we will assume they will send more ships into this fight, reducing their strength even further, we hope. So, this is what I think we ought to do. I need all of you to help me with this plan. We are going to send half of our forces on a strategic attack of the Morian base in the Juliet sector, and we will need to spread out the other half here to protect our solar system. The half that stays here, will pull back to a tighter parameter that will be out around Mars. All base personnel that are on our outer planets will be pulled back to the protection of our inner parameter. After the other half of you leave our solar system, we will again activate the protection barrier, but we will maintain scout patrols that will be going out in search patterns to detect any Morian ships that may be approaching our solar system. This will leave you free to do your job in destroying the Morian base. I want you to engage the enemy and stop them from coming back. We also know that the Hypertheans are sending a fleet of ships to help us in our battle, but they may be diverted to assist in the battle around the blockade. If we can destroy the Morian base and ships in the Juliet sector, the Morians will not have any reason to continue their fight with the Hypertheans around the blockade. So gentlemen, it is now your turn to give me your input."

There is a lot of conversation going on around the room. Finally, Admiral Fuentes speaks up and says, "Admiral, instead of heading straight for the Juliet sector, why don't we take a wider approach and come in from the side? It will take us a little longer to get there, but it may give us a greater advantage of surprise."

"Does anybody have a problem with this plan?"

Nobody speaks up, but Admiral Stark does have some concern about the extra time it will take, and even with taking a wider approach will we really be surprising them.

Finally he says, "Okay George, let's look at your approach. Work up the numbers, and let's see how much time it will add to our attack plan. I would like those numbers in the next six hours."

Admiral Fuentes leaves and has a team working on the approach. He does come back to Admiral Stark with his plan within the six hours. Admiral Stark gathers his admirals again, and Admiral Fuentes presents his plan for an hour, but Admiral Stark is not in favor of it.

"This plan will take an extra month to get to the Juliet sector, and I am concerned about the battle that the Hypertheans will be in. Adding an extra month getting there could put us in more danger. It could take more Hyperthean lives, especially if it puts too much pressure on the Hypertheans. If the Morians do send an attack force to Earth, they would be here a month before we got to their base.

No, we will take the direct approach."

He orders the fleet to get ready to execute his plan and be ready to leave within the week.

Stan says, "Admiral Fuentes, select the ships from the fleet that will be going to the Juliet sector and get them ready for battle. The *Hyperthia* will be staying here as part of the protection fleet. You will command the fleet going to the Juliet sector. Any questions?"

"No sir."

"Take Captain Stillwell with you. I recommend you make him your second. You will need his experience. Let me know what ships you will be taking and which one will be your command ship. I want your fleet on its way within the next six days."

Now Stan wants to focus on getting half of the fleet on its way with all the munitions and supplies it will need to sustain a lengthy battle within the next three months. He needs to have Admiral Duffy set up his supply routes for supplies and additional munitions. He also needs to provide these supply ships with the proper protection. Stan knows they will be running towards Morian ships that will be coming to Earth to attack us. Stan is working with Admiral Duffy to determine alternate routes that might be able to take them out of harm's way.

Admiral Duffy has his supply ships ready in three days and is continuing to supply the fleet that will be going to the Juliet sector. He starts his supply ships on the route that Admiral Stark's team has laid out, and Stan is providing them with ten destroyers to protect the supply ships.

The fleet that is headed for the Juliet sector has gathered at the edge of the Bravo sector near the outer planet rotation of Pluto. Admiral Duffy has supplied all the ships with the munitions they can hold and all the supplies they can carry for a three-month journey.

Admiral Fuentes has sent out six of his scout ships to do long range patrols to detect any Morian activity that they might encounter along their route. It is now time for the fleet to leave, and Admiral Stark is there to say farewell and to wish them God's speed and luck for the mission ahead of them.

Admiral Fuentes orders his ships to get under way, and they depart for the Juliet sector. Admiral Stark is on his way back to the *Hyperthia* and calls the command center.

"Captain Watson, as soon as all the ships pass the protection barrier, I want you to activate it. No ships are to pass in or out of the barrier without your permission and the proper codes."

"Yes sir."

"Once you activate the barrier, order all remaining ships back to their assigned parameter positions in the Mars orbital path. Also, order all personnel that are on stations outside of the Mars orbit to return to the *Hyperthia*. Then I want all the enemy drones that we captured, and converted, deployed in an attack pattern out around Saturn. Do not activate them, but hide them as best you can. I want them to appear as if they still belong to the Morians. I will be back on *Hyperthia* in the next couple of hours."

"Right away sir."

A month has passed, and Admiral Stark has received word that the Hyperthean fleets are now fully engaged in battle with the Morians. The Hypertheans still outnumber the Morians two to one, but the Morians are giving them a run for their money. The Morians are attacking on three sides with ships coming from the Morian home world and ships coming from the Juliet sector. These two groups have formed an attack force from the Hyperthean weak side. Ships, from the Hyperthean home world and DSS-3, are providing reinforcements from their strong side. The Morians are keeping the Hypertheans engaged twenty-four hours a day trying to wear them down and break through their defenses. But with the Hyperthean strong side ships that are damaged can pull out of the battle and are being replaced with other ships coming from the Hyperthean home world. Also, ships that have been engaged in battle for more than twenty-four hours can pull back and are replaced with another ship. This allows them time to get some rest and have time to replenish their supplies and munitions. For every Hyperthean ship that is lost or damaged, at least four Morian ships are lost or damaged. Currently, the Morians are losing the battle. Their attacks are slowing, and their offensive is weakening.

The battle has been going on for two months now, and the Morians have stopped fighting and are now just holding their positions. There are many ships in the field of battle with fires burning, smoldering, or just floating in space as piles of junk. Many lives have been lost on both sides because of the senseless desires of the Morians. The Hypertheans welcome the cease fire and are now trying to negotiate terms with the Morians.

Admiral Graham hears the stories of the battle that the Hypertheans have been engaged in. He remembers a couple of books he read while he was on his way to Hyperthia written by a captain that had been in a great battle with the Morians. From the books, he remembers a couple of things the captain wrote.

He said they had been fighting for three months nonstop. There was so much death and destruction on both sides. Out here you only have two options, live or die. Being wounded, you are one of the lucky ones. As he looked at his viewer screen he saw ships floating as useless pieces of junk. There were fires coming from them. They appeared in space as small blow torches. Other ships had blown up, and pieces of them were floating all around, like pieces of space junk. He could see bodies floating by with the horrific look of sudden death on their faces. So much useless death, all because of one reason. One race had become so egotistical, so brainwashed, that they felt they were the only ones that should be alive. Their only objective is to kill and destroy. They have no mercy in them.

When I read this, I had flashbacks to the training I had when we first started working with the Hypertheans. The horrors they presented to us was so profound it sickened my stomach. At first, I didn't want to believe it. I do now after having been in a couple of battles with them.

FIFTY-TWO

Scouts have reported that there is a fleet of war ships heading in the direction of Earth. They have told us that the fleet is made up of fifty-seven battle cruisers, around two thousand destroyers, and several hundred other ships of unknown designation. Now the scouts have determined that this fleet will come in direct contact with Admiral Fuentes fleet in about fifteen days. The scouts have also determined that the base in the Juliet sector is still well protected by at least two fleets of Morian ships.

Admiral Stark now makes a call to Admiral Fuentes, "Admiral, how is your cruise going? Enjoying yourself?

Admiral Fuentes grins, "Yes sir, we are having a nice trip. Balmy beaches, great entertainment, and the girls aren't bad either.

What can I do for you sir?"

Admiral Stark gets down to business and says, "George, I just received word from the scouts in the Juliet sector that there is a large fleet of Morian ships heading towards Earth, and you are in their direct path. I do not want you to engage them. Your job is to wipe out everything they are doing in the Juliet sector. From what the scouts are telling us, you will need every ship you have. So I want you to take a wide birth around them and make sure that you do not engage them."

"Yes sir, do not engage."

"I would say don't worry about us back here. We can take care of matters here. But I know all the crews will be worried about their families back here, but we will take care of them as best we can. You concentrate on your job and get back here safely. If you stayed on the direct path, the Morians would be upon you in about fifteen days, so you figure out a good course change and execute it now."

"Yes sir, we will keep you informed of our course change. A question sir? What if the Morians know we are coming, and they figure out our course change and come after us, what do you want me to do?"

"See if you can outrun them toward their base, but I am hoping they feel confident and arrogant enough in their fleet back at their base to take care of you and that they will continue on to try and attack us."

"Yes sir, good luck to you."

"And to you."

As George makes his course change, out of the Gulf quadrant into the upper sectors of Fox, he will now be taking his fleet into the lower left side of the Juliet quadrant. This approach might be a bit of a surprise for the Morians, since it is not a direct approach from our solar system. This change of course will add about a week in time before they can reach the Morian base.

As they continue towards the Morian base, Admiral Fuentes has his scouts out in the direction of the direct approach. They are following the Morian fleet that is passing by going towards our solar system. The scouts report that the fleet is not even changing course but are continuing their planned course. At their current speed, they should reach Earth in about five weeks. This is reported back to Admiral Stark. He now has his defenses set up, and he is ready for them.

FIFTY-THREE

The Hyperthean High Command had brought the entire federation to high alert when they decided to set up the barrier against the Morians.

Admiral Tern now contacts Admiral Graham and says, "Chris, your deep space stations are highly vulnerable to attack. We weren't anticipating the Morians wanting to go into this section of space when we set up the deep space stations. We have decided that the stations need more protection. Also we are sending you two more fleets of ships to protect each station. For DSS-7, we are sending you an extra fleet of ships. Your station is too important to the federation. We are not expecting the earth command to provide any ships. They have enough of their own concerns. These fleets will be under your command."

"Thanks Admiral. I will use them wisely."

The fleets from Hyperthia arrived when the Hyperthean battle with the Morians was going strong, and Admiral Stark has sent half of his fleets to attack and destroy the Morian station in the Juliet sector.

Admiral Graham is monitoring the situation with both the

Hyperthean battle and how the situation is with the Earth fleet. He feels helpless as he must sit there on his station, just watch, and monitor the situation. After days of agonizing over the situation, he has decided to take some action.

As he approaches his quarters door to go to the command center, he hears a commotion outside. He opens the door, and standing before him is a Morian with a weapon pointed at him. The two guards that had been posted outside his door are lying on the floor in a pool of blood. As the admiral raises his hands half way, the Morian starts walking toward him. The admiral starts backing up.

The Morian says, "Good afternoon admiral. Having a good day?" with a snarl in his voice and on his face.

"How did you get on my station?"

The Morian laughs and says, "That really doesn't matter, does it? In a few minutes you will be dead, but I want to watch you squirm and beg for your life," as he takes another step closer, but Admiral Graham stands his ground.

The Morian starts to move to the side, starting to circle the admiral. He is now about five feet away. Suddenly, the door opens, and Admiral Kleg is rushing into the room to see how Admiral Graham is after finding the two guards down. He has sounded the alarm, and security personnel are on their way.

The Morian turns his head, sees Kleg, and starts to turn his weapon to shoot him. As he does so I say, "Run, Kleg, run!" as I lunge toward the Morian hitting him and throwing off the two shots he makes and misses Kleg. The Morian and I are now on the floor struggling for the weapon, but he is stronger than me and pushes me off. He gets to his feet while I am still on the floor. Getting up on one knee, he grabs his gun from the floor. Now Harold rushes into the room, and again the Morian is startled. He turns towards Harold to take a shot, and again I jump towards the Morian as Harold dives for cover. This time he catches me mid stride and slams the barrel of his weapon against my head, and I fall back to the floor. Now two security guards rush into the room, exchange fire with the Morian, and finally kill him.

As I lay on the floor I am still conscious, but my head is spinning and all I hear is high pitch sounds, and my vision is blurred. I can see the two guards come into the room. I hear loud sounds but they sound like three to four pops. Slowly my senses are starting to return and I try to raise up a little but I start feeling dizzy again. I am now feeling this terrible pain in my head, and then I feel something warm running down the side of my face.

Kleg and Harold get up off the floor, rush over to me and help me up from the floor.

Kleg says, "Are you alright?" as he sees a large lump forming on the side of my head with blood coming from a wound.

As I get to my feet, with the help of Harold, and trying to clear the cobwebs, I say, "I think I'm okay but I'm still feeling dizzy."

Admiral Kleg turns to the security team and says, "Contact Captain Taylor and bring this station to full alert. I want everything locked down. I want four security personnel outside the admiral's quarters, NOW! From now on there will be four guards outside his quarters, and four to go with him everywhere he goes. They are to be fully armed.

Get Captain Dreg in here now."

Within seconds you hear General Quarters over the speakers, and the sound of the general quarters alarm being sounded. All personnel are scrambling to man their stations.

When Admiral Kleg ordered more security personnel to the admiral's floor, Captain Dreg was already getting additional security. He was headed that way when he gets the call to report to the admiral's quarters immediately. In a few seconds, he has reached the admiral's floor and sees two of his security personnel lying on the floor dead. He turns to the team he has brought with him and says, "Secure all entrances to this floor. Let no one in or out."

The team rushes off and secures all entrances to the admiral's floor. Captain Dreg hurries into the admiral's quarters where four of his team are standing at the door, and he sees the dead Morian on the floor. Admiral Kleg is with Admiral Graham as he sits in his chair. He is holding a towel to his head, still trying to regain his composure and senses.

Admiral Kleg sees him enter the room and says, "We apparently have Morians on this station. Double your security on the command center, and then go through every inch of the command center to make sure that a Morian has not entered the center. Recheck all personnel in there now, and make sure that a Morian hasn't replaced one of the team on duty. While you are doing that, have a team check the room and all surrounding areas for any bombs that might have been set. Arm all of your security teams and have them search every inch of this station. Double check all personnel to make sure they are who they are supposed to be."

"Yes sir," and tries to hurry off.

Admiral Kleg says, "Oh, one more thing, I have requested that the ships' doctor come here to make sure that the admiral is okay. I'm sure he will bring other medical staff. Have your team vet them and then let them in to take care of the admiral."

"Yes sir."

As Captain Dreg is hurrying out of the room he is already on his comm device barking his orders to all his teams. He arrives at the main command center and sees that the extra guards are in place with firearms. He enters and is met by Captains Sprot and Vog asking what is going on.

Captain Dreg tells them that Admiral Graham has been attacked by a Morian, and that the admiral is fine. He tells them that they need to go to each of their team members that are on duty and make sure they are who they are supposed to be.

As they start to do that, additional security personnel have entered the area. He orders them to start a sweep of the area.

While his teams are doing their jobs throughout the station, he goes over to the communication officer and tells him he wants a secure line to all station captains and all ships captains surrounding the stations and Admiral Tern.

He says, "Tell them this is a top priority message."

The officer immediately gets all of them on the comms, and tells Captain Dreg he has them. He tells them what has just occurred, and that Admiral Kleg has brought the station to full alert. He tells them that Admiral Graham is okay and that he would like for all stations and ships protecting the stations, be brought to full alert and for all stations and ships to be searched for any Morians or explosive devices.

Admiral Tern says, "Make it so immediately. When Admiral Graham is able, please have him call me."

"Yes sir."

Captain Dreg has also ordered all security personnel on all the stations to be armed. He has placed extra security on all command centers and security for all captains on the stations.

The ship's doctor has entered the admiral's quarters. Admiral Graham is now up, walking around, holding the towel to his head and talking with Kleg. The doctor goes over to the admiral and tells him to sit in his chair, so he can have a look at the admiral.

"I'm fine doc, I don't need to sit down."

The doctor looks at him, and firmly says, "Who's the doctor here, you or me? Now I'm in charge, and you will have a seat."

The admiral reluctantly complies, and the doctor takes the towel from him, cleans the wound, then pulls an instrument from his kit, and waves it over the wound to stop the bleeding. After he finishes he says, "You're fine, you hard headed German. You should be able to resume your duties when you feel like it. You will probably have a headache for a couple of days, but I want to see you tomorrow morning to make sure everything is okay. Admiral Kleg, make sure he does that?"

"Sure doc, tomorrow morning."

"Thanks doc," and smiles at him and continues, "Now get out of here before you do make me sick."

The doctor grins back at him, turns to the medical team and says, "Let's get three gurneys, take these bodies down to the medical area so we can examine them, and determine their cause of death as if we didn't already know."

Captain Dreg has returned to the admiral's quarters, and says, "Are you okay sir?"

"Yes, I'm fine. Give us a report please."

Captain Dreg updates Admirals Graham and Kleg on everything. He now tells Admiral Graham that Admiral Tern would like for him to give him a call when you feel up to it. He also tells the admiral that the security team is outside and will go with him everywhere.

The admiral thanks him, and he turns to leave to get back to his duties. The medical team has arrived to pick up the bodies and to clean up the blood that is on the floor in the admiral's quarters and in the hallway.

As everyone leaves, the door closes, and Kleg says, "Are you sure you are okay?"

"Yes, thanks Kleg, and thanks to you and Harold for showing up when you did. I would have been a goner.

If you will excuse me now, I need a few more minutes before I call Admiral Tern."

Kleg leaves the room, and I sit back down in my chair still trying to clear the cobwebs, and thinking about what has just happened. I feel I am back to normal, I think. I lean forward, bring up my comm device, and place my call to Admiral Tern.

I see Admiral Tern on my screen and he says, "Chris, are you okay?"

"Yes admiral, I'm fine. A lump on my head, and I have a terrific headache. This was a new experience for me. I think I need to get more exercise. The struggle with the Morian was a little more than I expected."

"That would be a new experience for most of us. I'm sure the

Morian was trained for infiltration and hand-to-hand combat. So don't judge yourself too harshly. I also want to let you know what has been going on over the last hour."

"I'm sure you have been updated by your staff, and I want to say they have done an excellent job in handling the situation."

"Thank you sir. They are an excellent team."

"The high command is aware of what has happened, and they have made all fleets aware. We are also searching for more infiltrators. So far, we have not found anymore. Apparently, they were just focused on your stations, and for good reason.

We are still trying to find out how they could slip through our security and get on your stations. We will find out.

When you are ready, you can bring your stations and ships down from general quarters, but I would keep them on high alert for the time being."

"Yes sir I agree."

"Good, you take care of yourself," and they both sign off.

As I get to the door to head to the command center, my comm signals me again that I have a call coming in. This time it is Admiral Stark.

"Hi Stan. I'm fine."

"Well, at least it doesn't seem to have affected you. You old grouch."

I sit back in my chair, relax a little, and say, "Sorry Stan, just too many calls about my wellbeing, and my head still hurts. But I'm glad you are one of them. How are you doing? Getting ready for a big battle I see."

"Nah, just a little one."

"Yea, right. Listen Stan, I was getting ready to head to the command center when this Morian showed up, but I will let you know now what I was getting ready to do.

I am going to break down the fleets around stations three, four, and seven, and create a fleet that I will send to the edge of our security area near your solar system. Should you need them, they can be there in about six hours, and if I need them back here, I can recall them. I know the Hypertheans are sending a fleet to help you, but I will keep them here when they arrive. This way I can have this fleet, that will be at the edge of our security area, ready to go at a moment's notice."

"Thanks Chris, I appreciate it. It will give me some comfort knowing they are there, if I need them," as Stan smiles in the monitor.

"Don't get too cocky now. Don't underestimate the Morians. You of all people know the Morians.

"Don't worry sir, we will handle things here, and thanks."

We say our good byes, and good lucks.

I head to the command center with my security team, and we all enter the command center. The security team stays just inside the doors, standing at ease, while I go over to my team that is gathered in the command center.

"I want all of you to support me in this. If you have a problem with it, I will make sure that it is noted in the logs. I want you to split up ships from the fleets around stations three, four, and seven, and form a new fleet. I want you to send them to the edge of our security zone near the Earth's solar system. They are to stay there. Should Admiral Stark need them in their fight against the Morians in the defense of Earth, I want them sent in to join in the fight. Should we need them back here, we can recall them. We have another fleet coming in to reinforce the ships we have moved to our outer parameter. Any problem with my decision?"

I look at them all, they are all silent, and then I say, "Then, make it happen."

Then I say to Counselor Centas and Commander Areg that I would like to speak with them, as the others along with Admiral Kleg go off to execute my order.

"Commander Areg, I have been receiving a lot of calls about my wellbeing and the incident. I would like for you to put together an article about what has happened here and at all our stations. Also, let them know that I am fine, and I appreciate their concern about my wellbeing and safety. Let me see the article when you have finished, and I will approve it. Then send it to your command for their approval, and if they are okay with it, I want it sent out to the entire federation."

"Yes sir," and heads off to start writing the article.

I now turn to Counselor Centas and say, "How is everyone handling the situation. Do you feel you need to sit with anyone and talk with them?"

"I don't believe that any of the team is too stressed by the situation. But I will keep an eye on them, and if I see anything, I will meet with them. If I sense any concern, I will let you know. You, on the other hand, is another story. You have gone through something that most people don't experience. Tell me, what do you feel?"

"I'm dealing with it. I think I will be fine, but you keep an eye on me. If you feel we need to sit down, please let me know. I will do the same."

"No problem admiral, you will be my special patient. I will be watching you."

"Thanks, now get out of here. You are starting to make me uncomfortable with that probing mind of yours."

We both smile at each other, and she heads back over to the team.

After two days of searching the stations and ships they have found and captured, or killed, at least twenty-four Morians. The captured Morians on the stations are now locked up in a highly secure brig. They are awaiting the arrival of a high security brig transport ship to take them back to Hyperthean command for "deeper" interrogation.

FIFTY-FOUR

Admiral Fuentes is now a half day from the Morian station, when he is met by two fleets of Morian ships. Rather than stop and have a standoff, he charges straight ahead into the Morian fleet, and the battle begins. As he drives straight into their fleets, he scatters the Morians into an unorganized bunch of ships, leaving wreckage along his path from both sides. He turns his ships around, and they start charging back into the enemy ships before they can reorganize. He charges through them again leaving more damage behind, but he is starting to suffer more losses. Again he turns, but this time the Morians are regrouping and are ready for a direct assault this time. George holds his fleet in check, waiting for the Morians to charge at him. They take the bait and start their charge at George's fleets. He waits until they get closer and closer. Then he orders his fleet to move left and right as the Morians are on top of them. The Morians don't have time to react to this and are forced to charge straight ahead. As they start to pass by them, he orders his ships to make a sharp turn and to charge right into the middle of the Morians. This tactic has completely caught the Morians off guard and they can't react as quickly as they would like. They try to pull out of the charge, but are caught by the attacking earth ships. This time George keeps his ships engaged in battle with the Morians, destroying just over half of the Morian ships in these three attacks while losing ten ships.

The battle with the Morians continues for another two days. The earth fleet continues to have the advantage and then on the third day the battle is over. The Morians continued to fight until they had lost every ship. In the process, George has lost about a hundred ships, but this is a great victory. But the big battle is yet to come. He must deal with the station now.

He reports the results back to Stan and everyone is pleased. The Morians know of the loss of these two fleets and now orders the ships, that had been sent to the Hyperthean barricade, to return to the station to protect it. These earthlings have proven to be a bigger challenge than they expected. As these Morian ships start to return to the station, the Hyperthean command orders two fleets of Hyperthean ships to go after them.

George pulls his fleets back together to assess their damage. Two cruisers and forty-eight destroyers are too damaged to continue. They want to stay in the battle, but George orders them to stay back, group up, and protect each other as best they can. He tells them to keep the ships with the most damage in the middle and the rest should protect them.

George continues to the Morian station. He isn't receiving any resistance for the next six hours as he approaches the station. When he is about thirty minutes away from the station they can see it. A large contingent of war ships are approaching him. He keeps his fleet as close together as they can to keep the Morians from charging into them. The Morians keep charging forward, and the battle begins. Our ships that are out front are taking on the Morians with all they have, but the Morians keep coming. They are trying to force a wedge in between our ships, but we are holding the line. The Morians are starting to collide with the ships, and the damage is heavy to both sides. The

Morians are starting to break through, and George decides to split his fleet to go both left and right so they can't be encircled by the Morians. As they do so, the Morians are breaking off and are giving chase to the ships. George's fleet now turns and starts to take on the Morians. As this battle continues, George orders one of his fleets to break off and take on the station. As this fleet breaks away, the Morians realize what we are doing, and sends some of their ships after them. George now takes some of his ships and starts to form a barricade to block them from chasing after this fleet. The battle continues fiercely, and both sides are starting to lose more and more ships. George orders his fleet to start using their trans-portal and laser weapons on the Morian ships. The fleet continues with its battle as they start using their trans-portal weapons. As the larger ships use this weapon, Morian destroyers are no longer engaged in the fight, and they are starting to drift. Then the ships move in, and destroy the defenseless ships. Our scouts that are cloaked are now engaged, but are not firing any weapons. They move in close to a ship, use their trans-portal weapon, and sections of the Morian ships have personnel completely disappear. This slows the ships in their battle with the earth ships. The cruisers are starting to use their laser slicing beam on Morian cruisers, slicing them in half, and the halves start drifting apart. Now the earth cruisers move in and start firing on the halves, making sure they are useless. The battle continues for another two days as they maneuver back and forth. Georges' fleet has gotten the upper hand by the end of the second day, but the Morians are not giving up. As with the first battle, they are bound and determined to fight to the end. George continues the fight for another half day, before the rest of the Morian fleet is destroyed. In this battle, George loses another one-hundred fifty destroyers, sixteen cruisers, three thousand fighters, and one hundred scouts. He also has three hundred destroyers and twenty-seven cruisers that can't continue the battle to fight with the station. He orders them to go back and join the other ships that have been damaged. Again, the commanders of these ships are reluctant to obey this order as they can see the Morian station and want to continue in the fight. George decides to let the less damaged ships stay in the fight but orders them to stay in the back of the battle. The other ships have no choice but to travel back to the other ships in their crippled state.

The fleet that George has sent to the Morian station is now fully engaged with the station, ships, and fighters, that are protecting the station. Some of the earth ships are getting through the remaining Morian fleet and are attacking the station. The station is so large they are only inflicting minimal damage, before they are destroyed. Captain Stillwell, who commands this fleet, decides to keep his fleet together and fight these Morian ships before they take on the station. Since this fleet is only a small portion of the fleet that was sent to take on the station, they are not making much headway in this battle. They are holding their own, but that is all they can do until Admiral Fuentes arrives with the rest of his fleet.

George now takes his remaining ships, and continues to join Captain Stillwell's ships. He gets there in about thirty minutes and joins in the battle with Captain Stillwell's fleet. George now takes command of the battle. To try and get this battle over as quickly as possible, he orders the fleet to use the transportal and laser weapons. All ships are now fully engaged in the battle, and they are starting to use all weapons that are available to them. The ships are fighting gallantly, moving in and out of the enemy fleet, and taking on the Morians. Enemy ships are starting to go dead in space, while others are being sliced in half. The Morians know we can do this, but have not come up with anything to counter our weapons. They are starting to separate from us, mostly trying to avoid getting close to our ships and trying to avoid our weapons. The battle is lasting longer, with the Morians trying to avoid our ships, but we can get in close to some and destroy them, or use our trans-portal weapons to disable them. We now outnumber the Morians and can encircle them and destroy them. We know they won't surrender. We give them a chance to surrender, but George gets no response.

George has destroyed all the Morian ships, and there is nothing to protect the station. He can take it on without worrying about other ships attacking him. George has received communiques from the Hyperthean fleet that they are chasing the two Morian fleets that are trying to return to the station. They are about three days away from the station. George knows he has three days to destroy the station, before he must engage another fleet of enemy ships.

George send scouts to circle the station to determine the best place to attack. They have found sections of the station that have not been completed, and should be vulnerable. George sends several of his cruisers and destroyers to these locations and has them start their attack. As George approaches the station, the Morians send out fighters to take on the ships. George counters by sending his fighters to take on these fighters to protect his ships. This is working as George starts his attack on other parts of the station. Fighters from the station are trying to fend off George's attack, but to no avail. The ships that are attacking the vulnerable part of the station are starting to have an effect. The station is starting to break apart, and George is sending in more ships to peck away at that part of the station. Other parts of the station that are under attack are starting to weaken. Fewer and fewer fighters are attacking George's fleet as they destroy them. They are now twenty-four hours into their attack, and the returning Morian fleets are now forty-eight hours out.

George steps up his attack on the station, and it continues to weaken as more of it continues to break apart. At least a fourth of the station has been destroyed, and other parts of the station are showing signs of weakening. George now focuses his attack on the weak points, hoping they can have the station destroyed before the Morian ships get there.

Another twenty-four hours has passed, and the Morian fleet continues getting closer. But the following Hyperthean ships are now about two hours behind the Morian fleet. Since the Morian fleet is aware of this, they are sending ships back to attack the Hyperthean ships in hopes they can slow them down, but this is to no avail. It is just decreasing the number of ships they must have to move forward.

George continues pecking away at the station and half of it has been destroyed. With each passing moment, more and more of it continues to fall apart. The station has received continuous missile and gun fire for the last thirty-seven hours. If the station continues to break apart under the constant bombardment, it should be destroyed in the next day, but the Morian fleet will arrive before they can destroy it.

As the bombardment of the Morian station continues, it appears the Morians are losing more and more ground. The firing from the station has decreased, as more of the station is destroyed. Distress calls from the station have stopped as their communication systems must have been destroyed. About an hour before the approaching Morian fleet arrives, George decides to break off. He has started to pull what remains of his fleet back together and regroup for the approaching Morian fleet that should be upon them in about an hour. Ships that are crippled refuse to leave the fight and remain with the fleet. They are now ready for battle.

Scouts are now out making sure the Morians are only approaching from one direction. George's sensors do not detect any, but he wants to make sure. Their long-range sensors show that the Morians are taking the same strategy as all their other attacks, the direct approach. They are now about fifteen minutes out, and George knows from the sensors they are greatly outnumbered. Their only hope of winning this battle is the approaching Hyperthean fleet, but they are now thirty minutes behind them.

George has decided to take a different approach this time.

With less than half his fleet left, he has decided to place his fleet among the rubble of the destroyed pieces of the station and ships, both from the Morian fleet and his fleet. They are going to sit there silently as part of the destroyed fleets. All the ships have been dispersed, just sitting there dead silent, no fighters out, just silent.

The Morians arrive, and see the station almost destroyed. They slow to a dead crawl being very cautious, especially with no ships attacking, or any seen to attack. They are not picking up any movement, just blips on their screens of all the debris floating around. They are now dispersing their fleet to start moving through the debris field. Moving slowly and cautiously, they approach each piece waiting for something to shoot at them.

All of George's ships are silent with no communications. Their sensors are active monitoring all the Morian ships. The debris field is very large, and George has his ships well dispersed, but they are ready to move at an instant notice, should one of the ships be detected.

The Morians appear to start getting nervous and are starting to get a little careless. They have been searching through the debris field for about ten minutes now, and they haven't found any of us. They got close to a couple of the destroyers, but went right by them. Another five minutes pass, they are now deep in the debris field. Their maneuverability is becoming more precarious, as they must take sharper turns to avoid hitting debris.

Crews on the earth ships are starting to get anxious waiting on one of the Morian ships to discover them and start firing. All crews have been at their stations for five days fighting the Morians, with only a forty-five-minute break before this new danger arrives. They know that the Morians have arrived, and has been searching the debris field for fifteen minutes, but not finding any evidence that they are there.

The Morians know that the Hyperthean fleet is now about

fifteen minutes out, and they are moving out of the debris field, because they don't want to be caught in there when the Hypertheans arrive. They want to be ready for the Hypertheans.

As they move out of the debris field, they can tell from their sensors that the Hyperthean fleet is about five minutes out. As they regroup, they start moving toward the Hyperthean fleet. Now, as they engage the Hyperthean fleet, George orders his fleet out of the debris field and attacks the Morians from behind.

The Hypertheans are taking the Morian fleet straight on, and the battle is underway. Ships are maneuvering in and out, firing at each other, with fighters going after other fighters and ships, when they can. The Morians are completely surprised when Georges' ships have started attacking them from behind. They are now greatly outnumbered as some ships turn to take on the earth ships. The battle continues for about four hours, with Morian ships being destroyed in great numbers. Those that remain finally decide to depart since they are greatly outnumbered. Now that there is nothing left to defend.

There is jubilation among the crews, but also a solemnness as they remember the crews and friends they just lost. The Hyperthean ships gathers with George's ships, and they move in to finish off the rest of the station. With the station destroyed, the Hypertheans help them as best they can. After the Hyperthean admiral speaks with George, he decides that he will stay with George's ships and escort them back to our solar system.

Admiral Fuentes and the Hyperthean admiral have joined with the ships that George left behind from their first battle. They are accessing the damages and determining which ships are salvageable and can travel, and which ones they will need to leave behind. After discussion with the Hyperthean admiral, George finds out that the Hypertheans are sending salvage ships to all the scenes of the battles and will be collecting graphical images of all the battle fields and debris for analysis.

The salvage ships will collect the debris and will bring Hyperthean, Morian, and Earth debris to a specified location within our solar system for us to go through and salvage what we can. We will be responsible for taking the rest and turning it into something useful. They will also be recovering all the bodies, allowing us and them to bury the dead. We will also respect the Morians and bury their dead.

George's communication center has been in contact with the *Hyperthia* the whole time they have been gone. Stan has been aware of the battles and the victories. But, George is worried about home, and now he can focus on getting back to our solar system and what is going on back there. With his crippled ships, it will take them about three months to get back to the solar system, or what is left of it.

FIFTY-FIVE

The Morian ships that bypassed the earth ships are heading toward our solar system, and should reach it in about five weeks.

Admiral Stark has his fleets set in a wide dispersal pattern just beyond the Mars orbital path. He is ready to bring them closer together once he determines what the Morians are planning to do. All personnel have been brought back to the *Hyperthia* from the outer stations. Stan has brought up the outer barrier shield, and the modified Morian drones have been set in place. Stan has ordered all personnel to leave all earth orbiting stations and report to the Texas base where they will find protection under the dome. He doesn't feel he will have enough ships to fight with and to defend these stations. He doesn't want their losses on his conscience. He has also ordered the *Hyperthia* to leave earth's orbit and to move just behind his fleet that is in the orbital path around Mars.

The Morian fleet is still approaching and is about two and a half weeks away. Stan is getting reports that George's fleet is now engaged with a fleet of Morian war ships about a half day away from the Morian station.

He is now in his command center, listening intently to the reports that are coming in about the battle, and watching his holographic views on his command table. Stan wishes he could be there to help George, but he knows he wouldn't reach them in time, and he must be ready for the approaching war ships.

Admiral Fuentes' battle was won about a week ago, and he is now on his way back to Earth. Stan knows that the approaching Morian war ships have reached the outer parameter of our barrier. As they approached, the Morian fleet has stopped. Their sensors have determined that the barrier is up. They were not anticipating that the barrier would be up since reports had shown that it had been down for two years now. The Morians have taken up positions and have started firing at the shield trying to punch a hole through it. Their continued bombardment lasts for two days before they are finally able to break through.

Now that the Morians have collapsed the shield, they are sending ships through and are now headed toward Earth. As they are passing Saturn, the Morian drones activate and start moving towards the Morian fleet. When the Morians realize these are their drones, they assume they were activated by their approach. Since these drones have been here for several hundred years, they were surprised they still worked and are glad to have them in this battle. The drones pull up alongside several destroyers moving in a parallel path. They appear like they are joining the fleet moving towards earth. After several minutes of traveling with this fleet, they receive a signal from the *Hyperthia* to attack.

The drones begin firing at the destroyers and are starting to inflict some damage. They are so close to the destroyers they are unable to fire on the drones. They try to maneuver away from the drones, but the drones are more maneuverable than they are. As the destroyers are starting to show some damage, the drones continue to fire at the damaged areas. Cruisers launch some of their fighters and come after the drones. Drones are now taking on fighters and destroyers. Eventually all the drones are destroyed, but not before they have done their damage. Seventy-two of the destroyers have been damaged enough that they must drop back. The Morians are being more cautious now as they approach Earth, uncertain as to what other surprises they might run into.

As they get closer to the outer orbital path of Mars, they have picked up the earth ships on their sensors. Instead of taking the direct approach, they have split their forces into three separate units. Stan must split his forces into three units to take on the Morians. As he splits his forces, the Morians are moving in faster trying to disrupt Stan's fleets before they can get organized.

As the Morians move in, the fighting begins. All three of Stan's fleets are hit at the same time. With each move that is made, there is a countermove. Fighters, destroyers and cruisers are going at each other. Death and destruction is starting to fill the vacuum of space that once was void of anything but space dust. Stan decides not to waste lives and ships on gallantry and orders all his ships to use the trans-portal and laser devices when they have the opportunity. This back and forth has been going on for five days now, and the Morians have pulled back to regroup. As they do, Stan is also regrouping his ships.

Stan is accessing his losses, and has determined he has lost about a fourth of his ships. He is not sure about the Morian losses now, as he needs to concentrate on what he needs to do next. His scanners and hologram show that the Morians have gathered in a central location about thirty minutes away from his fleet. They are probably wondering where these measly inexperienced humans with outdated ships get their stamina and experience to fight. It is starting to demoralize and anger these mighty and destructive Morians whose only defeats has come at the hands of the Hypertheans. They are their equals, but we are holding our own against them. They are glad there is not more of these "human races" out here.

While Stan is regrouping and waiting on the Morians next move, he gets a call from Admiral Graham.

"Stan, I know you are busy and need to focus on your situation. I just wanted to let you know I am releasing the two fleets I have at our outer area and sending them in to help you. They should be there in about a day. You hang in there until they get there."

"Thanks admiral. We will do our best, but hurry. I think we can hold them off until then but it depends on their next moves."

"Get back to what you were doing. I'll talk with you later."

Stan gives him an exhausted grin and says, "I hope so."

It takes the Morian fleet about three agonizing hours before they start moving in again. This time they have brought all their ships together and are trying the direct approach which they like. They are hoping to scatter us this time to see if they can get some ships through to attack Earth.

Stan has engaged the enemy, and his ships continue to hold their own. The Morian ships are now starting to try and go around the ends of Stan's ships. Stan must disperse them in a broader defense parameter to keep the ships from going around his ends. As he does this, it starts to weaken his position in the center where the main body is still coming at them. He decides to bring the *Hyperthia* up into the center of the battle. As he does so, he is now taking on at least twenty cruisers and dozens of destroyers. But the *Hyperthia* is no match for them. She is firing all her guns and launching missiles. He has launched thousands of her fighters, and they are all taking on the Morians. Destroyers are crumbling before this goliath of a ship, as she is still a formable foe. The *Hyperthia* is starting to use her trans-portal and laser cutting weapons, and hundreds of enemy ships are being destroyed. Again, the Morians are pulling back. This time they have lost at least a half of their fighting fleet.

As Stan pulls his ships back in to regroup, he evaluates his situation. By now he has lost half of his fleet, but the morale of his crews is high with the significant victories they have just had, but they know it is not over yet. We appear to be trading the Morians ship for ship in this battle, and we can't continue to do that if we are to save Earth.

Two hours have passed since the last battle ended, and the Morians are still holding their position. They must now be aware that there are approaching Hyperthean fleets that are about four hours away. If they are going to attack Earth, they must break through and get to Earth in the next couple of hours or turn back. I don't know much about the Morians, but I don't see them turning back. The Morians now order the seventy-two damaged destroyers to hold back the approaching Hyperthean fleet as best they can. The destroyers now turn and face the direction of the approaching Hyperthean fleet, knowing they will be destroyed within a matter of minutes.

They are now coming at us again, full on. Stan believes they are going to try and drive a wedge through us and have ships continue to Earth. He pulls his ships in tighter, with the *Hyperthia* in the middle. Trying to drive a wedge through a ship that is five miles wide and one mile high, Stan believes is an impossible feat, but the Morians arrogance and battle skills have shown some surprising results. Stan suddenly decides on a new strategy. He orders his ships to form a reverse wedge with the *Hyperthia* at the center. As the Morian wedge is headed toward the *Hyperthia,* they have a dozen cruisers in the front taking on the charge at the *Hyperthia.* Right behind these charging cruisers are about two hundred destroyers with about two thousand fighters ready to take on the *Hyperthia.* The cruisers act like they are going to sacrifice themselves and crash head on into the *Hyperthia.* Stan's fleet is now heading toward the Morian fleet from both sides before the Morians realize that this is a reverse wedge. As these cruisers are heading straight at the *Hyperthia,* Stan has ordered all forward guns and missiles to fire. As a thousand forward gun placements fire, another five hundred missiles are launched. They don't stand a chance against the *Hyperthia*'s fire power. Within minutes the cruisers and approaching fighters are destroyed, or so badly crippled that they cannot continue in the fight.

As the *Hyperthia* was in the heat of battle with the cruisers and the rest of Stan's fleet is taking on the rest of the Morian fleet, about two dozen destroyers and two thousand fighters slip by the *Hyperthia* and head toward Earth. While the forward batteries are taking on the cruisers, the command center notices the destroyers and fighters slipping by the *Hyperthia*. They order the rear batteries to fire on these ships and fighters, and they destroy about a dozen of the fighters, but the other ones got past them and are heading to Earth.

Stan is immediately made aware of it, and orders six of his destroyers to go after them and releases as much of his fighters as he can to support the destroyers. He orders his CIC officer to inform Earth command of the approaching enemy ships and for them to prepare for battle. It will take at least an hour for the Morian ships to reach Earth.

The Morian command realize that some of their destroyers and fighters got through, and are now fighting more fiercely than ever to keep the earth ships occupied so others can break through.

The Hyperthean fleet is now two hours away, and Stan suspects that the Morians need to decide within an hour whether to retreat or stay and fight to the death. Either way, the Morian ships headed toward Earth are on a suicide mission.

Stan's ships are continuing their fight and are holding their own. With the aggressive charge of the Morians, they are fighting with a devil take care attitude and are starting to lose ships at a three to one rate. They continue their fight knowing that the Hyperthean ships are now about ten minutes away and have destroyed the seventy-two damaged ships, and they have no hope of escaping. But that doesn't matter to them. They will continue to fight until there is not a ship left, planning to do as much damage as they can to the earth ships and to keep them occupied for as long as they can, to allow their other ships to get to Earth.

The Hyperthean ships arrive and join in the fight and within fifteen minutes all the Morian ships have been destroyed. Stan now has about a third of his ships left that are in fighting condition. Another third is so crippled that they can't continue in the fight. Stan is now concerned about the Morian ships going towards Earth and asks the Hyperthean commander if he would send some of his ships to Earth and help in destroying the Morian ships.

FIFTY-SIX

All the domes that were set up on Earth have now been activated. General Todd has contacted all heads of nations and has informed them of the situation and has asked them to bring their militaries to full alert. He has also asked those who have nuclear capabilities not to use them, except as a last resort. He has also told them which of their cities have the dome protection around them. He asked them to get as much of their populations into those dome areas as possible.

Within minutes all military forces on the Earth are at full alert. Missile commands are fully manned, military jets are ready to take to the air at a moment's notice. Other jets are on patrols, armored divisions are manned, all military ships are on station, or are heading toward their countries, if they are close enough to get there, or they will protect countries as best they can. Everything that can be done is being done. The Morians will be here in about forty-five minutes.

The earth ships that are chasing the Morians are keeping pace with them, but don't have a chance of overtaking them before they reach Earth. Some of the fighters that are with the Morian ships are turning back to try and slow the pursuing earth ships. Within minutes they are upon the earth ships, but our fighters take them on and destroy them within seconds. We didn't have any fighter loses. The ships are now twenty-five minutes out.

General Todd is monitoring the situation and has calculated that the Morian ships will be coming into the earth's atmosphere and hitting countries in Europe, and possibly moving on towards the Eastern seaboard of the United States. That is, if they continue to take the direct approach. He has made all countries aware of the approach and that they will be upon us in about twenty minutes. All the countries know what they need to do.

Jets are being scrambled, missile silo doors have opened and are ready to fire. Space fighters are up and headed towards space ready to take on the Morians before they enter the earth's atmosphere. As these fighters leave the earth's atmosphere and take up their defensive positions, they are now ten minutes out.

The sensors on the space fighters detect the approaching Morian destroyers and fighters. Instead of waiting, they charge toward the approaching Morians. Within minutes they are engaged with the Morian fighters, and the dog fights are on. Fighters are weaving in and out of each other, firing as they engage one other. Some shots miss, while others hit their targets on both sides. As the fighters are engaged, the destroyers continue towards Earth and are entering our atmosphere. While most of the Morian fighters are engaged with the earth fighters in space, some continue with the destroyers and are entering the Earth's atmosphere.

With a dozen Morian destroyers entering the Earth's atmosphere, they begin to split up. Two of them are now headed towards Moscow, Russia, two are headed to Paris, France, two towards Brussels, Belgium, while the other six are headed towards the United States. Missiles from many locations are being fired at the approaching destroyers. After the missiles have been fired, military aircraft are now taking on the Morian fighters and destroyers. The missiles have done damage, but not enough to prevent the destroyers from continuing on their mission. Now ground placements are taking on the destroyers, but they are doing less damage than the missiles. The destroyers have reached Moscow, Paris, and Brussels, and are now firing at the cities. As soon as they take their first shots, they realize that the cities are protected by domes. They continue firing at the domes, but their protection is holding, protecting the residence of the cities. Soon they find where the domes end and are now firing on locations that are not protected by the domes and destroying as much as they can.

As military fighters and ground weapons continue to pound away at the destroyers, the destroyers are starting to sustain damage. More missiles are being fired and more damage is starting to appear. Russia has been able to bring down one of the destroyers, and it crashes near the Baltic Sea while the other continues to destroy and attack cities, and populations around Moscow.

France is doing the best they can in fighting the destroyers and fighters. Fighters from surrounding countries are joining in the fight. The destroyers that were attacking Paris decide to split up. While one continues to attack the cities and country sides around Paris, the other goes after cities in Italy. The Morians are now trying to split up the Earth defenses by trying to thin them out as they try to protect as many cities as they can, knowing we don't know where they will be hitting next.

The same is going on with the destroyers that are attacking Brussels. After learning about the dome around Moscow, they only send one destroyer to hit the cities around Brussels. The other destroyer heads towards Berlin and its surrounding cities.

Taking on Berlin is too much for the Morian destroyer and its fighters. The defenses that are there are greater than they can handle, and soon this destroyer is destroyed.

Ships and fighters from England are now coming to the defense of the Belgium's, along with fighters from other countries. Everyone is joining in the fight to destroy the Morian ships.

The fight in Europe has been going on for three hours now, and the six destroyers and fighters headed for the United States reached the US shores about one and a half hours ago. As they were approaching, the US launched as many of its missiles as they could before the destroyers reached the east coast. US Naval vessels were firing on the destroyers and fighters as they approached. The Morian destroyers destroyed over three fourths of the naval vessels protecting the east coast, but not before three of the six destroyers were shot down. Knowing of the domes in Europe, they have decided not to attack the big cities. They are attacking the small towns on the east coast. They are destroying everything they can that is in their paths. US fighters are engaged with Morian fighters and destroyers, firing air-to-air missiles and cannons as they move in.

More ground-to-air missiles are fired at the Morian destroyers both in Europe and the US, as they are starting to have their toll on the Morians. Naval vessels that remained on the east coast of the US along the Atlantic coast of Europe, and in the Mediterranean Sea, continue to launch surface-to-air missiles at the destroyers.

Eventually the destroyers and their fighters start to dwindle in strength. Their fighter support has been destroyed, and the destroyers are taking the full brunt of the missile attacks. The two destroyers that remained to attack the US, have been shot down and are burning in the waters about a half mile off South Carolina. There appears to be no Morian survivors. Fighters from China have joined in the attack on the destroyer that is around Moscow. With missiles being fired at the destroyer over Moscow, and fighters from Russia and China attacking the destroyer, it will soon be over for the Morian destroyer. Within a half hour, this destroyer has been destroyed.

The destroyers that are attacking Paris and Brussels have had a little better luck in their mission. They have destroyed many of the smaller towns in France and in Italy. The destroyers that were attacking Brussels have destroyed towns in the southern part of Belgium and in The Netherlands. But with the gathering forces from the surrounding nations, they are eventually destroyed. The fight on Earth is over. There are many casualties. Towns and country sides are still burning as disaster relief and aid head toward them. Fighters are flying over all locations providing cover from above, should another attack come. The dome shields are turned off as people and equipment head out to help as best they can. There are many injured that will need assistance. Complete cities have been destroyed, and death and injuries is everywhere.

Military forces are gathering around the downed destroyers and fighters. There are Morian survivors coming out of the destroyers, and the earth's military is now engaged in ground combat with these survivors. The Morians will fight to the death, taking as many earthlings as they can with them. They are greatly outnumbered, but they put up a fierce and gallant fight against Earth's defenses. As far as we know, all the Morians lost their lives, but there are rumors that some may have slipped away. If they did, it may take us quite some time to find them.

The Hyperthean ships have arrived. Upon their arrival, they find that the battle is over and all the Morian ships have been destroyed. They are holding a position just above the Earth as a defense barrier, in case there are other Morian ships around.

FIFTY-SEVEN

This battle for Earth is over. Many lives have been lost, both military and civilian, but Earth remains. The Morians are probably more determined than ever to destroy us now. We have given them their greatest defeat. It wasn't just militarily, it was by a race that wasn't even worthy to do battle with them. So, their pride has been greatly damaged, and that isn't good. Our union with the Hyperthean Federation is stronger than ever now.

Admiral Stark along with the Hyperthean fleet, are now back in orbit around Earth. Half of the military personnel are back on Earth with families rejoicing they are all still alive and giving comfort to those who have lost loved ones. Many are helping in the cleanup of the damage that has been done and are glad they can do it.

It has been a couple of weeks since the battle, and things are starting to settle down. The Hyperthean fleet has stayed behind and is establishing patrols around our solar system. Other ships are on their way. Stan has been in contact with George, and he reports that things are going well. Everyone is battle weary, but they are all recovering, glad to be alive.

Admiral Fuentes is traveling with damaged ships and it is slowing their progress, but they should be home in about three months.

Luckily the Morians didn't have a chance to attack any of the bases on Mars or the moon, nor any of our stations out beyond Mars. The orbital station for our space exploration ships also remains intact. The Morians focus was on Earth. Stan has ordered that all these stations can be manned again, when their personnel is ready. It is up to the station commanders as to when they want their crews back. The crews that were on leave for two weeks have been asked to return to their duty stations. This will allow the other half of the crews to take two weeks to see their families.

While crews are taking their leaves, repair crews are starting to work on all the damaged ships. Unfortunately, all the ships have received some damage, so it will take quite some time for the damage repair parties to get everything fixed.

While Stan and all personnel are busy repairing things and trying to get their lives back to normal, Admiral Graham is checking on Stan.

Stan is walking around the *Hyperthia*, trying to avoid getting in the way of work parties. He's hearing the clanging of heavy hammers, dodging sparks from ark cutters and welders, when he receives word that he has an incoming call from Admiral Graham. He heads to his cabin where things are quieter and takes the call.

"Hello Admiral, how are you today?"

"Why are you yelling at me? I can hear you fine."

Stan laughs as he replies, "Sorry admiral, I've been out and around the ship looking at some of the repair work being done, and it was loud."

"How is that going?"

"Going slow but well. It will probably be another three months before the *Hyperthia* is fully repaired, but she is battle ready even in this condition."

"I imagine she is. That is one large piece of metal and machinery. From the reports, I see you lost quite a few ships and lots of people."

Stan replies in a solemn voice, "Yes sir, the loss of lives was very tragic and high. But morale is high, and we are still getting volunteers wanting to join up and serve. Ships, on the other hand, are another thing. We lost over half our fleet, and the other half is damaged. We have the materials to repair them, but it will take the repair crews at least two years to repair them all. I don't know where we are going to get replacement ships from for the half that we lost. Even if I could get them, it will take some time to get them here."

"I feel your pain. When is George planning on getting back?"

"I am expecting him to be back in about forty-five days. The Hyperthean ships that are with him will stay around and join the other fleet in the protection of our solar system. I understand they will be sticking around until we are ready to take over."

"Yes, those are my orders. I'm glad the Hypertheans are willing to do that for you."

"I'm glad, too. If the Morians came at us now with any force, I don't think we could defend Earth this time."

"I want to add one thing, in case you haven't thought about it. Even though morale is high and you have just come off a great victory, don't allow yourself and your crews to get too cocky with this victory. We know the Morians are a great evil force, and they have been embarrassed by you. They will not make the same mistake twice, nor will they let it go. Allow your people to enjoy the victory, but bring them back to reality soon. They don't have the luxury to relax their vigilance. It would also be a good idea if you had all the admirals go through the training again. It probably has been several decades since some of them had that.

Listen, I have received word from the Hyperthean High

Command that they would like to meet with us tomorrow at 1000 hours. You need to be in on that call."

"Yes sir, I will be there. Do you know what it is about?"

"Very little. What I do know is that they want to work with us on building a stronger federation and that we have shown ourselves to be worthy of a larger seat in their council."

"Good. I will see you in the morning. Anything else?"

"No, that is all for now. Talk with you tomorrow."

At 1000 hours the next morning, Stan is on his video display, and joins Admiral Graham and several others. The meeting hasn't started yet, and they are still waiting on the Hyperthean High Council.

Stan says, "Good morning Admiral. Anything happened?"

"Not yet Stan, we are still waiting on the High Council to join in."

Everyone is seated in their seats, waiting a few more minutes for the council to join in. Now the screen changes, and the council is on everyone's screen.

The leader of the council starts off the conversation by saying, "Good day to all of you. I would like to start by thanking the members of Earth for joining our meeting. I believe you are Admiral Stark, correct?"

"Yes sir"

"I would like to tell you how honored we are to have you as part of our federation. You have shown yourselves worthy, and we are pleased to call you friend."

"Thank you."

"I would like to tell all of you that because of this great victory that the earthlings have had over the Morians, they have pulled back from all their offenses. Unfortunately for the earthlings, we don't feel that is a good thing. The Morians did not feel that the earthlings were of any consequence and didn't feel they were worthy of any effort."

He points at Stan and says, "You have hurt their pride, and

they will do everything they can to get even with you. But, we have no intention of letting that happen.

The council has met, and we are making a few adjustments. As Earth's solar system is now part of our federation, that means we have expanded the size of space that comes under federation protection. We also see this area of space to be weakly protected.

Admiral Graham, if you please."

"Yes sir?"

"Admiral Graham, you are now a three-star admiral within the federation. You are now in charge of all fleets in the L241 Sector. This includes all the deep space stations, Earth command, and twenty-two other fleets that will be spread out in this new territory. Seventeen of these fleets need to be formed and assigned. You will also need to find a new base of operation to command your new Sector. You can't do it from DSS-7. You will receive more details later."

"Yes sir, thank you sir."

"Vice Admiral Kleg. You have been promoted to two-star admiral. You will take over for Admiral Graham as the admiral of the deep space stations and will report to Admiral Graham."

"Yes sir, thank you sir."

"Admiral Stark. Even though Earth recently joined the federation, you haven't been reporting to the federation. We finished signing agreements with your Earth council yesterday, and your solar system is now a full member of the federation. As of today, your command is now part of the federation, and we are promoting you to a two-star admiral reporting to Admiral Graham. With this promotion and being part of the federation forces, your area of responsibility will increase. Instead of just your solar system, you will now protect an area of space known as LG241-A, which covers one-half of your Milky Way system and includes your solar system.

"Yes sir, thank you sir."

"Admiral Stark, as you are probably wondering, and asking

yourself, how are you going to do that with an outdated fleet and with over half of it gone."

"Yes sir."

"We are not going to leave you and Admiral Graham to defend this with what you have. You still have a few of the new ships left that we provided you. Keep them in good working condition. We will replace all your older ships with new ships. In your world, you have what is known as "Mothball ships". We want you to set the older ships into a "Mothball state" in several locations so that you can reactivate them easily, should you ever need them.

This includes the *Hyperthia*. She is a great ship, but like your old earth battleships, she has her usefulness, and are no longer needed. With her being decommissioned, you will need a new base of operation. You can work with Admiral Graham on where that will be. Along with new ships for the seventeen fleets you currently have, we will provide you with seven more fleets of ships to protect your solar system. Admiral Graham has the responsibility of working with you to determine how many other fleets you will need to protect the LG241-A section of space."

With a huge grin on his face, Admiral Stark says, "Yes sir. Thank you, sir."

"In the meantime, the rest of the Federation fleet admirals will work with Admiral Graham in providing him with the necessary ships to protect that sector of space around the deep space stations, and the Earth solar system until such time that the ships and personnel are provided to him to protect this area of space. Understood, admirals."

From everyone that is present there is a "yes sir," and a round of applause goes up for the three that have been promoted and the decision that has been made. The council adjourns the meeting, and everyone signs off.

Within seconds Admiral Graham has his video display

beeping telling him he has an incoming call. He answers, "Let me guess who this is?"

There is a grinning face on the other end and with excitement, Stan says, "What just happened! I don't believe it. Someone pinch me and tell me I'm not dreaming."

"Whoa, slow down cowboy. If you were in a dream, I was in the same one."

Stan is now rubbing his chin trying to regain his composure. He takes a couple of breaths and says, "Yesterday I was wondering if we were going to be alive in six months, and now this. God is alive and well."

"I want both of us to take a day to let all of this sink in. You can tell your command, and Earth, what has just happened and about both of our promotions and changes of command. Congratulate them all for me on a job well done, and tell them that I am proud of them. We will get together the day after tomorrow to start formulating our plans. Again, congratulations Stan."

"Thanks admiral, and congratulations to you."

Two days have gone by, and I have had time to collect my thoughts, and I am ready to discuss things with Admirals Kleg and Stark. I have asked Kleg to join me in my stateroom, and Stan to join us via video at 1000 hours.

It is now 0950, and Kleg is at my door. I tell him to come on in. He sits at the conference table, and I join him. I ring for Harold and he comes into the room.

"May I help you sir?"

"Harold, would you bring me a drink, please."

I turn to Kleg and ask, "Would you care for anything?"

"Yes, would you bring me one too, please."

"Yes sirs, I will be right back."

Kleg says, as Harold leaves the room, "Are things starting to settle down for you?"

"Yes, much better now. I have had some time to think about

things, and that is the reason I wanted to have this meeting with you and Stan."

Harold comes back into the room with our drinks and sets them on the table, and turns to leave the room. We continue in some small talk until Stan comes up on the display.

"Good morning Stan, how are you doing today?"

"Very busy, but things are getting better. How are you two doing?"

"We are good. Stan, I have asked you and Kleg here today because we need to start formulating our plans. But first, I want to get some very simple things out of the way."

I turn to Kleg and say, "Kleg, with your promotion, you know these are going to be your quarters now. As soon as I can find some appropriate temporary quarters, I will move out and you can move in."

"Please sir, don't rush off on my part. I am perfectly fine where I am."

"I know, I know, and thank you. But for the change of command to work appropriately, I need to find another location to set up my headquarters. I don't want people to think that I am still here to override you. We need to have a ceremony before the command to signify that I am turning over command to you.

Also since two stars are hard to get out here, I would like for you to have mine. I will get my stars later."

"Thank you admiral."

"Stan, let's see, you are going to need to make several personal changes."

"Me sir, in what way?"

"First off, you're ugly, and we need to change that mug of yours."

Everybody laughs, and Stan says, "Thanks Chris, you look like you could stand some help yourself."

"Hey now!"

"Now, on to a serious note. Since Earth command is now

part of the Hyperthean Federation, you need to start wearing a federation uniform. So, we need to get you some new uniforms to go along with your two stars. I know all of you are proud of what you have accomplished and are proud of the uniforms that you have. I will let you make the decision if you want them to keep their uniforms, or if they need to change over to Federation uniforms. But, they will need to change at some point, soon."

"Thanks admiral, I will think about it, but my initial thought is to allow them to keep their uniforms. Then we can look at it again, a few months down the road."

"That's fine."

"With the decommissioning of the *Hyperthia*, have you given any thoughts where you would like to establish your base of operation?"

"No sir, not yet."

"Like me, you have had a huge responsibility placed on your shoulders. Your command area is going to spread far now. I know for myself, as I have reviewed the breadth of my command area, I believe I will have a command station built that will be strategically located to allow me access to all my commands and to the Hyperthean home world. I need to be able to communicate with everyone in a timely manner. For you, I believe you should consider something similar. If you agree, we will have it built for you."

"Thanks admiral, that sounds good. I will let you know of my decision."

"Good, now we need to discuss what your area of responsibility looks like."

I bring up a holographic display of the sector of space that Stan will be responsible for. We are all looking at the enormity of it and wondering how we are going to handle it.

I then say, "Stan, from what we have been told, it appears that the Hyperthean Federation has decided to, shall we say, defend a lot of space that has not been explored yet. And the responsibility to defend it has fallen to both of us but more to you. This is where our solar system is at."

I point to a small dot compared to what the rest of what Stan has responsibility for.

"We currently have, or will have, just enough ships to protect our solar system and some of the surrounding areas. The seven additional fleets you will receive, I expect you to use them to broaden the protection area around our solar system. This is a significant number of ships to fill with personnel from Earth. Currently Earth doesn't have that number of people to fill our needs. We lost a lot of people recently. So, we will combine personnel from all federation planets to meet the demand for these ships. This will allow Earth personnel to get to know other races, and will also allow them to go further into space.

Now to the rest of your LG241-A section of space. Since this is unexplored territory, my thought is that instead of trying to fill this space with military craft, we should first start off with space exploration ships. How do you feel about this idea?"

"I like it. This way we can intermix our crews. This will allow other races to visit earth and to get to know us, and we them. Also, it won't place a greater demand on our small planet to fill these ships with personnel from Earth.

Exploration ships! I hope we can get those from Hyperthean command. It would take us decades to build ships to explore space that far out."

"Yes, my thoughts exactly. The plans are still preliminary, and we will discuss it. We will get exploration ships from the Hyperthean High Command. I don't know of any reason why they wouldn't supply them for us, as they will benefit from this too. My thought is that we would ask them for a thousand ships. They would be manned by races from all the planets of the federation. Earth has been itching to get in on the exploration of space, and this is their chance. As we go deeper into space, we will build deep space stations for all our ships to rendezvous at. As we build these stations, we will provide military ships to protect them, and this will also provide protection for our exploration ships, should they run into any problems."

"I like it. I am getting excited."

"Okay Stan, I think this is enough for today. I will let you absorb this, and we will get back together in a week, unless you need something sooner."

"Thanks admiral, I have a lot of details to work out. I will talk with you later."

We sign off, and I turn to Kleg and say, "Well, what do you think? Am I headed down the right path for him?"

"He is very new at this, and we have given him quite a lot to be responsible for. He has done an excellent job in the defense of Earth, and in setting the Morians back. With this promotion, he will be more of an administrator and less of a military man. He is going to need a lot of help to keep his mistakes at a minimum."

"Yes, I agree with you. I think that is why the federation has left you in my command. You have been a great asset and friend to me, as I have grown through the years. The responsibility you now have has increased, but I will be giving you more as we take on this new opportunity. I don't see you staying here long before I move you to a bigger command."

"Don't worry about moving me to a bigger command. I will serve you as I always have, and we will make this a success."

"Thanks Kleg."

FIFTY-EIGHT

George is back in Earth space, and the excitement of the victory starts all over again, as his crews begin their celebration with the other crews. Just like Stan's fleet they split three weeks of leave, since they were gone longer. George is aware of the changes that has been made with Stan and he is excited for him.

After George comes back from his leave, he gets with Stan to discuss what the next steps are in getting things back to normal. As they meet up, Stan starts off their meeting after some cordial conversation, and they have sat down to relax in Stan's stateroom.

"George, you have kept up with the communiqués on the changes that have been made. As you know, the *Hyperthia* will be mothballed, and we need to establish a new base of operation for the command of the solar system. I have met with Admiral Graham and after some lengthy discussion, I have decided I need to set up my command center on a new station. The plans for that station have been completed, and Admiral Graham has approved them. Supplies for the building of this station have been ordered, and the station should be completed in about a year and a half. I have decided to have the station built in the Gulf sector of space. This is some distance from the solar system, but Chris and I believe it will be strategically located for the LG241-A sector of space that I will have responsibility for. I have met with Admiral Graham, and we have decided that since our stations will be so far from nearby planets, they will be built like small cities. Mine will be called Canterbury Station.

I won't be taking you with me because I will also be looking for a new second in command."

There is silence in the room for about ten seconds, and finally George says, "I don't understand sir. Have I done something wrong?"

"Don't worry George, you haven't done anything wrong."

With a grin on his face Stan says, "George, you will be taking over the fleets for our solar system. I am turning command over to you."

George lets out a sigh of relief and says, "Please sir, don't do that to me. I thought you were getting rid of me."

"George, I have been around Admiral Graham too long. You know how he can be a kidder at times, and it must have rubbed off on me. But, seriously, I would never get rid of you. Along with this new command, I am promoting you to a full one star admiral. You will also need to wear a federation uniform."

"Thank you, sir, I don't know what to say. I hope I won't let you down."

"You haven't so far, and I don't see you doing it in the future.

Now, I don't know if you know it or not, but all the original ships that the Hypertheans gave us will be mothballed. You will need to salvage what you can from them when you get replacement ships from Hyperthea. I would recommend that you decide where your new base of operation will be, get the plans drawn up, and have it built. With this promotion, you will not be in the heat of battle anymore. So, build your base where you are well protected; you're not to be involved with earth politics, and you need to provide all the support you now have on the *Hyperthia*. You may find that building a station like the one I'm having built is your best option.

On my station, I will be including an infrastructure like Admiral Graham has set up on DSS-7, for all the deep space scout patrols, but mine will include support for all the space exploration ships. All my fleets are to communicate with it. This will also be a relay point for all communications going to Admiral Graham's command.

We already have ships that are on their way to us and Admiral Graham. We should be getting ours, or should I say, yours in the next three months. I have an inventory of what they are, and I will have my new XO send them over to you."

"Who is your new XO?"

"I have decided to bring someone in from the Hyperthean fleet. We need to start balancing out our commands. On top of that, we lost a lot of human lives during our last encounter with the Morians. Our resources are starting to run thin.

I know this might be too soon, but have you given any thought to who your XO will be?"

"Yes sir, I have. With your permission, I would like to promote Captain Stillwell to vice-admiral and make him my XO."

"That is an excellent choice. I am pleased with your selection."

Time continues to go by, six months, and now a year. George has been able to get all his ships replaced from the Hyperthean High Command along with the additional fleets that were promised to protect the area outside of the solar system. Patrols have returned to normal, and new crew members are coming aboard ships daily. Crew members from the Hyperthean commands that brought ships here are starting to stay behind to become crew members with the humans. So far, the relations are going well between the two races. George has also chosen to have a station built like the ones that Admiral Graham is having built, but he will have two platforms. It is about half finished, and will be located about half way between Earth and Mars. He has decided to call his Windsor Station. In the meantime, he still has the *Hyperthia* as his base of operation until his is finished.

Stan's station is about three-fourths finished, and he has been going back and forth to it monthly to check on its' progress.

While George was receiving his new ships, Stan was also receiving new exploration ships and the fleets for the deeper patrol areas. He has also worked out an agreement with Admiral Graham, and the Hyperthean High Command that these ships would be here on a rotational basis. The agreement is that the ships would be stationed here for ten years, and then be rotated with ships back to Hyperthia space. This will allow the Hyperthean crews to go home every ten earth years.

The Hyperthean war ships have been sent to their patrol areas, and things are starting to fall into place. The exploration ships that arrived are being manned with a mixed crew, and training is underway for eight hundred of the thousand ships that will be sent out. Training will continue for another six months before Stan believes they will be ready to leave. He has also worked out a deal with George. The station that was built for the space exploration ships will be turned over and modified as a base of operation to go with the Windsor station. The exploration ships that were originally provided to earth will now report to Stan at his station, and they will be a part of that exploration fleet. Stan has also asked the Space Exploration Council that was located on Earth, to relocate to his station. They have agreed and will be moving within a month.

In the meantime, he is having his staff work with each of the exploration teams, defining what they will be doing and where they will be going.

Admiral Graham is also making progress on his command. He worked with Kleg on choosing an XO, and he has chosen an admiral that Kleg has recommended to him. Admiral Graham has chosen the makeup of his staff, and things are starting to take shape.

He has chosen a location that he sees as a good strategic one to command his fleets. There are no gaps of space between the last Hyperthean patrol area and where his command areas begin. His stations will be ready in six months.

Another six months goes by, and all Admiral Graham's commands are in their patrol areas, and patrols are routine. The Morians have been quiet, but Hyperthean command has ships monitoring their activity. Two years have passed since their encounter with the earthlings. Since they are being closely monitored, all patrols have been routine. Crews have been enjoying the quiet.

George, Stan and Chris are now on their new stations and settled in. Both Stan's Canterbury Station and Chris's Osborne station, with their four other stations that are nearby, are quite impressive. Admiral Graham's location has lots of activity moving from all five stations. The Hyperthean High Command has been very impressed with the setup and has decided to build similar setups in all their other remote command locations.

Stan's setup is quite impressive too. He has four stations surrounding his. One is to support the exploration ships, two stations will support the war ships, and the fourth for transports. The training for the exploration crews has been completed, and they are ready to be sent out. He has eight hundred exploration ships gathered around his stations in the Gulf Sector. It is an amazing sight to see this number of ships gathered together at one time. Stan and his team are meeting with the eight hundred commanders, and they are all going over their missions that have been defined by the council and are receiving their sets of orders. The commanders of the exploration ships have mixed crews, some from Earth and some from Hyperthea. Stan is quite impressed how well all the crews are working together.

A new chapter is now underway for Earth and the Federation. Protection for Earth has been reestablished, and space exploration is beginning. We have come a long way over the past several decades. No telling where we will be two hundred years from now.

GLOSSARY

Fleet
- 14 fleets to protect solar system
- Will take approximately 1,000,000 personnel to man ships
- Each fleet is made up of:
  - o 10 Battle Stars
  - o 60 Battle Cruisers
  - o 300 Battle Destroyers
  - o 1 Hospital Ship

Command Ship
- Name – *Hyperthia* (FCS-2014)
- Crew – 25,000
- Oval
  - o 5 miles in diameter
  - o 1-mile-deep at highest point
- 200 launch bays
- 50,000-gun mounts
- 10,000 missile launchers
- 10 laser cutters
- Trans-portal weapons

Battle Star
- Crew size – 3,000

- 1 Fighter Squadron of 7,000 fighters
- 7,000 fighter pilots
- Laser beam for slicing into enemy ships
- 500-gun mounts of varying sizes
- 120 missile launchers
- Trans-portal weapons

Battle Cruiser
- Crew size – 2,000
- 200-gun mounts of varying sizes
- 60 missile launchers
- Laser beam for slicing into enemy ships
- Trans-portal weapons

Battle Support Destroyers
- Crew size – 300
- 100-gun mounts and missile launchers
- Trans-portal weapon

Scout Ships
- Crew – 15
- Cloaking
- Speeds more than 200 pressers
- Appropriate amount of armament for their size.

Transport Ship
- Approximately 420 ships
- Crew – 50
- Minimal defensive systems

Scientific Ships
- 100 ships
- Provided by the Hypertheans for us to explore our solar system and then eventually beyond
- Minimal amount of armament for protection

Earth bases
- 42 Earth bases
- Each about 10,000 acres each
- Domed protection
- In remote locations
- 2,000 acres for base housing and training
- 5,000 acres for runways and housing transport ships and fighters

Botanical Ships
- Named – FFS for Federation Food Ships
- Crew – 250
- Civilians – 1,000
- Grows organic food supply for the fleet
- Small gun mounts for defensive purposes

Hospital Ship
- Crew – 200
- Doctors and nurses – 400
- No armament

Travel Vehicle
- Shape-shifter capabilities
- Can look like a normal car while on Earth
- Changes into a travel vehicle for space travel
- Capacity 2 people
- No weapons

Presser
- Measure of travel using new Laws of Movement known as space bending
- 1 presser of movement is equal to 90,000 miles/second
- Incorporating space bending and traveling at 90,000 miles/second you are moving through space at 1 light year per presser.

Antrip
- stands for <u>A</u>stro-<u>N</u>autical <u>Tri</u>angulation <u>P</u>oint (Antrip)
- Locations is space require three points of reference to pinpoint location.
- This has been established by a Triangulation Point.

Trans-portal Weapon
- Weapon capable of moving people into another dimension without harm.

Hypertheans
- The race that has befriended Earth

Morians
- An enemy race so evil that they do not like any other race and plans of destroying all.

Sporians
- Race of people who disappeared eons ago in the Hyperthean world
- Not much known about them except what is in history chronicles.

Veltans
- Race of people that are friendly but choose to remain neutral in all conflicts
- Not much known about this race.

Wrist Band
- 8 inches long, 1-inch-wide and 1/32 of an inch thick
- Monitors health and adjusts to correct health issues
- Life support system in space
- Knowledge transfer device
- Goes inactive upon removal.

Building of the new stations

Osborne Station

The building of these stations required the designers to consider many factors. They presented Admiral Graham with many options and these are the final considerations he chose:

1. The sphere would be three miles in diameter.
2. Since the station would be located a long distance from any inhabited planets, we need to create an environment that will be pleasant to live in.
3. People from all worlds would be working and serving on Osborne Station.
4. The environment would be like the home worlds of Earth and Hyperthia.
5. A clear dome structure that appeared like a sky.
6. Superstructures for people to work and live in.
7. Walking highways with no moving vehicles on them. There would be trams that moved along the walking highways to take people from one location to another.
8. There would be no flying vehicles within the dome.
9. The city would be protected by a dome, like the ones build on Mars to hold an atmosphere, and for protection. The dome would be surrounded by a network of protection buoys, like the one that protect the solar system, but would be setup in a network shaped like pentagons. From these pentagons, there would be suspended lights, to provide illumination for the city below. The lights would go out after fourteen hours to give the illusion of sunrise and sunset.
10. The middle of the station would be eighty feet high, with a base on top that supports the city above, and separating it from the bottom half of the sphere. This section would contain life support for the station. This

would have the power generation stations, oxygen and water generators, and all the other necessary support functions to keep the station alive.

11. The bottom half will be for shuttles, moving around to the other four stations. It is also large enough of an area that other space crafts can be repaired, and manufactured.

12. The four attached stations will be flat, about two miles across, but without the dome or shields to protect them. They will have a platform that will be eighty feet high, that will support an enclosed superstructure twelve stories high with landing bays. The middle section will have power generators, and other functions like the main sphere, but it will only be for the middle section, and superstructure. This section will also have a command center for personnel to handle the ships, that are coming and going. On top of these structures will be small domes, around each of the landing bays for space traffic control centers. There will be armament for the protection of the stations. Two of the platforms will be for the military ships to land and take off from. The third will be for fighters that protect all five stations. The fourth platform will be for transports that bring supplies, and to take people to other stations.

13. These stations will be about a quarter of a mile from the main station, and will be connected to the main station for personnel to move back and forth. Each of these platforms will be located every ninety degrees around the base of the main station.

14. The main station can be home for families, as the station will have schools for children to attend. Personnel and families can stay and live here, if they desire.

15. Should the station be attacked, the four platforms can break away from the main station, so that it can maintain stability while the fleets protect it.

Canterbury Station

1. This station will have a similar design as Osborne Station.
2. The main station will be built the same as the Osborne main station.
3. It will also have four platforms built around it.
4. One of the platforms will be for fighters.
5. A second platform will be for the space exploration ships.
6. The third platform will be for transports and cargo ships.
7. The fourth platform will be for military crafts.
8. The station that was built for the space exploration ships will be moved close to this station, and will be used now as a repair station.

Windsor Station

1. The main station will be built like the other two stations.
2. The Windsor station will only have two platforms connected to it.
3. One platform for transports and cargo ships.
4. The second platform for military ships.

ABOUT THE AUTHOR

Tim Eichholtz served in the US Navy after high school and then obtained a degree in business data processing from Texas A&M University. He built a fifty-year career in the oil and gas industry, working in information technology, and he retired in 2013. In May 1971, he became a Christian and has served his Lord faithfully. He and his wife, Patsy, have two children and eight grandchildren and live in Tomball, Texas.

Lightning Source UK Ltd.
Milton Keynes UK
UKHW02f0703310718
326548UK00009B/407/P